C000085564

LIGHT
EMERGENT

BOOK ONE
OF
THE TIRANIMEITH
CHRONICLES

R. Allen Jones

Copyright © 2020 R. Allen Jones

ISBN: 978-1-9163693-1-3

IREDAN PRESS
3 The Quay, Looe, Cornwall PL13 1AQ

LIGHT EMERGENT
ISBN: 9781916369313

First published in Great Britain
In 2020 by Iredan Press

CONTENTS

ACKNOWLEDGMENTS

To Amanda Miles and Kenneth Robertson for in-depth, invaluable, detailed, long-term help and encouragement.

To Hayley Rust for such excellent artwork. If you are interested in Hayley's work, she can be contacted through the author.

ABOUT THE BOOK

Please note that in this book some speech is in *"Quotes and Italic words."* This is to denote that the conversation is spiritual communication. This is a form of telepathic speech used by spirits and gods. The existence and content of those discussions will be known only to those few who can hear spirit speech. Everybody else will be oblivious.

MAP OF NORTH EAST
TIRANIMEITH

PROLOGUE

512 YEARS AGO - THE FALL OF THE SHANOVIAN EMPIRE

The Princess stood on the polished white stone balcony to her private quarters looking over the gardens of the imperial palace. The morning sun on her face is lovely and warm. For one of the few times in her life, she looked down at the sleeping infant son in her arms, with eyes full of love. The baby wriggled as her long blond hair tickled his face. Opening her white silk dressing gown, in one final act of motherhood, held him to the bare skin of her breast underneath.

Her family would not have approved the taking of a consort from her guard, but they were all dead now, a testament to how wrong her family's strategy of governance had been. To keep hope alive, she had secretly married her captain as soon as the pains of birth had started. There was now a legitimate male royal heir, the descendants of whom could one day lead humans back to their rightful place of dominance.

'Your, your, your Highness, I, I, I am terribly sorry to interrupt, but it is time. If I do not leave now, I may not be free of the area in time to save your son.'

The Princess looked down at the shaking stammering dark haired maid staring at her own feet.

'Do not be fearful of me anymore. While today I will kill thousands, it will not include you or your family. The service you do me is beyond measure. You may look upon my face for the first time. I will not behead you for it. You will be earning that privilege this day.'

'I, I, I, am afraid to say my father was unable to secure help for you from either the remnants of the priesthood or the Elves. He has secured some help though.'

'More soldiers?'

'No your highness not soldiers, but it will be just as useful. Please don't ask me what or who they are. Identification will not be acceptable. Sorry your highness. You will know the help when it arrives. It will deal with a good portion of the enemy.'

'Then, we have hope.' The Princess said and wordlessly handed her son to the maid.

'And the former Arch Priest's family?' The Princess asked.

'My father has already left with the youngest male heir. Their bloodline will be secure too.'

'The responsibility your family carry is overwhelming.'

'We will be successful, we always are. With your leave, your highness.' The Princess nodded with a heavy heart, then watched as the maid walked backwards out of the room.

Standing alone, the Princess thought reflectively. The capital and all other provincial capitals had long since fallen. Her city was the last unconquered provincial capital. It had withstood the siege for over a year and with ease. They were in the middle of a wide valley. Her troops regularly ranged out defeating the forces of evil and preventing any long-term encirclement. Her city was frequently re-supplied from the few remaining human villages and towns down the river.

However, as with many things, it was her success that was her undoing. By so regularly defeating the army of monsters sent to finish off the last free untainted race she had attracted the attention of The Lord of All Evil himself. The five thousand men of her army were fully trained and equipped professional soldiers supported by her magicians. They could easily cope with the local army of twenty thousand tribal warriors, but the hordes of evil were five times that at least. Looking back, she realised this war was lost one hundred years before it had begun.

Many millennia ago humans, dwarves and elves supported by the Gods of Light whom they worshipped, defeated and exiled the Lord of All Evil. Then came the Shanovian Empire. Formed from cohesive military tactics with skill at arms and supported by the discovery of magic, its army was the best ever seen. The rest of humanity and the other races had no defence against magical spells or regular trained professional troops and were conquered. Over the next one thousand years, the Royal Family slowly eradicated all priests of the Gods of Light in order to curb their power over the people. She now realised that the persecution of priests was a mistake that meant this war, the war of The Return of The Lord of All Evil, could not be won. The spiritual power bestowed by the priestly worship of the Gods of Light, no longer existed to defend humanity against the ghosts and spectres of evil.

However, there was now some hope of victory. While the old Gods of Light were the most potent opponents of The Lord of All Evil, they were not the only ones. It appeared the ever capable diplomats and master spies of her maid's family had secured some help. That was in addition to rescuing her family's sword from the enemy, a sword which she would be using today.

It was time now to get ready for the day ahead. The Princess put her clothes on and shouted 'Armour' which the attendant helped her with. Then she cast her spells of protection. Like most of her family, her royal highness was a skilled warrior and magician.

When she descended the palace's white marble steps, all one thousand of her mounted bodyguard were waiting, impeccably positioned in their ranks and files. The glint of the sun off their steel armour only marginally dimmed by the slight glaze of the magical protections they all had. It was a truly awesome sight. The impact a charge of her bodyguard could inflict on any regular army equipped with only bronze weapons was truly staggering. She knew though that as soon as the Lord of All Evil unleashed his ghosts and spectres, they would all die. No amount of magical protections can stop a ghost for they are spiritual and immune to all magical effects.

She led her personal guard out of the main gate and formed them into a line three ranks deep. The rest of the garrison deployed from the various other city gates and formed up also. Then behind them from the coast came the most horrific lightning storm ever seen. Constant ground strikes, roofs were blown off houses, walls hit, but still, it kept coming at her little army from behind. So this was the help, she thought.

She could hear the shouts of soldiers wanting to take cover and remembered her interrogations of captured priests.

'Stay in your places. Our enemy only controls evil spirits and the dead. This storm is not of his doing. Stand firm.'

Despite the distance and noise, her voice carried. To a man, her soldiers remained in their places as the storm passed overhead. She looked at her army. It had survived relatively intact.

The storm moved North West and hit the ranks of the hordes of evil with a vengeance never seen. Many bolts of lightning and massive tornadoes struck the packed ranks of the army opposite her. Then without orders, the trebuchet catapults and ballista from the towers opened fire shortly followed by a thousand longbowmen in the ranks of the infantry. Each firing with speed brought on by desperation, knowing it was certain death to their families if they failed. The combined impact of that one minute on the ranks of the horde was truly staggering. It looked like half the one hundred thousand hordes of evil were gone or dead.

This was it. If there was ever a time to use the best heavy cavalry the world had ever seen, this was it.

They Charged . . .

The scene outside the grey stone walled city was one of utter devastation, even the ground shook. Dismembered corpses of just about everything living and undead lay strewn across the mile-wide field of formerly pristine wheat.

Perhaps a half mile in front of the city stood a defiant lone plate mail armoured warrior, bastard sword in the right hand and tattered remnants of a large shield on the left. So much blood and filth of battle was covering the city's sole protector, you could not see who or what it was, although everyone in Tiranimeith knew it would be Princess Elgiva, the last surviving member of the Shanovian Empire's Royal Family. A highly skilled warrior and black mage. Opposing her was the last remaining enemy unit on the field of battle, the wraithlike soldiers of the Dark Legion.

Usually, she would have attacked regardless of the odds enjoying the thrill of taking lives, but today required a different strategy. Her human subjects were the last people unconquered, so to avoid slavery and death, they had to be given time to escape. Today was all about delaying the enemy. A strategy that would also give her infant son the chance of life.

The large humanoid black skinned translucent shape that she knew as The Lord of All Evil moved through the ranks of his prime legion. He was the god that had initially ruled these lands. A god that was now on the verge of ultimate total victory mainly due to the stupidity of her family, herself included. She looked over her shoulder at the cavalry disappearing into the distance as Captain Iredan of her personal guard took her family's sword to safety.

She felt the emanating weight of pure hatred approach, so looked the entity in those fire red eyes.

'You have fought valiantly, as is the way of your family and people. If you had not killed all your spell casting priests, you might have stood a chance. That mistake will now cost you your soul along with the souls of all your people. Like the rest of your family, you have failed utterly.'

'Victory is not always winning on the field of battle. There are many versions of victory, and we have ours today, for you shall not have my people this day, nor anytime soon.' Replied Princess Elgiva standing tall in the presence of the enemy god.

Then she felt the overwhelming compulsion to obey her opponent's command.

'Bow down to me now, worship me, your people worship me, and you all shall live. Defy me, and I will take your souls for all eternity.'

Suddenly, the compulsion to obey the command seemed to slide off her. Her magical protections could not do that. Then she remembered, a decade or so earlier she had strangled the last Arch Priest and head of the church of the Light Bringer. A guard caught the priest with a pretty dark-haired young woman from the Graff family. While dying, he had been muttering strange words with the last of his breath. His final act was to smile at her.

She was brought back to her senses by a series of loud detonations. She looked behind her to see the city walls collapse and houses fall.

'You won't get much out of my soul, it's almost as black as you are, or so I was told. My little army destroyed or routed all of your mortal troops. Undead cannot occupy the land, only terrorise in the dark. You may have the field, but I have won. After today, you will have to go home.'

'As you wish. I may not have destroyed the last humans today, but destroy them I will, one village at a time. I will take their souls, twist and corrupt them. Today I will start with you. Prepare for ultimate pain.'

The Princess could feel the force of his will building, pressing against some unknown shield. Similar to her magical one but different. The compulsion to bow down to him was growing. So this was it, no more time to be had. She created her magical focus, summoned every last scrap of magic she had in her, touched the ground with her hand, and quietly said the same magic words her magicians use to such great effect on the enemy mortal troops during the battle.

There was a great tearing sound as the earth split in two beneath her, many yards front and behind. As she fell, the ground closed up over her.

20 YEARS AGO – OWEN SHAMUS

Sergeant Michael walked through the Kersladen city streets in the pre-dawn on his way to the central barracks. He wore his long heavy hooded cloak more to prevent identification than protection against the weather.

Today was an important day for him. He was to undergo two tests. One to become the Sergeant Major of the City Guard, and the other, to become the only Blade Master in the valley for several generations. At the age of twenty-five years, it was a serious honour even to be asked by the hierarchy to take either test. Nobody had ever held both.

He was not worried about the Sergeant Major tests. They were about organising soldiers and the like. The Blade Master trials were a different matter. He was already a recognised master of two weapons in his dominant hand and had achieved mastery of some other skills as well. Sergeant Michael was already one of the youngest Lord Guardian's in the valley. Now he would have to fight in single combat each other Lord Guardian of the valley twice. Once with the dominant hand, and once using his off hand. He could not reuse the same weapon. The catch was, his opponents could use whatever weapons they wished. The final trial could easily kill. He had to fight three of them at once, though he did get his choice of weapons.

When noticing a medium height dark-haired man ahead of him, he stopped his musing. A priest of the Church of the Light Bringer he thought, judging by the cloak. Following the clergyman was a slightly taller unkempt man carrying a long narrow bladed dagger. He quickened his pace and drew his sword. The churchman stopped and turned to look at the man following him. Mistake, Michael thought. The dagger of the ruffian was thrust into the side of the clergyman who fell to his knees. Michael, who had now reached the pair, in his usual style, beheaded the ruffian in one blow.

Recognising the victim, he caught him in his arms as blood came from the mouth.

'I am sorry Owen, the wound is mortal.'

'Michael, please look after Dina for me. She's at the inn.'

'I will.' And with this, Owen Shamus died.

Twelve months later, Michael carries a baby to some visiting monks at the central market.

'Good day Brother. I am seeking a member of the Order of the Infirmary. Have I found them?' Michael asks.

'You have. How may we assist you?'

'I am Michael, Sergeant Major of the city guard. I have a request to ask of you.'

'I will see what can be done. What is your need?'

'This baby needs a home. His father was murdered a year ago, and his mother has died recently.'

'What is the baby's name?'

'Oswald Shamus.'

'Shamus you say. Oh dear, that is unfortunate. We cannot take a baby from that family. I am due to see the High Priest of the local church. I will take the baby to him and see what I can do.'

PART 1 – THE GATHERING

1 - THE PENANCE OF OSWALD SHAMUS

The ecclesiastical grey stone cell was a small neat well-ordered room with a bed, desk, chair, and large wooden chest. Opposite the door was a small window just large enough to put your head through. Below it, in an alcove, was a twelve-inch equal-armed wooden cross that had a three-inch diameter flat carved sun symbol pressed on the middle.

An outside observer's only complaint would be the damp cold smell one gets at the middle of the night in the depths of winter where the room has no fire. There was just a small candle to repel the darkness. A tall dark-haired man in his early twenties wearing the unadorned white cowl that signified him as an Initiate Priest, sat at the desk writing with his feather quill. He was a hopelessly incompetent clergyman whose nickname Shamus Badly fitted him entirely, or at least that was his opinion.

He looked over his shoulder at the wall next to the bed, staring at the myriad of first names of his ancestors scratched on it. Each name contained two or three dates. The first being the date of initiation, the second being the date of becoming a full priest. The last date, for the few that had it, was that of becoming Arch Priest, the now vacant post of head of the church. He looked mournfully at his name, the only one with just one date. Oswald hoped that one day he would be remembered for the extreme competency that attaches to the Shamus family name. In the silence of his own soul he asked for his god's assistance in being worthy of that desire.

He remembered the events of yesterday and shuddered. Not only did he say his words in the wrong order during the Mid-Winter Holy Day ceremony, he also managed to drop all the holy water onto the altar at a critical moment.

Everyone laughed, apart from the High Priest who was so red-faced Oswald thought he might explode.

He recollected the fate of the last culprit of such a severe error at a Solstice service ten years ago. The error-prone cleric had been stripped to the waist, stripped of rank, birched and cast out through the front gate. Oswald was surprised not to have been given this punishment as well. Instead, the High Priest of his Temple had set him the task of duplicating the entire scroll of Time and Service. Oswald could not have any sleep food or water until his manuscript was identical to the original. Despite working through most of the night, he had only completed about a quarter of the scroll.

Oswald accepted his punishment as fair, more than fair in fact. Though the penance was a tough one, secretly it was a task he liked. It was his best skill, he had not been beaten, and it was always possible that he might remember some of it, but he was exhausted.

I must keep going. It's so late, perhaps two hours to dawn. I must not sleep, I must not . . . he thought.

Ninety minutes later, he awoke with a start as his head rolled off his left arm and banged against the desk. *No! I must have fallen asleep. If I was seen. . . But surely, they will know anyway. A quick prayer by the High Priest to their God, The Light Bringer, is all it would take.* He idly wondered if one of the other churches of the gods of light would take him if cast out. Of course they wouldn't. All of the others were little more than penniless chapels if they even existed. Only the order of the infirmary had any presence.

So he did a quick ad-hoc prayer himself asking for The Light Bringer's forgiveness in the hope that the old stories of tolerance for those that believed were still true. The currently written doctrine clearly stated obedience to a senior priest was paramount. Still, his prayer was all he had now.

Oswald then reviewed his copy of the scroll. He knew

it must be accurate. Damn, somehow the timeline is all wrong. It's my only scroll, and I have written it all wrong. Damn! Damn! Damn! I am going to have to start again from scratch Oswald thought.

The worried penitent read further. His copy said you were supposed to be utterly drained after the ceremony as you had bequeathed your power to God.

Why did I put that? In any event, I've never felt like that, and neither has anyone else, as far as I know. He wondered while continuing to read his scroll.

The service is supposed to take place at sunrise on mid winter's day. What! Surely, I did not write such a thing, but that's in half an hour. Maybe I should pray at sunrise. No that's a silly thought, I can't go and pray at the altar at sunrise, can I? No one prays at dawn these days, so I won't get caught. If I am, I could always say I was praying to appease God for my utter failure at the service and in carrying out my penance. Plus, God may actually listen; you never know. It certainly couldn't make anything worse.

He left the large stone built initiates' house, walked the short gravel path to the open-sided stone built wooden roofed cloisters and headed to the church. It was the largest and most important church in the valley, so big that they couldn't make them that size any more. It was also old, dating back to the days of the old empire, or so it was believed. Except for the roof, it was made entirely out of stone blocks. It even had columns and curved stone arches. It then occurred to him that the orientation of the church was the main window to the sunrise so that the main altar would be illuminated about half an hour later. As his mind continued to churn things over, Oswald wondered if one of his early ancestors had ever presided over this church. Probably, he mused, as he came to terms with never being a priest himself.

He reached the North East Transept and checked the solid dark oak single door. It was unlocked. Gingerly he lifted the latch, door hinges creaking alarmingly as he entered. Sneaking along the side edge of the transept he then dodged behind several large pillars before dashing to the High Altar. I have made it was his first thought. No one else was about, so breathing slowly and deeply Oswald composed his mind and body for the prayers he had to do.

Kneeling in front of the high altar Oswald started to recite the ceremony asking for forgiveness, but his exhausted mind failed him. He tried his best to remember the words, but he was so very tired. Determined to finish the prayer despite feeling ever more drained, Oswald did what he did best, cut corners and improvise. He only used phrases that were of paramount importance while adding a few of his own to tie it all together. The feeling of a distinct lack of energy on top of bone-weary tiredness caused his head to spin. Knowing that the prayer couldn't be finished, Oswald decided to get back to his cell. He stood up, reverently backed away, staggered, tripped over the first step of the altar's plinth, and fell. His head hit the corner of the stone altar where he had previously spilt the holy water.

He lay on the polished marble steps to the altar, struggling to keep his consciousness. His sight was blurry and eyes blood covered. A dark shape of a man stood in the shadows at the side of the church near the South East Transept. The man, with a right hand inside his hooded cloak at the waist, approached. Oswald struggled to move but found that he couldn't even sit up. The hand of the cloaked man moved and drew a long narrow bladed dagger while he started to bend over Oswald. The blade went to Oswald's throat and began to press into the skin.

Just as the horror of realisation sunk in there was the sound of running feet and the commanding voice of Novice Peter.

'Stop with the dagger and run or die. The choice is yours.'

If there was ever someone to have next to you in a tight corner, it was Novice Peter. The only exception was

Brother Michael. A little younger than Oswald, Peter had received several years of adolescent warrior training before his family kicked him out. Destitute, he had joined the church.

The dagger was withdrawn immediately, and his assailant ran back the way he came. Feeling several helping hands around him.

'We will look after you Oswald. We owe you that for the years you have quietly helped and taught all us novices the things we didn't understand and saved the beatings from the master of novices.' Novice Peter said. Oswald succumbed to unconsciousness.

Somehow, despite his bleeding head, he slowly became a little aware of his surroundings, although unable to move or properly wake. He was being picked up by arms under his shoulders and dragged. Firstly he was taken across the smooth stone floor that must be the church, then he was carefully put down and the side door to what must be the transept opened. Although there was a little breeze, he could feel the colder air on his face. The stone floor he was now being dragged along felt like rough cobblestones. He was being taken through the cloisters. Then the stone beneath his feet was replaced by hard earth. The cold brisk wind of just post dawn at mid-winter confirmed it. He was in the vegetable and herb gardens, so was being taken to Brother Michael's infirmary.

Of course, a further attack would never happen with Brother Michael inside. Firstly, Brother Michael did not follow the Church of the Light Bringer but was a member of the monastic Order of The Infirmary. The primary reason though, as everyone knew, you never, ever, ever picked a fight with Brother Michael. Oswald didn't know what it was, but he had a history. His older cousin, Osgood knew but refused point blank to tell him.

Then there was a knock at a door.

'Brother Michael, it's Novice Mark, please help us. Novice Peter and I have Oswald Shamus, and he has suffered a head injury.'

'Bring him in.' The door unlatched and opened.

'Put him in the cot over there and get some water. I will get my things. What happened Peter?'

'We found him on the floor at the High Altar, which had blood on the corner. I think he collapsed while praying and hit his head. There was someone with a dagger stood over him. I frightened him off.'

'Good.' Brother Michael replied. Oswald felt strong, calloused hands on his head, realised he was safe relaxed and faded into full unconsciousness.

Later Oswald Shamus started to become vaguely aware again. He was being washed with a cold, wet cloth but couldn't seem to wake himself up. There were voices, but it was as if they were a long way off. Most of the words could not be understood. Some people seemed to be quite concerned about his wellbeing. He had severe trouble concentrating. There were a lot of unknown words and symbols flying around in his mind. He could also vaguely remember hitting his head on the high altar and seeing a strange white person shaped light saying to him.

"You have paid the blood price. Now I can look after you and your family."

Oswald thought to himself that he had lost his wits. Not only that but for an unknown reason, he was partially aware without being awake. While there was no voice now, there was a bright, warm glow inside as if something else was with him. He knew he would never be alone anymore. A second feeling was also present. An impression that the resting was over and things had to happen. His head still hurt, and he wasn't keen on doing anything but thought that despite his past actions, he did believe that he should do as his God asked, whatever it be.

"Done then." The ethereal voice said to him.

His head was suddenly filled with symbols. Hundreds of them it seemed with strange archaic words that were somehow familiar.

"Too much, too much." Was his inner reply.

"Alright, start with these." Six symbols remained at the front of his mind with matching archaic words.

"Concentrate on these. Use the symbols and the words with the power of your belief in me to summon my help. Each symbol does a specific thing when you invoke with the correct word. You will have to learn for yourself what each one does. I cannot remain long or my mad uncle, The Lord of All Evil, will know. Us Gods of Light are not strong enough for that yet. I will send you a companion spirit to help and assist you. I will try and guide you when I can. You must embark on a journey to return light to the world which humanity will need if it is to survive. Concentrate and learn what combining each of these six symbols can do."

All the other symbols faded into the back of his mind. He was left with six symbols, four overlapping ellipses, a point with eight lines at compass points, a jagged diagonal line, a pointing arrow, a stick man, and a shield. He was also left with six strange words.

"Why don't I teach this to my cousin, he is better by far than me."

"You cannot introduce others to me until you are a full priest. You are just as capable. Besides showing your cousin now would endanger him." The voice was gone.

Oswald thought carefully over what was said. The first thing he realised was that he could now think clearly. Then he considered how to invoke the power of his God. He would have to match the symbols and words to produce an effect, then practice each set individually to work out what it did. After that, it would be necessary to determine how to invoke each of them safely. All of this would require some considerable time and privacy. Oswald believed some of this could be carried out at the infirmary knowing he would be safe with Brother Michael, well safer than most places anyway.

He remained in this meditative state for what he thought was several days. His cousin regularly visited, with Oswald's daily care dealt with by Brother Michael and several novices. While in this state, he considered the symbols and words that had remained in his mind. There was a symbol of a single jagged line emanating from a central point. One of his six given words meant power in an ancient language or roughly that. Oswald decided to try that word with the jagged line symbol.

Calling the chosen symbol to the front of his mind, Oswald quietly said 'Grym', but nothing happened. He then reconsidered the instructions of the Light Bringer.

"Use the symbols and the words with the power of your belief in me to invoke my help."

So, he must do something to invoke the power of his belief in God. He remembered the vision of his spiritual meeting with the Light Bringer and the feelings associated with that. The palm of his right hand tingled. Again, he called forth the symbol of the single jagged line to the front of his mind then quietly said 'Grym'.

He instantly became full of energy. Even his hair felt like it was standing on end. After a few seconds, it dissipated in a kind of small explosion, causing him some pain. He practised various ways of casting the power symbol twice. After some time, he found that adding an extra jagged line to his image and saying 'Grym' twice made the effect more significant, although he was unable to focus for the third time. Oswald concluded the first-word symbol combination he had worked out provided the power portion of whatever he wished to achieve.

The next step must be to work out what one of the others did and then to try and add the power portion to that. There was a symbol of four ellipses at right angles to each other that overlapped. Oswald was aware that in ancient times this meant healthy, or something similar. There was a word given to him that had a comparable meaning.

Again, he remembered the vision of his spiritual meeting with the Light Bringer and the feelings associated with it. The palm of his right hand tingled. He called forth the image of the four overlapping ellipses and instinctively added the image of the jagged line for power he had worked out earlier. He then put his tingling right hand on his head and quietly said.

'Iach Grym'

An effect happened, in this case, his head improved a bit. Oswald decided to stop now in case someone saw him practising his new skill. God telling him that introducing others would only get them killed gave him some concern for his safety. The obvious choice was to keep quiet and practice in private. The first spell perfected used two of his six symbols. Oswald also thought that one of the remaining four unknown symbols represented light. He would have to experiment with that one in private. It wasn't much, but it was a start.

Hunger eventually overcame the ability to maintain his meditative state. Once Brother Michael had returned to his care and dismissed the attending novice, Oswald started to moan. When he felt Brother Michael come to him and check his head, he opened his eyes.

'Welcome back; you've been out a long time.'

'Brother Michael.'

'No no no, don't sit up you are much too weak for that just yet. How are you feeling?'

The door opened, and High Priest Cenric walked in.

'Your Grace, our patient has just woken up.'

Oswald Shamus tried to get up and fell over, being caught by both the High Priest and Brother Michael. The touch of the High Priest was somehow cold, black and oily. Two sets of symbols immediately came to mind, the power one and another, but thinking quickly, he resisted casting them. He was placed back in bed.

'Thank you, Your Grace. Brother Michael appears correct; I can't stand yet.'

'Brother Michael usually is correct on such matters. I have heard Initiate Oswald Shamus that not only did you severely injure yourself while praying at the High Altar at dawn on the Mid-Winter Solstice, but you were attacked. You should have been writing your penance scroll. If you had done so, then neither would have happened. Regretfully the captain of the temple guard found no trace of your attacker.'

'You are correct Your Grace. The patient sustained a severe injury when he somehow hit his head on the corner of the High Altar. He sustained no injury from the attack, the assailant being frightened off by Novice Peter.' Brother Michael interrupted.

'Despite the attack, I gave him a penance and want to know why he was praying instead of his appointed task. He was due the most severe of punishments. I want an explanation.'

Brother Michael nodded as if understanding. 'Your Grace, I suspect that he has cracked his skull just above his right eye. That is a serious injury. As with all serious head injuries, the long-term effects may not be known for some time. Even though he is conscious, it will be some considerable period before he is capable of withstanding any significant questioning.'

'Brother Michael, if he cannot answer me soon, I will have to expel him from the priesthood.'

'In his current situation, that would be harsh even for you, Your Grace.'

'His transgression destroyed our most holy of celebrations. In the absence of penance completion, there is no alternative.'

'There is always an alternative, Your Grace. Discipline is most important but expelling without the right or capability of reply only causes trouble and undermines the willingness of others to obey. I of all people understand that one.' The High Priest appeared to consider matters for a few seconds.

'I must have order and punishment where required. However, I am prepared to consider the alternatives. While you are conscious and appear to be of reasonable mental function, you are also clearly a long way from healthy. I, therefore, have a problem. I gave you a penance, and Curate Shanks has brought me your scrolls. While as ever the quality of your work is exemplary, your content is wrong in several important aspects. You have failed in your penance.'

'That is why I went to pray. I knew the punishment was either death or being cast out, so I took what I knew would be my last opportunity to pray to God to apologise for failing the penance.' Oswald Shamus interrupted.

One thing he had learnt in life was how to think quickly for excuses. While he knew he was lying to a senior priest, Oswald believed God might allow him this one in the circumstances. Then with a shock, he realised that the High Priest, wouldn't count as a Priest of Light and probably worshipped the Lord of All Evil, given his black oily feel and the pop-up symbols he had received.

'While that shows good intentions, you accept that you have failed in your penance. The normal procedure is a full clergy trial with the only available punishments being execution or casting out and stripping of priesthood membership. It would be a mockery of justice to put you on trial when you can't even stand. Brother Michael made it quite clear you would not be able to stand trial for some considerable time. Given what I have seen, I tend to think he is right, and it is not often we agree on anything. I cannot leave this to wait for your recovery or I will lose credibility and authority, do you understand that?'

'Yes, Your Grace.'

'I must give you a severe punishment, but as you cannot stand trial, I must take the severest punishments off the table. I am thinking of banishment but without stripping you of your priesthood membership or status. There is a little village at the head of the valley that has had no priest or religion in as long as can be remembered. I will give you a basic allowance and some equipment. Merchants trade that way and on occasion even as far as

Warameth, which will now be your home until you hear from me further. What do you think of the suggestion Initiate?'

Oswald considered the offer quickly. God had told him he must go on a journey, so Warameth it was to be. If there wasn't any priesthood up there, then he could practice his symbols in peace.

'I think your judgement is fair Your Grace and much better than I had believed possible. I could do with being taught how to preach and run a church though. I will need that knowledge if I am to be of any actual use at all.'

'I cannot have you trained for a banishment. Your opinion, Brother Michael?'

'The punishment is not legal. You cannot replace a right to a fair trial with a lesser punishment, but in the circumstances and due to the Initiate's agreement, you will get no trouble from me. As for the Initiate's training, how about his cousin? He is here several times a day anyway. It will not be as good as formal training. If his cousin agrees to go along with this, it will be the best option as the Initiate will listen to him.'

'Do you agree to this Initiate?' the High Priest asked.

'Yes, Your Grace.'

'Brother Michael, will you?'

'Yes, Your Grace, but it may be a while before he is well enough to travel that kind of distance regardless of the punishment being acceptable or not.'

'I understand, but he must leave with all haste well or not. Good day brother.' With that the High Priest left.

'Oswald are you alright with this?' asked Brother Michael once the door had closed.

'Yes, Brother, I am. I know I must leave and High Priest Cenric's suggestion is as good as any, if somewhat daunting.'

'You are probably correct. Somehow, I will need to train you in combat without being caught, and your cousin will need significant time with you too. You are going to be a busy man, but first, you must eat.'

A little later, his cousin came visiting and gave Oswald a rare hug. He felt a strange warm tingly feeling very different from the horrible cold one he got from the High Priest. That told him all he needed to know.

'I have just had a bizarre talk with High Priest Cenric. He says you have agreed to banishment for failing to complete the penance but that I am somehow to train you to run a small church attract new followers and give sermons. That is the strangest banishment I have ever heard of. Further, he says that you have agreed to this.'

'Yes, I have, cousin. I failed in my penance; I am due punishment. I have long believed that nothing can be achieved behind locked gates, as you well know. This punishment keeps me alive, removes me from causing family and friends trouble, and puts me where I want to be.'

The cousin nods. 'Alright, I will go along with this, but we start now.'

Oswald did not complain and listened intensely. He tried to commit as much as possible to his significantly improved memory, learning a great deal very quickly despite being bedridden. Brother Michael's training had to wait a few days, but when the time came, he was taught quarterstaff, and a large weapon called a maul. It was an enormous two-handed war mace. Brother Michael explained that the staff would suffice for local banditry, but up the valley, he would need the maul.

2 - THE FALCON AND WOLF

The bushes barely wavered as the unseen creature moved through them in the dark of the moonless night. If those being hunted had been observant, they would have seen a dark grey wolf about the size of a large male tiger. A species the humans called Great Wolves.

Freki could smell the evil now and didn't like it, not this close to his human and her pack. Circling the evil unseen, he approached it from downwind. Hearing a noise, the wolf slowly pushed his head through the bushes on the edge of the clearing. Oh, it was these odd looking sort of humans again. These creatures were hated by all animals as they served the Lord of All Evil. Wow, there was a lot of them, many times more of them than in his old pack. He always thought these things looked odd, sort of human but with the wrong skins and heads. If they tried, Freki was sure they could blend into the forest quite well, they had the skin colouring for it. These not humans didn't appear to want to though. They also weren't as tall as his human and her pack, but then again, very little was. Although there were a lot of these not humans, there was an awful lot more in his human's pack. If warned the wolf was confident they could handle it.

He looked around and saw some of his old pack across the clearing quietly watching. Wait, there were more of them. Freki looked up. There was a giant grey and white coloured gyrfalcon perched on a high branch of a tree. Great that looked like Helghyer bonded with another one of his human's pack. They looked at each other. Freki figured that Helghyer also knew what they must do. Slowly he crept through the bushes around this pack of not humans getting in front of them and avoiding their scouts. He was pleased that now it mattered all the years spent with his human had not lost him too much of his wild edge. His old pack had done the same, puppies and all. Tonight was going to be a tough one. If either he or the falcon could get through to his human's pack, then they all stood a chance. If not, they were all dead.

Freki looking up saw Helghyer scanning the area. As the great falcon started to move, the scout nearest to him put an arrow to its bow. Even at this distance, Freki could see the worried expression on Helghyer's face as the falcon took to the air.

The scout released the arrow before he could do anything about it. Thankfully these not humans were nowhere near as good shots with bows as his human's pack were. This one was on his own and not paying attention. Freki crept nearer and growled to distract it from releasing another arrow. Yes, that was it, the not human looked at him. Its face turned to one of horror at the sight of the huge wolf. Freki leapt, knocking the scout to the ground and then bit its throat before it could react. He looked up and realised his old pack had neutralised the neighbouring scouts. There was now an unobserved hole between these not humans and home. He looked at his old pack leader Geri; both knew what the pack must do. They all ran for it.

♦ ♦ ♦

A tall leather-clad female carrying the serious look of the focused hunter sat at a wooden table having some breakfast of bread and cheese. When times required, Luka was also a competent warrior, so this morning, she was part of the second-night shift watch. A massive crash occurred when her falcon flew straight through the window and pecked her on the ear.

'Ow.'

It then flew over to the weapons rack and knocked her sword over.

'Dad, Mum, something is very wrong here.' Helghyer kept squawking and tugging at the swords.

'I'm coming.' Her dad said, pulling on his chain mail

shirt. 'Let's go see.' They picked up their swords and followed Helghyer who squawking flew straight for the north-western gate.

'Dad, I know that call. We're in trouble.'

Luka and her dad ran to the low palisade. She looked out and saw a pack of wolves running towards the compound. The largest wolves were at the back with the cubs in the middle.

'I think that is Tara's wolf at the back next to that larger one. The biggest one appears to be carrying a green and brown arm!' Luka said.

'Guards, open the gates slightly.' She shouted.

'Yes Luka.' And the heavy bar locking the two large wooden gates was moved. As one half started to open, Freki ran at full speed straight to Tara's hut. The cubs and smaller female wolves followed him. Meanwhile, the biggest wolf stayed at the gate dropped the arm on the floor and turned around, then snarled at the wilderness.

'Luka, I don't need your affinity for animals to know there is trouble in the trees.'

'You are correct dad.'

'It looks like bits of a Goblin arm.' A guard shouted up.

'Then shut the gate now.' Ordered Luka's father.

◆ ◆ ◆

A blond haired, twenty years old woman with the muscular physique of a full-blown warrior lay sound asleep on a wooden framed bed. Some five years ago, Tara had been one of the youngest ever to pass the combat tests.

She was woken by a substantial weight on her chest. While opening her eyes with a groan, a sword hilt was dropped on her arm.

'Ow.' Then she saw the blood on Freki's face.

'Dad.' She shouted.

Entering the room, her father saw the wolf's face and ran back out. He returned moments later, pulling his chain mail shirt on.

'Arm yourself, Tara, and stay with me.'

'Yes, dad.'

She ran into the main room pulling on her chainmail shirt as she went, only to see her mother and younger sister get bowled over by a dozen or so wolf cubs that had charged in through the now open front door. Freki was looking at her hopefully.

'Of course we can look after them, can't we mum?' Her mother and sister smiled between face licks. Tara went after her father and ran to the low palisade by the Northwest gate.

While the palisade was low on the inside, it was a good deal higher on the outside. When the tribe had moved to the area some fifteen years ago, they had chosen to place the village here because of the low flat-topped hill. The slope had been excavated to create an earth wall around the circumference of the village, in front of which the tribe had placed large wooden posts with sharpened ends. It gave any attackers a significant barrier to overcome, and a ready-made fire step from the backfilled earth.

They looked over the palisade and saw hundreds of Goblins emerge from the forest some four hundred yards away. They were carrying scaling ladders and a battering ram.

'Secure the gate.' Luka's father shouted.

Some twenty people with ropes and leavers started to push two large stone blocks, each of some two cubic yards, behind the gates. Then some thirty Goblins carrying the battering ram ran straight for the gate. One member of the tribe started frantically ringing the gate's bell.

The few guards at the gate fired their longbows into the charging Goblins but caused insufficient casualties to stop them. A stone block slipped down the slope behind one of the gates just before the Goblins reached it. The attackers hit the now secured entrance with a crash and no significant effect. More archers arrived at the palisade and started firing their bows. With half of the Goblins attacking the gate either dead or dying the rest ran back to the Goblin lines,

Every warrior and hunter were now at the northwest palisade. A group of Goblins with a scaling ladder ran forward. The archery fire took its toll, and not one reached the base of the wall.

'Now what happens? I have not been in one of these before.' Asked Luka.

'We wait. The Goblin commanders will be looking for weak spots. When they think they have found one, they will attack it in force.' Replied Tara.

'So that's what the scouts are doing. Presumably, we want them to stay here.'

'With our chief and many of our warriors away, we do yes.'

Tara then heard Luka shout a command she had not heard before, followed by several arm signals. A fair number of hunters left their places following the palisade parapet around the village. The occasional bowshot from the hunters at any Goblin scout that got too close frequently caused cries of pain. The main body of Goblins remained where they were.

After several hours of unsuccessful Goblin scout probing, the enemy made an all-out attack on the north western palisade. With every defender using a longbow, a quarter of the four hundred or so Goblins who first rushed the palisade never made it to the base of the wall. Unfortunately, as soon as the ladders were up, the archery had to stop. At that point, all the Goblins rushed in.

Tara leant over the palisade and with a massive swing of her sword, severed both hands at the wrist of the leading Goblin climbing the ladder. It fell, knocking several of the others off. There was a swearing shout to get back as an arrow thudded into the wood next to her. Tara saw Luka in trouble. Two ladders had gone up near her position. Two Goblins were now on the fire step and another two climbing over the top of the palisade, the head of a fifth lay at Luka's feet with the bloody corpses of a further two nearby. Although she had done well, Luka was not a warrior with chain mail armour and would not survive four to one odds. Her falcon flew past pecking the eye out of one of the attackers causing it to put its hands to its face. Luka instantly put her long sword in the Goblin's throat.

Being free of enemies, Tara shouted 'Freki, help Luka.'

The wolf, who was already at her side leapt at the Goblin approaching Luka's flank impaling it on the palisade. Tara chopped at the ladder next to her, causing it to fall to the ground. Swinging her large sword again, hit the arm of the next Goblin climbing over the palisade near Luka. With a yell, it fell back over the parapet. Freki was distracting another who was desperately trying to avoid having its throat ripped out, leaving just one for Luka. She deftly parried a blow aimed at her chest then sunk her long sword under the Goblin's leather chest armour into his torso, causing him to collapse with a scream.

'Luka, we must get these ladders down, or our section of wall will be overrun, and the Goblins break through to the village.' Said Tara. Luka's response was to lean over the parapet and swing her sword at the ladder, taking a chunk out of one side several feet below the top. It snapped and fell. Tara downed two more ladders enabling them to return to archery fire on Goblins climbing ladders nearby. They could hear the pounding on the gate, but it did not sound like it was getting anywhere.

While there was fighting on the whole stretch of the northwest palisade, the Goblins had not secured any section. Some of the defenders had cleared a part of the wall of the enemy and were also using archery on those climbing nearby ladders. Like Freki, several of the wild wolves were fighting on the palisade fire step waiting for a Goblin to present an opening or attacking one as it climbed over the parapet. The tribe did not give ground and fought not only with the competent skill of generations of warriors but also with the bravery of the knowledge that retreat was certain death for not only them but their families too.

Traditionally the married women and mothers did not fight; this was now wholly disregarded as they did whatever they could to help their men. Many of the women were quite competent warriors in their own right before having children. The elder children climbed onto roofs firing their smaller bows at whatever Goblin presented itself as a target without the risk of hitting a tribe member.

The Goblin attack continued for what to Tara seemed like hours but was probably only about thirty minutes. She took several hits, but her chainmail armour absorbed most of the blows. Luka also suffered from many minor cuts giving the impression that she was covered in blood but looked much worse than it was. Then there was the sound of a large horn.

'The warriors are back.' Tara yelled with delight.

'It's not over yet' was the reminding shout from her father as an arrow buried itself in the back of a Goblin approaching Tara from behind. Tara looked around and saw her little sister on top of a roof holding her bow smiling.

The returning warriors burst out of the forest like a flood, mercilessly butchering the Goblins outside of the palisade trying to climb the scaling ladders. Some fled, but in a matter of minutes, hundreds lay dead. The warriors now leapt from their horses and started to climb the ladders of the Goblins. Within ten minutes, it was all over, the last Goblin going down to the tribe's chief as it tried to kill Freki's old pack leader. The two of them exchanged a long look of mutual respect.

The aching, battle-weary Tara and Luka both sat down slowly. Helghyer, gliding in the high thermals, could be heard squawking. Freki slowly padded over and nuzzled

Tara. She carefully felt all his body noting no issue other than the blood, filth and exhaustion of war.

Tara's father came over. 'You fought well my daughter, I am proud. You did too Luka; your father was also proud. We are all grateful for your animals. Without the help of the falcon and the wolves, we would not have survived this.'

'How is everyone?' Luka asked.

'Many are down or injured. I am afraid your father is unconscious, a club to the head it seems. The healers believe he will be fine given time.'

'That's great. In the end, I feared the worst.'

'We all did. We are putting patrols of warriors with hunters and trackers attached to check for others and our situation.'

'I need to check on my father then I will be ready.' Said Luka.

'We will both be ready in a few hours. We need some rest and get cleaned up. Neither of us is seriously hurt.'

'No Tara, you won't.' Her father said. 'Get yourselves clean first, then come and find me. The tribal council are discussing something else more important for you to do. I will leave it to you to decide if you will accept it. I am very much in two minds myself.' He then left.

Luka got up. 'I must go to my father and family.'

'Of course, you fought very well today far better than can be expected of any hunter.'

'Thank you, Tara. You warriors handle yourselves with such skill. I won't be accusing your kind of being a sedentary wasteful option ever again.'

'I need to clean Freki and check on the other wolves before I do anything else. See you later.'

◆ ◆ ◆

Luka glanced at the broken wooden framed window as she approached the sizeable circular wooden and mud hut that was her home.

An acceptable price, she thought. Then Luka noticed another experienced female hunter and scout similar age to herself covered in blood cuts and bruises, washing her bedridden, unconscious father.

'Katina, what are you doing here?' She said.

'Your father went down, protecting me. I killed the Goblins around him afterwards. I would be dead if it weren't for him. I would like to stay with him a while, at least until your mother gets back from speaking with the council.'

Luka sighed. She would have preferred family only but knew that thought was unfair in the circumstances.

'Very well, Katina.'

She grabbed her father's hand and whispered in his ear. 'I love you, father.' There was the faintest of squeezes back. 'I must go and get cleaned up now. The council want to speak to me.' There was another light squeeze of the hand. Luka was worried but pleased. Her father was still in their somewhere and to some small degree, partially conscious.

◆ ◆ ◆

Tara looked at Freki, 'Mind if we find my mum and sister first, then I clean you.' Freki pricked his ears up and looked across the compound. Off they went if somewhat slowly, only for the pair of them to get knocked flat by Tara's younger sister and a pile of wolf puppies.

Her sister talked excessively quickly about how amazed she was at having killed a Goblin with her bow. While Tara was pleased for her, she shouldn't be surprised. Her younger sister was better at both sword and bow than any of the other children, and some of the adults too. At fourteen years old she could already hit just about anything with her bow at one hundred paces and hadn't even started her warrior training yet. Tara hugged her mum, and yes, she was fine just a couple of bruises.

The older children had already obtained cloths and several buckets of water from the well. People were getting cleaned up. She went to the nearest pail of water, grabbed a rag and cleaned Freki off, then went in search of the other wolves. Those with skill in animal husbandry were trying to clean and bind the wounds on the wolves as many were hurt. There were no fatalities, so long as the wounds were cleaned and treated correctly. The wolves were prepared to be washed by her tribe but had a problem with bandages.

'Be careful. These are wild wolves. They helped us today out of a common need for protection from the Goblins.' Tara said to the immediate hands-off reaction from the carers. 'Freki, you know the bandages were temporary and safe from your stomach wound last year. Can you tell your old pack?'

Freki gave several barks, whines, whimpers and some barely perceptible body movements. The growling of the other wolves stopped. Tara thought there was a look of profound scepticism, but the wolves did allow themselves to be treated. Luka came over.

'You need to get cleaned up Tara. I can stay here.'

'Thank you.' and off Tara went.

Sometime later, Tara started to help Luka brushing down various animals. Tara's father approached them.

'Hello, ladies. Luka, have you seen your father?'

'Yes, he squeezed my hand on a few occasions when I spoke with him, so he is still in there somewhere.' She responded.

'That is even better. The council want to see both you two and Katina, now.'

A little while later, Luka, Tara, Katina and Tara's father stood outside the great hall. They could hear shouts and lots of heated arguments; mainly, it would seem from Luka's mother. Katina looked at the others. 'I thought we were done with the fighting today.'

Luka looked at Katina. 'It appears my mother doesn't agree with you.' Luka said, giving a smile.

'I had better put a stop to this.' Said Tara's father.

'Good luck, dad, you're going to need it.'

'You will be asked to do a task. Make your minds up.' He took his large sword off his back and banged the pommel loudly against the door to the hall three times. He entered without waiting, then shouted, 'This hall's deliberations can be overheard.' The hall silenced.

After a moment of peace, the chief was heard to say, 'Ask them to enter.' One of the warriors headed for the door. Luka turned to Tara. 'I am not looking forward to this.'

'We had better go in.' Tara replied. The three of them entered side by side without being asked or having the door opened. All three briefly bent down on one knee bowing to the chief and rose. Luka then said in a clear, loud and firm voice.

'We understand the council wishes to see us.' Looking straight and level gazed at the seated chief. He was an enormous man even by their standards and had a formidable presence. He was also the most skilled of his tribe's warriors, yet all three looked him straight in the eye.

'You are certainly your mother's daughter Luka.' Was the chief's initial comment and was followed by quiet giggles from some of the crowd. 'A large portion of the tribe's council of elders and I have an important task to ask of you three. It would be appropriate to say that a significant portion of the tribe and the balance of the council do not agree with my request, and that includes your own families. I would also say there is merit in some of the counter arguments I have heard so I will place matters before you and let you make up your minds.'

'Oh, that's just great.' Katina said in a voice that was not meant to be heard yet still managed to be carried to the farthest reaches of the hall and provoked many laughs.

The chief continued, 'As you all know a few years ago,

our lord guardian, our priest and an escort left us heading north to find better and safe lands to live. When they found them, they were to return and lead us to our new home. They have not returned. I wish you three to find them, then return and take us to our new home. Today's attack, the largest in years, made that task now urgent and imperative.'

An elderly man then stood slowly with his stick supporting him. He started shouting.

'This is ridiculous and dangerous. The only reason we survived today's attack was the forewarning by the animals. Send these three away, and the animals will go with them. The next attack we will all be dead. The connection between the falcon, the wolf and their owners are not as good as a black witch and her cat, but it is damn close. Without that, we don't stand a chance.' As if to emphasise the point Helghyer flew in and landed next to Luka, shortly followed by Freki who stood next to Tara. Several of Freki's old pack stood by the door with enquiring expressions on their faces.

Luka's mother then shouted. 'This is too much to ask of my daughter or my family. My husband is badly wounded; she must forage for our food. If I lose my daughter too, we will starve.'

The chief called for silence. 'The tribe will provide for you.'

'That is too large a burden. Things are hard as they are.' Was the comment made by a member of the crowd.

'Still, it will be done.' The chief commanded to some crowd grumbling.

'What if our priest and the guards are dead?'

'They are not.' Came the authoritative voice of the tribe's elderly shaman.

In the semi-silence that followed, Luka looked at Tara and Katina. Both had somewhat resigned looks on their faces. With a sigh, Luka broke the silence.

'There is no choice we have to find a new home. It

would only have taken two arrows, one for Helghyer and one for Freki, and we would never have known the attack was coming.'

'Even then I doubt we would have made it without Freki's old pack.' Said Tara. 'They will not stay long even if they wish too. The wolves will need to range to seek food as soon as the injured are well.'

'The tribe and our neighbours cannot remain here any longer we must all leave or die.' Was Katina's comment.

'There are too many Goblin tribes coming to the plains from the west. Even with our neighbours, we do not have the warriors to defeat all the Goblin tribes together. The only real questions are where to and when.' Added Tara.

The chief interrupted. 'The events of today have determined that we must investigate the fate of the former expedition. If we cannot locate the wanderers, then suitable alternative lands must be found. This time those sent must return promptly with answers. We need to know one way or another.'

The elderly man banged his stick and again interrupted. 'That may all be true, but it cannot be Luka and Tara. They and their animals are needed here.'

The three young women looked at each other, giving almost imperceptible movements that said a thousand words in an instance. They each knew what the reply must be.

Katina spoke first. 'We will go. Helghyer and Freki will increase our chances of avoiding unpleasantness with Goblins.'

'It will not be a typical search for those that went before. All we can do is make an educated guess at where the previous expedition went and whether we can find any place safe to live.' Luka informed the meeting. Looking questioningly at the other two women 'We will return in six months regardless.'

'Agreed' was the other two responses.

Tara's father looked at the women. 'You are decided on

this.'

'There is no choice, father. We are the most likely to succeed.' Tara's sister and mother ran forward with a cry and hugged her. Luka's mother did the same.

'It is decided then. Your bravery and skill may well save us all.' The chief replied.

'Or kill us all.' Was the response from the back of the hall.

3 - THE MINE

The earliest of Arturous' memories were the warm, safe feeling of being wrapped securely to his mother's front while she worked in the mine. There was always the kind loving face looking down at him no matter her tasks, tiredness or even injury. His first memories were from before he could walk. At this young age, he was not aware of his surroundings, just where his mother was.

Later in life, he realised that to retain vivid memories from such a young age was very unusual, but then so was he. Perhaps it was because he was an Elf of the Woodland Realm, but he could not be sure. The Goblins permanently segregated male and female elves. There were so few kinder (Elvin children conceived before enslavement) and no new ones.

Once he could walk, the slave masters no longer allowed his mother to carry him. Instead, he was placed on the floor behind her off to one side. She was still mindful of him, paying constant attention and smiling at him whenever she could.

He started to pay proper attention to his surroundings. Looking back, they were dark narrow wet cold and dangerous, but at the time he did not know of anything different. His life revolved around sitting behind his mother while she worked at the face, then walking the few hundred yards to the sleeping area. A place which was only slightly wider than the one mine cart width passage they worked in.

Night-time was still one of his best memories, though. Falling asleep cuddled into his mother's chest, her arms wrapped protectively around him.

The earliest of his bad memories was the food. It was dreadful. One meagre strip of some meat, grain and fat mix the Goblins gave the slaves twice per day. His mother did not receive any extra allocation to feed him. Instead, she had to break a piece off the end for him to eat. Even at this young age, Arturous noticed the size of the part she gave him was getting bigger and the remainder for herself smaller, despite the physical nature of her work each day. Strangely the water was clean pure and plentiful, this being due to the proximity of the underground waterfall more than any Goblin desire to be helpful.

His overall memory of those early years was the Goblin guards being cruel and vicious. Beatings were regular and without reason. Frequently an elf slave was beaten to a point where they could not work. Occasionally they were killed. He started to pay attention to what the guards were saying as much as possible to find a reason for the physical violence. There, of course, wasn't one, but he did learn the basics of the Goblin language just by watching and listening. By the time his mother told him he was three years old, he could speak the basics of both Elvish and Goblin. Spending his time in a dimly lit mine, taught him how to navigate in the dark by remembering how many steps it was between two points. This also by extension and continued application taught him how to count, as well as the beginnings of addition and subtraction with angles and the effect on distances. His mother taught him the very basics of the elven written language using patches of dirt on the ground on the rare occasions she had the time.

One day Arturous heard another group of Goblins and slaves coming. He woke his sleeping mother.

'Mummy, mummy there are more coming.' A group of about a dozen male elf slaves in chains were taken to a passage the women no longer mined as the rock was too hard for them to work. The men were carrying heavier equipment than his mother and the other women used. Much he didn't recognise.

'Arturous, see the one standing tall in the middle. He is your father. His name is "Almous." When you are older, and they take you away to be with the males of our kind, you must make yourself known to him.'

Arturous studied the man as he walked by and thought he noticed the merest hint of acknowledgement passing between them, missed by both sets of guards. From then for quite a time, he could hear the male group working with sounds of hammering and the passing of heavy carts. Slowly though, day by day, the sounds grew more distant as the two passageways progressed in different directions.

Some months later, shortly after Arturous' mother told him he was five years old, four new Goblins arrived one morning and grabbed him from his mother while they were asleep. He was woken by a callous, dirty hand being placed over his mouth while being swept away from his mother's arms.

Instinctively he bit the hand over his mouth as hard as he could, spat out a piece of the finger and screamed. He was instantly dropped by the Goblin that had grabbed him, who while cursing held his bleeding hand to his chest. He ran to his mother, who was quickly getting to her feet. Before she could ready herself though, two Goblins grabbed an arm each while a third attacked her with the large sticks they all carried. Arturous, crying and screaming hysterically, picked up the heavy stick dropped by the Goblin who grabbed him first. Then with all his strength, he swung it at the back of the legs of a Goblin hitting his mother. It didn't do much harm, but the legs buckled, and he fell over. After a few seconds of shock, the remaining two started to laugh at the sight of a five-year-old elf boy hitting the prostrate Goblin with a stick.

'A five-year-old kinder has put two of you out. Stop laughing and get the job done.' Was a new stern, gruff voice from behind the Goblins and could be heard over the screaming voices of the other women.

Arturous swung his stick again as hard as he could, aiming for the prostrate Goblin's head. It raised its arm to protect itself. There was an audible crack as his large stick hit the Goblin's wrist. Arturous was picked up from behind, slammed against a wall, then dropped and hit in the stomach. Crying in fear and pain, he lifted his head to see his mother covered in blood on the floor being beaten by guards with sticks. Desperately he picked up his stick and stood up tall preparing to rush in for the second time.

'Enough kinder. Do no more, and we will not harm your mother further, continue, and I will slit her throat myself.' Said the gruff-voiced Goblin haltingly in elvish.

'You are also not going to be harmed. We are simply taking you to the males of your kind because of your age, that is all.'

'Please let us say goodbye.' Said his blood covered mother.

'Yes, slave I will permit that. Go kinder say your goodbyes, but quickly.' Arturous ran over to his mother and flew into her arms.

'It is now time for you to find your father. We will be fine. You fought bravely, my valiant little warrior, but sometimes a fight can't be won, and we must do as best as we can to survive.' She hugged him fiercely for a few seconds before they were forcibly separated. Screaming Arturous was put over a Goblin shoulder and carried off into the darkness. The last vision of his mother's bleeding face burned itself into his soul.

He was carried through various dimly lit passageways to a larger room where he was dumped on to a used bedroll lying on the floor.

'This is your replacement slave.' The gruff-voiced Goblin said.

Arturous lay on the floor, crying on what he knew was now his home. An elderly male elf came over to him and gently touched him on the back. He winced.

'You're hurt, aren't you lad?' Arturous nodded.

'Then let's have a look.'

The elderly elf gently felt Arturous' body once his course cloth tabard was removed.

'How is he Madarn?' A voice asked.

'Cracked ribs, bruising to the chest and stomach. Can't

see where all the blood is from though.'

'It isn't mine.' Arturous said through the tears. There was a surprised look on the faces of the gathered elves. 'They tried to take me from mummy while we were asleep, so I bit his finger off.'

'You have had Goblin blood in your mouth. You must drink this. Do not swallow, just swill it around and spit it out.' The elderly elf told him. Arturous drank from the small earthenware bottle he had been handed. He was then washed down with the same vile smelling liquid and dressed.

'What is your name?'

'I am Arturous, son of Aebba. I am told my father is Almous.'

'Madarn, we must tell his father.'

'There is no easy way to achieve that. Right now, we must treat his injuries and keep him safe.'

The following day he started to shiver and sweat. Bouts of vomiting and dizziness were frequent. For the next week, he rested and was washed down with the smelly liquid daily. He was also made to swill it around his mouth twice a day. In time he recovered fully. One day the elderly Madarn woke him.

'Morning Arturous. I am afraid to say it's time for you to start work.'

'Yes, sir.' Arturous said and got up.

'Your first tasks will be fetching and carrying water for the rest of us to drink while working. This helps the team because it means we can keep going without having to stop to fetch water.'

'Yes, sir.' The elderly elf took him on a quite long but not to arduous journey for a five-year-old to the same waterfall his mother and the other women used. He added the route to his mental map. If he could slip away occasionally, then he might be able to see his mother.

'The ledge is very slippery. It is safest to refill the skins from here.'

'Yes, sir.'

Madarn gave him a knowing look while his back was towards the escorting guards. Arturous filled the water skins as instructed and was escorted back first to the sleeping area, and then to the work face.

He patiently waited until needed and then distributed his water. After which the skins required refilling. On this occasion and several more Madarn and a Goblin guard, escorted him. When he knew the way, Madarn let Arturous go on his own, with just the guard, carrying out his duties diligently, but not too quick.

Over the next few weeks, he carried out his daily work tasks to the best of his ability. He was also careful to maintain the slower walking pace when escorted by a Goblin. Then it happened, a trip to the waterfall without a Goblin escort. This time, however, he took no chances and did the walking at the usual slow pace through the dark corridors returning with refilled water skins.

Over time, the number of unescorted trips increased. It also occurred to Arturous that each group of Goblin guards had only one leader, and at best, it alone could count and even then, not always. Arturous thought he couldn't make use of it now due to his size, perhaps when he was fully grown.

One day his team were working later than usual, so he had to get additional water again without an escort. When clear of the guards, he ran to the waterfall, arriving very quickly, then on to the women's sleeping quarters. They had finished the day's shift, but the Goblin guards were still present, so he crept slowly up the passageway in the shadows. Seeing his mother sitting and eating, gave a hand sign for a kiss and a hug. She responded with a slight smile. Quietly he slipped back off into the shadows and ran back to the waterfall.

Although he filled the water skins without issue or detection, unfortunately, he slipped while running back severely twisting his ankle. Slowly he hobbled to the work area.

'That explains it.' The gruff-voiced one said to the other guards having spotted him hobbling.

'I am sorry, I slipped at the waterfall.' Arturous replied in Elvish. The guard shrugged, and Arturous distributed the water.

Eventually, the iron ore ran out in their passageway. The area where the ore was last found was widened out a few yards in all directions taking several weeks, but no further deposits of any kind were found. The following morning while they were still eating breakfast, the gruff-voiced Goblin returned.

'This area is worked out. You are being split up. Kinder come with me, the rest of you wait here others will come to take you to your new teams.' Arturous picked up his bedroll and few belongings, looked at Madarn and the others, gave a thankful smile and followed the leaving guard.

He was taken through various corridors and passageways, frequently having to run to keep up. When trying to fill in his mental map, noticed that he was walking in circles, but said nothing for fear of exposing his unusual ability. Although they walked for a long time, he believed they had travelled about half a mile from where they had started. Arturous recognised the group the Goblins had been taken to, and his heart jumped.

'Slave, I have your new water carrier.' The gruff-voiced Goblin ordered. A tall slave walked over.

'Hello. My name is Almous. I am the team leader. Your prime job is to fetch and distribute water and food to us adults. When you are bigger, you will help move rocks, and when fully grown, you will help mine ore. I will teach you the ways of mining and the dangers involved, so be mindful. What is your name?' The tall slave asked.

'I am Arturous, son of Aebba and born in the mine.' Arturous replied with a respectful bow. There was a stunned look on Almous' face and some of the miners.

Arturous smiled a bit and nodded slightly trying not to give anything away to the watching Goblin guards.

'You have your mother's eyes.' Was his father's barely audible reply.

There was a loud crash sound behind them. As the guards turned to look, Arturous gave his father a quick hug. He let go immediately so as not to be seen by the guards.

'After being taken from mummy, I was placed with the work gang of an elderly elf called Madarn. He taught me the basics. I carried and fetched water as well as food and helped with collecting small rocks.' Arturous continued.

'The old thorn is still going then.' Was the reply with a slight smile.

'Yes, sir. They are being moved and split up as our area is now played out.'

'Enough talk, you have work to do.' A guard said.

'Sir, can you please show me the way to the water. I don't know the route from here.' Arturous asked in elvish. The gruff-voiced Goblin motioned to one of the guards.

As with Madarn's crew, to start with, Arturous was escorted to the waterfall all the time. A few weeks, and sometimes they didn't. A few months, and he always made the trip on his own. He used the unescorted trips to learn the skills of stealth and quietness.

Collecting the food packs was different. There were always at least two guards. This had nothing to do with him, but with other Goblins trying to steal it for their gangs.

He did, at one point manage to get a few moments alone with his father. Just enough to tell him that his mother was alive when he last saw her, and he knew where she had been a few months back. His father was overjoyed. He did not tell him about his special memory and navigation ability, or his mental map.

Over the next few years, his father showed him what the various tools were and how to use them. He was taught the methods of mining and breaking rock, how to cut passageways and shafts, how to support both, how to spot the risks such as the danger of collapse and gas. Despite his training, at this young age, he carried out only the ancillary tasks.

By the time he approached puberty, the mining had hardened his muscles. The constant practising of stealth in travelling through the corridors in the dark had made him quick and agile. Remembering the map of the mine, counting of steps, continually working out where he was, and learning of both Elvish and Goblin languages kept his mind active and quick of thought. By the time he was twelve years old, he was strong, lean, agile and intelligent.

Arturous entered elvish puberty at about thirteen years old. When this happens, the physiological changes for elves are far more radical than with humans. Humans and elf are very similar in outward appearance, but how elves mature physically is very different. The final height of an elf is mostly achieved before puberty, whereas the adult muscle mass, and body shape all occur afterwards. Another important difference is the ageing. Body ageing slows down dramatically once puberty starts. So dramatically that for every elf year of ageing, something like thirty human years has passed. In other words, an elf in his mid-twenties is approximately four hundred human years old.

In his thirteenth year despite other work, he still fetched the water when needed. It was on returning from one such trip.

'Almous, I am getting a hint of a strange smell.'

'All of you stop work.' Arturous noticed the Goblin guards had developed a worried look.

'Where are those caged rats.' A guard had already gone and retrieved one. He wordlessly handed it to Almous who put it on a ledge near the work face. He waited a few seconds then.

'We leave now guards and all.'

'You don't give orders slave. You will stay here as long as we tell you to.'

'You can remain if you want, but we are leaving. We will go back to our sleeping quarters and await further instructions. If you doubt my reasoning, look at the rat.' They all looked at the cage, and the rat was lying on its side.

'Almous, I don't feel well.' A fellow worker said. Then as if to emphasise the point, he collapsed. Arturous, who was further away from the work face took a deep breath, ran in, grabbed the worker's arm and pulled. His father grabbed the other arm, then everyone ran for it, guards and all.

'What was that, Almous?' Arturous said to his father once clear of the area.

'That was one of the types of bad air I told you about. Stay in that, and it kills you.' Arturous looked at the elf unconscious on the floor.

'He will be fine in a while. A terrible head tomorrow though.'

'We were lucky Almous, a few more minutes and we would all be dead.' Another elf said.

'I know.'

Then there was a deafening explosion that echoed through the mine. A few minutes later, the gruff-voiced Goblin came in.

'What are you all doing here?'

The guards went over to him. They spoke quietly and quickly while looking at Arturous and grovelling profusely. The gruff-voiced Goblin seemed to consider matters for a minute, then looked at Arturous.

'You appear to have a good nose. I need that now come with me.'

'Lead slave, some of the guards are going to have to see the mine supervisor and report this. Stay here cause no trouble, and you will receive extra food.'

'Yes, master. If we go back, we will all be dead before

the first mine cart. You will get no trouble from us, but we will not go back.'

'The guards will make sure the mine supervisor knows your opinion.'

Arturous went over as ordered, was blindfolded, led away, and then taken a reasonable distance through many unfamiliar passageways. Eventually, there was a whiff of fresh air. Then a light appeared beneath his blindfold shortly followed by a very unusual warm feeling on his face. Arturous realised he had been taken outside for the first time. He also added the route to his mental map though it was quite a long one. Unfortunately, there were the sounds of many dozens of Goblins, including possible women and children. The reluctant conclusion was that no escape was possible this way.

After a further one hundred yards or so he was told to halt. His ankles were shackled, and so were several other young male and female elves he could hear around him. Then, still blindfolded and now shackled, the group was led outside the mine for a mile or two. When Arturous could smell burning, they were halted.

'Slave scum, close your eyes.' Arturous did so just as his blindfold was forcibly removed. The bright light stabbed at his slowly opening eyes, but it did improve over time.

'Listen, slaves. There has been an explosion and a collapse in a new mine. You six are to enter the mine, retrieve gemstones that have already been mined and dig out more. You will also remove the fallen rock and stabilise the entrance. Now get going.' The shackles were removed.

Arturous quickly looked around the valley through eyes, hurting from the bright light of the sun. He noticed the mine complex was vast. They were near the head of a valley several miles across at this point with a river running through the middle. There were camps on both sides of the river with evidence of Goblin families as well as other slaves. Further up the valley was obscured by thick smoke from many large chimneys.

'Slave get on with it.' Came a hoarse shout of a Goblin that was accompanied by a crack of a whip on his back. Arturous winced from the pain then followed the two boys and three girls walking slowly over to the collapsed mine entrance.

They were still quite low on the mountain, so a significant amount of earth had been taken away to make the new entrance. It had been randomly piled up nearby rather than properly removed. Arturous also considered they had not cleared enough of the earth from above the work area. As a result, the explosion caused the overhanging earth to cover the collapsed entrance.

The first thing the six of them did was clear earth, small stones, and loose rocks. Once this had been achieved, they saw small gaps between large blocks of stone near the top. He signalled to the watching guards and after an acknowledgement climbed the fallen rocks with his companions to a small gap.

'One at a time. I will go first.' Arturous said to the other slaves.

Holding a candle in one hand, he put his arms ahead of him and crawled in. The gap was very tight. If he had even been slightly bigger, he would not have got through. There was a strange whiff to the air.

'Do not follow me.' Was Arturous' quick shout back to the others. He kept crawling through receiving many cuts and abrasions on the way. When he climbed out the other side and stood up, the scene was one of total devastation. The place was littered with shattered timbers and burnt corpses of many Goblins. The smell was also much stronger here but not overpowering. It wasn't the same bad air as Arturous had experienced this morning, so according to his father's lessons that only gave one option, burning air. He also noticed a lot of crystals lying around in hands, bags, pockets and loose on the floor.

The strange smell was getting stronger. Picking up a

crystal in his other hand, Arturous left. After some time, he crawled out, holding the crystal and candle in front of him.

'We can't go in. It's unsafe. The air on the other side is bad and can catch fire. That is what killed all the other Goblins. It's dreadful in the mine, but there are loads of these.' Arturous said, opening his hand to expose a clear jewel that was shimmering inside.

'Get back in there now.' A Goblin ordered Arturous as the crystal was snatched from his hand.

'Most honourable master, we will be killed if we go in. The air will burn.' Arturous was whipped instantly and hard. He screamed.

'I am not deliberately refusing you, sir. Almous, our team leader, has taught me about this stuff. There are two types of bad air, the stuff that kills by breathing, and the stuff that catches fire. A single spark and the air will burn. The first one of those smells I caught this morning. There is a strange smell to the air inside and lots of burnt bodies behind the collapse. It must be the second one.' Arturous said while he continued to be whipped.

'Hold.' Said the gruff-voiced Goblin who had returned to the back of the group unnoticed while the attention was on Arturous.

'Slave go back in and bring back evidence of burning. Quickly now.' The gruff-voiced Goblin ordered. Arturous nodded and scrambled off. As he did so, he heard the gruff-voiced Goblin say to the other guards.

'Given what we already know if he comes back with proof, we must accept what the slave says as true. If he fails, kill him.'

Crawling through the gap again, Arturous remembered a charred severed arm near the entrance. Having not taken the candle with him, he felt around in the darkness for the limb. Finding it quite quickly, Arturous grabbed it and retreated. Once he had crawled out, he merely handed the arm over to the gruff-voiced Goblin. It was burnt almost beyond recognition. The Goblin nodded.

'There is a pool downhill a little way, get yourself cleaned up. While you are doing so, come up with a way to work this out. The crystals must be recovered, and more mined no matter the cost to slave or Goblin. Whatever happens, you six are going back in.' The gruff-voiced Goblin told him. Arturous nodded and followed the first of two Goblins downhill. Deep in thought, he washed.

Oblivious to his open surroundings, he cleaned the cuts and scrapes as best as he could. After a while, he was escorted back.

'And?' The gruff-voiced Goblin asked.

'As the bad air builds up over time, a single flame or spark will ignite it, and we all die. You too probably judging by the size of some of those stones. No jewels for anyone.' The gruff-voiced Goblin and a new leader type nodded.

'I think it is entering from the mine face at the back. The only way I can think of is to cause another explosion then, clear a new way in and get out what we can before the bad air builds up too much again. We won't be able to take candles in or use tools as the sparks will cause trouble. I don't know how more can be mined. Any use of tools and bang.' Arturous suggested.

'The crystals must be recovered, but we will do it your way for now.'

'The second explosion may collapse everything or blow all that clear and kill the lot of us anyway.' Arturous said, pointing at the collapsed entrance.

'The crystals must be recovered no matter the cost.' Was the reply.

'I need a long pole about three times my height and some twine.' Arturous asked. The ornately dressed Goblin waved a hand, and a guard trudged off downhill towards their camp muttering. After a while, he came back carrying a long thin tree branch about two inches in diameter.

Arturous sighed, took the tree limb and tied the candle

too it. Then he lit the candle while protecting it from the wind and started to carry it towards the narrow entrance.

'Halt slave. We are not letting you in their unescorted.' The ornate Goblin said. 'You take the pole and deal with it.' He said, pointing to the Goblin with a whip.

For a second, it looked as if there would be a challenge, but the rasping sound of the gruff-voiced Goblin's sword being drawn stopped that. Gingerly the Goblin took the branch from Arturous and climbed the bank of debris. Arturous, on the other hand, retreated rapidly. The Goblin slowly inserted the candle end of the long branch through the entrance. It was unable to resist the temptation of looking in. There was a massive explosion with a scream. The now incinerated Goblin was sent flying through the air along with much rock stone and earth. They all dived to the ground behind whatever cover was available while being showered by small stones and earth.

It took several minutes for things to settle before everyone got up.

'It appears our slave was correct my chief.' The gruff-voiced Goblin said while looking at the devastation. The one referred to as chief, just nodded.

Arturous got up and with the other five elves went to where the entrance had been. While rocks had been blown clear more had fallen blocking the old narrow crawlspace. With the help of the other slaves for a second time, they cleared a passageway in.

'I will go first. I know what the danger smells like.' Arturous told the other slaves. 'Can you please shine some light through the hole, but don't put the candle inside or we are all dead.' Arturous said to the two senior Goblins with hindsight somewhat too firmly. Surprisingly to Arturous, they took it well as they happened to be looking at the burnt corpse of the whip master.

Arturous squeezed through a hole back into the new mine. This time the devastation inside seemed much worse. More rocks had fallen. Remembering where one of the dead Goblins had been, he decided to search the body. Steeling himself for the unpleasant task, he touched a squashed wet mess partially covered in rocks that had a gemstone in one of its pockets. Like the other one taken out earlier, the gem tingled the hand when touched. He crawled back up to the entrance hole.

'You can come in now.' He shouted up the gap. One by one, his companions joined him. They sat on nearby rocks until all were present.

'I will put something in each of your hands. It is what we are looking for.' Arturous said quietly.

'It tingles.' Said the soft female voice of the first person he gave the gemstone too.

'That is probably the best way of knowing if you have picked up the right stone. Pass it on please.' Once they had all handled it.

'Does it tingle for all of you?' They all confirmed it did. 'Then feel your way around and place in your bags everything that tingles. Check the dead too. I got that one from an inside pocket. When we start to get a funny smell, we must all leave immediately. No arguments.' There were various sounds of agreement.

They separated. It was not quite pitch black. Each of the slaves placed gemstones in their sack and cast other stones aside. Slowly Arturous noticed the strange smell return. He left it as long as possible knowing the beating they all would receive when they left.

'We must all leave now. Don't try to keep any. The Goblins are bound to search us.' Arturous said to the others. There were a few moans, but Arturous was insistent. Reluctantly various additional gemstones were placed in sacks. They all crawled out.

'The smell is back. I am sorry, we could not stay any longer. We have brought these out for you.' Arturous said bowing humbly and pointing at the six, part full sacks. The leader signalled a Goblin who scrambled up the slope and sniffed at the entrance hole. He turned towards the leader and nodded.

The sacks were taken from them. Arturous believed they had retrieved several dozen gems of varying sizes.

'Now strip completely while we search you all fully. Have a very good look, boys. It's the only time you will see a naked female elf in your miserable lives.' The head Goblin said, laughing.

Arturous saw the three girls look at each other and nod. They started to undress. Arturous turned away out of respect and got whipped instantly.

'Relax, it's alright, we are all in our twenties. Female elves develop slower than you boys do.' A soft female voice said to him. He undressed and turned around.

The girls had made no attempt to cover themselves, stood quite openly before the boys with blushing faces, and smiling looked them all up and down. In doing so, they put the boys at ease. They were all searched as were their clothes. The process took a significant amount of time. No hidden gems were found.

'You have done well. Take your clothes, go down to the pond, get cleaned up and dressed. You can each have one of these. They are an edible fruit called apples. Also your teams will be given extra food for a week.' The ornate Goblin stated.

Once cleaned up, they were blindfolded and shackled again, then led away. Arturous could smell that he was being taken back into the mine. He was made to be stationary while he was unshackled. There was another earth-shaking explosion.

'Idiots.' Was the comment of the gruff-voiced Goblin.

'I don't mean to speak out of turn master, but I can't think of a way of mining the stuff without being blown to bits before you get anything out.' Arturous said while bowing humbly.

'Neither can we. That is why you weren't all killed for refusing to mine it.'

He was escorted further along many corridors. His

mental map indicated he was being taken back to the sleeping area for his team. Eventually, they arrived back, and his blindfold was taken off.

'Stay here. The rest of your team will be back shortly.' The Goblin guard told him and placed a small bag of ration bars on the floor. Arturous counted them, two additional bars each. He lay on the floor, resting for what seemed like hours while thinking over the day's events. His guard leaned against the wall, bored watching him only occasionally. Eventually, the others returned.

'Arturous, you are safe. When we heard the other explosions, we feared the worst.' Almous said to him holding his hand in his two, firmly.

'All six of us are fine. The second explosion was planned. Don't know about the last one.'

'Quiet slave, no talking. You are bound to silence, or the extra food will be taken away.' The guard interrupted.

'Yes, sir.' Arturous responded, handing out the additional food.

Once most of the team's guards had departed, the remaining two guards talked to each other and paid the slaves little attention.

'Where were you taken and what happened?' Almous asked quietly in elvish.

'We were taken out of the mine complex, along the side of the mountain a few miles to a new shaft started by the Goblins.'

'By the sound of it, they had problems.' One of the older workers said.

'The Goblins did not prepare the entrance and supports properly. When they met bad air, it exploded and collapsed the mine entrance killing all the Goblin miners inside. We had to get some gems out, so we deliberately caused a second bang to clear the bad air and get out what we could. We didn't mine any more gems. I couldn't think of how to do so without killing everyone. So, they brought us back. The third bang was after we left.'

'Can you remember how to get out of the mine.' One of the elves asked.

'That is unfair he was blindfolded.' Almous responded.

'Sure, I can.'

'Could you guide us out.' The elderly elf asked.

'Sure. Won't do any good though, it leads straight to the main Goblin camp.' Arturous responded as his father erased the map on the floor. There were several sighs.

'You could take messages between slave gangs if you could slip away.' The elderly elf suggested, hopefully.

'No, he would be missed here and caught. They can count.' Almous said in a very firm, quiet voice.

'Actually father, only the team leader can count, and not all of them.' Arturous added quietly.

'Still, he would be noticed, especially now.' Arturous' father replied. The others nodded.

'What my son must do is make a map of what he knows. We have some spare leather. It must be kept well hidden. It must not be found.' Almous stated. Arturous nodded.

Once given the leather, a nail, and some charcoal, very surreptitiously and over a great deal of time, he made a basic map. When complete, he gave it to his father. What none of them noticed was him making a more detailed map of his own. This one had where he thought the outside was.

After continuing to work with his father for perhaps a hundred human years, it was agreed he could make an occasional trip to find others. Luckily the over-clever gruff-voiced Goblin and his two superiors had long since died of old age. Their replacements came and went. Overall, they were crueller, a lot less intelligent, and less attentive. All slaves were whipped most days, were less productive, and generally not adequately observed.

Although the entrance to their sleeping area was guarded, they weren't watched continuously. During these unobserved periods, slowly a secret language was developed amongst Almous' team based on elvish but different with various discrete signs. When the whole team was proficient, about once per month Arturous would slip off when not observed. Sneaking quietly and cautiously he would locate another group, insert himself into the team for a day or so, teach them the rudiments of the new language, then when shifts changed slipped away and returned to his team. Despite the hair-raising risks he was taking, and the extreme caution required, it worked quite well. His map grew too.

Then Arturous decided to go further afield, but grew careless, forgetting that in mines things change. One trip he fell down a hole due to lack of care on his part, severely cutting his leg. Hearing a patrol coming and stifling the cries of pain, he crawled up a side tunnel and hid. Waiting for about an hour, he then staggered back to his father's team as stealthily as he could muster, adding himself to the returning mine cart pushing team. When they arrived back at the face.

'Almous, this stupid young one has dropped some rocks on his leg. His companion stated loudly. The two Goblin guards laughed.

'Endar, deal with that.' The elderly elf came over. His wound was cleaned, washed and bandaged tightly.

'How did you get hurt?' Arturous was asked quietly.

'I grew careless and fell down a hole.'

'It was bound to happen sooner or later.'

After that, Arturous was a lot more careful. Over the years, several dozen teams of elf slaves were discovered, and his map expanded considerably. He found about one thousand elves.

Arturous' tasks as a slave miner continued for several decades, each day mining more rock and ore. Then one morning when Arturous was in his eighteenth elf year (approximately one hundred and sixty human years) several dozen Goblin guards arrived. Arturous and another elf new to the team were forcibly removed. The complaints were met with beatings by guards with sticks. The two of them were blindfolded and taken to the main entrance. They were part of a group of a dozen or so elves. Arturous noted there were at least two Goblin guards per elf.

The group was led several miles upriver to where the road crossed it. Onwards, it led to a large castle nestling between two mountains half hidden by rain and mist. The wooden bridge crossing the river had collapsed. All that remained of it were two small portions lying one on each bank.

'You slaves, on to the bridge. Retrieve the wagons and supplies. If you fail, you will be killed, and your fellow slaves will starve, as this is your food.' A large Goblin master ordered. The Goblins followed up with the sticks they carried.

'Sir, that is too dangerous.' Said an elderly elf Arturous had never previously met. The response was instant. He was hit on the side of the face by a large wooden stick and collapsed unconscious.

'You are slaves. We don't care if you live or die. Now do as ordered or die right now.' Replied the Goblin master. There were several seconds of silence.

'We will not be able to move them laden. We will have to unload the carts first.' Was the groggy response of the collapsed elderly elf who was starting to come around.

'That is acceptable. Now get to it.' Was the reply. Arturous and the other elves were forced onto the remains of the collapsed bridge.

'Form a chain and pass the supplies up to the top of the bank and off to one side.' The elderly elf ordered. Arturous noted the other elves obeyed the elderly elf without question. Two elves climbed onto the nearest cart and were quickly handing down bags of supplies. Everything creaked alarmingly but otherwise went smoothly. The second cart was in the middle of the river, so the chain of elves was extended. Again, being unloaded without incident.

Next, the elderly elf had them recover the first cart. It was large, with four wheels and high sides. Its rear wheels were in the river's mud up to the axle. The elderly elf looked underneath at the back of the cart.

'It may just be strong enough.' He seemed to think out loud and after some consideration.

'Retrieve those planks and beams.' The elderly elf said, pointing at some broken timber that was stuck a little way downstream. Arturous and several others collected the wood as ordered. The elderly elf's instructions for creating a ramp between the river bottom and remains of the bridge for the cart's rear wheels were followed precisely. On his orders, the back of the cart was lifted out of the mud and slowly lowered on to the temporary ramp. Arturous and another elf were sent to the front to steer the wagon while the rest pushed from wherever they could manage. Slowly the cart moved forwards and onto what remained of the bridge. From there, the cart was more easily pushed up to the top of the bank. The elves collapsed with relief and exhaustion.

'Get up now slaves and onto the next cart or die here.' A Goblin screamed while hitting Arturous with a stick. They all reluctantly got up and hesitantly climbed down the slippery bank to the other four-wheeled cart stuck in the middle of the river.

'Clear the wheels of stones and mud, then altogether turn the wheels a bit at a time.' The elderly elf ordered.

Those and other orders were carried out promptly despite being neck deep in rushing freezing water. Cautiously the other cart progressed towards the ramp created for the first. Slowly the front wheels rose up the planks of wood towards what remained of the bridge. In time the rear wheels left the mud and steadily climbed the planks also.

When the rear wheels of the cart reached the end of the bridge, both the bridge and back wheels of the cart collapsed. The entire weight of the back of the cart fell onto an elf's legs, crushing them completely. He screamed, and the Goblins laughed. Arturous and the other elves who tried to help their injured comrade were beaten back. They were forced to watch as the screaming elf slowly faded into unconsciousness.

Eventually, the Goblin slave master let Arturous and the other slaves lift the broken cart off the stricken elf. Arturous went over to the unconscious, dying elf and held his head gently.

'Kill him.' Was the order from the slave master. A Goblin drew his sword.

'Not that way. Slowly, painfully, you know how it's done now do it properly.' A senior Goblin ordered. Several Goblins then attacked the unconscious elf with sticks and feet. The anger that rose in Arturous was immense. He was about to try and take a Goblin sword when he was grabbed by two other elves.

'You cannot win this young one. We must endure and survive.' The elderly elf whispered to him. Held fast he was forced to watch as the helpless elf was beaten continuously until finally, his skull collapsed.

Arturous squeezed blood from a cut in his hand and quietly whispered 'I will not rest until every Goblin, down to the last baby, is dead.' There were sad looks from the elderly elf. Then he remembered his mother's teachings, that no good could come of such decisions. His thoughts were interrupted.

'You should not think such. We are here because of our own choices.' The elderly elf stated sadly.

'We must be free, or else our race will cease to exist. I will escape and then start my killing.' Was Arturous' response.

They lifted the rear of the second cart and pushed it off the remaining bridge. Then sombrely loaded the first cart with as much of the supplies as could fit. The remaining oxen were harnessed to the first cart. Then two Goblin guards drove it to the mine complex.

The remains of the second cart's broken wheels were recovered. Using some available basic tools and a nearby fallen tree, eventually, two temporary replacement wheels were fashioned and fitted to the cart. The second cart was then loaded with the remaining supplies and hauled back to the mining camp. Their fallen comrade being left behind unburied. Despite having worked through the night, they were returned to their teams to work through the next day without either food or rest.

"I must escape, I just must." Arturous thought to himself.

4 - OSWALD SHAMUS' FIRST JOURNEY

Two weeks after his injury and Curate Shanks curtly escorted Oswald out of the temple complex. As soon as his feet passed the threshold, the heavy oak double gates shut behind him and the locking bar put in place. He stood there ashen faced and shaking as he stared along the broad cobblestone paved street that led past the temple. Rarely had he been out of the temple complex and always in the presence of others from his order. The throng of people, ignoring him, moved past the temple complex and the opulent three-storey timber-framed houses on the other side of the street. I must walk alone he thought and held his cross for comfort. Then he felt the warm glow inside and the reminder that he was not alone.

Walking, with his meagre possessions on his back and using his quarterstaff as a walking stick, Oswald threaded his way along the main thoroughfare that led past the temple, through the central square, and on to the principal market. Oswald approached the nearest trader.

'Excuse me, sir, I am wondering if the merchants from up the valley are due to be here soon. Would you by chance know?'

'You are in luck priest. They have just sold me some wool and are now in the next row buying woven cloth for the return trip. Those you seek are taller than the rest of us.'

'Thank you very much, sir.' Oswald said and hurried off.

He forced his way through the crowd of people. Turning into the next aisle, Oswald could see a small group of men head and shoulders taller than anyone else. Thinking that must be them he approached. Suddenly there was the sharp pain of a blow to his shoulder that also knocked him to the ground. Remembering his recent training, he rolled onto his back, and despite the discomfort swung his quarterstaff with all his strength.

He hit his dark-haired assailant in the ankles, who with a cry fell sideways. Oswald scrambled to his feet and ran between two traders' stalls. The assailant cursed, got up and started after him. However Oswald was now trapped, his path blocked by the backs of other traders' stalls. Looking around quickly to see if there was another way out, he realised the few seconds that he had gained were now lost. Expecting a fight to the death, Oswald turned to face his enemy, only to be hit by significant amounts of blood. The assailant was now falling to the ground sporting a large gash in the side of his neck.

'Don't worry priest, he won't be bothering you anymore. You need to be more aware though. No names here, we can do introductions later.' said the man now standing in front of him.

Oswald, who was taller than just about everyone else, looked up at his rescuer. He was blond and muscular, wore a thick heavy long woollen coat beneath which was the small glimpse of chain mail armour. The sword, now being put away, was significantly longer than others Oswald had seen used one-handed. The rescuer handled it with the same familiarity that Brother Michael had shown during training.

'Thank you for helping me, but isn't that likely to be a problem.' Oswald commented, looking at the body on the ground and the surrounding worried-looking traders.

'Not likely, he was trying to kill a priest. The city watch will not wish to get caught up in that level of politics. It would be wise to move on though. They would much prefer we had left when they get here.'

'I am looking for the merchants that head upriver.' Oswald said.

'Then you had better come with me and meet my boss.' Oswald followed the tall stranger to a group of three men, one deep in discussion with a trader of cloth.

'Are we agreed on this master trader?'

'Yes sir we are on this occasion, but you drive too hard a bargain for me to repeat it. There is too little in it for me.'

'How about I come back with a good quality set of shears from Treenys at cost only when I am next in town.'

The trader thought. 'Good quality and properly sharpened, they are useless at that here. Yes, that can be agreed.'

'Sir, we have a problem.' Said Oswald's saviour.

'I saw, we must leave. Master trader, please deliver within the hour.'

'Certainly, Sir.'

'Welcome Priest. We must talk, but not here.' Said the merchant.

Oswald followed the merchant and his three guards to the walled warehouse complex at the top of the market. Two carts with horses were waiting, and several saddled horses as well. Three further guards were also present. Bolts of cloth, sacks of grain and barrels of ale were being loaded onto the wagons. All of the guards and the merchant himself were wearing the same heavy cloak as his rescuer. All carried similar swords to the one used with such brutal efficiency a short while earlier.

'Master Priest, I am Ablamon. We saw profit in becoming traders between this city and the villages upriver. It is profitable but somewhat dangerous. Having managed to attract an attempt on your life within yards of the temple gates, I think you are fairly unpopular and presumably are someone who needs to travel.' The merchant said.

Oswald considered that being dishonest would potentially be very dangerous. If they were heading up the valley, even if he travelled with them only part of the way, it would improve his chances considerably. He would need to tell them the truth, well some of it at least and certainly not lie.

'I am Oswald Shamus, an Initiate of the Church of the

Light Bringer. I have been sent to set up a church in a village called Warameth. I was hoping to travel with merchants that head up the valley. Am I correct in assuming that you are indeed them?'

'Warameth eh, well then. We certainly are those traders, and we are travelling there eventually, but not directly this time. We are heading to a mountain community first and then onwards up the valley to your village.'

'May I travel with you please?'

'If you are, then you must pull your weight. You must defend yourself when we are attacked. Everyone is required to share in the night watch and the cooking.'

'That is the most reasonable offer master merchant.' To be allowed along without paying was better than expected. They were going to where Oswald wished to be, so he didn't care that much which route they took.

'I will be happy to share the tasks you request. I have received some training in quarterstaff and maul.'

'Maul you say. An odd choice.'

'Brother Michael, who gave me my weapons training, said that I would need it up the valley. I don't have one yet. Apparently, there is someone in Treenys who could supply it.'

'Your Brother Michael is probably right about the valley. He is correct about Treenys too. I know a weaponsmith there, one of the few of any quality. Get on one of the wagons we need to leave before the gates shut for the night.'

Oswald climbed aboard a cart placing his belongings immediately behind him. Each carried two people with the merchant and another in front and an additional two at the back.

'Hello, master priest. I am Ternan. We will be travelling together for a week or two.' His companion said.

'Hello Ternan, I am Oswald Shamus. Pleased to meet you.'

'The chap riding at the front next to Ablamon is Hawken, the two in the cart behind us are Felon and his brother Calston, the two at the back are Reath and Tarie.' Said his companion.

The heavily laden wagons then slowly trundled along the cobbled stone streets around the outside of the market, turned onto the main thoroughfare and headed northwest away from the centre of the city towards the upriver gate. As they approached, a guard stopped them.

'Hello Ablamon, you are taking a passenger I see.' Said the gate guard.

'Priests should not be travelling alone these days.'

'And neither should anyone else.' Laughed the guard. 'I haven't heard about the fatal fight at the market a little earlier, so I will let you through the city gates.'

'Thank you, sergeant.'

Oswald Shamus looked on at the approaching gatehouse with trepidation. Although his companions passed through the upriver gate in the city walls without issue, it was a huge moment for Oswald Shamus. He decided to shut his eyes as his courage failed him.

'Everything all right?' Ternan asked gently.

'I have never left the city before. The only view of outside I have had is looking across the river. My first trip is to a distant village I may never come back from.' Oswald replied with his eyes still closed.

'They are good people. You will be fine. We are outside now. You might as well open them.'

Oswald took a few deep breaths and slowly opened his eyes. The first thing he noticed was the farms, large neat and orderly bordering the road with substantial stone walls surrounding each of the farm buildings complexes. Then, to the north, the trees of the Great Forest that ran the length of the entire valley, or so rumour had it. Beyond that the distant shimmering image of the northern mountains. Looking the other way across the river, he could see the farms there too. Then the grassy plains, and in the distance, the southern mountains.

The small caravan followed the road that led upriver for several miles until they entered a small forest that stretched both sides of the wide river.

'We will be stopping soon. It is not safe to travel at night.' Ternan told him. They pulled over to the side of the road, the watch was agreed, the night passed without incident, and they moved on in the morning. The farms continued for ten miles beyond his city, but after five, they were poorly maintained and worked.

After an hour or so on the road in the morning, Oswald started to get bored and looked around. He would not have noticed anything but happened to be looking at his companion driver when he swapped hands with the reins and put his right hand on his sword hilt. Oswald also noticed similar movements on both the merchant and companion ahead of them. With his left hand, he freed his quarterstaff from its stowage.

Suddenly an unkempt assailant rushed at him from behind the bushes to his left. A cudgel swung at his hip. He quickly put his right hand on the quarterstaff and turning in his seat to the left, parried the blow with his hastily raised staff. Oswald's assailant was now jumping for the cart. Holding his quarterstaff across his body, he punched his assailant in the nose with the middle of the staff. Blood pouring from his face, the attacker fell off landing on his back. Dazed and face bleeding, his attacker lay on the side of the path.

Oswald quickly looked about. He noticed six attackers on the merchant and his guard at the front. However, in only a few seconds, one was headless, and another two were already falling. His companion had taken the arm off his first attacker, who lay screaming on the floor and knocked the other two attackers off the side of the cart. Oswald spun round to look behind him. Four also attacked the other cart, but they had fared no better than those who attacked him. Two were on the ground already.

He couldn't see the back two guards clearly, but several were down from the group who attacked them.

His companion urged the horses forward, and the heavy cart quickly accelerated towards the front two horsemen, the cart behind following up the escape. The remaining attackers then fled, leaving various screaming and dying comrades on the ground.

Oswald, pale face and shaking from the fear of his first real combat, thought reflectively. His travelling companions had repelled an onslaught of twenty or so attackers, odds of over two to one against, disabling about half the number in a couple of minutes tops with no apparent injuries. He had thought that they were merely a group of experienced and well-equipped merchants. They were far more. Despite being outnumbered three to one, his companion was not even vaguely concerned.

'You performed correctly master priest, well done.' Ternan complimented him.

'But I did not kill or wound him just knocked him over.'

'You took him out of the combat and checked for others needing assistance. Neutralising an opponent quickly without getting hurt yourself and checking if others need help are the important points, well done. Going for a body count does not get the job done and usually gets people killed.' His companion advised.

They all stopped a little way up the path.

'Is everyone alright?' asked the merchant. There were various positive indications. 'How did our priest do?'

'He spotted what I was doing and prepared himself quickly, put his opponent on his backside without running away or getting hurt himself. Not a bad start for anyone, let alone a priest.' Oswald's companion replied.

'Praise from you, what is the world coming too.' Muttered Fellon to a general round of laughs. Oswald's companion shrugged.

'It was his first outing. He did as much as could be

expected of anyone in that situation. The praise is deserved. Are we going to turn off yet?' looking at the master merchant.

'No, not yet. The bandits must think we are going straight to Treenys. We will pass the bridge and turn off a little later. There are places further upriver.' said the merchant.

Oswald decided to give a prayer of thanks for his deliverance. This time he put in more effort. The small merchant train continued past a rickety wooden bridge and crossed the river about a mile or so upstream on a broad, shallow stretch. The riding horses it appeared could be left without being tethered and would just stay put. Getting the heavy carts safely into and out of the river took all the effort each of them could muster. They were all soaked by the time the carts were on the other side. The others took off their long heavy coats draping them over the sides of the wagons exposing their chain mail to dry in the winter sun.

The wagons continued across the grasslands towards a vast forest in the foothills of the southern mountain range without incident. Ternan was ever watchful. There were wild cattle and horses, even a pack of wolves, although nothing bothered them. After a few days or so Oswald saw smoke coming from the forest in the foothills.

'That doesn't bode well.' Oswald said to his companion.

'It doesn't, but probably not in the manner you mean. It looks as if someone got the charcoal burning wrong.'

'Charcoal burning?'

'Yes. There is an old castle that is occupied by some miners. They dig for iron ore in the hills and smelt it into iron ingots. We trade food and money for that iron which we take to Treenys and exchange with the blacksmith and weaponsmith for tools and swords. We then exchange the tools and cloth at the two upriver villages for spun wool and leather. Then take the wool, leather and swords back to Kersladen to sell. We are making a reasonable if eventful living.'

'Are there any other travelling merchants?'

'No, we are the only ones who go upriver. The others go between Kersladen and Porarpen. The absence of upriver trade is why we decided to give this a go. The villages existed without proper tools or equipment. We take food to the miners, metal to the smiths and tools to the farmers. It has improved the entire area beyond mere subsistence farming. So long as we don't get greedy, we do quite well out of it, and every one of the villages are happy to see us.'

As they approached the castle, Oswald commented 'They live in that?'

'It is better than living in the open. The walls are decrepit, but they mostly still function. They keep off the worst of the weather and hostile creatures out.'

Oswald thought hostile creatures, what could that mean. The merchant approached the nearest wandering miner.

'Hello, I am Ablamon. We are here to trade food and ale for metal. Do you still have someone I can negotiate with? Last time I dealt with Vikarr.'

'How much are you after, sir? Any of us could provide a sack full or two.'

'I am hoping to buy a cartful of iron and to sell a cartful of food and ale.'

'That would be most welcome. The best person to speak with would be Walgund. Vikarr was killed in a raid a few weeks back. He is in the mine I will ask his son to get him.'

They pulled up in what had been the courtyard and ate their midday meal while waiting for Walgund. Oswald prayed in his usual ad-hoc manner, giving thanks for food and deliverance.

As they were finishing their meal a stocky dark-haired man of middling years approached with a badly pitted pickaxe over one shoulder and flanked by two other miners of senior years. Ablamon got up and met them halfway then took the three miners to the food cart. It seemed to please the elder two a great deal, although the one Oswald assumed was Walgund looked far from convinced. Ablamon opened a door in the other cart previously unnoticed by Oswald. Several iron pickaxes were pulled out together with a large two-person saw, smaller hand saws, a few chisels and some hammers. The young boy from earlier was sent running off to a shack while further discussions took place. He came back holding an iron ingot, which Ablamon examined carefully and seemed pleased.

'That looked like too tough a deal Ablamon. We have to make a profit, you know. It will cost a fortune to replace those tools.'

'Not so much as you might think. The iron is a lot better quality than previously. We are also getting a full cart of it. The trade is worth it. We must help them fix the food storehouse too after being damaged in the last raid. It will delay us a few days but not cost us anything other than time.'

Before he had a chance even to turn around, Oswald found himself leading one of the now unhitched cart horses, pulling aside burnt beams and lumps of stone. In the space of a week, the community rebuilt the food storage building while despite a substantial rainstorm, the inside remained dry. The food and iron ingots were exchanged. Daybreak the following morning they were off, if somewhat more slowly, with the heavy iron-laden carts.

They travelled across the grassy plains towards the island village of Treenys. The river running through the valley widened considerably at this point leaving a sizeable island in the middle about half a mile wide and a mile long. In the distant past, someone had put large cut stone blocks at the upriver end of the island, and down each side, for several hundred yards. These only stopped river erosion and flooding, but they also had been adapted. A bargeman operated an impromptu ferry service from a small dock when required. They stopped on the south eastern side of the river and waited for the ferry to arrive.

It took several trips with Ablamon, the iron cart and a few guards going first. By the time Oswald's cloth cart and the balance of the guards were on the island the merchant appeared to have completed his negotiations. The blacksmith received two-thirds of the iron who set aside various shovels, farming tools, parts for ploughs and a few pickaxes in exchange.

They moved on to the weaponsmith who was already with a customer, one who had several bodyguards.

'I can assure you I will be able to supply the swords you wish your Honour. I have just agreed to purchase a significant quantity of iron which is arriving this morning. It will easily be enough for your purposes.'

'Can I trust you on this?' the purchaser enquired.

'Yes. The deal I have agreed required me to supply some weapons. Your requirements will take the rest with a margin for failures. The sample you have just purchased is from the previous batch of iron. This next batch is much better.'

'Very well, then. I will return in due course.' The customer left.

'Master Ablamon.' The weaponsmith said.

'That is a lot of swords you have just sold.'

'He is from the temple guard in Kersladen. They are expanding it. The price is good.'

'If they pay.'

'If they don't, I have other options. In times such as these people will always find the money for a good sword. My apprentice is working on your special order. We haven't made one before. I had to look it up in my old scrolls. It has its uses I would imagine, in the right circumstances. It will be ready in the morning.'

'Very well, then. I have your iron.'

'And I have your weapons from the last batch of iron you supplied.'

'Good.'

'When will you be around again?'

'Probably a month, maybe six weeks.'

'Can we by chance agree on the same deal? It's working quite well for me.'

'I certainly can for the next batch as I have already agreed to buy more iron from the mine. I haven't got a permanent deal with the mine yet.'

'Good, that means I have enough iron to work flat out for at least the next three months. That's about as much guaranteed work as anyone can reasonably expect these days.'

The remaining iron was exchanged for several bundles of swords. The group stayed the night at a local inn taking turns to watch the carts. There were no incidents. In the morning they returned to the weapon smith's shop when a very bleary-eyed apprentice brought out a wrapped large two-handed war mace.

'It is a gift for the priest good apprentice.' said Ablamon. Oswald who unwrapped the course cloth covering. It was certainly well made. A large flanged metal head and a four-foot metal shaft.

'I am afraid the shaft is not as good quality iron as I had hoped. It is detachable so can be repaired or improved if needed.' The apprentice said.

'Thank you, sir. It is much appreciated.'

'You are most welcome master priest.'

They picked up a set of shears from the blacksmith and headed for the ferry. Again, it took several trips to cross to the northwest bank, but the carts were not so heavy this time, making the crossings easier and quicker. The group headed up the river on the established trail. As mid-day approached, they passed through one of many large copses that covered the northwest bank of the river. It was fast expanding to re-join the vast forest on the low hills of the northern mountain range.

When near the middle of the copse, there was a bang followed by a crack. A large tree fell in front of Oswald's carthorses. His companion stopped the cart with some curses. Ablamon and his guard were the other side of the fallen tree. The second cart and rear guard were behind Oswald's cart. Before they had time to think there was a hail of arrows. Oswald had already grabbed and lifted his quarterstaff. An arrow buried itself heavily in the middle of the staff that would otherwise have hit his head. There was a cry next to him as his companion keeled over, clutching his right shoulder. Then all went dark. He could hear lots of shouts of alarm and running feet. Oswald then got a voice in his head.

"Get to it, Oswald. You are an Initiate Priest of Light, counter this."

It was not the voice of his God he had had while injured. It seemed somehow a lot nearer. Ignoring, for a while at least, the disturbing thought that he was now hearing voices in his head, Oswald realised it was time to get to work. As he had done in Brother Michael's infirmary, he created his focus by concentrating on the memories and feelings attached to when he met his God. His right-hand started to tingle as the power of his belief flowed through him. In his mind, he added the jagged vertical line of the power symbol to the four overlapping outline ellipse shapes of the symbol for curing, creating a mental image of the spell. He pulled the arrow out of his companion's shoulder, who gave a loud cry. Placing his right hand on the wound, Oswald said the words.

'Iach, Grym.'

The power flowed into the shoulder, and the arm warmed up. Multiple shouts of alarm and clashes of iron were interrupted by a loud

'What the.' from Ternan.

Oswald knew he had to do something about the darkness. A spell to produce a light somewhere away from him. There was a symbol he had not used that may move the focus of his spell somewhere else. Despite his worries, there was no choice he would have to try that.

All previous attempts to combine three symbols having failed, Oswald felt somewhat daunted at the prospect of casting his first successful three fundamental spell in combat. Not only that, but he would need to do this at least twice. Directing his mind to the task at hand, his fears were banished. Again, he created his focus by concentrating on the memories and feelings attached to when he met his God. The palm of his right hand tingled. Then he called forth the memory of the symbol for light, a central spot with a gap around it followed by eight straight lines at compass points. To that, he added the now-familiar jagged line symbol for power. Also, he made an extra addition to his existing complicated spell image in his mind, the pointing arrow for the symbol he believed was for moving the focus away from his hand. He pointed the arrow symbol away from his spell image to a visualisation of the tree branch in front of them. Oswald then said the words

'Golau, Grym, Pellter.'

The light shot forth from his hand, causing the end of the tree limb to glow white with light. It radiated out, evaporating the darkness around it. On the other side of the fallen tree, he could see both Ablamon and his guard having been pulled down off their horses were surrounded by at least half a dozen slovenly looking dark haired leather armour-clad attackers. They were desperately covering their heads and necks. Stood off to one side of the road there was another man, slumped shoulders in a hooded cloak, holding a foot-long dark wooden wand.

Now they had light; things were changing quickly. One opponent who was about to bring the sword down on the merchant's head got bitten heavily on the shoulder by Ablamon's horse. The opponent dropped his sword. Another opponent got kicked in the lower stomach by both rear hooves flew backwards, landing on his neck with a loud cracking sound. Ablamon then swung his large sword across his body, hitting both ankles of a third opponent. The other horse equally assisted its rider, Ablamon's companion Hawken. As soon as the light appeared, the horse rose up on its hind legs. It then brought both forelegs, and its full weight down on the head of an attacker, who was concentrating on his prone opponent didn't see it coming. He went down instantly, bleeding profusely. The guard rolled to his feet, drawing his sword and advanced on the remaining opponents. Oswald figured the front of the column could now look after themselves.

Turning to look towards the rear of the merchant caravan Oswald saw only at the last second an attacker swinging a sword at him. Desperately he tried to parry the incoming blow with his staff, but only partially blocked it. The sword hit his unarmoured leg, causing a deep cut. Oswald screamed as the pain and fear bit him.

"Relax my initiate for I am with you. Normal fear does not affect those in my divine priesthood, so long as you just relax." Came the reassuring words of his God.

Oswald felt the fear dissipate as he swung his quarterstaff, hitting his opponent's neck with a crack. The unkempt dark-haired ruffian stumbled backwards falling over.

Oswald figured that would perhaps give him a few seconds. Deciding to try another spell, he focused his mind as before. Feeling his hand tingle, Oswald recalled the eight radiating straight lines symbol for light and added the jagged line symbol for power. Again he included the arrow symbol, pointing it to his visualisation of the back of the second cart. Finally, he then said the words

'Golau, Grym, Pellter.'

The glowing light appeared in his hand, then burst forth illuminating the second cart's tailgate.

Before he had time to consider the situation or see

what was happening, Oswald got a sharp pain in his other leg. The unkempt ruffian had returned. He swung his quarterstaff, hitting the man on the ear, quickly followed by a solid jab to the stomach. The thug went down groaning.

His companion, having dismembered several opponents, jumped down off the cart and ran to the back of the group. Oswald tried to stand and fell over. He saw Ablamon and his guard had re-mounted their horses and were riding to the end of the caravan to engage the remaining bandits. There were several screams and the sounds of flight. Oswald more slowly brought himself to his feet and moved to the back of the group using his quarterstaff as a walking stick. He could see now that the attackers were dead, dying or dispersed. By the time he got there, it was all over. Felon, Ablamon, Tarie and Calston were injured. Stomach arm and head wounds.

'Wherever that light came from, it saved our bacon.' Ablamon said.

'It came from our priest here.' Ternan replied. There were sounds of shock from the others.

'From a priest, that can only be spiritual miracles. The old gods honour us. Amazing.' Said Hawken.

'Then you have earned your war mace master priest.' Said Ablamon. This statement was shortly followed by 'NO' as Oswald reached to pull out the arrow shaft sticking out of Felon's stomach.

'Leave him to do his thing Ablamon, he can heal wounds too. He has done this to my shoulder already.' Said Ternan.

'What.' Was the stunned reply of Ablamon. 'He has been a busy priest then.'

'Not busy enough judging by his legs.' Said the injured Calston.

Oswald grabbed the arrow shaft in his left hand, created his focus with the thoughts of his God, called forth the symbols for curing and power in his mind, placed his right hand on the wound and pulled out the arrow with his left. He quickly added another symbol for power and said the words.

'Iach, Grym, Grym.'

He could see the blood stop escaping from the wound. Oswald tried to add the jagged line for power for the third time, but when he applied the symbol, he lost concentration and the spell image faded.

'Sorry, that is the best I can do for him.'

'Don't worry Oswald. It is no longer bleeding, and although there is still a cut, it is much shallower than before. I can deal with it now.' Ternan told him. Oswald went to Calston.

'Good.' Said Ablamon. 'Treat and bandage the wound and put him in one of the carts. Lie him flat, no bending over, or it won't heal properly. If my memory of the teachings of our High Priest is correct, despite not being fully healed, the wound will mend quickly, so he must lie still.' Ternan and Tarie helped their companion to the back of the cart that was carrying cloth.

'Truly a miracle and a privilege to behold.' Added an awe-inspired Hawken.

'Master priest, you appear to have been keeping secrets and have some additional abilities. You are an ancient style warrior priest, aren't you?' Ablamon enquired.

'Actually, I am just an Initiate Priest, as stated earlier. The Light Bringer has seen fit to grant me some minimal powers. I only have six of the symbols, and I can only actually use four of those. Today was the first time I have been able to combine more than two.' Oswald stated with the slurred voice and slumped shoulders of one close to exhaustion.

'Still, even that is unheard of in hundreds of years. Although perhaps basic, they made the difference today.' As Oswald said the words on the arm of the last injured guard, he felt decidedly strange lightheaded and passed out. The last thing he heard before fading into unconsciousness was Ablamon saying.

'It looks like he has done too much. Clean and bind his wounds and put him in one of the carts also.'

Oswald woke the following morning and groaned. 'Where did they come from?' He asked his companion looking back at three prisoners being dragged at the back of his cart.

'Three survivors of the attack that have admitted to being part of a group hired by one of the Lord of All Evil's servants to stop us from reaching Warameth. They had the Lord's coins and used a dark spirit wand. It was supposed to keep the place without light for fifteen minutes. They are being taken for trial and execution.'

'Oh. Is conviction certain then? In Kersladen, you get to plead your case before the Mayor and seek clemency before execution.' asked Oswald.

'Guaranteed. There is clear evidence of the group using dark spiritual spells and being in service to the Lord of All Evil. In our tribe, that is clear grounds for execution. We are approaching Izellameth. With these three in tow and what happened yesterday, we will not stop this time and should make Warameth by this evening.'

'Will we have any more trouble?' Oswald asked.

'I doubt it. We must have killed over forty this trip alone. I would suggest you heal your legs as best as you can. I have a strong feeling you will need them very soon.' Replied Ternan. Oswald did this and rested again as he still felt quite weak. He awoke when tapped on the shoulder.

'We have stopped for food and to rest the horses. Some of the bandits had reasonable armour and weapons. Have a look at the back of the cart. There are a few bits that might fit you.'

Oswald did that and found a hard leather helmet, breastplate, skirt, and grieves for his legs. With some assistance, he put them on. It appeared that the guards now considered him an equal. While clearly, he was nowhere near as proficient as they were at combat, his spiritual spellcasting ability could be decisive in the right circumstances, and that was good enough for them.

They approached a large village. Like the one they had just passed it nestled between the wide river and many hills with sheep grazing on them. The nearest hill, also the largest, had a stone tower on top and in the distance near the top of the village a large stone bridge crossed the river. As they crossed the grassland Oswald noticed the occasional remains of large cut stone blocks partly sticking out of the ground. The buildings looked of solid construction, the bottom few feet of stone and the rest of oak darkened through the years. There were several streets off a sizeable central village green. Oswald breathed a sigh of relief and thought, *"I have made it to Warameth."*

5 - THE TEMPLE

After about an hour of loading the horse and extended goodbyes Tara, Luka, Katina, Freki and Helghyer departed. A little later, having left behind outside assistance, they decided to discuss the best approach.

'Do we try and follow Katina's uncle and the others?' Tara asked.

'Which is more important, finding someone from two years ago, or a new safe home. It would be great to find my uncle, but a new home must come first.' Katina stated.

'We have no chance of tracking them by conventional means, not after two years. If we head in the general direction and find people, we can question them. Perhaps we can find Katina's uncle and the others that way.' Replied Luka.

'A new home it is then.' Tara said.

'Any safe place would have to be either a long way away or the other side of some significant natural obstacle. Heading east to the sea is pointless. Even if we discover an alternative place, there is no means of getting to it, let alone the whole of the rest of the tribe. The south and west were just plains as far as anyone has travelled with no indication of anything else.' Katina said.

'That only leaves north to the mountains. We could see if there is a way through them.' Luka responded.

'I think my uncle and the others went in that general direction on leaving the village. I don't know how long the mountain range goes on for.' Replied Katina.

'When we reach the mountains, head away from the sea for a week, find out if there is a pass through it. If not, we could go the other way for a while.

They travelled roughly north for several days through an ancient forest. It had a wide variety of trees, with frequent clearings. Freki and Helghyer ranged out ahead as scouts. Luka and Katina took it in turns checking the area for signs of Goblins or other hostiles. They also hunted wild game to preserve the food stocks. Heated discussions about progress and leadership were frequent, but after several days the group had gelled into a co-operative where each knew their duties.

After about a week when they had left the lands known by their tribe and neighbours, the evidence of Goblin activity became more pronounced although historical. The occasional rusty sword or Goblin skull being clear evidence that they were no longer in "friendly" territory.

◆ ◆ ◆

The first one to spot actual "Not Humans" was Helghyer. One morning before they had broken camp and while Katina was taking her turn at foraging for food, Helghyer was out looking for her breakfast. While flying at treetop level, the falcon saw a group of four not humans dragging a human woman behind one of two very ill-looking horses. Helghyer thought the human was already dead, so started to screech. Gliding silently towards Freki, landed on a low branch in front of the wolf. After looking towards the prey, the falcon took to the air and headed back to her human.

When she approached, her and Freki's human were talking. Her human lifted an arm for her to land on and gently stroked her head. Looking in the direction of the enemy Helghyer squawked. As always, her human caught on immediately. The falcon looked in the direction of the not humans, squawked and tapped her hand with her beak four times. Again, her and Freki's human caught on instantly, had a quick discussion in surprised tones and secured the packhorse. Deciding to re-join Freki, she left the two humans creeping through the undergrowth heading for the group's quarry.

When Helghyer returned to where the not humans were, she silently glided to a suitable perch on a high branch of a tree and looked down. Those being hunted were oblivious. The great wolf shook its head in disgust at the unaware not humans too busy hurting a corpse to ensure their survival. He started stalking his prey unseen from downwind and behind, silently moving from bush to tree keeping as low to the ground as possible. Helghyer had seen this wolf tactic often and knew the death it would bring. Still, four not humans to one wolf, even a Freki sized wolf was not good odds, so she waited for her chance to swoop in and attack.

The wolf was in position now, crouching behind a near bush. After a few moments, the huge wolf leapt knocking one not human flat to the ground, bit another, then growling with teeth bared he ran at the terrified horses. They pulled desperately at their tethering ropes, which broke, and they bolted.

Helghyer seeing one not human prepare its bow to fire at the departing wolf, dived from her perch, wings folded, covering the distance to her prey in a few heartbeats. At the last instant opened her wings, unfolded her talons, and with the beak too, hit the not human on the side of the head. The target, now missing an ear, lost its balance and dropped its bow. The falcon flew off back to her perch and looked down.

Now the large falcon could see her human running silently through the undergrowth almost as well hidden as the great wolf had been a few minutes earlier. The two terrified riderless horses galloped past her in the other direction. Her human readied her bow on the move, then stopped and released her arrow at the one injured earlier. The not human went down with an arrow sticking out of where its ear should have been. Helghyer could see three others shout with alarm as her human ducked behind a tree.

Deciding to keep the pressure on the falcon again dived from her perch. This time she got an eye, which Helghyer spat out as it tasted even worse than the earlier ear had. Helghyer departed flying low and fast dodging tree trunks and branches, followed by several arrows, none of which came close. When clear, she circled climbing to the treetops well out of bowshot.

Then there was the unmistakable cry of an Iredan warrior about to impart death. Helghyer landed on a low branch to watch, well for now. There had been further archery exchanges between her human and the three remaining prey. Helghyer saw a not human hastily raising its bow to parry the warrior's attack as she charged through the undergrowth. Her enormous sword went straight through its bow, biting deeply into the not human's abdomen.

The one next to it, panicked by the sudden attack, was trying to nock another arrow to its bow before the enraged plains warrior could close on it. The first wounded Goblin, however, had now recovered its wits and, with a wicked curved sword was advancing on Tara. None of them was paying attention to her human and presented easy targets for her archery. She shot at the unwounded Goblin, her arrow penetrating its chest deeply from the side. It went down. Deciding to attack, Helghyer dived, then saw Freki leap at it from behind biting its neck as she with talons and beak bit heavily into a leg. Like Freki, Helghyer decided to clear the now prone not human as the warrior's heavy sword sliced into its shoulder. The warrior then went on to behead all the not humans, although Helghyer thought they were all already dead.

The falcon then watched from a nearby branch as her and Freki's human discussed the corpse. They were correct. She was not of her human's kind. A lot shorter and dark-haired. They talked about her with sad faces then recovered the used arrows and left the female human unburied returning to camp. Helghyer followed them.

◆ ◆ ◆

Katina returned to camp after an early morning forage

for food. A successful trip with two rabbits, a small deer plus root vegetables and a fair amount of wild wheat. Enough for a week's worth of meals and bread. Not bad for a few hours work.

'High guys, judging by the squawking I heard earlier you have been busy.'

'Yes. Nothing we found overly taxing, just four Goblins. You have too by the looks of it.' Replied Luka.

'Yep. I have had a successful hunt plus two Goblins and recovered horses. They are in a bad way though and won't be rideable for some time.'

'On your own without backup or telling us.'

'Really, you make such a comment of me Luka. I am a hunter and scout of Iredan. As you well know.'

'We are a long way from help is what I think Luka is getting at.' Commented Tara.

'Alright, noted, but there was only two. Easy for any of us.' Responded Katina.

'We could fashion some litters for the saddles and supplies to keep the horses backs free for a few days. If we clean the wounds and feed them properly, they should be alright after about a week or so.' Luka suggested.

'We need to be moving like now.' She added looking at Katina. 'With your two that makes six we have killed this morning. We cannot remain near so many dead Goblins. There must be at least another six, mounted probably. That twelve will not have been alone. A major party will be within half a day.' Tara ordered.

Despite the health risk to the new horses, reluctantly the others agreed to move on immediately. Camp was broken quickly, removing as much evidence as possible. Then they headed off at a slow run for several hours, each leading one of the new horses. As always, the tribe's horse followed closely automatically.

The group made good time that day and although there was evidence of other Goblin patrols, none were near enough to matter. That evening the litters were constructed, the new horses were fed and had their wounds cleaned. They were ravenous, so the food and water fed to them had to be appropriately managed to avoid causing additional problems. The ladies took a few hours' sleep each, taking turns at keeping watch.

When they were all awake, the new horses were examined. Although they were still pitifully thin and exhausted, they looked a lot happier. The litters were attached, and supplies loaded. Starting slowly, they headed North East and sped up to the usual slow run after a few miles. This continued for about a week, each night stopping at a convenient clearing in the forest, each day the new horses looking that bit better and less thin.

The ancient woodland continued day after day. Where possible, they avoided dense areas of undergrowth. The trees remained varied and old. Progress was good, but periodically it was necessary to clear a path through thick brush. All three took it in turns to hunt, forage, make camp and extend the tribes' map to include the new areas. Notes were taken on how many days it was between landmarks, the terrain conveniently having the occasional rocky outcrop or hillock, which they used as reference points. The scouting spotted many Goblin parties which with care, were avoided. By the end of the second week, they could see the mountains in the distance.

After a few more days the forest changed. The undergrowth and bushes were unusually thick, and the trees were extraordinarily tall with enormous trunks.

'We can't hack our way through this, we had better head northwest and try and go around.' Tara commented. Then Helghyer flew in from that direction and landed on Luka's arm squawking quietly.

'I think that's the Goblin squawk.' Said Katina.

'It is. I had better go and have a look.' Replied Luka. Leaving her horse behind she headed off northwest.

'I will go and look the other way.' Offered Katina.

'Please keep an eye out for Freki. He should be out that

way somewhere.' Requested Tara.

Luka crept silently through the undergrowth skirting the outside of the heavily overgrown area. Within fifteen minutes, she heard several Goblins inefficiently standing watch. There was a lot more noise than a few guards, so Luka cautiously crept closer to get a good view. There were hundreds of them in a large clearing.

We won't be going this way then, she thought to herself and silently crept back to Tara. When she got back, Katina was also returning being followed by Freki.

There is a large clearing about a half mile northwest of here. There are several hundred Goblins in or around it.' Informed Luka.

'It's much the same to the southeast, but the clearing is about a mile away. We can't go that way either. About a quarter-mile, there is what looks like the remains of a path into the bushes.' Said Katina.

'So with Goblins on either side, we either take this path or try to go back.'

'Neither group of Goblins is looking for us, so if we are quiet, we might be able to try the path and hideout.' Suggested Luka. 'All we have to do is pray the horses don't make any noise.'

Katina took Tara and the horses to the possible path while Luka attempted to erase evidence of their presence in the area.

'Here it is. I think it once may have been a road. There's not much left now. It's all covered in brambles and weeds.'

'It's not much Katina, and we can't hack through that, it will be seen.' Said Tara.

'Let's try and pull the plants apart. Here, I have a small gap.' Katina continued before carefully moving the vegetation aside. She worked quickly in the dimmed light of a winter's afternoon. The only noises being the bird and animal sounds of the forest, the horses being quiet in response to Tara's attention. After a short time, they cleared a path one horse wide and some twenty feet long.

'Damn, a stone wall covered in creepers.'

'Check for a door or break in the wall.'

'This wall is big. The stones are huge. Hold on. I have the side of a doorway or something. The door is long gone, but there is lots of rubble.'

Luka slowly approached covering the party's tracks as she went. When the nearby traces of the group were erased, she looked after the horses, while Tara went to help Katina clear a collapsed large gateway. After about half an hour enough stones had been shifted to get one horse through at a time. Behind the gateway, there was a heavily overgrown courtyard, which was in areas passable. The horses were brought through and secured nearby.

'I will go back out, cover our tracks in and try and replace the broken bushes.' Said Luka.

'We will start replacing the stones in the gateway while you are working.' Replied Tara.

Once the entrance was secured, they took it in turns to keep watch from a vine-covered spot on top of the wall. The horses were tethered in a dilapidated building further into the compound.

It was a tough few days. Keeping watch was especially tricky, as it rained incessantly. Tent canvas was used as an impromptu roof to keep the worst of the rain out of the one building they used as a camp. With just one room for the horses, supplies and themselves, none of them got much sleep. They made the decision not to explore the compound and risk upsetting whatever was in residence until after the Goblins had left the area. They lit no fires and ate cold meals.

During the next few days, several groups of Goblins came close to the gate area, but none discovered the entrance. Thanks to the cold heavy rain and Luka's covering of the tracks it soon became impossible to spot that anyone had passed through the area recently. None of the Goblins even gave the area a second glance, appearing to be more interested in getting out of the rain. By the third day, the Goblins had moved on. The rain stopped, the birds and animals came back, and life returned to normal.

'Ladies, I am thinking that we should consider staying here a few more days. There is something like five hundred Goblins within a few miles of here. We should let them move on before we do. It would have been nice to know where they were going.' Tara suggested at breakfast

'True.' Agreed Luka 'They are heading towards the coast and the lands of the Agrini.'

'Should we warn them?' Asked Katina.

'There's not enough to worry them. We should stay on mission. Besides this place must have been something important in years past. We haven't explored much yet, but it wouldn't surprise me if it is bigger than our village.' Responded Tara.

'Could we have found our new home? These walls are tall and the stones large. Some repairs on the walls and a ditch at the base with some sharp stakes and this place could hold Goblins off with ease.' Asked Katina.

'It would require too much work to start with and too many people to hold. We would be swarmed under before we were ready. Even if we did complete the repairs, we could never withstand a siege here. It's a good place to hold out for a while, though.' Suggested Tara.

It was soon discovered that the perimeter wall was about fifteen feet high and as thick. Some of the fire step was cleared of thorns, but the crenulations themselves were left overgrown with brambles. This made keeping watch without being seen more comfortable while maintaining the abandoned appearance of the place.

'Why don't you two explore while I keep watch for a bit.' Katina said as she climbed up the wall to her vantage point.

Further investigations discovered the fortified wall surrounded a very overgrown area the best part of a mile in diameter with a very large broken down building in the middle. It was made from white stone, was at least three hundred feet long and fifty feet wide. The walls were breached in several places, and none were anywhere near their original height. The far end had walls up to about forty feet high with what looked like remains of columns. They entered the building.

'These must have supported the roof.' suggested Luka.

'This place is enormous. There are lots of fallen stones, but no evidence of internal walls. This building was a very significant meeting place.' Replied Tara.

'I wonder if there is a chief type seat or table at one end like in our meeting hall. If so, it may give us a clue as to who lived here.'

'I think it is from the time of the old empire. No one can work or transport this size of stone since then.' Said Tara looking at a huge stone block.

With that Helghyer landed on Luka's arm. Freki also padded up next to Tara. They kept on exploring through the undergrowth.

'The remains of this pillar are a lot bigger than the ones further back.' Said Tara.

'There doesn't appear to be any more this side either.'

'This must have been the main area you were talking about earlier Luka.'

'By the looks of this, a large stone statue has fallen onto a huge stone block. Let's clear some of the undergrowth away and take a better look.'

Some fifteen minutes later and the worst of it was cleared.

'She is a big lady. The statue must be some fifteen feet tall. In its day, it would have looked very nice. I think it's polished marble.' Suggested Luka.

'That would have taken some serious work. Can we even do that now?' asked Tara.

'Whoever built this place believed in this lady big time. It looks as if there is a door on the back of this.' Observed

Luka. Helghyer stopped her investigative flying and landed on the stone block. 'Can you help me with this door?'

'I'll try.' Said Tara scraping through from the other side of the enormous fallen statue. Freki jumped up on top of the stone block joining Helghyer who was now looking curiously at the two struggling women. After both using their daggers as leverage, there was a rusty click sound, and the door opened slightly.

'Ow. Shit that hurt. The damn thing has cut my finger open.' Said Luka.

'There is something inside, but I can't get to it. The door is in the way. Can you?' Responded Tara.

Luka shook her bleeding right hand briefly then reached in her left to retrieve a small statuette and a piece of parchment. They both crawled out from underneath the statue. The statuette had large lumps of dirt and clay stuck to it, making it difficult to see what it was.

'Careful with the parchment, it is very fragile. We will only be able to open it once I suspect.' Suggested Tara. They carefully opened just part of it and even then, only slightly. They peered in.

'I can see a map. It looks like a symbol for a temple, some mountains and maybe a castle. If this place is the temple, then the castle is in the middle of the mountains, east-northeast of here.' Tara observed.

Luka, while trying to clean her finger, suggested 'If the castle is in the middle of the mountains, then there must have been a pass or valley through them. Otherwise the castle wouldn't have been built in the middle to block it.'

'Looks like we had better try that way then.'

'Agreed, I want to clean the statuette first though if only to remove the worst of the mud and clay.' Luka inadvertently pulled at the clay around the head with her cut finger.

'Yep, it's a small statue of the big one. I thought it would be.' Luka observed. With that, her finger bled again. Several large drops of blood fell onto the head of the statuette. Helghyer screamed and Luka dropping the statue raised both hands to her head as she fell to the floor. Tara dropped the parchment and dived forwards, catching the statuette but missed Luka who hit the floor with a crash, screamed and passed out.

'Freki, get Katina.' Off he ran. Tara, despite the growing tingling sensation in her hand, carefully put the small statue down on the polished marble block and went to Luka. She was very pale. Her eyes had become deep-set, her hand was bleeding badly, and she was out cold.

A little while later, Katina and Freki returned. Tara had put Luka's head on her lap and was cleaning the bleeding hand. So Katina went to Helghyer and checked her over. Like all hunters, she had a capability with animal husbandry.

'She seems alright, physically. Breathing is strong, no damage to wings feet etc. Helghyer is just out cold. What happened?'

'I haven't got it properly worked out yet. We spotted the statue and cleaned the area up.'

'Oh.' Katina interrupted.

'Anyway, Luka spotted a large stone block under the statue's head, so we cleared stuff away, and it turned out to be polished marble with a door on the back buried under the statue itself. We opened the door, but Luka cut her finger. Eventually while cleaning the statue, some of Luka's blood got on it and bam out they both go.'

'Is she alright?'

'Just unconscious, I think. Breathing is strong.'

'Have you touched the little statue also?'

'Yes I have. It tingles but hasn't bitten me like that yet.' Said Tara.

'They did try and teach me to be a shaman, but I didn't take to it. If I remember things correctly, this must be one of the large old temples dedicated to The Huntress. The polished marble block would be the altar making the small statue the altar's religious relic.' Said Katina.

'Well, you would know more about that sort of thing than me. I never paid much attention to those lessons.'

'Have you fully cleaned Luka's hand? We are a long way from help if it goes wrong.'

'Yes, I have. No dirt or clay left in it, it's fully clean. After having a final bathe in hot water, it should be fine. At least that's my thinking.'

'Do you want me to help carry Luka?'

'Can you take Helghyer back to camp first, please? Freki will go with her. Get Helghyer warm and leave Freki to guard her, then come back and help me with Luka and the other bits.'

'Other bits?' Katina said emphasising the plural.

'Yes, we found a map too. It's an ancient parchment, but we managed to take a little peek. It has a clue we can discuss later. It looks like we will be here for a while anyway.'

Katina carefully picked up Helghyer folding her wings into her body. 'Come on Freki, let's get her back to camp.'

When back at their impromptu home, Katina carefully put the falcon onto a sizeable dry pile of soft grass and leaves.

'Can you keep watch please Freki while I go and help bring Luka back.'

'Bark' was the response.

It was quite clear to Katina that following the events of recent weeks both the falcon and the wolf were far more than well-trained animals. They were on occasion almost human in action and understanding as well as being far more reliable than a fair few humans she knew. Katina had started to treat them accordingly, which appeared to be appreciated by both the animals.

Katina, having returned to the temple, said.

'All done. Can we pick up the small statue or do we leave it?'

'We certainly can't leave it to the Goblins, so we must take it.'

'I suppose it had better be me that picks it up. Oh well here goes.' Katina said, picking it up somewhat gingerly. 'This looks like the obsidian our old shaman's ceremonial knife was made from, but gold coloured. I didn't think you could even get gold obsidian much less carve it.' She wrapped it carefully in a cloth and placed it in her leather bag. 'It's still filthy and will need proper cleaning. This must have been an important place of worship to have a fifteen feet tall statue, polished marble altar, and carved obsidian statuettes. Someone put in an enormous amount of effort here.' Said Katina.

'It's a shame all the tribes can't move here. It would suit us well, but it's just not strategically viable.'

'It's a hell of a place though.' They carried Luka back to the stone building being used as a camp. They wrapped her in woollen blankets and did their best to keep the place warm and clean.

The neighbouring building was cleaned out, and the walls made stable. After some work, they discovered both buildings had decent stone floors and suitable stones for window and door lintels. They also found a useable well and an abundance of rabbits and fowl. Within a few days, both buildings had walls to above door height. At that point, the conditions improved dramatically. Helghyer was the first to come around a few days after that.

◆ ◆ ◆

Luka suffered an enormous stabbing pain in her head and what felt like someone tying a knot in her brain. She remembered falling to the floor and Tara diving to save her, but that was about it. Some unknown time later, she seemed to become partially awake. Aware of her surroundings to a limited degree but was unable to wake up. Luka realised that she was being cared for, cleaned and covered in blankets. It also sounded like the building was being repaired and the floor swept.

Her mind had a strange dream or vision of a semi-transparent lady similar in appearance to the giant statue.

"Hello, Luka of Iredan. I am the goddess you call 'The Huntress' and am here to offer you guidance, comfort and if you agree, to allow you to become a proper worshipper of mine with all the benefits that this brings. Do you agree to this?"

"So, you are real then. We have all wondered what happened all those centuries ago. You say benefits, like the spiritual powers of old?"

"What you describe from your legends was the most powerful of miracles and magic. What you would receive in return for regular worship would be of a basic nature."

"I would be able to invoke miracles, but at a novice level."

"That is as good a description as any, so yes." The spirit replied.

"Then I agree," said Luka.

"You have paid the blood price and are bound to me now. In time, you will be able to ask for my help when in need. You will learn to cast miracles to invoke my power. There are symbols and words you will need to learn as well as proper dates for worship." The spirit informed her.

"There is one who worships the god you call 'The Light-Bringer'. He is not a full priest yet but has enough knowledge to start you on your way. Each Lord Priest or Lord Guardian of any of the Gods of Light has a special spirit attached to them called a Guardian Spirit. They help you cast your miracles and will allow you to see and deal with hostile spirits. Helghyer has requested to be yours. You cannot have one at this time, but should you become either a Lord Priest Lord Guardian or Shaman then she will become your guardian spirit." Luka was advised.

"As you are not a priest of any type but have paid the blood price to one of my most sacred artefacts, the binding has taken you a lot harder than it normally would. In time, you will recover and be stronger for it." The spirit continued.

"When you discuss this with your friends please reassure Tara that the Gods of Light are most pleased with her. I have not offered the binding to her, as I am not the one for her. She would make with

experience and further training a truly excellent Lord Guardian of the one you call 'The Warrior God'. I have not seen him in some fifteen hundreds of your years. The Light Bringer and I will try and find him and guide you."

"We are looking for a safe new home for our people. That must be our primary aim. I will happily worship you in return for your help, but we must find a new home."

"Any new place you find will not remain safe for long. Wherever you go will eventually be overrun. Only by restoring our power to the world can any home be safe. I cannot come like this again. The Gods of Light lack the power to openly challenge our deranged uncle just now but, know that I will be watching you and will help when I can." And with that the spirit departed.

Luka considered what had been said to her and thought *I've gone mad.*

Shortly after, when still in this not quite awake stage, she could feel a weight on her chest and a gentle pecking on her nose and cheeks. Somehow, Luka knew it was Helghyer, tried to wake up but couldn't. Something was stopping her. She considered matters but had great difficulty concentrating. With effort, slowly it started to return.

The pecking continued.

Somehow, she didn't feel at one with her own body. How was that one going to be solved?

The pecking continued.

There were vague sounds of speaking, but very far away. Luka thought about flying with Helghyer.

The pecking faded.

Then ouch, what was that. There was a very sharp pain and a split-second vision of her biting her own nose. Luka also felt the emotion of a very worried Helghyer. "Oh you stupid girl, think about the sensations of your own body." She concentrated, concentrated, concentrated on the continued pain in her nose and the blood running from the cuts.

The pecking continued.

Then a rushing sensation as if she was being pulled through a whirlpool. I'm back Luka thought. Giving herself a few seconds to get acquainted with the feelings of her own body Luka then opened her eyes. There was a loud squawk followed by

'Look who's back. How are you feeling?'

'Very strange Katina. My head is full of wool, and I am exhausted.'

'Not surprised, you've been out for over a week. We managed to get some water in you, but you haven't eaten anything in ages. Sit yourself up, clean your face from Helghyers ministrations and I will get you something to eat. Tara and Freki are out foraging but should be back soon. Tara put together an oven from some conveniently shaped stones, so there is bread. There is also some cold cooked venison. I found some herbs suitable for tea, and there is hot water too.' Said Katina.

'You guys have been busy. Decent stone floor and repaired walls. Are we staying then?'

'Tara doesn't think it's viable long-term, unfortunately. We had the time, so we thought we would make the place more habitable.'

'You have done well.'

'What happened?' asked Katina.

'We had better wait for Tara and discuss it all together. Did she tell you about the map?'

'Yes. We haven't tried to look at it further due to its condition. In the past, there was a castle in the mountains east-northeast of here. Therefore possibly a path through.' Luka had eaten her meal and was drinking her tea when Tara and Freki returned.

'Another small deer, some potatoes and more of that tea herb you found earlier. Ah hello, Luka, you are back with us again, I see. How are you?'

'Very fuzzy-headed and weak, but a lot better now Katina has given me something to eat and some warm tea.'

'What happened?' asked Tara.

'I have become mentally unstable. I had visions and great difficulty in waking up. I very nearly didn't make it back. If Helghyer hadn't been pecking me and finally bitten my nose at the right time, I wouldn't have woken up at all.' Luka went on to explain the dream and the advice given including finding the not yet priest. 'As I said, I've gone mad.'

'Probably.' Was Katina's answer. 'You have had some nasty experiences lately and have been hurt badly too. If any of those Goblins had spotted us, we would all be dead. We have seen it on some of our warriors before from time to time. However, let us consider alternatives.'

'Alternatives, what alternatives?' questioned Luka.

Tara interrupted. 'We have already worked out that this is a temple to The Huntress and a damn important one. Given the stone block's location and polishing, it must have been the altar. That makes the statue you put your blood on the temple's holy relic at the very least.'

Katina went on 'We all know that the Lord of All Evil has bad spirits and mortal beings capable of spirit magic at his command. My uncle and his escort killed the last pack of Plains Devils that came into our area a few years ago. We know from the old stories that the Gods of Light bestowed humans and others with spiritual capabilities. The kinds of things you talk about would have been possible if not frequent in those times.'

'Maybe but it's not been done in at least a thousand years.' argued Luka.

'True, but that makes it unlikely, not impossible. You come across as pretty rational, despite your dream. I think we should at least consider it possible The Huntress visited you.' Was Tara's final thoughts.

'What I would say though is that you shouldn't be going on any more spirit walks Luka. My Shaman made it quite clear that even in the times of old, only the most experienced of Shamans did that, and you learnt by lessons from an experienced spirit-walking shaman. Any other trials killed you.' Katina informed her.

Surprised at her friend's support and views Luka went on to say 'Well in which case if we are to consider the dreams as possibly true, Tara, I have a message for you from The Huntress. She is well pleased with you but said that she is not the correct god for you. She believes the god we call The Warrior is one that would be to your liking. The catch is they haven't seen him in the last fifteen hundred years. They are going to try and find him.'

'That's kind of her, but I don't see how worshipping the warrior would help much currently. We should see if we can find this castle in the mountains and if we can, then check what is on the other side. This new Light Bringer priest can't be round here.' Tara said.

The others agreed but also insisted that Luka would have another day's rest first. Instead, they spent the day replenishing supplies and clearing the exit to the northeast end of the complex while Luka cleaned The Huntress statuette.

When Katina and Tara returned. 'Hey, guys look what I found at the base of the statuette. Eight symbols two on each side of the base. The Huntress said something about symbols and words to cast spirit magic.' Luka informed them.

'That will be what this new Light Bringer priest is to teach you then. A few basic symbols and words.

6 - WANDERINGS OF TARA & LUKA

They left the following day heading out of the North East exit, replacing the fallen stones and bushes behind them in the same manner as when entering the other side of the compound. Being cautious, both Freki and Helghyer immediately went scouting. They travelled towards the mountains, but did not go directly to where they thought the pass was just in case they were being followed. Instead, they headed nearer to the coast. After a week of cautious travel, they passed through the foothills and discovered a cliff some five hundred feet high before a further mountain range rose high above. They continued north-west along the base of the cliff but even after several days found nothing.

On occasion, they decided discretion was the better part of valour and despite their instincts hid from scouting parties of Goblins rather than engage them. Concealing themselves in bushes or caves became common, and progress was slow. Thankfully all the animals kept quiet, even the new horses that after the now extended period of rest and feeding were back to health.

They each took it in turns scouting, even Helghyer and Freki. On the falcon's return from one trip, she perched on a nearby branch squawking erratically at Luka and Tara.

'Helghyer is flustered. Something has bothered her.'

'Alright, Luka why don't we go and have a look.' Tara asked. The two women followed the falcon creeping cautiously through the bushes until she perched on a low branch and looked down at the mud.

'I don't recognise the tracks.' Commented Tara.

'Neither do I. Which means it's neither animal nor Goblinoid.' Replied Luka.

'That only leaves one option. Some form of Plains Devils.' Said Tara.

'So much for finding a safer place to live.' Commented

Luka. They went back to the cave they had spent the last few nights.

'Katina, we have to leave now.'

'What's up, Tara?'

'Plains Devils are in the area.' Was Tara's reply.

'What!'

'Well, we think so. The feet are bigger than Goblins by about a third, with four claws instead of toes. At least that's what it looks like.' Said Luka.

'Sounds like what my uncle described for them. If we have to fight them, they will be most unpredictable. Also, we can't send the animals out, especially Helghyer. A dark magic spell killed one of my uncle's warriors. Freki may be alright, he's huge and could probably take a couple, but Helghyer is only a bird.' Replied Katina. There was a derisory squawk.

'Unpredictable, what do you mean by that?' Asked Tara ignoring the animal noises.

'I can't say for sure, Tara. All I know is that Goblins are essentially the same in terms of strength, size, combat ability, and intelligence. They don't have schooling, training, or skill specialisation that we do. They learn on the job, making most of them less skilled, less brave, and with inferior equipment. There is a lot more variation amongst Plains Devils. Some cast dark magic, some are exceptionally strong, some are exceptionally skilled, being equivalent to our Lord Guardian's or Warrior Priests of old.' Said Katina.

'We must avoid them if we are to complete our mission.' Replied Luka.

'After your meeting with The Huntress, it is more important that we get through and find this trainee priest of The Light Bringer to return the power of the Gods of Light to the world. That way, maybe we can make a safe new home.' Said Tara.

They packed up camp and continued the search for the pass while playing the game of hide and go seek with the

Goblin scouts. There were a few close calls, but they were able to avoid any personal encounters. They concluded that the Goblins were conducting a precise search pattern. That made them predictable and easy to avoid.

'We must have passed it by now.' Luka concluded while setting up camp one night. The others agreed.

'We can't find it from the ground, that is clear. It is highly unlikely you would both miss a path, even a hidden one. Maybe there would be a clue from the top of the cliff. Can you make Helghyer understand a search from up there?' asked Tara.

Luka started drawing pictures on the ground for Helghyer, who completely ignored them flying off shaking her head.

'I don't think she's got it and appears to have gone off hunting.' Luka said.

'It's supper time Luka.' Tara replied.

'I don't begrudge her that, I am just disappointed is all.'

'We'll find it. It's just well hidden, and that is no bad thing in itself.' Was Tara's opinion while brushing Freki down. They took it in turns keeping watch. In the morning while breaking camp, Helghyer returned. She pecked Luka on the cheek and flew off northeast perching on a nearby branch squawking.

'I think that means "follow me".' Stated Katina.

'She's found it.' Was Luka's reply. They spent the rest of the day following Helghyer along the base of the cliff. About ten miles away, she led them to an area of heavy rock falls, dense bushes and trees.

'I guess that it's through that!' said Luka.

'Look up. There's a crack in the cliff. There might be something on the other side.' Said Katina.

'We will have to go over it. We dare not clear it, or half the plains will follow us through.' Said Tara.

'It's afternoon already. We will have to get a move on and if necessary, proceed through the night without torches.' Replied Luka.

'Great.' Responded Katina.

'No choice.' was Luka's answer. Slowly but surely, they quietly moved the laden horses through the bushes doing their best to cover the tracks behind them. They clambered over the rock pile. One by one, pulling and pushing the reluctant horses through places they didn't want to go. Everyone got bitten and kicked, but having worked through the afternoon and all night, by sunup they were through. Looking up at the light Luka said

'We can't stop and rest, can we?'

'No, we can't.' was Tara's reply. 'We daren't risk the Goblins hearing us and finding the pass.'

'Thought so.' Replied Luka. They continued through the break in the cliff despite being weary, battered and bruised. The "Pass" was simply a crack in the cliff that ran through the mountain itself, littered with rocks and boulders brought down by the stream in its middle. In places, it was very, very wet and only six feet wide. By evening they reached a narrow valley and stopped to eat.

'Look what I see.' said Katina.

'It's a castle, well sort of. Looks a bit overgrown.' Replied Luka.

'We had better wait until morning. We don't know who's in there. We hide tonight, no fire.' Said Tara. They found a small area behind some large rocks near the pass' entrance to the valley. They rested there that night taking turns at watch, then approached the castle in the morning.

The valley widened to a steep-sided five hundred yard wide area. The castle had stout stone walls some thirty feet high though badly overgrown and neglected. There was a tower at each end of the wall protruding from the nearly vertical sides of the gorge. A large gatehouse in the middle gave entrance to the castle. With the horses secured, the three ladies proceeded on foot. Both Helghyer and Freki remained nearby. The gatehouse was in a lot better condition than the walls and looked reasonably maintained. Proceeding with caution, and swords drawn, they passed through the gatehouse. Seeing some young children playing, they sheathed their swords.

'Hello. Can we have a word with your mums or dads please?' Asked Katina. The children looked at them for a few seconds and collectively ran off shouting 'Dad'.

On the other side of the gatehouse was a large area with several hundred yards before a similar set of walls and towers facing the other way. These though were in much better condition. Inside the castle walls, there were various buildings. Some were dilapidated, others in a good state of repair. On the other side of the valley to the keep was the entrance to a mine. Several men of senior age came out. All the men were carrying pickaxes and covered in the dust and filth of mining.

'They are dark-haired and a good deal shorter than us, not quite six foot I would imagine. They are not of our origin.' Luka observed. The leading man, seeing the swords had now been put away pleasantly said

'Good morning, ladies, we do not see people come from that direction. How may we help you?'

'We are from the south eastern plains and are trying to find a group of our tribe that headed this way a few years ago. Some ten or so men, blond-haired like us but a few inches taller. They are skilled warriors, would have been armed and wearing chain mail.' said Katina.

'I don't know about a few years ago, but we may know them. There is only one group that matches a description like that I know of, a merchant and his guards. He trades food and tools in exchange for our iron from the mine. Beyond us is a wide valley with a large river running down it to the sea. There are various towns and villages situated on the river. As I understand it, they take our iron to village blacksmiths where they exchange it for tools and weapons. These they take to various villages, which they exchange for other goods. Those goods are then taken to the city at the seaward end of the valley for sale. They can defeat the banditry in the valley, so we all do quite well.'

One of the others said.

'From here they will have gone to a place called Treenys to our North East. It is on an island in the middle of the river. From there they will have travelled along the road that is parallel to the river to the upper villages.'

'Thank you' said Katina. 'When did you last see them?'

'About a week ago.' One of the miners said. 'They took our iron North East to the blacksmith at Treenys. They will be somewhere in the upper villages by now. In any event, they will be back here in a few months.'

'Thank you most sincerely.' Said Katina.

'No problem. The merchant has done us well. We now have enough food, so we don't have to waste time farming but can concentrate on mining and smelting.' Replied the lead miner.

'I would suggest you repair the southern gate though. There are lots of Goblins where we come from. They haven't found the base of the pass yet but . . . .'

'Thank you. We will get right on it. We have some of them here too, and bandits.'

The miners let them through the other gate. The group mounted the new horses and were soon in the low hills on the other side of the mountain range, travelling north east along the edge of a vast oak forest and onto the rolling plains of the valley.

'I think we should continue heading north east until we meet this road and head up it.' Suggested Luka.

'Agreed Luka, we should attempt to find my uncle and the others. Once we have done so and know why they haven't come home, we should go home ourselves and tell the tribe.'

'Probably right Katina, but we need to know what's happening here first.'

They kept the usual scouting routine, eventually seeing the river and village.

'It looks like the village is in the middle of the river and no bridge.' Said Katina.

'There is a small jetty though upriver, see.' Said Tara. They headed towards the jetty and rang the bell. A little while later, the small ferry docked.

'Good day to you ferryman. We are looking for some merchants who may have passed this way a week or so ago. Can you help us?'

'I took them to the north bank and the road some three or four days ago.' Replied the ferryman.

'Thank you. We are not from around here. Our tribe uses bartering for trade, so we don't have any local coins to pay for the crossing. Could you see to taking us over anyway.' Asked Tara.

'Bartering you say, well then.' Looking shrewdly 'I see you have some venison. It has been a long time since my family have had meat.' Tara gave him two large steaks. 'Across to the north bank, it is then. Thank you, ladies.'

The crossing progressed smoothly, and they were soon on the road riding upriver at a steady canter. A few hours later, while they were resting the horses, Freki comes back barking. They approached the copse he had come from with caution.

'There are signs of a serious fight here despite carrion-eating most of the bodies.' Commented Tara.

'There are cart tracks. The bodies are not our tribe either.' Observed Luka.

'Can we be sure.' Asked Tara

'Yep.' Replied Katina.

'The bodies if whole would not be tall enough for starters.' Stated Luka.

'The real clue is that the three heads all have black hair.' Replied Katina.

'That would be why the others have not come back then. Not a safe place to live.' Theorised Tara.

'We should catch up with them soon. Two heavy carts against horses.' Observed Luka. 'We need to get moving though, we shouldn't stay here.'

The group proceeded at a steady canter in an upriver

direction. On reaching the next village, Tara asked a shepherd if the merchant and his carts had gone that way. Indeed they had but had not stopped, instead heading directly to the Sheriff at Warameth with three prisoners. The shepherd hoped the merchant would stop on the way back as the village had food and wool to trade.

The group continued upriver. The heavy cart tracks were visible in the dirt road. After proceeding at a steady canter, by sundown, they could see dozens of houses nestled between the river and several hills with various farms around the outside.

'That must be Warameth.' Said Tara.

'Strange place. Stone tower on top of a hill and a large stone bridge.' Added Luka.

'Let's ask that shepherd.' Suggested Katina.

'Excuse me sir, is this Warameth?'

'"Sir", not been called that before. Yes, mam, this is Warameth.'

'Can you tell me if the merchants are here?'

'Yes. They are staying with the magistrate. It is the large house at the top of the green.'

'Thank you, kind sir.' Responded Katina.

The three of them slowly rode into the village. Many of the inhabitants were going about their daily business but looked at them warily saying nothing. The village square was a large oval grassed area with happily grazing sheep on it. They rode across to the large house at the top, dismounted and knocked on the door. A little while later it opened. In it stood a tall blond-haired man of middling years and a wise face. He was at least six foot six inches tall and wearing chainmail armour on his chest. He carried a long sword at his waist. After a few stunned seconds of silence, he shouted

'Daxx, you had better come out here. We have visitors.'

Another even taller and more muscular man entered the hallway of the house. Katina gave a scream, ran through the doorway and leapt at the second man, nearly

knocking him off his feet. Amidst a big hug cried.
'Uncle Daxx.'

7 - ARTUROUS LEAVES

Arturous worked through the day deep in thought despite the tiredness from the bridge incident. He knew they had once been a free people. He also knew that slowly they would all die here if they didn't become free again. What he had been told so far was that they were slaves due to bad choices made when they were free. If he was to decide a course of action, he needed to know more. When they were eating after the shift, he decided to ask questions.

'Almous, Endar, can I ask you something, please? We were once free, weren't we?' Arturous asked quietly. His father's face frowned.

'We must answer him Almous. He has seen many horrors. If we don't, his hatred will turn him dark. That cannot be allowed to happen to one of the last.' Endar spoke quietly to Almous, who responded with the resigned sigh of someone who knew he must do an unpleasant task.

'In the very distant times, even for us, there was The Lord of All Evil. He is a God who at the time, controlled all. Those who lived then were not of any fixed race or shape and were the offspring of the Lord of All Evil's original creations. There was no decency or kindness. Evil was all that existed. Some started to produce offspring of a consistent shape and more moderate temperament. The result was us elves, dwarves, goblins and humans, all of whom are free of the Lord's desire to twist and corrupt everything that exists. We found and worshipped other gods we now call The Gods of Light. They taught us compassion, kindness and civilisation. They also taught our priests special spiritual magic to protect us from the hideous creatures of The Lord of All Evil. The four true-bred races fought the Lord and his cohorts. With the gods of light supporting us, the Hordes of Evil were defeated, and the Lord banished. Peace existed for thousands of years.'

'Then the humans turned to evil. A different kind of evil than had been seen before, a structured, organised one. They built an empire with great cities of stone and an army of professional soldiers who did nothing, but train, follow orders and kill. They practiced magic from the natural elements rather than the gods of light. They left the dwarves and us alone in our enclaves.'

'Then the Goblins abandoned their god and worshipped The Lord of All Evil, allowing him to return. The humans' professional soldiers could fight the Goblins and other creatures of this world but could not fight his spiritual demons and devils of evil. They no longer served The Light and did not have the protection of the gods. Some of us begged to help the humans as we still had the spiritual knowledge, but our leaders said no in fear we would be killed. Once the humans were forced away from our lands, we were surrounded and enslaved. We have been dying ever since.' Almous informed the listening Selvin, Promik and Arturous.

'Did any escape?' Arturous asked.

'No. Ours was the last enclave to fall.' Responded Endar.

In his occasional travels, he relayed to other elders the story his father had told him. They all confirmed the story's accuracy. He found Madarn again, quite by accident, and relayed the story to him too. His response stunned Arturous.

'You must also know that it was the elders of your family who tried to get us to side with the humans. They fought with incredible skill, courage and professionalism. They damn nearly won on their own using just their determination and elemental magic. If our priests had helped them, then the humans would have won. We would not be slaves, and so many of us would not have died. We did very badly in not following your family's advice. Not only have we our dead to be responsible for, but for the entire human race too. We don't deserve to live. One council meeting in which we let our fear and prejudice overrule reasoned actions cost more lives than can be counted.' Madarn told him.

Arturous considered matters further. So, they were slaves because of their fear. The current situation was of their own making, and the elders believed they must pay the price for the bad choices made. His questioning did not indicate any free elves and not even a rumour of anyone capable of rescuing them. With the segregation of males and females, there would be no more kinder. He was one of if not the last elf to be born. In the long term, they were facing extinction. That could not be allowed to happen, no matter the past mistakes. The only saving grace was the extreme longevity of their species. In those circumstances, there was no choice but to escape themselves and find others willing to help his people.

So Arturous continued his routine while starting to plan. The river downstream must go somewhere so he could follow that out of the mountains and hope. Trying to escape via the main entrance was not viable. He had to find another way undiscovered by Goblins. On his first trip outside Arturous had not been blindfolded. Due to his exceptional skill with distances, he added to his soft leather map where he thought the outside was. It showed that one of the mining faces was quite near the edge of the side of the mountain. So quietly one night.

'Almous, Endar, I think there may be a way out.' He told them. They looked at him with instant attention. He opened his map when not being observed by guards. 'This face is quite close to the edge of the mountain. I believe there is a fissure near it. There may be a hole, or perhaps we could make one. It would be a way out unknown to the Goblins. A few of us could get out.'

'It is too risky, Arturous. The Goblins will kill you if they catch you. I am not prepared to risk that.' Almous replied sternly. Arturous nodded glumly.

It was in Arturous' two hundred and eighty second year

(roughly twenty two years old in human age) a friend, Selvin, found a small hole that produced clean air. By this time Arturous was a fully grown and developed adult male elf roughly five feet seven inches tall, muscular but with the lithe, thin physique of an elf, long dark brown hair, deep, deep brown eyes, and the slightly green tinge to his skin that all adult elves carried. Ignoring his father's command, Arturous and Selvin worked to enlarge the hole while trying to avoid detection. Over many days the pair were able to create a small opening at an angle behind some rocks, then expanded it to allow one person through at a time.

They had saved a little food each day for a week. The pair decided it was time to leave. Shortly after everyone was asleep, Selvin woke Arturous.

'Quietly now, do not wake the others. The guard has gone for a walk or something. If we are to go, we must be quick.' Selvin whispered. Arturous grabbed his belongings, including the map.

'I will go first. If you see any light, hide.' Arturous whispered. He gave his sleeping father one sad long look, turned his back and led them both up the narrow passage.

'Light, hide. There are small alcoves on either side. Move.' Arturous hissed. They scampered to the sides crouching in the alcoves just in time. Two armed guards passed them by, not paying attention as usual. Once the danger had passed, they proceeded quietly as before. Within a few minutes, they entered a corridor that had the faintest of whiffs of fresh air. Arturous went for the hole in the rock.

'I will go first and wait on the other side. Once I am through, pass my equipment to me.' Selvin said, handing Arturous his belongings and crawling through the hole. Arturous passed him his meagre possessions, then followed himself. Within a few minutes, both were clinging on to the rock face, their few belongings strapped to back or waist. The hole came out deep inside the crevasse and was not immediately visible to the outside world. Thankfully it was dark, so their eyes did not need much adjusting. Unfortunately, it was also raining, which made the rocks slippery.

'I recognise that path above us. It leads off the mountain to a track heading to the river. The collapsed mine with the crystals is down that way too.

'We should climb to the path and follow that, but not for long as the Goblins are bound to find us that way. As soon as we get to the top hide against the cliff face.' Selvin suggested.

They both scaled the vertical cliff in the ravine to the narrow path above them. Selvin arrived first and crouched against the rocks out of sight. Arturous arrived next and hid also. A patrol of six Goblins left its nearby hiding place in the side of the mountain and saw the two elves.

The Goblins instantly drew swords. Despite being unarmed, Selvin grabbed the head of one Goblin and spun around, causing the body of his opponent to hit the cliff with incredible force. The Goblin's neck snapped. Arturous leapt at another two hitting one in the face very hard mid-jump. It fell instantly, moaning. The other Goblin in a panic wildly swung his sword at Arturous but missed. Seeing an opening, he barged the panicking Goblin hoping to knock him over the edge. The idea didn't work, but the Goblin did stumble and lost his footing while trying to avoid falling off the path.

As Selvin broke the neck of a second Goblin, Arturous grabbed another and threw him over the edge into the ravine. Unfortunately, a further Goblin had approached unnoticed and tried to stab Arturous in the side. While dodging the attack, he fell over the edge into the ravine. His assailant though had overextended its sword arm when attacking, Arturous grabbed it pulling the Goblin over too. The last a horrified Arturous saw as he fell was Selvin get stabbed by the remaining two Goblins. With an audible thump, Arturous' head hit the edge of a rock, and all went black.

When he woke, Arturous was cold, covered in blood, hurt everywhere, and had the putrefying remains of a dead Goblin laying on top of him. Most of the blood was from the Goblin. Arturous noticed he was sweating profusely, shivering, and feeling quite ill, then remembered, Goblin blood is poisonous.

The pair had landed on a tiny ledge a hundred feet or so above the ground. Arturous carefully crawled out from underneath the Goblin resisting the temptation to throw it over the edge. The cut to his head was quite severe, but the blood had congealed over it. The rest of him was covered in bruises and grazes. Considering the state of the Goblin, the frost on the ground, and being ravenously hungry, Arturous realised he must have been unconscious for some time and was very lucky to be alive.

There were no signs of his friend or the supplies and tools he had brought with him. Searching the dead Goblin, he discovered some spoiled food and a water skin covered in mould. He threw both away. The Goblin's belt had a pouch with a few coins in it, and a dagger with a scabbard. He took these, putting the belt on. The Goblin also had a small pack over his back that contained a wooden bowl, surprisingly clean for a Goblin, a flint with a little box of dry tinder, and best of all, a clean, dry waterskin.

Arturous then started the arduous task of climbing down the remains of the cliff face without being seen, heard or falling. What he did hear was the noisy and argumentative approach of a Goblin patrol along the path some fifty feet above him. Quickly manoeuvring himself to be half hidden by the ledge he clung desperately to the cliff face with his head looking down. Several tense minutes were spent just waiting, hoping not to be seen by the patrol on the path above him. One Goblin made a joke, and another gave a furious reply. They left in silence. He waited sometime before continuing his descent.

Due to his injuries, exhaustion and lack of food, the

hundred feet climb down to the base of the cliff took many hours. By the time he reached the bottom, it was dark, not that meant much to Arturous. He did need rest though, and finding a small alcove risked a few hours' sleep. He was woken by the sounds of a Goblin patrol nearby. It was still night. Quietly he packed his things and moved from the alcove to a nearby large bush and boulder. Then sneaking from bush to bush continued his escape. Despite his lack of familiarity with woodcraft, his luck held, the patrol did not see him and moved on. Arturous suspected that this was more because they were not looking for him than any level of skill.

He remained hidden for the rest of the day watching patrols come and go, several hours gap between their passing. When the late afternoon patrol had passed, Arturous risked everything and made his move. He headed to the riverbank intending to fill his water skin and to wash. On the way, he found an apple tree with many ripe fruits. Those on the lower branches he grabbed and ate ravenously, then he climbed the tree to recover apples from the higher branches placing them in his pack for later consumption. After it was full, he continued to the river, washed thoroughly and filled his waterskin.

Several things occurred to him. First, while the patrols were not looking for him, they were up to something. Patrols of twelve went out, but less than that came back, so someone else must be around. If they could be located, they may help free his people. Secondly, because of the patrols, blindly following the road down the river was not sensible, it was too extensively travelled. The apples would not last long. He would need to forage for food which could not be carried out near a well-travelled road without being seen. Crossing the wide icy cold river in the dead of night Arturous headed for the southern mountains in a downriver direction. He hoped this way he would avoid Goblin patrols and find wild food.

From where the mine was at the narrow meeting point

of the two mountain ranges, the valley was no more than a couple of miles wide. Some ten miles downriver from the mine and the valley was at least ten miles across. The signs of regular Goblin patrols ceased at the edge of the foothills of the southern mountain range. By the time Arturous had travelled about twenty miles from the mine, he realised the need to find somewhere safe to stay for a few days while foraging for food.

Between two low hills, Arturous found a tree protected clearing containing a lot of large boulders and a stream. A temporary dwelling could be built here that would not be seen from more than a few hundred yards away. Using the stones and sticky earth clay from the stream bank, he was able to make four low walls with no gaps quite quickly. His first real night of freedom was spent looking up at the stars, the worst of the cold wind kept off him by the valley's trees and his four low walls.

The following day he increased the height of all four walls but, made one wall higher than the others. He scavenged dead branches split from trees for the roof supports. Placed sticks and grass on the beams to form a sloping roof. It was just large enough to sleep in and have a small hidden fire.

Although it took several days to complete and looked very haphazard, he was quite impressed with his first home. Using the knife obtained from the dead Goblin, he fashioned a short hunting spear and caught some small fish from the stream. Lighting his first fire took extensive time practice and patience. However, he did it and ate his first ever cooked meal of the fish and the last of the apples. Catching skinning and cooking rabbit took longer to learn, but eventually, he managed it.

At the end of his first week, he had built a small place to live, created his fire, caught and cooked both fish and rabbit. His cuts, bruises and grazes had healed, and his illness had also gone. By the end of the second week, Arturous was in the best shape he had ever been. His head wound had healed. He slept in his shelter next to a warm fire and ate cooked food. All self-taught, Arturous in one respect, was very pleased with himself, but another side of him was still very much in turmoil. He felt lonely and frequently very sad, not only was he no longer in the company of other elves but had also seen Selvin stabbed by two Goblin swords.

He stayed there for several months learning the skills of survival and woodcraft that were second nature to his ancestors. The need to hunt his food allowed him time to learn the craft of moving silently and without trace through the forest. Then he decided to explore a little further.

Several miles downriver and further into the southern mountains he found a group of trees and tall bushes that didn't look right. They were too well organised and regimented for natural woodland. All the trees and shrubs were equally spaced for one thing. Although he had previously decided not to take risks, curiosity got the better of him. He approached the tall bushes with caution, then slowly forced his way through. After many yards of thick undergrowth and small trees, many scrapes and scratches, he found the entrance to a hidden valley in the gap between two mountains.

The entrance to the valley was roughly thirty feet wide, the corridor he had forced his way through was some one hundred feet long with cut vertical sides about fifty feet tall. The valley had a flat middle some four or five hundred yards wide, then rose slightly over a similar distance on each side. Small trees mostly populated the area. A vertical cliff rose on all sides of the valley. Arturous believed it had been artificially created or at least heavily modified.

Towards the top of the valley, he found two large cut stones lying on the ground. Together they were some six feet six inches long by three feet wide. One contained a plaque, so Arturous cleaned it to expose the carved writing. He found two sets of scripts.

"Here lies Korrigan. My beloved husband and the last of the true Elvin priests."

Then, it said

"If you are an elf in need, you may find my husband's belongings useful, but must seek permission first or they will kill you. Please handle his grave with respect for he was a good and brave man."

Arturous tried to move one of the cover stones. His hands stung as if he had grasped a bunch of loose nails. He then stopped and thought. Korrigan was the last of the true Elvin priests. That means the occupant of the grave could cast spells. The god of the elves would protect the grave. Somehow, he would need to ask permission.

He looked again at the two cover stones and noticed on the sides a series of symbols and strange words. He considered his situation carefully. He didn't recognise any of the words or most of the symbols. He did remember one though, a symbol Endar used to draw into the ground and pray to each night before he went to sleep. He put the palm of his hand on the symbol as Endar had done and tried to remember the words used.

'Oh Lord God of the Elves, please hear my humble prayer.'

The palm of his hand tingled. He considered what to do next.

'I am an escaped slave who has very little to his name. May I please use the items of Korrigan?'

A disembodied voice replied

'You are not an Elvin Priest and do not have the temperament to be one as you do not honour life. You should not be allowed to use the weapons inside, but I will bargain with you. Will you hear my proposal?'

'Please tell me your desire, my lord.'

'Inside is a religious artefact of mine and some weapons. I will let you use the weapons if you agree to look after my relic until you can hand it to a proper elf priest.'

'Is there one?' Arturous asked in surprise.

'Yes, there is someone who could get things moving again, but he won't want to.'

'So this person will need persuading. I will try. How will I know who?'

'You will know when the time comes. He is the only elf that still knows the symbols and words.'

'I will agree to your proposal my lord.' Then realised with shock that he probably knew who was being talked about.

'Then, you may proceed. Do not try and use the relic. It will harm you.'

Although it took some effort and leverage from a broken tree branch, Arturous was able to move one of the cover stones. Korrigan's body had been carefully wrapped. He had a bow and quiver on one side and a long sword on the other. In the middle of his chest was a small statuette of an elf. There were also a few small personal items. Arturous considered the situation and didn't like the idea of grave desecration but felt there was little choice. He took the bow, quiver of arrows, sword and statuette, but left the personal items. After replacing the cover stone, he vacated the hidden valley and returned to his house.

On arrival at his camp, he examined all the items. Despite having large amounts of dust and dirt-encrusted on them, all were sound in structure. While the sword would be the most useful against Goblins, it would need the most work, so he decided to try the bow first despite never having held one. Remembering where there was some sand, he started the difficult process of cleaning.

Despite his initial misgivings, everything seemed to clean up well and tingled to the touch like the gemstones all those years before. He started with the bow. Arturous restored it quickly. The arrows were more of a chore, but that was due to their number. The sword needed considerably more work using water and sand, taking over a week to be usable. Again, reaching a point where it tingled to the touch. For the statuette, he used just water and his fingers. Once cleaned, the bottom plinth revealed strange symbols.

After cleaning the bow, arrows, sword, and statuette, Arturous scrutinised the arrows trying to establish how they were made. With some practice, he was able to work out the basics of fletching, though the arrows were of poor quality. With experience, that improved. He spent weeks practising his new bow with his home-made arrows. Firstly, against tree trunks, then ever-smaller branches and later ever-smaller animals. He then turned his attention to familiarising himself with the use of the new sword. Having acquainted himself with the weight of the sword, he fashioned a wooden practice stick and trained extensively against various unoffending trees.

After another few months, Arturous noticed Goblin patrols starting to come into his area. They did not come too near and mainly headed downriver. He also saw that less came back than went. This presented the opportunity to learn how to spot the tell-tale signs of Goblin movement, watching them pass, then observing the ground once they had moved on. To a limited extent, he was able to tell the number of Goblins and direction of travel. His skill at this also improved with practice.

Though he liked his first home, Arturous decided the area was no longer safe. Further, he wasn't going to be able to find anyone capable of freeing his people by staying in the clearing. Arturous decided to trek downriver to see if he could find anything "Non-Goblin". So, with his pack filled with supplies, his newly learnt hunting and archery skills, Arturous headed off.

Looking back in later years, Arturous realised this was the moment he stopped being an escaped slave and became "The Elf". It also signalled for him and the others he would soon meet, the start of a truly incredible series of events which win or lose Arturous felt honoured to have participated in.

He carefully proceeded southeast in the foothills of the mountains and soon caught signs of some Goblins in the wilderness. With care and consideration, he tracked down their direction of travel and a little later their location. Moving silently through the undergrowth, Arturous proceeded to within about a hundred paces. Crouching behind a convenient bush, he watched as a group of twelve split into two groups of six. One group headed towards the river, and the other went into an ancient woodland. He decided to follow the group heading into the woods and lowlands of the mountain range.

Initially, Arturous stayed at least half-mile behind to avoid detection, following by sound and tracks. Although his woodcraft skills were improving rapidly, he didn't need to worry about that as the Goblins were not being observant. Realising it was possibly a stupid choice he decided to destroy the patrol, starting by whittling their numbers down. Waiting for nightfall and the posting of the watch he sneaked closer, to about fifty paces and bided his time.

The watchman was not paying attention. While the other Goblins settled, Arturous waited quietly and unnoticed. He, using one of his Elvin arrows, then took very careful and lengthy aim on the watchman.

His first shot in anger with a bow was an incredible one. It went straight through the neck of the Goblin watchman and came out the other side. Arturous saw him fall. Elated at his first shot, he retreated through the forest to a safe distance amidst shouts of alarm, being sure he had killed one of them. Staying clear for several hours, he slowly returned to his previous fifty pace distance and again bided his time as before. Two were on watch this time. From his hidden position slowly aimed and released the arrow. Another good hit, to the head this time. Without the lengthy preparation, his next shot at the other watching Goblin only hit a leg.

Like before Arturous retreated, but not far this time.

He had killed two of the six for sure, and a third would be indisposed for a while. That left only three. Hiding behind a large tree, he prepared to shoot again. Hearing several Goblins coming he went down on one knee, came out from behind his tree and fired at an approaching Goblin. A hit to the stomach as it dived behind a tree, moaning. The other two also hid, but not well.

Various Goblin arrows hit the tree Arturous was hidden behind. Since one Goblin was only protected by a bush, he shot again and ducked back behind his tree. There was a moaning sound. As Arturous was not skilled at battle tactics, he decided to retreat a bit to another tree while he was doing well.

The remaining uninjured Goblin was creeping up to Arturous' original tree. Again, not thinking about his task correctly, had not considered his opponent might move. Now side on to the Goblin he released another arrow, again hitting a leg causing it to fall to the ground. A second shot at the prone moaning Goblin, penetrated the chest deeply, killing it.

Arturous then went hunting Goblins, finishing two wounded ones with his sword. On returning to the Goblins' camp, the last remaining one was trying to bind his injured leg. It neither heard nor saw what was coming. A further arrow at the unobservant enemy hit it in the chest. It collapsed with a moan and was finished off by the sword.

Arrows were then retrieved, and the bodies searched. The Goblins only had a few water skins and some copper coins. Proceeding towards the river, Arturous started to track the other six Goblins heading downstream.

Because of the time spent with the first half of the patrol, it took Arturous over a week to find the other half. When he did, there were only four Goblins, but they were beating and abusing two people. A naked woman and a man wearing some short woollen trousers and a heavy course woollen cloak. He wondered if they were the extinct humans his elders had talked about, although, having never seen one before he wasn't sure. The two weren't either Goblin or elf.

The first thing that occurred was the lead Goblin who had been doing the beating, berated two other Goblins for not keeping watch for "The Sheriff". A term Arturous had not heard before. Although the others argued they turned around to keep watch. One immediately saw him. Arturous swore at himself for being careless and losing the opportunity of surprise. He released his arrow, but the Goblin ducked. It hit a log near the two prostrate beaten people. The lead Goblin pulled the arrow out and cried

'Elf.' They started to get their bows out.

'You stupid idiots you cannot have an archery battle with an elf while standing in the open.' The Goblin leader shouted again with significant additional swearing. Everyone ran for cover.

Arturous released another arrow, hitting the lead Goblin in the back who fell over swearing badly. The leader was more inconvenienced than suffering any severe injury. Arturous ducked back undercover and moved position. Various enemy arrows went into the tree and bushes that he had previously been hiding behind. After retreating a significant distance, he returned for his second attack and now approached the group from the other side.

The Goblins could be heard calling to each other checking if they could find the elf. The lead Goblin had by now sorted itself out and was crawling to the others. Arturous from his new hidden position aimed and released another arrow. Not where he had planned to hit but a brilliant shot anyway. Straight up the arse from behind. Very appropriate considering what the lead Goblin had been doing to the female captive. The Goblin leader screamed and went down. Arturous backed away again. This game of cat and mouse went on for many hours. Slowly but surely, he whittled down the numbers of Goblins until the last one just ran. He caught the panicking

Goblin and killed him quickly with the sword, deeply penetrating the Goblin's leather chest armour.

Arturous returned to the injured, frightened creatures that he now believed were humans. A wife who was stripped naked abused and crying looked at what Arturous assumed was her badly beaten, husband. He untied the wife first and then went to the man. The wife's physical injuries were just as significant as the emotional ones she was obviously suffering. Despite that, she immediately tried to go to her husband and then screamed with despair. She was wrong, though, he lived as he was still bleeding. Arturous knew from the mine injuries that all damaged clothing and mud had to be removed from the wounds immediately, followed by them being cleaned with water, stitched and bandaged.

He went to attend the man. The hysterical wife tried to speak to him and cuddle her husband. Arturous could not understand her and could not waste time with communication problems, so he somewhat forcefully removed her from her husband and signed her to shut up and help. He was pretty sure she did not understand much of what he had tried to tell her, but she did come to her senses.

Over the weeks since his escape, Arturous had scavenged or found many items abandoned from Goblin patrols. He had cleaned some materials which at a pinch could do for bandages. He used these as best he could for the husband. Arturous was able to clean his wounds and bind them to stop the worst of the bleeding. To her credit, the wife did not care about her situation but instead helped him save her husband's life. She spent nearly an hour naked in the cold rain assisting Arturous stop her husband from bleeding to death. This taught Arturous that not only were there still humans about but some of them at least, were not what he believed they were. They, like his race, were worth saving and knew the concept of helping others.

They did have a severe communications problem. The woman did not speak either elvish or Goblin, and Arturous tried both on her. He did not speak the human tongue either.

Once the husband had been stabilised, Arturous took off his knee-length shirt and gave it to the woman. It wasn't much, but she was appreciative anyway. She took a quick swim in the nearby river to clean herself off and got dressed.

Arturous tried to explain that they needed to be moving immediately. Using the best he could come up with for sign language and drawings on the ground he told her there would be more patrols. It took a while, but she eventually understood the concept and agreed.

They half carried, half dragged the wounded husband a few miles to where Arturous had made his overnight camp. He uncovered the previously used sunken fire pit and lit a small hidden fire. The wife took the few wild vegetables, a raw pheasant, a piece of metal for a spit and a bowl he had poorly carved. The wife skewered the pheasant and using some shaped rocks hung it up to cook. She put vegetables on large stones near the fire. Then she went back to check on her husband.

Arturous tried to explain to her that he needed to look around for other patrols. Again, this required pictures to be drawn on the ground, but eventually she understood. He first checked the area nearby, then travelled at a slow run ranging out several miles in a circular pattern around the camp before returning. Arturous checked the husband's wounds while the wife worriedly watched. The bleeding had stopped. Between them, they cleaned and re-bandaged him before erasing the camp and moving on.

The wife then drew pictures on the ground of the two mountain ranges, the river, trees, and two groups of stick people on the river. The upriver one she put an X through and an arrow pointing to the lower one. Arturous indicated where they were currently and drew a circular route along the edge of the hills. She nodded. They picked up the injured man, one of them under each arm and slowly headed for the hills.

It became clear that her husband could not travel well, and he was at risk if they continued. When they had walked about ten miles, the husband started to bleed again and could not continue. They carefully laid him down while Arturous went in search of a new campsite. After about an hour he discovered a sheltered spot in a group of large stones near a stream not far away.

They stayed there for many days. Arturous ranged out patrolling the area and hunting for food. He picked up some wild vegetables and fruit, supplementing them with wildfowl, while the wife cooked and tended to her husband. The arrangement worked quite well. She was a much better cook than Arturous was and that left him much more time to forage for food and search for Goblins.

After a week near the fire and the constant attention of his loving wife, the husband came too, although weak. His wife cried with joy and hugged him fiercely amidst a groan. The wife fed her husband a small meal. Only when he had eaten did she try and tell him what had happened, speaking very quickly and enthusiastically. Once he had got through to her that she needed to slow down, he appeared to understand.

Beckoning him over, the husband started to try and teach Arturous their language by pointing at things and saying words. When he had worked out what the husband was doing, he drew some pictures of objects on the ground. The husband then spoke the human word for them. The three picked up a basic level of communication quite quickly. Arturous discovered he was able to learn the human language with incredible speed.

After some effort, Arturous worked out that the husband had a cousin who ran something called an "Inn". If he could safely get them back, then his cousin would give him accommodation for a reasonable time and Arturous could probably find paid work to support himself in lodgings, food, clothes and equipment.

Arturous considered this was a good start for an escaped slave, so he agreed. It took a few more days of rest before the husband could travel, so the lessons in the human language continued. Eventually, they made their way down the river hiding from one Goblin patrol, both on its way down and back. Although Arturous was itching to engage them, he knew the safety of the two humans was more important. Eventually, after many stops and diversions, the wife pointed across a grass plane to a village the other side of a wide river.

'That is Warameth. We have made it. There is a large stone bridge across the river. We can use that.' The wife said.

'The villagers have not seen an elf before, you had better put my cloak on and put the hood up.' Added the husband.

They crossed the grassy plain and approached the stone bridge. It was a solid construction of many large blocks, a flat road surface about ten feet wide with stone walls either side. It had many arches supporting the roadway and was narrower at the village end. He crossed the bridge with a sense of relief.

PART 2 – AND SO IT BEGINS

MAP OF WARAMETH VILLAGE AREA

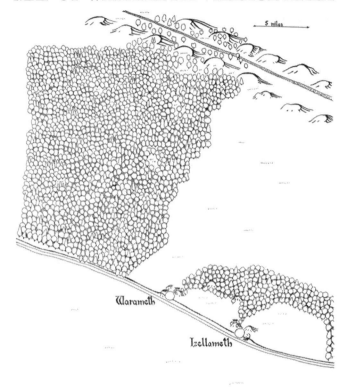

8 - THE FIRST MEAL

They rode along the dirt road. All three prisoners were being dragged behind now. Oswald did not know if they were alive or dead. The others appeared not to care either way. As they continued a young teenage boy tending a field of potatoes took one look at them and ran ahead shouting for his father. When approaching the village green, people stopped their daily chores and came to watch the arrival.

'We have plentiful supplies of the usual goods to trade, but we must take these prisoners to the Sheriff first.' Ablamon shouted.

'And what are their crimes?' came a booming shout of a tall, muscular blond-haired man the same height and size as Oswald's companions.

'My Lord Daxx, it is good to see you.'

'And you too Ablamon. You have had an eventful journey judging by the bandages.'

'We have my Lord Sheriff. I will give you and the Magistrate more details later, but these three are the survivors of a band of some thirty bandits that attacked us using dark magic from this wand.' Ablamon said with a loud voice holding the wand up. There were gasps of shock from the crowd. 'I also introduce this representative of the Church of the Light Bringer, without which we would have suffered many casualties. He refers to himself as an Initiate but has proved far more useful than just about any full priest I have ever come across. He wishes to set up a church in Warameth. I believe he would be of much use to the village.'

The Sheriff came over to Oswald. 'Master Priest, my greetings.'

'And mine to you, My Lord Sheriff. It is a pleasure to make your acquaintance.' Oswald responded, knowing that this exchange would determine how the village viewed him.

'An Initiate is a rather low rank to be starting a church, but you come with praise from Ablamon, which is saying something, so never mind about that for now. I am Sheriff Daxx. You will need to discuss your desires with the Magistrate and me in more detail later. You will not be allowed to do anything until approved by the village council, the Magistrate and myself. You need to be introduced to certain family elders to see if the village is willing to accommodate you.' There were murmurs of approval from the crowd. 'You are injured, I see.'

'Thank you, my Lord.' Oswald's companion gave him a sharp look and a thump on the leg. Oswald realised there were things that they didn't want to be said yet. 'I am Oswald Shamus, an Initiate of the Church of the Light Bringer. I asked my masters to allow me to preach basic guidance to the people on the values of my God. They sent me here. As for my injuries, I overextended myself in our last encounter. I will be fine in a few days.'

'We must talk of such matters later.' Replied the Sheriff sternly. 'Ablamon may I borrow a few of your guards to assist with the escort of the prisoners to the jail pending the magistrate's pleasure?'

'Certainly, Lord Sheriff.' Ablamon replied, making a curt gesture to some of the guards who then dragged the prisoners off. Ablamon then turned to Oswald

'Master Priest you had better come with me, so I can introduce you to some of the people we do business with here.'

Oswald went after Ablamon, listened to all the various discussions, was polite and made a point not to be overbearing with his views or requirements for his church. When asked, said that he would be more than happy to conduct services periodically on the green and had no intention to intrude on working time or village buildings. Overall, it appeared that so long as he was useful to the village and did not get in the way, they were at least willing to consider the idea.

Ablamon then negotiated various deals to exchange tools and cloth for leather and wool. The blacksmith, however, was a problem. He wanted Ablamon to supply him with iron ingots. Ablamon, already being committed to providing Treenys, could not do Warameth as well. After much discussion, Oswald asked if the blacksmith could reuse the metal from the various swords, other weapons and equipment they had left behind at the last encounter. The blacksmith replied that he would need to build a new type of furnace for that, which would be a lot of work. Ablamon commented that to be able to melt down and reuse metal from elsewhere would be an advantageous capability to have. The blacksmith wasn't keen, but Oswald suggested if he could borrow a cart, he could lead an expedition to see what they could retrieve from the deceased of the last encounter. The blacksmith could then melt this down for reuse. That seemed to appease him, or at least he agreed to see what could be retrieved.

By the end of the afternoon, Ablamon had agreements for most of the cargo he brought with replacements for travelling back downriver.

'We are keeping some back for trading with the other village we bypassed while bringing the prisoners here.' Stated Ablamon. 'I will introduce you to the innkeeper in the village square and see if we can negotiate a long-term rate for you. He is difficult to bargain with. Max Graff is even quicker off the mark with replies than you are. Despite his failings, he is a master brewer, a good cook and baker. If travel were more widespread, he would make a good living.'

Oswald approached the Inn with Ablamon to see a larger than average dark-haired man in his mid-forties leaning on the doorway. 'Good afternoon master Ablamon, you have brought me the priest I see.'

'Indeed' replied Ablamon. 'Subject to the desires of the Magistrate, Sheriff and village elders he wishes to set up a church here. He will need somewhere to stay. Can you accommodate him?'

'Well now master priest, many of your kind are against the consumption of alcohol. What say you to that?'

Oswald gave up on the correction of his status. He also remembered a particularly horrible illness of his childhood.

'As a child, I found out to my peril that most of the water, certainly in Kersladen is polluted. I was ill for a week in a manner I will never forget. Fermentation is the only safe way of drinking anything down there. Prohibiting such things on public health grounds alone would be foolish. Having said that, excessive alcohol consumption is unwise and prevents meaningful work.'

'I can live with that.' Was the innkeeper's reply. 'My name is Marion Graff, but people call me Max. I can rent you a basic room and simple gruel for one penny a night. You will need to pay me separately for evening meals and ale.' Oswald was about to agree when Ablamon replied 'I believe you will find him very useful to have around, we certainly have. Can you do any better?'

'How can a priest be of any use at all?'

'Trust me. He will.'

'Alright, for now, five pennies a week.'

'That will be fine, Master Graff'.

'I will take you to your room. Please come with me.' Both Oswald and Ablamon followed the innkeeper. The room was tiny. Big enough for a small bed, a small chest and a washbasin and that was it. Oswald was happy with it, though. It was certainly enough for him.

'The room will be fine, Master Graff. Here is a week in advance,' and handed the innkeeper five pennies. 'The only thing I am missing from my cell back in my old temple is a writing desk. Do you mind if I improvise something?'

'You can read and write?' asked the innkeeper in a surprised voice.

'Yes, I can. It is a requirement for becoming an Initiate in any town-based church. If I may get my belongings now.'

'Certainly sir.'

Oswald looked at Ablamon and said, 'Thank you and your men for all the assistance in bringing me here.'

'And thank you for your assistance too. You're travelling with us has been mutually beneficial. We usually eat the evening meal with the Magistrate and Sheriff. They will want to discuss matters with you. I suggest a short time after sundown will be appropriate.'

'If they wish it, I would be happy to dine with them.'

Oswald walked to the cart he had travelled up in and saw his companion. 'Hi. Ablamon has secured me a room at the inn at a reasonable rate so I will be collecting my belongings now. Thank you for being such a great companion in difficult times. Will you be around long?'

The companion looked around. Seeing that the pair of them were alone, he replied 'It has been a pleasure to travel with you and an honour to witness the return of the ways of the old gods. It has set us all thinking. You have been of significant use. Can you not travel with us long term? Those spells are mighty useful, and you are reasonable in combat too.'

'If I had just been sent out wandering, I would have been happy to, but I am to set up a church here if I am allowed. I can still assist you when you are here again, which will be of some help if somewhat belated. I would be grateful if you would keep my spells to yourselves.'

'Certainly. We will most likely be here for a few days anyway. We stay with the Magistrate, Lord Kasa Mord. The Sheriff is also a senior warrior in our tribe.'

'I see. Ablamon said that they might desire my attendance at an evening meal tonight. I will treat both the Sheriff and the Magistrate with proper respect.'

Oswald collected his belongings and returned to his room. He wrote a brief letter to the High Priest, which required careful thought. His Grace had given him a horrible black oily feeling when he had met him. The

Sheriff, on the other hand, had not. He decided the knowledge that the Magistrate and Sheriff, were senior tribe members should not be imparted to his former church. Oswald wrote the following letter.

"Your Grace, greetings.

I have arrived at Warameth. The village elders have agreed to a council meeting to determine if they will allow a church to be set up in the village. I have met most of them this afternoon, and they appear willing to consider the idea if I am of general use to the village. I will attempt to discover what the village would desire me to contribute to be allowed the church. It will not be money as they do not think that way. It will be one or more services they don't have or are having difficulty in obtaining.

I have secured some short-term accommodation. The journey was eventful as bandits beset us several times. The merchant's guards handled matters on both occasions.

The merchant I travelled with is returning to Kersladen to trade the goods they have exchanged here. He has kindly agreed to deliver this to you although I suspect it may be some weeks before it reaches you.

Regards

Oswald Shamus"

Having completed the letter, Oswald decided it was time to pray to seek guidance. He looked through his small bag of belongings and retrieved his religious symbol. It was a carved hardwood equal-armed cross about six inches wide with an ornately carved three-inch diameter sun secured onto the front.

After unpacking his cross and clearing his head, he started to pray by reciting the general prayer of thanks, adding special thanks onto the end for honouring the prayers for light and healing during his last combat. Aside from actually being grateful, it was appropriate. He then added a question about what he should tell the Magistrate and Sheriff. The voice from the last bandit raid then entered his head.

"Relax, you are not going mad. In the olden times, the chosen God allocated full priests and shamans a spirit guardian or guide to accompany and assist them. I have been allocated to you early because of the odd situation here. When you are a full priest, I will be able to lend you some assistance in the casting of your spells and miracles. You are not a full priest yet, so I can't do that. We normally go in an animal that accompanies you, but there wasn't a suitable one about, so I am in your cross for now."

"That's a relief." Was Oswald's reply. *"Is there any guidance from God on what I should tell the Sheriff and Magistrate. I don't know if you caught it, but the Magistrate is important to his tribe, and the Sheriff, the main warrior. I need to know what I can tell them."*

"That level of guidance requires the most complex level of miracles and lots of praying in the highest rank of a properly consecrated church. No chance of that yet, it's far too big an ask of you. 'The Huntress' now has a true worshipper also, and she is on her way here with a few others. This Magistrate and Sheriff of yours must know that a second God of Light is now in play too. You are to help this true worshipper become an Initiate of The Huntress and teach her the process of casting spirit magic the same way you do. There are a significant number of spirit magic fundamentals and divine miracles that are the same for all the Gods of Light. Only a few spell components are unique to each God. For now, you can help each other out by combining what you know. She will be here shortly."

"You will have to tell them what you did to become connected, what you believe of the High Priest in Kersladen, especially the merchant Ablamon and his guards. If you don't, they will be killed as soon as they get back to the city. That's my guess anyway."

"I agree, they must be told." Thought Oswald. He stopped praying to notice Ablamon standing in the doorway.

'An unusual time to be praying master priest.'

'I needed guidance.' Said Oswald.

'I hope you received it. It is time for dinner. The Lord Magistrate has requested your presence.'

Oswald looked up to see it was already dark. 'Sorry, I did not mean to be so long, and yes, I did. There are matters I must discuss with you all.' A surprised looking Ablamon led the way taking him across the village green to a large stone and wooden house. Unlike the other buildings that abutted the green, it was set back from the road, its boundary marked being a four-foot-high stone wall. He knocked slowly on the sturdy oak door and entered without waiting. Oswald followed him. The hallway was big but not overly so and well-lit with wide wooden stairs in the middle.

'Lord Mord, I have returned with the priest as requested.'

'Bring him in. Dinner is ready.'

Ablamon took Oswald through a door on the left into a large dining hall. Ornate wall hangings adorned the wood panelled walls. A haunch of beef, various vegetables, and a small cask of ale were already on the solid wooden table that could seat a dozen or more with ease. Two servants, a man and a woman both middle-aged, of dark hair and medium build, were serving dinner. A place was set for him in the middle of the long table with Ablamon opposite. The Sheriff was at one end of the table with an unknown man at the other. He was tall, well-built and blond like Ablamon and his guards.

'Good evening. I am Lord Mord. I act as the village's Magistrate, but formally was the head priest of my tribe, though I do not practice that here. I have heard a great deal about you but would prefer to discuss matters over dinner. You already know Ablamon and my guards. I also believe you have met Lord Daxx, the village Sheriff. He is also from my tribe and served as there Lord Guardian, a title given to the tribe's best warrior. Ablamon and the guards as you have already discovered are also very capable. Ablamon was Lord Daxx's second. The others were my guard. Now, master priest, please be seated and tell us about yourself.'

Oswald decided to take a chance. He proceeded to the chair indicated, which was next to his companion from the cart. Before being seated, offered his hand to the Magistrate in greeting. He noticed a small grin on his face, while he took his hand and shook it. Oswald noted a warm, pleasant feeling when the hands touched, but different from the previous feelings he had had.

'That confirms it, my friends, he is a priest of old. Daxx, please shake our guest's hand too. It should put him at a bit more ease.' The Sheriff did so with a knowing smile. He got the same feeling as he had had previously. The Magistrate continued

'It is a little-known skill of the old priests, that they can feel the aura of those beings connected to a god by physical contact with them. What our guest here has just done is to test our auras to see whom we worship and whether it is a god of good or evil. His aura is quite white and judging by the fact that he has not put spells of protection up, we have passed too.'

Oswald's former companion asked, 'I am confused, I have not heard of this before, sensing auras?'

'We keep it secret. It is why the servants of the Lord of All Evil never infiltrate the neighbouring tribes or us Iredan. All the elaborate rituals we carry out on those exposed to our enemy are designed to do is give the High Priest an excuse to touch the exposed so we can see the aura. Our guest here circumvented the lot by simply being polite. We should have thought of that.' He concluded with a wry grin.

He looked at Oswald and said, 'Regretfully it is the only ability of old we still possess.'

Oswald replied 'When it boils right down to it, after the events that gave me my limited abilities, it is the reason I left my church. I was injured while praying at the high altar and taken to the infirmary. The High Priest of my church came to see me. When he touched me, I got an oily black feeling, not pleasant like the contact with my cousin, or yourselves.'

'Presumably Lord Mord, this oily black feeling is what you are looking for in our rituals and represents a servant of evil.' One of the guards asked.

'Yes, it is.' was the reply. 'I know you have some powers and Ablamon has told me the manner you used them in your last encounter. Are you willing to explain more?'

Oswald replied 'That is why I was praying earlier, to establish what if anything I can tell you. There are things you need to know or Ablamon and the guards will be killed when they next return to Kersladen.'

There was a stunned look around the room. Lord Mord saying 'Then please proceed with what you can tell us at this time.'

Oswald took a deep breath and said 'Well here goes. It is probably best to start at the beginning. My task at the mid-winter holy day ceremony was to carry holy water. The service is held at sundown on the day before the Winter Solstice. I was to hand the water to the High Priest at the culmination of the ceremony. Unfortunately, I tripped and dropped a full jug of holy water on the altar. My cousin, who is a full priest, had spent several hours of ceremony that day purifying and blessing the water. Carrying it was my only task, but I managed to get that completely wrong.'

'The usual punishment for such a mistake is to be defrocked and cast out, but instead, the High Priest ordered me to copy the scroll of Time and Service remaining awake and without food or water until I completed the task. Unfortunately, not only did sleep befall me but my copy scroll was different from the High Priest's version in both timing and words.'

'So, knowing my fate was severe, praying at the high altar for forgiveness seemed appropriate. This happened to be at sunrise on the Solstice. When praying, my strength failed me, and I fell, hitting my head on the high altar in the process. Then someone tried to stab me at the altar. Two novices frightened my assailant off, and I passed out. It was about a week before I woke. During this period, The Light Bringer visited me, and I agreed to worship him properly. God then told me that now I had paid the blood sacrifice he could look after my family and me. It was then that I received the spirit magic symbols and words from my God. When I woke up, I got good feelings from my full priest cousin, but a horrible feeling from the head of our church, the High Priest.'

Oswald's former companion then piped up 'That explains a lot. Presumably, your former master got this white-based feeling off you, knew you were now tied to light and what you were likely to be able to do.'

Ablamon nodded and said 'Hence the assassination attempt in the market square at Kersladen and the ridiculous level of banditry we encountered on the way here. They want you dead.'

The Sheriff then interrupted. 'And badly would be my estimate. The last thing our enemy wants is for spiritual knowledge to return.'

Oswald intervened. 'I am not sure he sensed me that way. He gave no clue if he did. It was probably one of his subordinates, seeing what happened at the altar gave me away. A man called Curate Shanks would be my guess. One more thing though, my God when he spoke to me made it clear I am not a priest. I have certain abilities, which seem to be getting stronger, but I cannot make other priests or consecrate ground or conduct various other tasks until I am a full priest myself. That was made very clear. That is why I try to resist people calling me a priest.'

Oswald's former companion then opined 'My Lord Mord, if it's that important a difference and there are things he will be able to do when he is a priest, why don't you just put him through the ceremony now and have done with it?' Oswald gave a shocked look.

'He certainly has proved himself. Regular prayers that the Light Bringer answers, I heard that myself, religious knowledge, correct temperament. He's got a lot going for him.' Ablamon added.

'I am afraid it is not that simple. If Oswald were to be a regular priest, I would have no problem with advancing him even based only on what has happened today, let alone the last bandit attack. Back home, overhearing the clear answering of prayers coupled by a correct aura and the ability to sense it in others would be enough. However, he is to be an old-style priest of a different religion, and we have no consecrated ground to conduct the ceremony. It simply wouldn't work for his new powers.' The Magistrate replied. 'If you don't mind me asking how does the spell casting work.' The Magistrate went on.

'I may not have it all correct, but this is how I think it works. You must have agreed to worship your chosen God, paid a small personal blood sacrifice onto an appropriate blessed religious object, and on one of the holy days be engaged in heavy prayer. If your God accepts you, then you can use fundamental elements to invoke the power of your God and cast a spirit magic spell.' Oswald replied.

'Fundamental Elements?' The Magistrate enquired.

'My name for them and purely descriptive.' Replied Oswald. 'I have in my memory six symbols. Each symbol has a matching word. Say the word while thinking of the symbol causes an effect. One set is raw power, another is a distance element, a third is light, and the fourth is healing. There are two more I haven't worked out. When I cast a spell of say healing, I create a focus in my hand by remembering the meeting with my God. I imagine the symbol of healing, then imagine the one for power and say the words for healing and power to manifest the spell.'

'I see. The wand Ablamon brought me had symbols on it.' The Magistrate left the room and came back after a few minutes with the wand. He showed it to Oswald.

'The top two symbols and words are distance and power. I don't recognize the last one. Given what happened, I would imagine it is darkness.' Oswald said.

'I think that is enough for now. We had better eat before the food gets cold.' was the Magistrate's reply.

They discussed matters further over dinner. There was a knock on the door. As the servants were still serving food, the Magistrate went out to the hall and opened the door. There were a few seconds of silence followed by 'Daxx you had better come out here.' The Sheriff went out to the hall. Oswald heard an unknown female shriek.

'Uncle Daxx.' Followed by a thud and a groan. Then with excited shrieks of 'We've found you.'

Oswald then heard the Magistrate say, 'You ladies better come through.' The Magistrate re-entered the dining hall and looking at the servants said 'Find additional seating for the ladies and some bowls and mugs for ale. Also, the falcon and wolf will need something to eat too. They have come a very long way.'

'Certainly, my lord.' Was the respectful reply. 'If I may be so bold as to ask my lord, are my wife and I correct in assuming they are all from your old tribe.'

'You are. Do not be deceived by them being female. Our tribe is very different from your valley folk. It is the way of our tribe that they are trained as warriors or scouts until they are with child or apprenticed to an artisan. These three were highly capable even before we left all those years ago. They will kill without a second thought. The one on the right is Lord Daxx's niece and is called Katina. She was, at least when we left, a capable scout and wild hunter. Good on tribal lore and alchemy in addition to her hunting skills. The one on the right is Luka, also a capable scout and hunter. She has such a strong affinity to that falcon they can almost understand each other. The taller one in the middle is Tara. She comes from a very long line of highly capable warriors. As soon as space became available, she would have been on my guard. She communicates with the huge wolf just as well as Luka does with her falcon.'

'We will treat them with a suitable respect, my lord.' The servant husband replied bowing reverentially. 'With your leave, we will get the additional seating, and food.' And with that, the servants left.

Lord Mord then looked at the three ladies 'I am known as the Magistrate here. What we call "The Valley Folk" are predominantly peaceful people and are not warriors as we are. Aside from something called "The Goblin Raids" that took place several decades ago, there have been no significant war or large-scale combat in living memory. However, the monsters are on the move and banditry is rife. Ablamon and my guard are just about the only group that travels the entire valley as traders and merchants. The other merchants were wiped out years ago. Why are you here?'

'My Lord Mord, if I may be blunt, the chief and tribal elders are unhappy that you have not returned. Your mission was to find a new home and return so we can relocate before the Goblin tribes overrun us. There are now full-scale attacks on our villages. If it weren't for the advanced warning given by Freki and Helghyer, we would never have survived the last attack. If nothing else, the tribe needs its priest, his guard and the two Lord Guardians back.' Tara replied.

'That is just not appropriate yet. We were sent to find a new home. The only other humans we found are here, and I believe the tribes can move here, but not yet. Ablamon in his role as the merchant is improving the economy and combat capability of the entire middle portion of the valley. The top end is already overrun, but what we have done has stopped it spreading further. Plus, today has seen another important arrival. May I introduce you to Oswald Shamus, an Initiate Priest of the Light Bringer. He is looking to set up a church here. It is probable that the village elders will allow it, or at least allow him to conduct services on the green on holy days.' Said the Magistrate.

Oswald rose from his seat and shook hands with the three new arrivals. The one called Luka had a pleasant aura like the Magistrate and Sheriff. The other two had no such aura. The servants brought in three stools, some bowls and jugs for the ladies who ate hungrily.

After a while, the Sheriff asked. 'You ladies had better explain what has been happening back home.'

They talked about the recent attack on the village and the decision to find a safe home. Luka informed them of The Huntress' temple and her bonding, concluding the story with the pass through the mountains and trip up the river. She then asked about the new trainee Priest of the Light Bringer who was to teach her. After a few seconds of silence, the Sheriff said.

'I suspect you have found your priest.' Pointing to Oswald Shamus. 'It must be him The Huntress was talking about. He can cast spiritual magic and had to do so getting here, or Ablamon and the guards probably wouldn't have lived through their last combat. We know of no other spellcasting priest.'

'I will pray tonight before sleep to seek guidance. If my God approves, I will teach you what I can. Somehow though you will have to be ordained as an Initiate of The Huntress or it won't work. Only a priest can do that. You have paid the blood price, but you will have to be properly ordained.' Oswald replied.

'I am the tribal High Priest, and we have the statuette artefact the ladies found. I could try initiating her and see what happens.' Said the Magistrate.

'I agree.' Said Luka. 'I would be obliged if you would say your prayers and see if the Light Bringer will agree to the request of The Huntress that you teach me.'

'I will ask my spirit guide tonight and discuss matters in the morning.' Replied Oswald.

There was a commotion outside of the house with lots of people shouting and cheering. Then the male servant entered.

'Excuse me my Lords, but the innkeeper wishes to see you as a matter of urgency.' He asked Lord Mord.

'Bring him in.' Replied the Magistrate. The innkeeper entered with a massive smile on his face. 'I take it something important and good has happened.'

'Yes, Lord Mord. You know my cousin and his wife were taken by Goblins a few weeks back and the farm destroyed.' Said the innkeeper.

'Yes, I do.' Replied the Sheriff sadly. 'There were clear indications he had killed several though.'

'Well, a stranger has just brought them both in alive, though my cousin is in a bad way. He has many wounds and is weak, but the stranger has cleaned and bound them well. His wife only has the stranger's shirt and has been treated horribly. They are both being looked after by my wife. I wanted you to know my lords. One last thing, he hasn't taken his cloak off, keeps his hood up and speaks very little, but I believe the stranger is an ELF.'

'I must go to them immediately and see if I can heal him.' Oswald said.

'Daxx and I must also. Friends, this has been an incredible evening. We will be back as soon as we can.'

They left the others talking while the innkeeper led the three of them to the room where the injured couple and stranger were. On entering Oswald Shamus saw a wounded man lying on a bed with a very concerned lady washing him. A hooded armed man in a cloak was standing in a corner, and the inn keeper's wife was heating water over the fire. The man on the bed looked terribly weak. His bandages, although well fitted, were covered in blood.

'Madam, if you wish to get washed and dressed, we will tend to your husband in your absence.' The Sheriff said.

'No.' The lady replied. 'I am not leaving my husband. I have been so close to losing him so many times in the last few weeks I am not leaving him now no matter what.'

Oswald went over to her. 'Madam I need to tend to his wounds. We must remove these bandages, or they will become diseased. Are there new ones?'

'There are more bandages master priest.' Replied the inn keeper's wife.

Oswald looked at the Sheriff and Magistrate. 'I will tend to the stomach wound first and then one at a time as many of the others as I can.'

They removed the bandage from the stomach wound, which started to bleed immediately, but it was clean and not infected. Just as the two women were about to try and put fresh bandages on, the Sheriff and Magistrate held their arms and asked them to wait. Oswald cleared his mind and prayed. He called forth the image of curing, shortly followed by the symbol of power, which he invoked twice. Then said the words

'Iach, Grym, Grym.'

The warmth passed through his hand onto the abdomen of the injured man. The wound closed amidst gasps from the others in the room. The wounded man's wife suddenly burst into tears as the emotion of the possibility that her husband would not die, overcame her.

'It is how it was described to me by Ablamon.' The Sheriff said to the Magistrate who gave a nod of agreement in reply. Oswald repeated the healing with several other severe wounds before saying.

'That is as far as I can go. So long as he is kept clean and warm, the others should heal normally. I am tired now and must rest.' Oswald told everyone present.

The man's wife gave him a big hug and said, 'Thank you.'

'Please wait a minute before you go master priest.' The Magistrate asked. Then turning to the cloaked stranger continued. 'I have been told you rescued them from a group of Goblins, have brought them through the wilderness for some considerable time with courage care and skill. The innkeeper is most grateful for returning family thought to be dead. He also thinks you are an elf.'

Through the tears of joy, the injured man's wife then replies. 'That is all true. I saw him kill four Goblins, with both bow and sword. His name is Arturous. He only partially speaks our language. I have taught him some during our journey. He is an escaped slave from the Goblin mines at the head of the valley.'

'I see.' Replied the Magistrate. Looking at Arturous, he continued 'Presumably you have no money to pay for lodgings if you are an escaped slave. However, you have done this village a great service. For a limited time, we can find you lodgings to get yourself established, but in the longer term, you will need to pay your way. The Sheriff and I have some ideas on that.' Looking at the innkeeper, the Magistrate said, 'Presumably you are full of family and priest.'

'Actually, I am not. My wife and I have just finished renovating the abandoned room. It lacks decoration but is dry and has a basic bed. He can stay there for a while. Given the favour, he has done me. I can manage a few weeks without too much issue. I don't have the money to go beyond that.' Replied the innkeeper.

Somewhat haltingly and slowly Arturous replied 'That would be fine sir. Being dry and warm is far better than I am used to.' Turning to the Magistrate, he continued. 'I have some coins taken from dead Goblins and have acquired some items along the way, including an Elvin Sword, Elvin Bow and some Elvin Arrows. The four Goblins the good wife witnessed me kill were part of a group of twelve I was tracking. They separated into two groups. I killed the other six before I met this farmer and his wife. There was a second group of twelve I avoided. As for being useful, I have learnt how to make arrows and find food. My mining knowledge will not be of any help here, and neither will my treatment of wounds after what I have seen tonight. I am willing to do whatever I can to assist the community and help pay my way.'

'There may well be something you can help within the immediate future. A few days cart-drive downriver of here the merchant caravan was attacked by a group of about thirty bandits. I have asked the priest to lead a party to retrieve what metal is possible for our blacksmith to reuse. I would like you to accompany the priest. Tonight has also seen the arrival of three female warriors from my tribe. I will order them to accompany you as well. I will find someone from the village to drive a spare cart.' The Magistrate informed him.

'I will help.' Replied Arturous.

9 - THE FIRST TRIP OUT

In the morning, a polite knock on the door from the innkeeper's wife woke Arturous. She indicated that breakfast was ready. Acknowledging the call, he got dressed and on leaving the room discovered the lady waiting for him outside.

'I will show you to the room where we serve breakfast.' The innkeeper's wife explained slowly. 'The Priest has asked if you would be so kind as to join him.' Arturous nodded his agreement and followed. The backroom had a fire set in the hearth, a table, several chairs with the priest sat at one. He rose and presented his hand for greeting. Arturous shook the hand and said.

'Thank you for inviting me to have breakfast with you, that was kind.'

'I am Oswald Shamus and am pleased to make your acquaintance. I understand you are willing to accompany me to retrieve metal and weapons. Thank you. Aside from the two of us and the three female warriors mentioned last night, I have been told a young lady from a local farm will be driving a cart borrowed from her family.'

'I gather that you were attacked in force, will six be enough.' Asked Arturous.

'If I am honest, the thought does worry me. However, of the thirty bandits that beset us, at least twenty of them were either killed, badly wounded or captured. I can't see they will turn up. If we encounter those that are left, there won't be more than a dozen. Judging by what I have heard about you, and what I have seen of the combat ability of the warriors from the Magistrate's tribe, the skills of those I travel with are far superior.'

Breakfast arrived. Rather than being the expected gruel, it was proper porridge with toasted bread, sausages bacon and beans. They both ate heartily. When it came to leave the innkeeper brought a small parcel of bread and cheese for them. He said

'I imagine you will be away overnight, so I have brought you a small parcel of food instead of tomorrow's breakfast. You both take care, it's a nasty world out there just now. My wife and I have not said anything about what happened last night, who you both are or where you are going. It seemed sensible, but secrets like the events of last night can't be kept long.'

Oswald replied 'Thank you sir, and we shall. I don't know about the local girl, but I travel with experienced warriors, so if anyone does come looking for trouble, they will find it. Knowing where we are going, if we leave soon this morning, we will be back late tomorrow.'

They both said their goodbyes and left the inn. Seeing a cart on the side of the road with a beautiful long brown-haired young lady in her mid-twenties sat in the driver's seat waiting patiently, they approached. She was wearing leather armour and had a bow and quiver of arrows slung over her shoulder. They both walked to the cart. Oswald introduced himself by saying

'Good morning, I am Oswald Shamus, an Initiate Priest of the Light Bringer. My friend here is called Arturous. He is experienced with wilderness matters. We were to meet some others here I wonder if you are perhaps the local lady who was to supply the cart?'

'I am. My name is Agnes Partten.'

Just then a falcon landed on the cart's tailgate and squawked. It was shortly followed by the biggest wolf Arturous had ever seen. It jumped up onto the back of the cart and lay down. The animals looked at them. They turned around and saw three very tall women walking over with the Sheriff and Magistrate.

Arturous looked at the two animals 'Are you two bonded with those ladies?' There was a squawk and then a bark.

'I will take that as a yes then.' Was Arturous' comment.

'I certainly wouldn't want to get on the wrong side of

that wolf; it's huge and would make guarding my sheep really interesting.'

'He kills only for food, to defend his pack or my tribe. You will have nothing to fear from him.' Was the comment of the tallest of the approaching women.

'Unless you happen to be a Goblin, he is quite good at killing them.' Was the comment of another of the women.

The tallest woman continued. 'I am Tara of Iredan, a tribe of the southern plains which is on the other side of your mountains over there.' She said, pointing to the mountains to the southwest. 'I run with the wolf whose name is Freki. This is Luka who is twinned with Helghyer the falcon, and that is Katina. The Sheriff and Magistrate have asked us to accompany you.' She continued.

'I am Agnes Partten. My father has asked that I bring our farm's cart to assist with the return transport of recovered items.'

'We are pleased to meet you. Forgive the impertinence, but in our tribe, only fully qualified warriors are allowed such a sword as you carry, are you competent with it?'

'We are heading into potential danger, no offence taken. These both belong to my father, who was a soldier in the Goblin raids some years back. He has let me borrow these for this trip. I have received basic training in both but would not classify myself as a skilled warrior.' Agnes replied.

'I thank you for your candour, Agnes. If we are attacked worry only about keeping yourself alive, the rest of us are experienced in combat and will assist any other who happens to need it. When we get back, I will arrange for your training.' Tara said, looking at the Sheriff who nodded. Turning to Oswald and Arturous, she continued 'Master Priest. We have been told of your exploits on your trip up. Clearly, you can look after yourself. I also have no problem with you, master elf. Anyone who can take out a whole raiding party on their own, clearly needs no second-guessing from me.'

'It was not in one go, they split themselves up, and it took about a week.' Replied Arturous.

'They are still dead, though, and that's enough for me.' Responded Katina who then turned to the Sheriff. 'Uncle Daxx, we had better get moving, the day wears on.'

'Agreed and good hunting to you all. You shouldn't encounter anything before the next village. It's below that.' Replied the Sheriff. Oswald got onto the cart next to Agnes, and Arturous jumped onto the back with a snoozing wolf. Katina, Tara and Luka mounted their horses and moved ahead of the cart.

The group proceeded out of the village without attracting much attention. After a few hours when they were approaching the village of Izellameth, the falcon appeared to stop snoozing and squawked. The wolf stood up and looked about. Arturous called out

'Ladies, your animals' sense something.'

Luka looked at her falcon. 'We've got company. Non-human is my guess. Helghyer go have a look and be careful.' There was a derisory squawk, and off the falcon flew.

'I will go too, but I don't speak falcon yet.' Arturous said.

Tara added in a resigned tone 'Go on Freki.' To the wolf that was jumping off the cart before the sentence was finished.

Arturous was running quickly and quietly through the tall grass following the falcon to the edges of the forest a few miles away from the road and river. He was quickly caught by the wolf who ran effortlessly into the fringes of the forest and stopped. Arturous noticed the falcon taking a wide circle above the trees. When Arturous arrived a few minutes later, the wolf looked at him and then looked in a slightly inward but downriver direction.

'I go that way.' Arturous replied. Freki went directly onward.

Arturous proceeded with more caution deeper into the

forest, looking for signs of movement in the area which did not take long to find. There was an old rusty sword, the remains of a deer, eaten raw by the looks of it, and many Goblin tracks. Feeling he was being watched, he looked up and saw the falcon Helghyer standing on a branch. Arturous considering the rather odd situation of working with animals looked at the falcon and said

'You had better go get your human.' The falcon flew off.

Hearing a noise behind him, he saw Freki approach from in the forest. Looking at where Freki had come from he saw tracks coming from that direction. The area under the branch on which Helghyer had been perched also had tracks. Arturous looked at the wolf.

'Let's follow them for a while.' Freki went on ahead. After a couple of miles of cautious movement, Arturous heard noises. Freki instantly hunched down and with a stalking stance edged closer. Both hid behind bushes at the edge of a small clearing. It was a full scouting party of twelve. Arturous listened as he could understand some of the Goblins speak.

After a while, Arturous heard Luka approach. She looked at the Goblins and nodded. He signalled them to withdraw, which they all did quietly. When at a safe distance, Luka said to Arturous.

'You were tempted, weren't you?'

'Yes, I was, but it would not be sensible. There are too many for me on my own in one sitting, and it would alert the Goblins to our presence.' Arturous said with a wry smile.

'You are correct. Were you able to get any indication of where they are going?'

'Yes. I speak some Goblin. Picked it up in the mines.'

'We had better get back to the others quickly.'

Off they ran, the wolf and falcon following along. When they got back to the cart.

'We have company.' Luka said.

'There's a scouting party of twelve or so Goblins which are heading downriver of the villages looking for something.' Arturous added. The others looked questioningly at the elf.

'I partially speak Goblin. A survival requirement in the mines.' They all gave an understanding nod. 'There are other groups of Goblins about. I heard them referred to. They didn't seem that keen on finding what they were looking for.'

'I think we must consider travelling as quickly as possible to the combat site, retrieving what we can and return during the night. Helghyer and Freki can help with scouting. They are better at night than the rest of us, apart from possibly our elf. I have heard stories but do not know of the truth.' Tara said.

'I am good in the dark yes, but that is mainly due to my working in the mines I think.'

Oswald asked, 'You are thinking strategically here, what is the problem, I am not familiar with that aspect of life.'

'The Goblins are used to moving around in the valley unhindered. There are several groups each of twelve or more. They also don't know we are here. Better for us to get the weapons back to the village quickly and let the Sheriff know what is happening.' Tara said

'As sooner or later they are going to come knocking at the village.' Added Luka.

'At which point our hosts will need the weapons.' Oswald said with an understanding nod.

'You learn quickly master priest.' Concluded Tara.

'We are going to have to locate the usual paths and discourage freedom of Goblin movement.' Added Arturous.

'Yes, but not today.' Concluded Katina.

They continued along the road as fast as was practical, proceeding straight through the village of Izellameth without stopping. Arturous, Katina and Luka took it in turns to scout ahead with Freki and Helghyer. Evidence of

Goblin movement was abundant, but no further encounters occurred. During Arturous' second scout forward, Katina approached and said.

'We are very near the site of the attack judging by what we saw on the way down.' They continued together, proceeding on the sides of the road behind bushes and trees. As they approached, they saw about a dozen men looting the bodies from the battle with Ablamon and his guards. Helghyer and Freki returned to the rest of the group as Arturous and Katina took cover behind bushes and trees. They could hear the cart and horses approaching, and Tara's booming voice say

'The deceased were servants of the Lord of All Evil. The Sheriff of Warameth has ordered their bodies and belongings seized. Leave everything you have taken and begone.'

Oswald Shamus jumped off the cart and walked beside the horse. Tara was mounted, and on the side near Agnes, with Luka also mounted and on the outside of Oswald. Freki took position near Tara and started growling with bared teeth.

From his hiding position, Arturous thought the group looked quite impressive all by itself without him and Katina. Tara and Agnes had drawn their bastard swords, which were considerably longer than standard ones. The two-handed war mace of the priest looked genuinely horrible, and everyone was armoured in either leather or chain mail. Arturous thought that if the looters had any sense at all, they would drop everything and run. Initially, the looters formed a ragged line across the road. Then several seemed to eye the group up and down wearily. Then one said.

'Two of you are Southern Plains Warriors, aren't you?'

'Yes we are, of the Iredan tribe.' Tara said.

'That does it for me. I am surrendering to the mercy of the Sheriff. I suggest you all do too.'

'What.' Said another with a look of shock on his face.

'Look at them. Fight them, and they will kill without mercy. Run, and they will ride you down. Surrender and you may get to see tomorrow.' He threw down his sword, as did two others. The rest ran.

Agnes said 'Your surrender is accepted. We will take you to the Sheriff and Magistrate of Warameth where you will have to plead for your lives. Fail, and the village will execute you. We are entitled to take everything you own as bounty.'

'Please be merciful, we have eaten precious little in weeks. There's no chance of making an honest living here. All we want is a decent meal each day and a dry place to sleep.'

'Your case must be presented to the Magistrate and village elders. That is their decision, not ours.' Agnes replied.

'Leave the others to go, concentrate on our task.' Ordered Tara.

The captives and deceased were searched for coins and other valuables. The prisoners possessed very little. The looters had nothing belonging to The Lord of All Evil, but those from the previous battle did. By the time the group had finished, they had a cart full of metal weapons and some leather armour.

Helghyer returned squawking. 'That means Goblins, doesn't it?' suggested Katina.

'That it does, we need to move out now.' Replied Luka.

Oswald Shamus looked at Tara 'Ideally someone should scout ahead, but I don't suppose we can afford the time.'

'You do learn quickly master Priest. You are correct we run the risk of walking straight into a trap, but we need to get some distance.' Replied Tara.

'We could always go straight for the nearest village and stay there until morning, have a look around that sort of thing.' Suggested Arturous.

'Has mileage. We go there now, then see how the land

lies.' Agreed Katina.

They turned the cart around and preceded at a fast pace through the night. The captives were tied up and placed in the back of the cart. It was a hair-raising journey. Within minutes of leaving Arturous spotted several groups of Goblins appear where the fighting had taken place.

After a crazy few hours of fast, bumpy driving, they reached Izellameth. It was about midnight when they stopped in the village square. An older man of superior bearing, broadsword buckled at the waist, approached them.

'You are travelling very late. What is your business here?'

'Sir, we had trouble on the road and decided to continue here and rest for the night.' Agnes said.

'I recognise you now. You're Agnes Partten of Warameth. You are welcome here.' The man said as he returned to his walk.

'Thank you, sir.'

After a brief rest, Arturous and the two hunters Katina and Luka went scouting. The others guarded the cart. Half an hour later, all three returned having gone in different directions.

'I went inland back the way we came. I saw evidence of two groups of Goblins, probably the ones we saw when we left.' Stated Arturous.

Katina added 'I went in the direction we will be going tomorrow and saw evidence of one group but not recent.'

'I found a group of Goblins about three miles inland from the river waiting. They did not see me.' Said Luka.

'So, we have at least three groups of Goblins. Two are behind us, and one to our side. Arturous, how many to a group in your experience.' Asked Oswald.

'Both in the mine and my wanderings, they seem to operate in groups of about a dozen.' Was Arturous' reply.

'So, we are looking at facing at least three dozen Goblins, but probably not in one sitting. At first light, we head towards Warameth. That way, there will only be one group facing us.' Tara ordered.

10 - THE PRICE OF EVIL

The group returned to discover three men chained horizontally to posts set in the ground on the village green. More for the benefit of the crowd than the prisoners, the magistrate shouted.

'You have been tried and convicted of being servants of the Lord of All Evil. Your pleas for mercy after conviction were unsuccessful. You have requested an appeal to the village elders for clemency. I will, therefore, ask those of the village now, is there anyone who believes they should not be executed or that the manner of execution is speedy.'

There was a cry from one woman of the crowd, 'They are followers of evil. Let them burn in hell and suffer.'

'Is there any other opinion?' Bellowed the magistrate. There was silence. 'Let the sentence begin.' Ropes attached to four horses were tied one to each limb of the first captive amidst cries of

'No please have mercy please please please.'

He then screamed as the four carthorses pulled at the ropes. With a blood-curdling shriek first his arms were pulled off at the shoulder, then the legs at the hip. The ropes were then detached from the severed limbs, which were placed on the victim's chest.

As soon as it was clear that the sentence was to be carried out, the other two victims started to writhe and scream. The crowd beat them with sticks until they stopped struggling. The same sentence was carried out on each of the other two prisoners. The screams of all three prisoners continued for some time before they bled to death.

Oswald Shamus looked on in horror at the carrying out of the sentence, as did the three prisoners the party had brought with them. They drove the cart towards the blacksmith and in the process caught the attention of the

R. Allen Jones

crowd who saw the three prisoners.

'Three of a group that we met when we tried to retrieve the weapons.' Oswald Shamus said to the gathered crowd of people.

'Are they servants of evil too?' Asked a female voice.

'That will be for the magistrate to determine. They might be but have done nothing to indicate such an allegiance. They could be simply bandits looting dead bodies. That is what they claim to be.' Oswald replied.

'I don't believe them, Let's execute them now.' Said another voice from the crowd. 'We have all lost loved ones to these servants of evil.'

'That may be the case, but you have a system of justice here. No other place in this valley can claim that. Guilt or innocence is for the Magistrate and Sheriff to determine not us.' Oswald continued.

'That is enough discussion. I will take the prisoners into custody where they will be imprisoned pending trial. Katina, Luka, Tara, retrieve the prisoners and bring them to the jail. If they try and escape, kill them.'

'Yes, Lord Sheriff.' The three women responded in unison and removed the prisoners from the back of the cart. Each taking a restraining rope. Quietly when leaving the gathered crowd Tara said to the Sheriff.

'We need to speak to both you and Lord Mord in private immediately. If our scouting and that of the elf had not been so good, we would not have made it back.'

'I see. I will go and find Mord. When you are done with the blacksmith, go to his house.' Was the reply. With swords drawn, the were prisoners poked forward to the jail.

Oswald Shamus, Arturous and Agnes Partten had remained at the blacksmith's unloading the cart. Agnes suddenly dropped the items she was carrying and ran saying 'Father.' Giving him a big hug.

'I am pleased to see you return safely.' Her father replied.

'You must have your armour and sword back immediately. I will go and get changed now.' Agnes continued.

'No, my daughter, you will need them more than me. I have not used them in over a decade. I am sure there will be more trips.'

'They will be more useful in your hands.' Said Katina. Agnes' father looked both surprised and disappointed. He started to speak.

Tara interrupted. 'Do not be upset. Your daughter did you credit. We are all pleased with her. Her driving of the cart was exceptional in difficult circumstances. As soon as we are finished here, she can discuss matters in private with you. We will be doing the same with the Sheriff and Magistrate. She has told us you were formerly a soldier. You may need that skill soon.'

Katina looked at the blacksmith and his apprentice, who appeared not to notice the exchange of conversation. 'I hope master blacksmith that you will be able to make use of these.' She said.

'Once my son and I have finished the new furnace we will yes. The metal quality doesn't look good, but we shall see what can be done with that.'

'Then good day to you.' Katina concluded.

Tara, looking at Agnes' father, said 'Agnes will need to sleep this afternoon as we travelled through the night. However, if after that we go on another trip, can we take her with us? I have arranged with the Sheriff for her to receive additional training if she wishes it.'

'I will discuss it with her, but short trips such as this one where she is not away from the farm for long shouldn't be a problem if she attends to her training.'

'Thank you. We must go and see the Magistrate and the Sheriff now. Can we call on you later and discuss matters further?' Asked Tara.

'Certainly.'

Agnes followed her father back to the farm. The others

went to the magistrate's house, knocked on the door and entered when opened by his servant. They went into the main hall to see Lord Mord, Lord Daxx and Ablamon sat at the table.

'I understand there are things you wish to discuss. I did not believe that a few bandits would be a problem.' Said the Magistrate.

'They weren't. I'd imagine that any we missed are either already dead or will be soon.' Replied Tara. The group told Lord Mord and the others of the events of the trip.

'Luka confirmed a single group travelling parallel to us. I found evidence of movement between us and inland, but could not tell if it was the same as the ones we had already seen or not. Arturous understands some Goblin speak because of his time as a slave under them. They are looking for something, but the group he overheard were not keen on finding it.' Concluded Katina.

Oswald looked at Ablamon and said 'If you are to get to Izellameth then you will need to fight your way through. There are at least two dozen Goblins in your way.'

'There may be more, having found those groups our scouts left it at that. We could not take the risk of further searches and becoming too distant from the cart.' Tara advised.

'Daxx, we need to clear the road to Izellameth so Ablamon can continue back downriver. We must arrange that for tomorrow. I would suggest we send two groups without carts. One being Ablamon and my guards, the other being Tara's six.' Lord Mord requested.

'Tactically unsound Mord.' The Sheriff replied. 'We need to make sure we know what's coming and secure the safety of the outlying farms. We cannot afford to lose any more farms like the Graff's while we send the bulk of our warriors elsewhere. Tara, you and your group, get some sleep and tomorrow do an all mounted patrol of the inland farms and beyond to establish movement and safety. Track down where the three known groups are first and if still about, get the farmers into the village. Once that is done try and see how many groups are out there.'

'Yes, Lord Daxx.' Replied Tara while looking at Oswald who nodded.

'Uncle, obviously we will see you through the current issues, but at some point, Tara, Luka and myself must go home and tell the tribe what is happening here. We are already a good way into our six months.'

'I see, but not yet please.'

'Certainly Uncle.'

Oswald looked at the Lord Daxx and Lord Mord and said 'I have another problem. I am afraid I have some issues with the manner of execution. It is barbaric and should not happen in a civilised society.'

'You are correct it is barbaric, but so is our situation now.' Lord Daxx replied.

'What Lord Daxx means is that the benefits offered by the Lord of All Evil for service are many and bountiful. He will offer youth, beauty, wealth, magic, and a lot more.' The magistrate said.

'But only while it suits him.' Ablamon interrupted.

'We know that, but others don't. That manner of execution is designed to show that the penalties for service to the other side are greater than the rewards.' Said Lord Daxx.

'I understand that those who serve the evil one must be executed, if only for our safety, but isn't a straightforward hanging enough?' Asked Oswald Shamus.

'I am afraid not, master priest.' Lord Daxx continued. 'In our tribe's experience, those who serve him are not afraid of dying, as they may return in the form of ghosts or other undead. The pain and suffering they are put through is a strong deterrent, plus those that die in such pain and dismemberment cannot return as Ghouls, Zombies or the like.'

'I understand your reasoning. I think it is wrong to treat people that way, regardless of what they have done. We should be civilised about it and rise above such barbarism.' Oswald continued.

'Once the Lord of All Evil is defeated, we will be able to do that, but not before. In the meantime, a discussion of sentences for various crimes should take place with the village elders. I suggest you all get some sleep. Tomorrow will be a busy day.' The magistrate concluded.

'We need to see the Partten family first. Then we shall rest. My lord, we have all been on the road for a long time. For Luka, Katina and I the road here was long, tiring and dangerous. From what I have heard, the roads travelled by both the priest and Arturous were no less fraught. If we are to be effective, the whole group will need some time out, or we will lose our edge. We must also arrange for our training and for Luka to be initiated very soon.' Tara said.

'And I must start the preaching I was sent here for and teach Luka the first symbols.' Added Oswald Shamus.

'That is true. You guys haven't had much downtime yet have you.' Replied the magistrate.

'Unfortunately, I will have to overrule that. Necessity requires me to know what the three Goblin groups down the river are up to. Whether they are coming here or going home, and whether there are any more. That knowledge is a tactical necessity. If they are going home, then you can have your rest and training.' Concluded the Sheriff.

The group left the magistrate's house and headed for the Partten's farm. It was very close to the village on the landward side near a hill on which they grazed sheep and goats. They approached the stout stone walled farm complex and saw Agnes, her father, a woman, and a teenage boy of about eighteen years outside the front door of the farmhouse talking. It, like the barn, stables, and many other buildings in the village was a stout structure with sturdy stone walls for the first three feet or so followed by seasoned oak framing, and a stone tiled pitched roof.

'Hello. Let me introduce you. You have already met my

father. This is my mother and younger brother.' Said Agnes. Both the mother and younger brother were looking anxious.

'Thank you all for coming. Agnes has explained what happened. More bandits killed or captured on top of the dead from the previous encounter, with Goblins too banditry is becoming a dangerous occupation.' Said Agnes' father.

'Between us, Ablamon and the guards over fifty have been killed or captured in the last week or two. I can't imagine many are left. But all voids of power are soon filled, by Goblins it would appear on this occasion.' Said Tara.

'So, it would seem.' Replied Agnes' father.

'I tried to have us taken off patrol duties for a while so we could rest, gather our wits and train, but the Sheriff has overruled the magistrate on this one. He wants us to do a patrol tomorrow to find out where those Goblin scouts we spotted have gone, and what is happening inland up the river. The intention is for it to be a fast-moving, fully mounted trip with no cart. Not a kill mission but a look-see one. If you are willing, we would like Agnes to come.'

'The Sheriff is worried they are coming here then.' Replied Agnes' father.

'I believe so, yes. From what Arturous could overhear, they were looking for something and followed us back. Coming here for it must be considered.' Said Tara.

'If you think she will be useful, then Agnes must go with you. She is very green and has no experience of fighting on horseback.'

'But she does know the area beyond the village?'

'Yes.'

'Good, she can be our guide. Arturous, Luka and Katina will do the actual scouting when we get closer. Provision should be made for several days scouting.' Concluded Tara.

'That tower would make an excellent lookout point.'

Stated Luka, staring at the top of the nearby hill.

'Yes, it would.' replied Agnes' father. 'It's over seventy-five feet across and a good twenty feet high. It would make a great defensive position too. Unfortunately, it has no door.'

'Really, that's a surprise. I suppose that will have to wait for some other time.' Luka said disappointedly.

'We all need to rest now.' Oswald reminded them.

'Yes, you do. We will keep watch. Bowen, get some food and head up the hill. Eyes sharp now, boy, Goblins are green and brown. They are not easy to see if they don't want to be.' Said Agnes' father in the commanding tone of a soldier used to being obeyed.

'Yes dad.' Said Agnes' brother, who immediately departed.

Katina, Tara and Luka left for the Magistrates house, while Arturous and Oswald returned to the inn. After a brief explanation to the innkeeper, they went to their rooms and fell asleep quickly.

A few hours later, Oswald woke when the bar room became noisy. He went for some food and found Arturous doing the same thing. The pair proceeded past several dozen men heading for a table in the corner at the back trying to avoid attention. Most of the customers just looked at them, nodded an acknowledgement and let them proceed without issue. A few quietly said 'Hello'. After they were seated, the innkeeper's wife came over.

'They are curious. Despite our attempts at keeping things secret word is out about what each of you has done in saving the lives of my husband's cousin and his wife. They will not bother you.'

Oswald looked at Arturous who shrugged. 'That is fine madam. The village is a lot friendlier than I had been led to believe would be the case. It hopefully will assist when I start my once-monthly preaching and service.'

'You have both earned it. I doubt that will be an issue. What is your pleasure?' the innkeeper's wife asked.

'Something modest to eat and drink please.' Asked Oswald.

'And the same for me please.' Added Arturous.

'We have some gammon and vegetables with a medium ale.'

'That will be fine madam. Thank you.' Oswald replied.

The food was delivered quickly and was of good quality. Arturous and Oswald ate hungrily, and after a short walk around the village to familiarise themselves a bit better with it, they returned to their rooms. Oswald took the opportunity to pray and give thanks. This time at least there were no replies. After concluding his prayers, went back to bed.

He was woken in the morning by a gentle tap on the door.

'Breakfast is ready.' Mrs Graff said.

'Thank you.' He replied, got dressed and said a quick prayer. When he arrived in the dining room, Arturous was already present.

'Good morning, Arturous, I hope you slept well.'

'That I did master priest. I am worried about today's expedition, though. I don't know how to ride a horse. I have never done so and doubt chasing Goblins is a good time to learn.'

'Hmm. In your last scouting, you ran into the forest at quite a rate. Can you keep that up long term?'

'With ease, why?'

'Then my suggestion is we take a horse with us for you just in case. Given the nature of the scouting, you will be on foot for a large portion anyway checking for Goblin tracks. We are due some downtime, you can learn then.' They ate breakfast and left the inn to see Agnes walking her horse across the green with her family. They also saw the wolf Freki lying down on the grass nearer to the magistrate's house. As they approached Agnes and family, Katina Tara and Luka came out of the back of the house leading several horses.

'Arturous has informed me that he can't ride. It occurs that this trip is probably not the time for learning. Given his speed, during the last outing, he will most likely be able to keep up if we travel at a trot. Let's take the horse just in case.' Oswald said when they were all together. The rest agreed. Agnes' mother and brother gave her hugs while her father approached Oswald and Tara,

'Bowen spotted Goblins down the river watching the village last night.'

'Thank you. Can you report that to the Sheriff, we will head up the valley and see what we can find. We will check that position last. Come on all. We had better head off.' Replied Tara.

While the others mounted their horses, Arturous started at a steady run only to find Freki was following him. They were several miles beyond the village before the rest of the party caught up. Just before the others arrived as Arturous and Freki crested a hill, they both hit the dirt. The others were still at the base of the hill when Luka spotting the change called a halt.

'Something's up.'

'I will go and have a look.' offered Katina. She dismounted quickly and ran up the low hill dropping to the ground as she approached the crest. Calling quietly 'What's up Arturous.'

'Goblin attack on the farm underway.'

Katina saw what looked like the mother, and two young daughters were being dragged from the house and barn, while the father and two sons were attempting to fight off the Goblins attacking them but were facing odds of three to one against.

'We need to act now.' Said Katina.

'Look at the trees beyond.' Replied Arturous 'There are at least two groups at the edge.'

'Just how far can you see, that's over a mile away.' Katina said. Arturous shrugged. 'Can your elf bow hit the near group from here?'

'No too far. Maybe halfway.'

Katina ran back down and quickly explained the situation to the others.

'If we are to intervene, we need to hit fast and get back to the village before the others arrive.' Tara said. The rest agreed.

As soon as Arturous heard the others start to gallop, he moved quickly through the tall grass taking his bow from his shoulder as he went. The Goblins were paying no attention to their surroundings at all, just continued to terrorise the farming family. Both the sons and the father were now down with the females being dragged by their feet.

The others crested the hill as Arturous believed he was now in range of the nearest Goblin who was dragging one of the daughters into some long grass. Arturous stopped his run, he knelt, aimed and released his arrow hitting the Goblin in the back of the leg. It let go of the young woman and turned around swearing while holding the wounded limb. Arturous aimed a second arrow and released again penetrating the Goblin's stomach deeply. It went down groaning.

The rest galloped past to shouts of alarm from the Goblins. Agnes spurred her horse on faster crossing the few hundred yards in seconds. Drew her father's bastard sword from her back and to shouts of 'NO' swung it sideways across the front of her horse. Luckily, she hit her target, her sword biting deeply into the Goblin's chest. Continuing her mad charge running over a second Goblin before engaging a third who was stood over the mother of the family. Her aim was not so good this time, and the Goblin parried the blow easily.

Tara followed Agnes' mad charge. Riding between two Goblins used overhead swings killing both. Freki seeing his human gallop into combat ran at full speed beside her leaping at the Goblin trying to fire his bow at Tara. Luka and Katina also engaged several Goblins, distracting them from continuing to harm the family. The few remaining were targeted by Arturous and disabled quickly through archery fire.

With all the Goblins down, Arturous ran around to the other side of the farm buildings, took a quick look and came running back.

'They are coming.' He said.

Luka looked at the frightened family and said, 'We all must leave now. Far more are coming.'

'But Cecil and my sons are injured.'

'More Goblins will be here in less than five minutes. We must move now or be overrun.' Replied Tara.

'We must go two up for the village and leave now. We cannot wait to heal wounds.'

'She is right Sibble we must be out of here. We are not that bad we will be fine for a few hours.' Looking at Luka, he continued 'We must warn the neighbouring farms. Without that, they don't stand a chance. Nearest is downriver.'

Luka looked at Tara and said, 'That is directly away from the Goblins.' Tara nodded. Looking at her falcon 'Helghyer scout ahead towards the next farm. We will follow you.' Luka instructed.

The family were put one each behind Katina, Luka, Agnes, and Oswald. With the two sons put on the spare horse. Tara was unaccompanied, who with Arturous and Freki hung back to cover the escape of the others and continued to act as a rear guard. The group rode off at a canter down the valley to the next farm.

After a few minutes, the farm came into view. A young boy was tending some cattle. Agnes rode towards him and shouted

'Cedric, I need to speak to your father right now.'

'Yes, Agnes.' And ran off shouting 'Dad, Dad, Dad.'

A man came out of the barn, looked at the horses with multiple riders and said. 'Hello, Agnes, what is wrong?'

'You must all leave now. Right now.'

'What?' Was his reply.

Tara interrupted. 'Sir, we have just a few minutes until Goblins will overrun you. There are several dozen coming.'

He looked at his son. 'Cedric get all the horses now.' He then shouted for his wife, 'Mable. Come quick.' His son ran off to the barn. As his wife and daughter came out

'We must leave for the village immediately.' His son came back out with two large shire horses and a young foal. 'Both of you get on the mare.' He said to his wife and daughter

'What about the Hamlyn's.' She asked.

'That's the other side of the wood.' The farmer replied.

'Arturous, Freki and I will go and check. The rest of you go with the farmers to the village. Try and arrange medical attention for the injured. Oswald, you had better save your skills for now. We may need them later.' Tara said. Oswald nodded.

'I will tell Uncle Daxx there are at least five bands of Goblins around the village. We will wait for you on the green.' Said Katina.

Most of the group went off towards the village at a quick pace while Tara, Arturous and Freki headed out at Arturous' fast run pace around the top of the wood towards the last farm. As they crested the top of a small hill, Arturous called a halt.

'We have company, look.' Tara could see the farm in the distance and vaguely a group of something not quite between them and the farm, but close. 'If we go through the wood and travel parallel to the road we may still get through.' She responded.

They proceeded through the wood, but several hundred yards inside its edge to avoid being seen. When they approached a part that was near the road, Arturous went scouting. Tara dismounted and with Freki proceeded quietly behind.

'They appear not to have closed. The grass is tall if you

lead your horse we might be able to get through without being seen. Can't see how we can get back though with a farming family.'

'It will be difficult Arturous I agree, but we must try.' He shrugged.

They proceeded quickly but cautiously travelling as low to the ground as possible. Whether the Goblins spotted them was never known. None closed on the farm. It had been abandoned in a hurry. A cart heavily laden with grain and early apples was in the yard. One very old horse was waiting patiently, tied to a fence next to a water trough. It became very excited at the sight of the enormous wolf.

'Freki, you had better keep an eye on the road and plains for Goblins.' Said Tara to the wolf who obediently padded off.

'Arturous do you think we should try and save this food and cart.'

'It would help the village a lot if we can, but it will be hazardous. If we get caught at best, we would be four to one against.'

'We will have to try, though we may need to abandon it and run. You have a quick check of the farm while I hitch the old horse to the cart.'

Arturous found only evidence of a hasty departure. He also saw Goblins approaching from the other side of the fields. Tara found the old cart horse obedient now the wolf was gone, appearing to know precisely where he was being taken.

'Tara, company is coming from downriver. They are at least a mile off though.'

'Time to be going then. Freki we are leaving.' A single bark was the reply. Off they went, Arturous getting his first experience at driving a cart. He tried to get the horse to move to a look of "You idiot" from the horse. Once Arturous stopped what he was trying to do, the horse looked at a leaver on the right-hand side of the driver's seat and kicked his back leg at it.

'Oh I see, take the brake off.' Which Arturous did and the horse, slowly at first headed off at a fast walk. After about five minutes, Freki came back, gave a quiet bark and looking towards the plains away from the river gave a low growl. Arturous could see another group near the farm they had just left. Standing up in his seat, he could also see a second group running through the grassland.

'Tara, we have one group at the farm and another crossing the plains about a mile and a half away.'

Tara swore. 'Make that thing go faster.' Arturous didn't have to though as the old horse with supreme effort hastened to a trot anyway without command.

'The horse seems quite capable of making this trip on his own.' Observed Arturous.

They continued at a fast pace along the road to Warameth, but the Goblins closed quickly.

'Tara, we have riders from the village, about ten.' The Goblins on seeing the additional riders stopped their pursuit and watched. When the riders approached Arturous saw Luka, Katina, Agnes, Oswald, the Sheriff, Ablamon and his guards.

'My Lord Daxx. Thank you.' Tara said.

'That was very risky.' He replied, looking at the cart.

'Yes, but with the other farms abandoned we figured the village would need the food.'

'Probably true.' Was the reply

'The farming families?' asked Arturous

'The Hamlyn's spotted the Goblins last night and arrived at the village shortly after you left. The others are being treated. There is an old widow on the green that has a large house. She is allowing it to be used for treating the sick and injured. The lady is good with herbal cures anyway. She believes they will all be fine in a week or so.' Replied Lord Daxx.

'My Lord, we have at least two groups chasing us, one inland and one approaching from the Hamlyn's farm.'

'We best get moving. We will cover your rear.' The cart

proceeded to the village at a steady trot arriving safely.

MAP OF WARAMETH VILLAGE

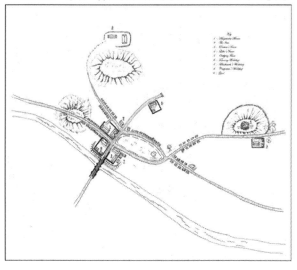

11 - ALL LEGENDS START SOMEWHERE

Tara and Arturous returned to the village with the cart full of food flanked by the Sheriff and the guards. They saw the wife of the first farm waiting on the green

'Thank you for saving us. My husband and sons have been treated and are resting. This is Mr Hamlyn, from the farm you visited last.'

'No problem madam.' Was Arturous' reply.

The Sheriff looked at Mr Hamlyn. 'We may need to commandeer your produce for the good of the whole village. The area is unsafe for outlying farms until the Goblins are cleared. I can arrange a suitable payment.'

'I will be happy with the usual merchant price, but I am willing to reduce due to the circumstances for the betterment of the village.' The farmer replied.

'Thank you, Mr Hamlyn, we can discuss that later.'

The farmer nodded an acknowledgement and left.

'Arturous, do you know how many Goblins are at the head of the valley.' The Sheriff asked.

'That I saw, maybe four or five tribes.' He answered.

'Any ideas how many Goblins that is?'

'The tribe that looks after the mine had about two thousand adults I think.'

'Alright, so as one in five tend to fight, there are about two thousand warriors up there. Thank you.' The sheriff concluded.

They had now been joined by Luka, Oswald, Agnes and Katina. 'You know what is coming, so prepare yourselves. Tara, please put Agnes through her paces. She has performed well, but this will be a serious fight, and I want to be sure she is ready. If not, she will need to sit this one out. Arturous, Luka and Katina, please have a look around and see who is about. No more than half a mile out and come back to me. Quickly now, the day wears on.' The Sheriff said.

Arturous, Katina and Luka moved away from the group and had a private discussion. From what Tara could see, a rather heated one. After a while, they headed out in various directions.

'Is there any chance they will follow my orders.' The Sheriff asked Tara.

'Not a hope in hell, my lord. They will look until they find and then come back. None of them will be willing to come back and say "I don't know". If they find a dozen or fewer Goblins, they will kill them and then come back.'

'That is not what was wanted. I need a quick local look to make sure we are not in any immediate danger, and then have the scouts rested before using their archery skills tonight.'

'I understand the strategy of your order, my lord. Us warriors are taught the importance of overall strategy and obeying orders. Hunters are not. I believe that is a problem in a situation like this. They are trained at being self-sufficient and deal with what they see, and ours are very capable. They will deal with that before thinking about the importance of communication.'

'I will need to go and discuss things with various others. I want your group of six, Agnes being with you, to cover the road to Izellameth. I will ask the Partten's to cover the stone bridge with a few guards added. The rest of the guards and I will cover the road upriver.' The Sheriff then left.

Tara looked at Agnes and said 'Don't expect yourself to be fit for full-scale battle straight away. We spend a year in training before we earn that privilege. Let's go to the green and get started. We will stop when the scouts get back.' They headed off to the green where Tara put Agnes through her paces for several hours. After a short while, both Agnes' brother and father joined them for practice. The group were watched reasonably frequently, by various villagers. Agnes learnt a lot and finished with sore muscles. She was told to eat and rest if she was to have recovered by the evening. Her father, who nodded agreement, sent her back home.

'Mr Partten, your daughter, while not yet at the level we would call a competent warrior is still reasonably proficient and learns quickly. She does you proud.' Stated Tara.

'Thank you. I hope she will not need it.' He replied.

'I'm afraid she will. Katina and Luka are excellent scouts. The elf Arturous while not as experienced, has incredible eyesight and other advantages too. If they say the Goblins are there, then you can guarantee they are.'

'I thought you were going to say that.' He replied regretfully.

'If you don't mind me saying, you are extremely proficient yourself.'

'I have ten years spent dealing with Goblin raids and The Battle of the Southern Plains to blame for that one.'

♦ ♦ ♦

Katina headed off on the road downriver. After passing the last of the inner farms, she headed a few hundred yards inland away from the road. Arturous had described to her roughly what was in the area and where he had thought it was. There were a few more miles to travel to get to that point.

Proceeding with caution and a constant eye out for watchers behind trees, she travelled towards Izellameth, keeping hidden in the long grass of the plains that lay between the woods and river. When getting near to the place Tara and Arturous had met the Sheriff, she proceeded with her best caution and stealth. Where Arturous had described, she could hear the guttural speech of Goblin scouts. Going over her knowledge of their tactics, Katina recalled they did not do scouts unless several groups were acting together. That was as much as could be done here, but she would still need to find the first group they had escaped from before going back.

Returning to the road a little upriver from the meeting point, she continued downstream on the river's edge, creeping cautiously through various river plants and bushes before silently crawling back inland to look around. There was no need to look far. Very quickly, Katina could hear the tell-tale guttural mutters of Goblins from either side of the road. This was a different group from the ones on the grasslands. Realising it was time to go back, she retreated with caution and stealth, then followed the riverbank upstream for about half a mile, crossed the road, went through the grasslands and into the wood while continually checking to see if the Goblins had made it that far. They had not. She returned to the village through the farms to try and obscure any Goblins seeing that someone had been "Out".

◆ ◆ ◆

Luka had been chosen to look inland. With the assistance of Helghyer, the pair would be able to cover far more area than the others could. Proceeding to the hill with the tower on top, she approached the crest, dropped to her tummy and carefully watched the surrounding area. There were no signs of hostiles. So, what to do next. Her forceful choice was that they should stick to orders, do the half-mile and return. The other two had said there was no point in coming back saying they had found nothing when they all knew the Goblins were out there. She now cursed her scouting companions who had forced her to go against orders and seek Goblins. There was no way she was going to be the only one saying that she had found nothing.

Scanning the area Luka could see the hill above the farm where the earlier rescue had taken place. Calling to Helghyer, she indicated her intended next position. Her great bird flew off. Looking at the tower, The Partten family were right, no doors or entrances of any kind. How strange. Still, save that one for later, there's a job to be done.

Proceeding with more caution and making an extra effort to hide in the long grass, Luka continued to the hill above the farm. Again, crawling on her tummy, she crested the hill. Her falcon was flying various large circles all around, giving Luka the exhilarating sensation of flying, which was a strange feeling when lying on the ground. Still, it meant that Helghyer was not worried so, at a crouch, she went to the farm.

On arriving there were clear signs of new activity. The dead Goblins had been removed for starters, and the farm investigated. Still, that was unimportant currently. There were many Goblin tracks, at least two dozen heading downriver. Helghyer returned, squawked and looked in that direction. They followed the tracks. After a while, it became clear that they were going to avoid travelling through the wood by going around it inland. With no Goblins in her area, she decided it was time to go back to the village.

It didn't take long for Helghyer to catch up. She noticed a single tall movement between the wood and the Partten's farm. That would be Katina, she thought and proceeded to the village square.

On arrival, there was a very unhappy Sheriff Daxx waiting.

'Where are the others?' he asked.

'I believe I saw Katina coming through the farm back there.' Luka said, pointing back the way she had just come. 'She will be here in a few minutes.'

'We will wait then.'

After a short while, Katina ran to the green. 'I am not happy you disobeyed orders. I said half a mile. You have both been gone for hours. I wanted a short trip out and back. If you do that again, I am sending you home.' The Sheriff said loudly and sternly. Having seen the two ladies return and hearing the Sheriff's voice, a crowd started to gather from those going about daily business in the village.

'Uncle, there was little point in saying where they weren't. I can tell you where my lot is, and no doubt Luka can do the same. Probably better knowing that falcon of hers. That is far more useful to you than saying "There is nothing within a mile".'

'You are wrong, my niece. All I needed to know was whether they were far enough away to allow you lot a few hours of sleep. When they come, it will be a tough fight at night, and you have been awake with little rest or food in over thirty six hours. That kills people.'

'We will be fine, uncle. There is no sign of attack within the next few hours. We have time for food and maybe some rest.' She then looked at the Sheriff sternly and continued. 'There are a lot out there, though. One group is inland of where you met Tara and Arturous earlier. They have six scouts out, so that means at least a further two dozen Goblins positioned the other side of the wood and parallel to the road. Also, further down about half a mile, a similar-sized group is positioned across the road. I believe there is about sixty between us and the next village down.'

'Luka what did you find?' Asked the Sheriff.

'I went as far as the farm we rescued the family from earlier. The Goblins we killed have been removed with abundant tracks of more recent activity heading the other side of the wood. None stayed in my area, they all went down the river, several dozen I think.'

'So, we have the group you escaped from yesterday plus another group of similar size blocking the road down the river. Get something to eat then I may need to send you after the elf.'

'Unlikely to work. If the elf has got into trouble, he will hide, and there is no way we will find an elf if he is hiding in woods. Not while dodging Goblins at any rate.' Observed Katina.

They were interrupted. 'I will feed them now, if I may

sheriff.'

'Alright, Max, the arguments about following orders can wait for later.'

Max led Luka and Katina off to the inn and arranged for his wife to supply them with a plate of food and a pint of ale each.

◆ ◆ ◆

Arturous, being more familiar with the terrain than the rest of them, ran off upriver ignoring the half a mile order. It was just not far enough to be useful. He didn't believe the Goblins would camp nearby but was sure they would have used the road to travel. A few miles away from the village, Arturous saw far more tracks than could be counted. It looked like the Goblins had driven several large carts through the undergrowth. He was able to follow the tracks with ease. After about two miles, it became apparent to Arturous that he was now behind many Goblins. At least three groups of a dozen or more were between him and the village. Finally, he understood why he had been given the order not to go more than half a mile. If the Goblins attacked, now they would arrive before his warning if he even made it back to the village at all.

Carefully and quietly, he returned to the road and travelled down the river doing his best to remain hidden. The Goblin scouts were spreading out. It was touch and go, but Arturous was still able to sneak past without being seen. If he went along the road, the Goblin scouts would spot him approaching the village, so he decided on a different route. After going along the riverbank itself, a very wet elf made it back somewhat late for his meeting on the green. At least it was still light.

Arturous climbed up the riverbank at the edge of the village and headed for the green. He spotted a very angry looking Sheriff. Remembering the orders to go only half a mile, he figured it was time to face the consequences.

'Ah, master Arturous I want a word.'

'Certainly Lord Sheriff.' Arturous replied. When they had separated from the gathered crowd a little, and before the Sheriff had a chance to berate him, he said

'Sorry, I am late. I have found evidence of a large group of Goblins a little upriver of here. At least three dozen, plus scouts. They have spread out from the road inland. I am late because by chance I managed to get behind them and had to crawl along the river to return to the village. I now understand your reasons for the half-mile limit. I have made it back with valuable information.'

'More importantly, I wanted you back to rest before what will likely be a very long night.'

'I understand, but I am fine, thank you. I suffered much worse in the mines. Some food and a change of clothes and I will be alright for tonight.'

'In your case, you are probably right. I am unhappy that you did not follow my orders. If you are to work for me, then you must follow orders. Now get something to eat.' The Sheriff turned his back and left.

Arturous saw Tara and went over. 'He is used to getting his own way isn't he.'

'Oh yes, and for a good reason. We have all been awake a long time now. The Sheriff needs us all to be in top form when the Goblins come visiting, especially those good at archery. That is why he didn't want you guys wasting several hours looking. Yes, you came back with lots of information, but we didn't need that yet.'

'I understand, but I am fine. Let's get something to eat while we have the chance. Sooner or later, we are going to be busy.' Tara nodded, and the both of them went to the inn to find Luka, Katina, Oswald Shamus and Agnes sitting in a corner finishing a meal with Helghyer perched on the back of a nearby chair. Arturous was given a fresh spare set of clothes by the innkeeper and changed quickly in his room before returning. Tara waited patiently, then they both joined the others.

'Good evening, all. I am surprised to see everyone gathered together.' Said Tara.

'Why? We are going to be busy. It is far better to start in the same place.' Replied Luka.

'Do you two want some food?' The inn keeper's wife interrupted.

'Yes, please.' Replied Arturous.

'That is true I am afraid Luka. Lord Daxx wants us to cover the road downriver tonight.' Tara told everyone.

'How many did you scouts find down there?' inquired Agnes.

'Around the fifty to sixty mark.' Replied Katina.

'For just six of us.' Commented Agnes in a surprised tone.

'Combat tactics will be critical.' Observed Tara. 'There are four of us good with a bow. We should be alright if something can be put across the road to slow them down. Then we incapacitate as many as possible with archery fire. A few good legs or stomach shots each with a bow will reduce the odds significantly. They won't all charge in at once anyway.'

'How about the cart Arturous brought back placed sideways across the road, that would help.' Suggested Oswald.

'Good idea.' Replied Luka.

'Before I met up with Arturous, I sent Freki up the river to check things out. Once I have eaten, I must wait for him on the green.' Informed Tara.

Luka looked at Helghyer. 'Can you see what is going on down the river.' Helghyer looked back at Luka, stretched her wings and flew over the heads of other customers straight out the door. 'Typical, she's gone the wrong way.' Observed Luka.

A little while later. 'I can feel the exhilaration of flight. Helghyer is coming back, time for us to head outside.' The group headed to the green,

Luka drew her sword, put the point to the ground and rested her hand on the pommel, locking her elbow. Helghyer flew in and landed on the outstretched arm, looked to the road heading to Izellameth and did a specific squawk once. She then looked slightly further round towards the last farm and squawked again. Luka saw the Sheriff come over and said to him

'Looks like we have company, two groups one along the road and another slightly inland through the farm.'

'I see.' Was the reply. With that Freki jumped up at Tara, licked her face then looked at the road heading up the river and growled.

'That would be Arturous' group coming to visit from the up-river road.' Tara informed the group.

'That level of animal training and communication is unreal.' Said Agnes.

'But a serious help I'd imagine. I could have done with that back in my day. It would have saved thousands of lives.' Responded Agnes' father.

'It's a spiritual link. Still very new but already has proved seriously useful.' Said Katina.

The Sheriff looked at Mr Partten. 'Please get your group together and cover the stone bridge. I will send a couple of the merchant's guards over to help. Myself, Ablamon and the rest of the guards will cover the road upriver.' He then looked at Tara and said. 'Take your group to cover the road to Izellameth. A little way past the green, but not too far.'

'We will put the cart crossways adjacent to the end houses and make our stand there.' Tara replied.

Various people went to their specified locations. The new mismatched group positioned the cart on the road to Izellameth. The houses along that road each had a platform at the front that slightly raised it above ground level. Arturous and Katina grabbed a few part full barrels placing them at the end of the raised platform on the left side of the road near the tailgate of the cart. They then ducked down behind them, bows in hand and waited.

Luka went to the raised platform of the house on the righthand side of the road, upended a large wooden planter, moved it to the end of the platform and knelt behind it. Helghyer perched on a convenient box nearer the green and watched. Meanwhile, Agnes and Oswald followed Tara, who was hiding behind a wheel of the cart bow in hand. Freki lay down a few feet behind her.

Tara looking at Oswald and Agnes said, 'Now we wait.' And to the frightened Agnes.

'It is perfectly alright for you to sit this one out. You have only been doing this for a few days and tonight will be very intense. We get at least a year in training before you're let loose on anything like this.'

She looked at Oswald and continued, 'Sorry priest, you are in this up to your neck.'

'I will serve my God; however he requires it. If I must stand in line and fight, that is how it will be. I have had some training from a Brother Michael at my church and some interesting experiences on the way here. I will do my bit.' Oswald replied.

'I suspect your bit will be curing people. If they all close hand to hand, the three of us from my tribe and the elf will defeat them, all you two need to do is keep them off our backs and heal those that get wounded so that we can hold the line.'

Tara then looked at Agnes, whose face showed the fear associated with sitting and waiting for overwhelming odds to arrive. Her face then stiffened as the emotion was forced away.

'I will stand and fight. I will do my bit to defend my village.'

'You are a credit to your family. Just remember this is your first outing, so play it safe. You do not have to kill much, hold the line, put them out of combat by any means at hand and stop them from getting past. If you can do that, in time, they will run.' Tara replied.

'Quit yacking and get ready. If Agnes' father is half as good as he appears to be, he will have already taught her this stuff. She wouldn't be here if she weren't prepared to stand. Get ready they are coming.' Luka said sternly.

Luka saw Oswald touch his cross and start to concentrate. He glanced under the cart in the darkness to see a spot up the road from Arturous and Katina. Staring for a few seconds finally said the words.

'Golau, Pellter.'

A tall stone sticking out of the wall up the road shone with light. Luka then saw him look at another spot slightly further up the road on her side but shook his head. Then concentrated again and after a few seconds uttered the words 'Golau, Pellter, Pellter.' A second stone further along the road lit up in the darkness. All the Goblins were now clearly visible.

◆ ◆ ◆

Little Isaac was a tall boy for his age, only five but already quite well built. His younger brother Evan was only three. Mum had picked up Evan from the front porch and was holding him while dad was locking and barricading possible ways into the house. Isaac had slipped away upstairs and was looking out of a window. The whole green as well as the roads heading to Izellameth and upriver were visible from here. Agnes, the new priest and the tallest barbarian lady were ducked down, hiding behind the cart talking. The elf and another barbarian lady were hiding behind some barrels. The last barbarian was on the other side, hiding behind an upturned wooden box.

Then there was the hoarse blood-curdling cry on the road from Izellameth and sounds of lots of people running. It was very dark now. He could see the new priest chap concentrating hard. Light shot out from his hand. A stone on the top of the wall down the road lit bright as a torch. He did it again, and another stone on the other side of the road lit brightly also.

Isaac could now see hordes of green and brown things come running up the road waving swords and other weapons. He was terrified, but the desire to see what he knew would be an important moment gripped him entirely. Shaking with fear, Isaac stood at the window and watched. His father was calling, but he ignored him. Those hiding behind the cart and barrels waited. He could see they intended to act. Arrows were put to bows, and swords quietly drawn. Even "Tubby Aggy" as the kids called her prepared herself for what she must do. He could see that. He now realised he knew what fear was and what bravery was in the face of what must be unstoppable odds against them.

Then he saw when the green and brown things were perhaps the length of a small field away the elf and barbarian behind the barrels, the barbarian behind the wooden box and the tallest barbarian behind the cart jumped up and started firing their bows. He had never seen anything so fast. Each of them was firing a shot every three claps, perhaps four at the outside. Within seconds several rows of these green and brown things were down. Every single shot seemed to count. They kept coming, though. His dad was now calling with an anxious voice.

'I am fine dad. I am up here. All of you come up and watch. Our defenders are amazing.' He called back. He could hear his dad come running up the stairs, followed by the lighter footsteps of his mother. 'Look out of the window.' With curiosity getting the better of them they crowded around, and all looked out.

The green and brown things were now at the cart, leaving many behind on the road. Then just as they were going to go around the cart, he could see Tubby Aggy and the priest jump up into the space that was between the back of the cart and the barrels. Tubby Aggy jumped into at least six of the green and brown things slamming two with her shield knocking them backwards which in turn knocked a third off balance. Tubby Aggy casually slid her sword into the third's stomach as a fourth got hit on the shoulder by an enormous two-handed "Thing" the priest was carrying.

Isaac saw that just as Tubby Aggy and the priest had jumped up, the tallest barbarian had dropped her bow, casually slid her left hand into the armholes of her shield and with her right hand grabbed her enormous sword from behind her back. In what seemed to be one move she swung her shield as Tubby Aggy had done, hitting an enemy and knocking him over, while in a single movement pulled her sword from its scabbard over her shoulder, sliced through the neck of one enemy and on into the right arm of another. He watched as the others dropped their bows drew swords and engaged.

In what seemed like just a few seconds, Isaac saw more green and brown things around the cart were down than he had fingers to count. Many more were coming, though. They surrounded both the tall barbarian on one side of the cart and Tubby Aggy on the other. Still, the defenders held their ground.

Then two arrows hit Tubby Aggy in the chest. She collapsed to her knees but raised her shield and sword to cover her head and shoulders from the incoming blows. With a gleeful look, the Goblins closed in. On the other side, the sheer weight of numbers was pushing the taller barbarian back. A green and brown thing approached from her side, preparing for a killing stroke. Isaac's heart dropped as he thought those watched would lose.

But the green and brown things were not quick enough to press the advantage. They had had about half a second, but they had missed it. The one approaching the tallest barbarian, while gleefully looking at striking her side had paid absolutely no attention at all to what was approaching it. The Goblin got hit squarely in the neck by a wolf that was the length of a small pony and way taller than Isaac himself was. The green thing and several others went flying. The other green and brown thing that had got side on to the archer next to the tall barbarian didn't fare much better either. He was hit squarely on the side of the face by the biggest falcon Isaac had ever seen. All claws, talons and beak. There was blood everywhere.

The other side of the cart also appeared to recover quickly. The priest hit his opponent on the head with his enormous "Two-Handed War Mace" as his father had called it. Then dropping his weapon, he bent over Tubby Aggy and pulled both arrows out, causing her to scream. Isaac then saw what looked like the priest's hand glow as he placed it on her chest.

She seemed to recover from her wounds immediately. Tubby Aggy swung her shield to cover both of them and swung her sword at ankle height, causing several of her enemies to jump back out of the way. They both stood up and advanced into the gap swinging sword and war mace at anything that came in range. The green and brown things looked at the priest's now glowing hands with fear.

Slowly the green and brown "Goblins" his dad had said, were beaten back with terrible casualties. Slowly yard by yard the line of six advanced up the road leaving a trail of headless and limbless corpses in their path. After a few more minutes the horde broke and ran.

Isaac looked the other way and could not see the Sheriff or the guards, just a trail of Goblin bodies. 'Dad, have we won?' Isaac asked.

'It looks like it son.' He then turned to his wife and said, 'We had better help the wounded and remove the dead.'

She looked at him, sternly and replied. 'We need to stay together as a family in case of more trouble. There are things out there that our children should not see.'

'We should go to the green then and see who wants to do what. Certain things cannot be left long and will need burning.' Was his reply. She nodded, and they all went to the green.

Once his dad had unbolted the door, Isaac ran out before his father could grab him. As soon as he was clear of the house's raised front platform, he saw some of his friends and started shouting enthusiastically to them.

'Did you see it; did you see it. Weren't they amazing.' Several of his friends indicated that they had been watching too and saw it all. He then looked at them all sternly and with his best adult face said,

'I don't think we should call her "Tubby Aggy" anymore.' The other children looking somewhat glum agreed.

Various mums corralled the children into the middle of the green where they all talked excitedly.

12 - THE CLEAN UP

After Freki and Helghyer had joined in, the priest had healed Agnes and continued to advance on them with a glowing hand and gruesome war mace, the Goblins resolve shook. It finally broke after they had been pushed back a few yards passed the cart, losing several more of their number in the process. Agnes had been unlucky to be targeted by the Goblin archers, but in seconds and before the Goblins could do any further damage, Arturous had neutralised them with brutal efficiency. Both Freki and Helghyer appeared alright if somewhat dirty.

While Arturous, Katina and Luka retrieved arrows and killed wounded Goblins Tara went to speak to Agnes.

'How are you?' She said, seeing both Agnes' father and brother appear behind her.

'Yes, my daughter, how are you? I saw you go down and get back up again.'

'Our priest did not fully heal the wounds, but they no longer bleed and are a good deal less serious than they were.' Agnes replied while being hugged by her brother.

'If properly bandaged and kept clean, she will be fully healed in a couple of days if not less judging by what has happened in the wounds I have healed so far.' Added Oswald

'That is wonderful, but how are you? That was your first proper fight.'

'If I am honest, I was seriously frightened. Tara told me to concentrate on holding the line and keeping myself alive. To only strike when it was safe to do so. I think I was doing alright until those arrows hit me. I can't be certain, but I think I put a few down, but nothing like the others.' The ashen-faced and shaking Agnes replied.

'Yes Agnes, you did put several Goblins down. Not that that matters, you held the line. Without every one of us holding that line, we would have been split up and died.'

Said Katina, who had now joined the discussion.

'Don't be hard on yourself either. Our tribe have been training and killing Goblins for a thousand years and more. Each of us has had a full year of basic training and several years in the field before we end up in a fight like tonight.' Added Luka. 'You have performed very well and have learned much in a matter of a few days.'

Agnes received a gentle tug on her skirt. She looked down to see little Isaac and a few of the other children. He looked up and said

'Mistress Agnes Partten, please accept this apple as thanks from us children. You and the others were amazing. There will be no more horrible names, we children promise.' Agnes beamed a smile of joy, bent down with a bit of a grimace from her wounds, picked Isaac up and gave him a big hug to much cheering from the gathered crowd.

Tara, looking at the crowd said 'Please get your families to safety as soon as possible. There may well be other attacks tonight. Goblins rarely attack just the once. I will need to talk to the Lord Daxx about what he wants us to do next. He will need to set a watch, and us warriors will need to be ready to defend our spots for a second attack.'

'Scouts will also need to be put out to see what is happening. My team will handle that. We will keep watch here while you go find out what happened to the Sheriff and his team. Don't take too long we need to do our scouting. Your team are pretty much played out and need a break before round two.' Said Agnes' father.

'Mr Partten, you both say they will come again. Is that serious, we thought it was all over.' One of the crowd asked.

'There is rarely just one attack in this kind of thing. Having said that the new team put a fair-sized hole in the attackers' numbers. From what I saw they got over half, perhaps two thirds, so maybe not this time.' Mr Partten replied.

Tara took Oswald and went looking for the Sheriff, just in case there was a reason he had not come back. She left Agnes to rest and the others to continue the clean-up.

As Tara and Oswald approached the other end of the green, they saw a trail of Goblin bodies. This trail went somewhat up the road. They saw the Magistrate, and one of the guards, each with a sword in hand stood around the three captives from the earlier expedition. The prisoners who held a Goblin sword each were sat on the ground, exhausted, covered in blood with several dead Goblins around them.

'Lord Mord, may I enquire what has happened here?' Tara asked.

'Once Daxx had beaten off the attack and began to chase, a smaller second group came up behind and tried to attack the jail. The prisoners fought back and killed several but are wounded. Master priest, can you check them over please.'

'Certainly, Lord Mord.' Oswald ostensibly looking at wounds placed his hands on each of the prisoners.

'There's no feeling at all, my lord.'

'As there is no clear allegiance to evil, and they did participate in the fight, are you capable of stopping the bleeding. I saw quite a lot going on at the other end of the green. I am not sure what you can still do after assisting Agnes. You must not exhaust yourself too soon. We may be busy again tonight.'

'I am not tired yet. I can provide that level of assistance and still be capable of doing more later if needed. Given the prisoners have fought against the Goblins, I believe I should assist if possible.'

'Please do so then.' The Magistrate requested.

While each had several wounds, they also only had one serious injury each. Oswald cleared his thoughts, composed his now-familiar healing prayer and gave a simple cure to the most severe injury on each of the three prisoners. They looked at him with stunned surprise. He advised them to get cleaned up with hot water to prevent infection.

'Hello, Tara. What are you two doing up here? You should be at your barricade' The Sheriff asked.

'Lord Daxx, the other four are covering, along with Mr Partten's group, so there is no risk. Anyhow, I was concerned. I couldn't see you or your team, so I came to check. I also came to report. We have beaten off our attack. Regretfully we only took about two thirds down. There is the best part of twenty-odd Goblins from my group still out there. My most severe apologies.' Tara replied.

'Two-thirds is adequate. Especially from a group that has not fought together in a situation like that before. How are they all?'

'Agnes stood her ground and performed well. Unfortunately, she was put down by two arrows to the chest. Oswald healed her and she was back up quickly. Although weak, she is still combat-capable. Considering her lack of experience, Agnes is doing remarkably well. Her courage in the absence of serious training is quite something. Our priest here stood in line next to Agnes, and he also took a few Goblins out in addition to healing both the arrow wounds very quickly. Our hunters performed well as is expected, the elf too. While he doesn't have our training or experience, his superior eyesight, agility and speed make him easily an equal to our hunters.'

'I see. Try and stand Agnes down so she can rest and give the curing a chance to take hold, but keep her close just in case another serious attack happens and you need her back.'

'Yes, My Lord.' Replied Tara.

'I am sorry, but the three scouts are going to have to go and have a look around. We must know if they are coming back.'

'My Lord, Mr Partten said his team would handle that, so that mine may rest.'

'He is a farmer. We need experienced scouts.'

'My Lord, he wasn't always a farmer. He said he was previously a soldier and is certainly quite competent with a sword judging by what I saw.' Tara said.

'He mentioned the experience of fighting in the Goblin raids of a few decades ago.' Oswald Shamus added.

'Hold on, did you say Mr Partten, a soldier who fought in the Goblin raids.' One of the prisoners interrupted.

'You are not serious.' Another added looking at the first.

'Yes, I damn well am. It must be.' The first replied. 'I want to see him right now.' The Sheriff, Magistrate, Tara and Oswald all looked puzzled by the outburst.

'My most honourable lords, if I may explain. What my impetuous colleagues meant to say is that while they respect and honour your gallantry and competence, they both fought as conscripts under a Major Partten, known as "The Hawk" in a series of battles some fifteen plus years ago South West of the city of Kersladen. That campaign resulted in the extermination of some five thousand Goblins and the routing of another of similar size. They would much appreciate the chance to meet their former commander before you behead them for rudeness.' The last one pleaded.

'That routed portion would be the group wiped out by the Agrini.' Postulated the Magistrate.

'Quite possibly, the timing would fit. We wondered where those Goblins came from.' Looking at the prisoners 'You are all campaign veterans then?' The Sheriff replied.

'Somewhat long in the tooth now, but those two are yes. It's all they ever talk about around the campfire. Annoying after a while. Major Partten was the best swordsman in the valley and an incredible cavalry commander. The Goblins could never work out where he was going to attack them from.' The third one replied.

'You said "The other two", what about you?' Asked Oswald Shamus

'Me, I am an unemployed armourer. Lost my position on allegations of deceiving people and not supplying the armour requested. All true I am afraid to say, but at that time you didn't need proper armour I could make shortcuts for profit. That appears to have changed now. I can do a good job if you wish. I should think I could put together a fair few suits of reasonable leather armour from all the dead Goblins. Previous experience and a look at these chaps at our feet I would think one decent human suit of leather armour per four or five Goblins in return for keeping my head and not being imprisoned.' The third prisoner said.

'So long as your work comes up to the mark, your offer is worth considering. The Magistrate and I will consider it privately at another time. I will discuss it with the village elders. Your proposal will be subject to serious consideration. Now let's take you all to see our farmer Mr Partten.' The Sheriff concluded.

The three prisoners were led to the green accompanied by the Sheriff, Magistrate, Tara and Oswald. When they got there, Agnes' father, brother and a few others on horseback were being yelled at by Agnes, angry at not being able to go with her family. Her father was trying to say that she had already been in combat, was injured and needed to rest. This, it would appear, was not going down well with Agnes.

'That's him, unbelievable we've found him.' One of the prisoners then yells out.

'Major Partten, may we please serve you for a second time. It would be an honour and a privilege to get to serve twice the greatest cavalry commander of all time and the general that won the battle of the southern plains.' Another then yells out. The villagers gave stunned stares at Agnes' father.

With a somewhat sheepish look, he responded 'I suppose it was bound to come out sooner or later. Although your declarations are somewhat exaggerated.'

'If you are the commander known as "The Hawk", they aren't exaggerating by very much.' Was the response of the blacksmith.

'The only reason my strategy worked is because the Sergeant Major of the Kersladen City Guard managed to keep the infantry together and facing the enemy.'

'Yeah, he kept chopping heads off until everyone obeyed him.' One of the prisoners said.

'While you led half the Goblins around in circles and attacked the other half from the rear.' Added another prisoner.

'The other half as you call them were fully engaged with the Sergeant Major's infantry and weren't looking behind them. Anyway, I recognise two of you,' Agnes' father said, looking at the prisoners, 'but not the third.'

'We were conscripted soldiers in your third company.' The first two responded.

'I didn't fight. I was an apprentice armourer at the time and therefore needed elsewhere.' Added the third prisoner.

'Anyway, why is this relevant to three prisoners?' Agnes' father asked.

'Having killed several Goblins in tonight's discussions. On overhearing your family's name, they offered to serve you again in return for a pardon, food and lodging. That is under consideration and will be subject to discussions with the village elders, but introducing them to you seemed reasonable.' The Magistrate said.

'I can confirm to you that they did indeed serve under me in that campaign. That, however, is irrelevant now, we must get a scouting patrol done. The three usual candidates have been busy enough recently and need a rest. My six have yet to see action so I would suggest we do a circular half-mile look and be back within the hour.' Mr Partten requested.

Looking at the Magistrate, the Sheriff said 'We agree, make sure everyone comes back in one piece, please. No risks.'

Mr Partten nodded at the Sheriff. Looking at his daughter continued 'Stay with your team, Agnes. You have been wounded, but with rest and care, you will be fit in no time.'

His group of six rode out inland passed the tower hill and out of sight. The innkeeper's wife then said to the sheriff 'I must take Agnes now and get her wounds cleaned and bound.'

'Yes, certainly, but quickly she will be needed at the barricade again tonight I suspect.' Was the Sheriff's response. A very glum and worried-looking Agnes followed the inn keeper's wife while looking back down the road her father and brother had just ridden up. The remaining of Ablamon's merchant guards split into two groups with half on the up-river road and a half on the inland road.

Tara and Oswald went back to their barricade to see Arturous, Katina and Luka already keeping watch with Helghyer and Freki apparently asleep under the cart.

'We think there is still movement out there, but a lot more cautious. It's difficult to tell. I can't see squat that far away, but Arturous believes something is moving.' Luka said.

'All right.' Responded Tara who with Oswald took her place behind the cart.

After about half an hour Arturous released an arrow. Some cursing from up the road followed. The archery exchange with the Goblin scouts continued for some time. The enemy's arrows either falling short of the group or hitting the barrels or cart. The defenders' arrows were more accurate with some shouts and curses.

Mr Partten's mounted scouting party indicated significant but cautious groups of Goblins both up and downriver. Each group was considerably less in number than they had been, but still large enough to cause trouble. Following instructions, he did not engage either set of Goblins, but periodically did go out and see who was where. The Goblins did not attempt to meet up nor leave. A tactical discussion between the Magistrate, the Sheriff, Agnes' father and a few of the village elders decided that at first light a mounted attack on the Goblins upriver by Mr Partten's team together with the Sheriff and some of the merchant guards would take place. Tara and her team would advance on the downriver Goblins to keep them entertained and focused on the village. The aim is to give Mr Partten and the others time to swing around and catch the downriver Goblins from behind to minimise any escape.

'They have not been specific on how we are to keep our lot "entertained", so how do people feel about an archery battle.' Observed Tara.

'We use the buildings' posts, dead bodies etc. as cover to get closer but do not charge in as the archery fire of the Goblins could hurt us badly.' Suggested Luka. After some discussion, the others agreed.

They all rested as much as possible and obtained what other arrows they could. When the cavalry group was preparing itself just before dawn, Tara's group unilaterally moved out. They manoeuvred the cart with Tara, Oswald and Agnes pushing it back up the street, providing them with significant cover from the Goblin's archery fire. Meanwhile, on one side Arturous and Katina dodged from large stone to gatepost or other item firing their bows at any Goblin stupid enough to raise its head. Luka did the same on the other side of the street. They took it slow and cautious but still managed to get halfway before war cries could be heard from inland as the other group charged the Goblins.

The other group didn't kill many of the Goblins. As soon as the charge became apparent, the Goblins turned to face and stood up, resulting in Arturous, Katina, Luka and Tara slaughtering them with archery fire. Between the two cavalry style charges, the upriver group having been effectively run over, only about a dozen Goblins had escaped from probably about a hundred.

Oswald had to cure several injuries mainly from archery fire rather than combat. With the sun now up and the Goblins defeated, Agnes, Arturous, Luka, Katina, Oswald, and Tara went to bed for what was agreed to be a well-earned rest.

PART 3 – ANOTHER JOINS THE GAME

13 - THE MASTER SCOUT

Arturous looked at Oswald who was sat on the road with his back up against a stone wall. He recognised the posture of bone-weary exhaustion he had seen so often in the mines. His face though carried a pleased and proud look on it.

'Oswald, aside from tired, you have a strange expression on your face. May I know your thoughts.'

'I have been awake so long I am beyond tired. It has been an amazing few days for me though. I can now say that I have fought in the line against evil. Also, I have fought bandits and participated in the recovery of equipment. My spell casting has been extensive and frequently under extreme duress. In about three weeks, I have developed from a meek petrified incompetent initiate that had just left the temple for the first time to an experienced something. I can't say I am a warrior priest yet. I am a long way from that, but I am pleased with myself. Finally, I feel I am some of the way toward being worthy of my family name.' Was the reply.

'If you are not yet as competent as others of your family, The Lord of All Evil is in serious trouble.' Arturous said with a smile on his face.

Oswald tried to get up off the ground so Arturous helped him.

'Thank you, but why are you not exhausted like me.' Oswald asked.

'I am a little tired, but not that bad. In the mines, we were forced to work for days without rest or food. I suppose my body is used to it. You however are not and must sleep.' Arturous responded in a commanding tone.

'That is true, I do need rest, but some things must be set in motion now, then I can sleep.'

'I had better help you then, who first?' Arturous asked.

'The Magistrate and Sheriff. We must get things

moving for Luka. I also need to make arrangements to write down what I have learned so far.' Oswald replied. Arturous put his arm around the bone-weary initiate and led him to the middle of the green where the Sheriff was organising various people into groups clearing the dead and undertaking repair tasks.

Before Oswald managed to get a word out, Arturous said

'Lord Magistrate, Lord Sheriff, Hawk. Our exhausted priest here wants a word. I have told him he needs to sleep, but he is having none of it. At least not until he's spoken to all of you. If you could take some time out from your discussions, we can get this over with, and I can make sure he gets a few hours' sleep.'

'We had better listen then.' Replied the Magistrate and they all looked at Oswald.

'I know you are all busy with practical matters of the after-effects of the battle, but there are a few things of a priestly nature that we must undertake promptly.' Said Oswald.

'There are several I can think of.' Replied the Magistrate.

'The last four weeks or so, I have been subject to some profound knowledge with significant consequences. That must be both passed on and recorded in the immediate future. If anything had happened to me in the various combats that have taken place recently, all would be lost. Your god has permitted me to train Luka. She must be initiated into your religion immediately so that I can start her tuition. I need the facilities to record the spell casting symbols and words we have discovered, together with what they can do and how they can be used. Then there is the need to record the other ones I have come across for research later. Finally, there is the new forms of service and correct worshipping dates to be written out.' Oswald said.

'While you have been of significant use to us in combat

situations, you were sent here as a Priest weren't you. At some point, you need to start doing real priest stuff.' Luka said from behind Oswald.

'You will need consecrated ground for that. Do you know how?' asked the Magistrate.

'I am afraid not. I will pray for guidance.' Was Oswald's reply. They all nodded.

'I can teach you our ritual if that will help. While yours should be quite different, far more formal I would imagine, we both worship Gods of Light so it should give you some indication.' The Magistrate offered.

'Then, Luka must be initiated immediately after that.' The Sheriff suggested.

'For Luka's initiation, you may not need a consecrated area. We still have the statuette, and she has already completed the touch with blood, chat with god bit we were told about when we first arrived. Our priest here,' Katina said, looking at Oswald 'won't need consecrated ground to start to preach. Surely, we can start things off, get Luka initiated and begin her training. Full consecrated ground and proper service can wait until later. I am sure our two gods won't mind that much, in the circumstances.'

'It's worth a try.' Oswald suggested. 'At the moment, I am the only one who can cast divine spells of any kind. If I die before we can train another, we lose everything.'

'You must sleep first and prepare for the ceremony.' Arturous reminded everyone. 'As must all humans.'

'What about you?' enquired the Sheriff.

'I am fine for now. The slave mines shifts were long and arduous, usually lasting for several days in one go. This recent stint is no worse. I could do with a decent night's sleep tonight, though.' Arturous replied. 'In the meantime, I can do some local scouting while the others sleep.' He continued.

'Not far now.' Commented the Sheriff who then looked at Mr Partten. 'Can you guys keep an eye on the elf from a distance? Don't get in his way, though.'

'We will.' was the reply.

Arturous nodded to the Sheriff and led the exhausted Oswald Shamus back to the Inn. On seeing the innkeeper's wife, Oswald asked to be allowed to sleep until about noon but no longer, requesting he be brought a pail of warm water for washing when woken. Arturous took the initiate to his room and shoved him in.

Arturous grabbed a drink of water, checked his equipment, retrieved and repaired arrows and checked his bow. The elf then went to the shore and scanned upriver of the bridge. Creeping quietly for about half a mile he proceeded up the river. Taking no chances, he crawled up the bank on his belly then realised there were no birds about, or for that matter any other wildlife. There were no rabbits or hares, and none of the smaller creatures. Everything was hiding. He froze before getting up. Looking around, he saw no sign of Helghyer or Freki. Not surprising they would be with their companions, so there must be something else. Looking slowly and carefully, he scanned every yard of terrain within a mile. Yes, there was something. He couldn't make out what. Anybody looking from the village would not be able to see the watcher. It was lying in a hollow behind a small hump in the grassland just watching and waiting.

He spent another half an hour observing to make sure. Arturous was convinced there were no others. That was odd, though. While he was pretty sure Goblins, if they put their mind to it could be that careful, they never were. They were also never on their own like that. Arturous decided on discretion, slowly backing away and returning down the river along the bank to the village.

Re-entering the village via his usual hidden path near the stone bridge he went looking for the Sheriff. He found him organising the disposal of the dead.

'Lord Sheriff, may I have a word please.'

Taking one look at the soggy elf he replied 'Certainly.' They moved apart from the crowd of working villagers.

'We are being watched from upriver. Very well hidden, so well in fact that I couldn't see what was doing the watching.' Arturous informed the Sheriff who looked concerned.

'The Goblins I have encountered aren't that careful and never act alone or at least not very far. Whoever this is, it is a lot more competent than I have encountered before.'

'What's it doing?' asked the Sheriff.

'Just watching and waiting. If I hadn't realised the absence of birdsong, I would have missed it entirely.'

'Any chance you could creep up on it?'

'None whatsoever. I get the feeling of extreme competence. It is all but invisible in open grassland behind a small rise.' Replied Arturous.

'Are you alright with checking down river and inland? It will be useful to know if any more of those watchers are around.' The Sheriff asked.

'I am fine and can look but can't guarantee I will find them. Our new enemy is very good.'

'Indirect signs will do for now. You know what you encountered before. No risks, it's been a long few days. We can leave the strange beast hunting to another time.' The Sheriff concluded. Arturous left the Sheriff and headed downriver to the outlying farms.

Proceeding with caution, Arturous entered a barn in a farm at the edge of the village. Climbing into the hayloft, he carefully looked out of a small window at the end of the barn. Gazing across the grasslands down the river, the first thing Arturous noticed was the lack of wildlife. There was some, but not much. There were no signs that anything was watching the village. Things were still way too quiet though. With care, he could enter the nearby wood unseen. Deciding to investigate further, he left the barn, sneaked behind various walls and hedges, and in time reached the long grass outside the village.

While remaining hidden Arturous considered his situation carefully. If there were a watcher out there, he would be observing this stretch, so extreme caution was necessary. It was perhaps a country mile from the end of the last farm to the edge of the wood down the river. He virtually crawled through the long grass being as careful as possible. It took ages, but the closer he got to the forest, the quieter the animals were.

When he got halfway, all animal activity ceased utterly. Stopping Arturous realised this, so something was there. It would be within a mile or so of his current position. That means the village end of the wood. He would be seen if he went directly into the forest. His two choices were, going back and saying something was there, but he wasn't sure where or trying to get into the wood from inland and discover more information. He decided on the latter.

♦ ♦ ♦

Mr Partten and his son, having watched an extremely cautious elf from the riverward side of an up-river hill decided to find the Sheriff. They cautiously backed away from their position and, using the cover of the hill returned to the village. They saw him on the green, deep in thought. He noticed their approach.

'I wonder if you have seen anything?' The Sheriff asked.

'Afraid not. We spotted the elf watching something.' The son said.

'Only just though, he was virtually impossible to see. We only saw him because we knew he was there.' The father interrupted.

'He was taking a good deal of care to watch something, but we couldn't see what.' The son continued.

'Thank you. Can you continue to keep an eye on our elf, please? Don't leave the village we mustn't cause him trouble.' The Sheriff requested.

'Certainly Daxx. We will watch from one of the farms.' Replied Mr Partten and left the Sheriff to his thoughts.

A little while later, Mr Partten and his son were hidden in the end barn of the last farm trying to watch Arturous.

'He's hard to follow dad.'

'Quite frankly son, given the care he is taking, it's a miracle either of us can see him at all.'

'I'm not sure I can see him. I am following a trail of barely moving grass. I can't see him. He's changed direction, and it's taken him several hours to move about a mile and a half.'

'That's a good point. It's time to fetch Daxx – with extreme caution. I may try and head inland to keep my eyes on him. Something is not right here. The elf is being extremely cautious. Way too cautious for a bunch of defeated Goblins.' With that, his son slowly backed away from his side of the window and quietly left.

After a while of watching a path of barely moving tall grass, Mr Partten heard footsteps up the ladder. 'Be careful hidden and silent.' He said to the unknown arrival.

'It's me, Mr Partten.' The Sheriff said gruffly.

'Be silent and approach the window from a hidden angle.' Mr Partten replied in a commanding no-nonsense tone. The Sheriff complied with the orders without taking issue with them.

'I think we are being watched and our elf is hunting the watcher. I have never seen anyone be that cautious. Do you see him in the barely moving grass parallel to the wood about a mile and a half away?' Mr Partten informed the Sheriff.

'They don't call you The Hawk for nothing do they, I am afraid I can't.' replied the Sheriff.

'Never mind that. Our elf left here, headed cautiously for the wood, then halfway stopped and went inland even more cautiously than before. He is hiding behind small hillocks and the like. There is no way what's in those woods will have seen him.' Mr Partten continued. 'Our new three scouts are competent, aren't they?'

'Few in our tribe can match Luka or Katina and even

fewer that are better. More than competent, I would say.' The Sheriff replied.

'That's what I thought, and our elf here is at least as good as your tribe's scouts.'

'Yes.' Replied the Sheriff in hushed tones. 'Though I told him not to engage, just find out if anything was watching us. Something Arturous couldn't describe observing from upriver. Arturous couldn't see it due to the care our enemy was taking in its hiding. I sent the elf down the river to see if anything is that way too, but not to engage.' The Sheriff answered.

'So, it isn't Goblins then. The elf is being far too careful for that to be the case, and it won't be a human upriver. Our elf believes there is something at that end of the wood. He may simply be checking what and where.' Mr Partten continued without taking his eyes off the barely moving grass. 'He is turning into the wood now from the back. It's taken him nearly three hours!'

◆ ◆ ◆

Arturous had weaved his way behind tall grass and small humps in the ground for cover. He had noticed a small raised ridge no more than a foot high and had followed behind that also. It ran inland at right angles to the river about a mile or so downriver of the village. Another hill at the end of the ridge had allowed him to continue inland without being seen. When past the end of the wood, he had circled around to approach from the other side.

There was no noise or wildlife sound, so something was here. He proceeded through the wood, watching every single step making sure he did not even break a twig. There were strange footprints on the ground. Quite a bit bigger than the standard human or Goblin foot and appeared to have some sort of claws for toes. It also had a long stride meaning it was most likely taller than the average human or Goblin.

Arturous followed the tracks through the wood, exercising the same care as he had earlier. When the edge of the forest was about three hundred yards away, he felt an extraordinary weight in his mind. It was as if someone had put a small bag of flour on the back of his head. Crouching down behind a tree, the elf cautiously peered forwards. Something moved. He ducked down, keeping himself well hidden behind a large bush and some tall grass. Arturous looked from low to the ground. It was quite difficult to see what the enemy was. It seemed to blend in with the surroundings. Not entirely, but enough to make it awkward to see. What he could see was that it had two arms and two legs, was quite tall perhaps as big as the barbarians he now associated with, had the skin of a reptile that changed colour to match its background, and had a large bird-like head that was too big for its body.

The creature looked around directly at him for a long time with eagle-like eyes. He froze barely even breathing. It appeared not to notice him and went back to watching the village. He couldn't see its feet. It had clawed hands, but with a prehensile thumb. There were a curved sword and a dagger attached to a belt. The thought that a thing like that could use weapons concerned him.

Feeling something else Arturous cautiously backed away. His enemy had hidden down in some thick bushes and was not searching for him. Now further back and definitely being watched he scanned the area. Noticing Helghyer perched on a high branch, he gave the falcon a long look. After a few seconds of eye to eye contact, he returned his gaze to where the enemy was hiding. Helghyer looked in that direction and nodded. She continued to watch both him and the new enemy.

Arturous wondered if he should attempt to kill the creature. The first thought was yes, but then the sense of the order not to engage became obvious. If Arturous got back, what and where it was would be known to the village, yet the enemy would not know they had been discovered. He now understood the overall strategy of the Sheriff and signalled with hand movements to Helghyer that he was heading home, quietly backing off, bow in hand and arrow nocked just in case. Helghyer seemed to shrug.

He continued his retreat being as cautious as before, but working on the assumption he was in danger of being seen. He never did find out if his new enemy spotted him. After a while, he noticed Helghyer flying low inland and circling around to tower hill.

It took him at least another hour to carefully extricate himself from the area. The oppressive weight at the back of his mind had gone as soon as he reached the wood's edge. He headed towards tower hill from inland. Arturous having gone around the back of it saw the Sheriff, Luka, Katina, Tara, Freki, Helghyer and Mr Partten.

'Good afternoon Arturous.' The Sheriff said. 'Helghyer via Luka has informed us that you found something and took an awful lot of time extricating yourself without being seen. Mr Partten watched you early on, cross the field, then turn inland and approach the wood from the back. In a short time, I have known you I realise you are a quite capable scout and given that, I am interested in the reason for the extreme caution. I am also interested in knowing why the falcon could not tell Luka what it was.' The Sheriff queried.

'I have never seen anything like the humanoid I was tracking. That is probably why Helghyer didn't have a clue either.' Arturous responded.

'Can you describe it?' Asked Katina.

'Not properly. It is quite tall, probably about the height of Tara, maybe a bit bigger it is difficult to say for sure. It has two arms and two legs.' Replied Arturous.

'It is not a promising start to need to describe how many arms and legs it has. Is having two arms and two legs that odd?' Observed Mr Partten.

'In this case, take nothing for granted. It has scaly skin and the ability of the skin to change colour to blend in with its background. This makes it difficult to see. It has eagle-like claws for fingers and judging by its tracks, for toes too. It has a bird-like head which is too big for its body and eagle eyes. Despite that, I believe I was able to remain hidden from it.' Arturous informed them.

'There is more. I believe it is more intelligent than Goblins, certainly more careful and thorough. It also has thumbs and uses weapons. The one I watched had a curved sword and a dagger. Further, as I said earlier to the Sheriff with the one watching upriver, all wildlife runs away when it's around. That was the giveaway when I approached the wood. Lastly, when I did get near it, I could feel a sort of weight at the back of my mind, which didn't clear until I left its vicinity.' Arturous concluded finally.

'Plains Devils.' Said Katina.

'Agreed.' Added Luka

'We discovered tracks on the way here near the pass through the mountains to the castle.' Explained Katina.

'Plains Devils, what are they?' Asked Mr Partten.

'Spawns of Evil and serious trouble. Who has run into them?' Said the approaching Magistrate.

'Our elf here has managed to spot two and get out without being seen.' Said the Sheriff.

'I'm impressed master elf. Few can do that.' Replied the Magistrate.

'It requires extra special caution and patience. I can't guarantee it didn't see me. It certainly saw Helghyer but didn't appear to realise the significance. Those claws look nasty, it carried a small curved sword and a dagger, but I doubt it could hold a decent weapon like you use.' Informed Arturous.

'Plains Devils are intelligent, and some use dark spirit magic and rituals. They are a potent enemy. Luka we must get you initiated immediately. Our priest Oswald cannot possibly handle this alone.' The Magistrate instructed. Luka looked at him and nodded sombrely.

'You have rested and eaten. Now get that statuette of yours and meditate immediately. Learn your vows. I want you initiated by sundown. I will find our priest.' Commanded the Magistrate who then left.

'Do you want attendants to help you prepare, Luka?'

'That would be kind Katina, thank you.' And with that, the three ladies left while the Magistrate's servants were ordered to commence preparation.

'Chameleons with claws and eagle eyes, that's just great.' Commented Mr Partten's son.

'We will be fine, my son. We know now and can set appropriate watches.'

14 - THE HUNTRESS RETURNS

The inn keeper's wife woke Oswald by a shake. 'Sorry master priest, but it has been nearly six hours. There is a large group of people talking to the elf Arturous who has been out scouting. They are looking quite worried, which is not a good sign.' She informed him.

'You are correct. It's not a good sign.'

'I am not trying to be forward, but you have been in battle several times are dirty and covered in blood. I have brought you some warm water and homemade soap. Would you like some assistance? I know the southern plains ladies are helping each other. Do you wish some help? The way you are moving indicates you are very stiff and sore. You will need help to clean yourself and your wounds properly. I can send my eldest daughter to attend you. Not ideal, I know, but it's the best I can offer in these circumstances.' The lady indicated. Oswald thought she was correct, he would need assistance. However, no one had ever attended him, let alone a young woman. The lady was right though he would need help. Well so be it Oswald thought.

'As a man of the cloth I do have concerns, but you are correct, I am stiff, sore and dirty so help will be appreciated.' Oswald replied.

'My daughter is in her late teens. I will advise her on how to act appropriately.' With that, the inn keeper's wife left. Oswald took the soap and gave his hands a thorough wash. Just as he was finishing, there was a polite knock at the door.

'Come in.' Oswald called. A just adult age, medium height, dark-haired, well-built shapely young woman entered the room carrying a bundle of clothes. Oswald looked and realised his outer garments had been removed and by the looks of it washed and dried. She put them on the table and closed the door.

'Hello. I am Emily. My mother has explained the situation to me and that I am to assist you in washing, cleaning your wounds and dressing. I have been given me some very stern advice on how to act properly in such circumstances.' She said in a somewhat downcast stuttering embarrassed voice. 'You were asleep, so I took the liberty of washing and drying your clothes for you. Except for your cloak, which is not dry yet, I have a full set of clean outer and under clothes. I also have clean sheets for the bed.'

'Are you comfortable with this?' Oswald asked.

'My mum has ordered me to help you and told me how to behave. After your actions last night, I am happy to help, but will admit to some embarrassment. I will have no issue with conduct from the village elders as my mum has told me to help you and few will challenge her. No man has expressed an interest in me, so I won't have any issues on that score either.' She concluded.

'Thank you for your openness. I am likely to have a busy evening, so we had better get on with it.' Oswald concluded.

Emily helped Oswald remove the knee-length shirt he was wearing and obtained a second bucket of water. He noticed she also had brought several cloths. Using the warm water bucket and soap, Emily started by washing his back thoroughly, rinsing the cloth in the second bucket, then moved on to the arms legs and finally his chest. She turned her back while he cleaned various private areas.

Emily then changed the cloth and dried him. Finally using a further cloth, she paid particular attention to his various wounds and bruises. Every limb had at least one cut and several bruises, but none were that serious. Emily anointed each wound with a liquid that seemed to sting briefly. Neither spoke the entire time, not trusting words in this awkward situation. Oswald admitted to himself that Emily had done an excellent job. She then helped him dress but became completely confused with his leather armour. He had to explain what went where and how to attach it.

'I will now deal with bedding.' Emily stated.

'Thank you for your help, but I must pray first.' Oswald replied.

'I will not disturb you, but must clean your other clothes.' She stated firmly. Emily nodded politely picked up the dirty clothes and left.

Oswald knelt to pray. He took hold of his wooden cross and cleared his mind commencing the silent ritual prayer of introduction and forgiveness of sins. His thoughts about Emily while she washed him needed forgiveness, such thoughts and actions were forbidden by the High Priest. Oswald continued his prayer with thanks for deliverance from the attack last night.

Having dealt with all the usual stuff, Oswald asked for confirmation of the training of Luka and gave details of how he intended to do it. He asked why others couldn't be trained, such as the Magistrate or the Sheriff or even Ablamon. There were also issues surrounding the ritual of consecration. To his surprise, he got an immediate response. Initially, the reply from his cross spirit was *"Keep praying. I will go ask."* Then a little later, he received a proper answer.

"The victory last night was very much of your own doing. None of us had anything to do with it. With regards to matters of the female persuasion, while unbridled wayward lust is a sin, proper monogamous marriage was allowed under the old religion provided you were both willing to have children that worshipped your chosen God. It is how we were able to get most of our spell casting priests as the children tended to have similar abilities to their parents." The spirit continued yes, he should train Luka of Iredan as soon as possible. No, he should not teach any others as cross religion training is forbidden. Any spells or miracles cast would not be honoured. Luka is a special case with direct approval between both gods. As for the consecration ritual, he will need to work this out for

himself. His mind would be improved far more by working it out than by being told. The Iredan ritual is a long way removed from the original ones but does still have some critical points in it. Establish what these are, and experiment on small objects. When it is correct, he will feel it. Oswald thanked the spirit for his information.

He stopped praying and realised he was being watched. Looking around, he saw Emily standing there back to the door. He noted she had made his bed but was very red-faced, embarrassed and shocked.

'I am sorry master priest. I tried to make your bed without disturbing you. I am afraid I heard your prayers. The asking for forgiveness and the response of a god to all your questions, including the prayer about me. Given the response that you are allowed to marry, I don't know what to say.' She stammered.

'You heard the spirit speak?' A shocked Oswald asked.

'Yes, I am afraid I did.'

'Then you must be completely overwhelmed. Nobody has been able to do that before. I am truly sorry you overheard my prayers. I will not press anything I assure you. The reply was not God himself, but one of his guiding spirits which is helping me out. I wasn't aware that anyone could overhear my prayers.' Oswald assured her.

With a sterner decisive manner and voice, she appeared to make a snap decision.

'Master priest, I am not against being pressed appropriately. You are a good honest, intelligent man, whom I am aware is good looking. Any woman would do well to catch you. I am not against it in principle but am completely overcome. Last week I didn't even know gods existed, now not only can I hear his servants speak, but God has approved me to marry and have children with the only spellcasting priest since the days of legend. It's a lot for a young girl to take in.'

Oswald, relieved by Emily's tone, replied 'Of course it is. My road of enlightenment has also been remarkably quick. I am not against a closer relationship either long term but think we both have other things to do right now. We should keep this to ourselves for the time being. There are some aspects your parents need to know though.'

They both went downstairs and found the innkeeper and his wife in the taproom, talking and preparing for the rest of the day. No one else was present.

'Mr & Mrs Graff. Thank you for allowing your daughter to attend to me. She acted appropriately and correctly throughout though needed guidance fitting the armour. Mrs Graff, you were correct I was far too stiff and sore to be able to attend to matters myself adequately, I certainly needed help.'

'I am most pleased my daughter acted correctly.' The innkeeper replied.

'There is one matter that we must discuss between us privately and quickly.' Oswald continued.

'Then we are at your immediate disposal.' Mrs Graff replied, having glanced round the room for visitors.

'Emily was able to overhear my prayers to God and the responses. That is priest level spiritual communications. Aside from the cultural shock having not believed gods exist to being able to overhear communications, she has an aptitude for matters like this. If known, it will put her in enormous danger. You have seen how popular I am lately. I will seek guidance, but you need to be aware of the aptitude and risk.' Oswald responded.

'Do you recommend her going away to become a priestess then?' Mrs Graff asked in a worried voice.

'She is an intelligent woman who knows her own mind. That decision must be hers alone.' Oswald replied. 'If Emily wishes to be trained, then somehow I must manage it here. Going to Kersladen will only get her killed.' He continued. 'I am not high enough rank to train her officially. Once I have found my feet, she can assist in the ceremonies and be taught how to read and write. A good way to start would be to write out our ceremonies teachings orders of service and similar.' Oswald advised.

Looking at his daughter 'What is your view, Emily?' her father asked.

'If it can be fitted in around my duties here then yes, please. I have no suitors. I am considered too strong-willed, intelligent, and stubborn to make a good wife, which is probably true. The local men of my age are all frightened of me. The priesthood would be a good choice for me, but it must work around my tasks here. With so many new people you will be busy and need help.' Emily replied.

The door opened, and the Magistrate entered.

'Ah good, you are up master priest. We need to talk.'

'That sounds ominous.' replied Oswald.

'May we talk privately please?' The Magistrate said indicating the corner of the taproom. Oswald followed him over and sat at a table in the back of the room.

'We need to conduct Luka's initiation immediately as there is more trouble afoot.' The Magistrate said quietly and in a concerned voice.

'I have no problem with that and have received permission to do so, but please understand teaching her the symbols, words and correct use will take time. It won't be a matter of initiate her in the afternoon, and she will be casting miracles by this evening. I must teach her the symbols, which she must learn so well she can picture them in her mind. Then there are the correct ancient words for each symbol. Also, there are issues of their effect and correct use. Plus learning the teachings of your religion and keeping her scouting skills up to scratch. That's a lot on her plate.'

'All true, but still, it must be done.' The Magistrate continued.

'I dread to ask, but why is it necessary?' Oswald queried.

'You know of The Lord of All Evil obviously, are you aware that he has minions that serve him beyond mere

Goblins.'

'I know they exist, but no more than that.' Oswald replied.

'Well, Goblins are a true-breeding race like humans and elves. They are not affected by the lord's mutations. Other races are affected and are completely subservient to him. Most of our knowledge of them has long since gone, but there is one type my tribe have experience of recently which we call "Plains Devils". A bipedal clawed reptilian creature about the height of us southern plains people. They appear to operate on tribal lines and are more thoughtful and careful than Goblins. They also have access to the lord's equivalent of your spells. Further, they have mutations which means individuals have some unique ability or effect. Some appear to have tough skin, some are exceptionally strong, some acute senses, and some like the ones Arturous spotted while you were sleeping seem to be able to blend into the background. He has seen two, probably scouts. One upriver a couple of miles and one in the woods down the river.'

'Arturous has been out scouting again! Doesn't he ever sleep?' Oswald enquired.

'Apparently, it's a side effect of slave mining. They did many long shifts. He does want tonight off though.' The Magistrate replied.

'Does Tara, Katina and Luka know how to fight these things?' Oswald asked.

'I don't think so, but they do know about them though. May I ask if you can teach me too, being a full priest already, it would have advantages.' The Magistrate requested.

'I have already asked the question, and my god said no. Cross religion training is forbidden. Direct discussions between our two gods have given Luka special dispensation. Once I have trained Luka, she will have to ask for permission to train you. Sorry.' Oswald informed the Magistrate.

R. Allen Jones

'I thought that might be the case.'

'Only the first of each religion is entitled to special treatment and direct communication with your chosen god.' Oswald continued 'I also asked about you teaching me your ritual of consecration. Yours has departed too much from the original to work, but does still have some of the key factors. My spirit guide believes if I learn yours, it should be possible to identify the key areas you still have and from that work out a ritual that works. I will know when it's correct.' Oswald concluded.

He then realised why his God had chosen him and not his more intelligent cousin. His cousin had a brilliant memory, was very intelligent and a great orator, but was useless at improvising or working something out off the cuff. He though was always able to establish critical parts of any religious teaching or service and improvise the rest. That is what was needed now. Once he had worked it all out and written it down, his cousin would be able to implement it a lot better than he could, but Oswald had to do it first. Well so be it he thought.

'If we are to do this service today, I must prepare now.' Oswald told the Magistrate.

'There are things that I must do also. Just before sundown on the green?' The Magistrate asked.

'Agreed. The initiation is to start at sundown.' Oswald suggested. The pair parted with Oswald returning to his room to prepare notes for his first service.

A few hours later, having requested Emily be involved too, Oswald was ready. He got out his white robe, and the innkeeper's wife cobbled together something for Emily. His cross was attached to his quarterstaff with twine. He discussed with a very nervous looking Emily what she was to do keeping it basic and straightforward. A small table at the top of the village green with a large white cloth over it doubled as the altar. A hole was prepared behind the table for Oswald to put in his quarterstaff with the attached cross.

They prepared themselves at the inn and once a small crowd had gathered on the green Oswald led the way holding his quarterstaff and cross vertically in front of him. Emily followed behind white cloth draped over her outstretched arms with Oswald's book of teachings on top. The Magistrate wearing a brown cloak and carrying the statuette of the Huntress in outstretched arms followed. Luka followed with a sombre, reflective look on her face also wearing the brown cloak of the Huntress. Flanking and slightly behind her were Katina and Tara.

Oswald walked through the crowd and up to the "altar". Going around behind the altar, he pushed the staff firmly down into the prepared hole. Emily placed the book of teachings on the altar opening at a pre-determined page. Oswald then returning to the front of the altar turned his back on the crowd, knelt and looking up at his cross uttered solemnly out loud the first words of all of his prayers, altered slightly not to offend his southern plains friends.

'Light Bringer, the god that brings us light, I beseech thee, hear our prayers this day and grant us your blessing.'

On the conclusion of his words, his cross seemed to have a shapeless white form cover it. He could hear the gasps of the crowd and the sounds of many people kneeling. Privately he suspected the spirit in his cross was playing games.

Then before Oswald had a chance to do anything and while he was getting up, the Magistrate who was now behind the makeshift altar stepped forward holding the statuette up high and facing the crowd said.

'Our beloved god The Huntress, I beseech thee, hear our prayers this day and grant us your blessing.' In what appeared to be a direct plagiarism of Oswald's improvised words. Still, the statuette was now covered in an amorphous glowing semi-translucent blob. Luka was kneeling on the grass before the altar muttering what appeared to be prayers.

Oswald projected a thought to his guardian spirit. *"Are you playing? If so, thanks."*

The response was *"Not me gov."* Then more sternly. *"Be very careful here, both our God and The Huntress are here witnessing the service. That hasn't happened in a very long time. We don't want to be offending anybody. Forget your training and do what you do best, improvise."*

A somewhat shaken Oswald glanced around and saw a very stunned Emily who had clearly also heard the exchange with his spirit. Luka was still praying on the floor with her two attendants behind her. He then looked at the crowd.

'We are gathered here today to offer thanks to the Light Bringer and The Huntress for their assistance and deliverance over the last few days. We are also offering The Huntress her faithful servant Luka of Iredan as her initiate priest.' Oswald then looks heavenwards and with outstretched arms said.

'Light Bringer we are gathered here today to offer you our thanks for your recent help and blessings to our warriors. God of Light hear our prayers.' Oswald then looked down in reverence.

After a few seconds, the Magistrate holds his arms out to the crowd and said

'The Huntress we are gathered here today to offer you our thanks for your recent help and blessings to our warriors. Huntress hear our prayers.' The Magistrate then also looked down in reverence.

Oswald then looking at the gathered crowd concluded that some explanation of what happens next was in order.

'It is customary for a short extract from the book of teachings to be read out to remind us of an aspect of conduct in our life. I will now read a section from an early portion of the book.' He noticed that both his cross and the statuette were still glowing. Nerves finally got the better of him. To conduct ones first service in the presence of a High Priest was terrible, but nothing compared to two gods. With a wavering crackly nervous voice, he read a section on the acceptance of praying in private as well as at a formal service. He then left a moment's silence before continuing.

'I will now ask you all to pray privately to your chosen god for the forgiveness of sins against others and god.'

After a few minutes, Oswald looked over the gathered crowd who were mostly it appeared, praying and started his first-ever sermon. It only lasted about ten minutes having to cut it short after putting about a quarter of the crowd to sleep. He concluded that they would now stand witness to the inauguration of Luka as an Initiate Priest of The Huntress. The Magistrate then in a booming voice.

'Luka, daughter of Ardan, child of the Iredan tribe, senior huntress declare that you hold no other allegiance than to your tribe and that you desire to forgo that only allegiance to serve The Huntress for the rest of your life.'

'I do so declare.' Luka said in a humble voice. The booming voice of the Magistrate continued.

'Lord Daxx, Senior Lord Guardian of Iredan and Surrogate for our lord chief do you permit Luka, daughter of Ardan and child of Iredan to be free of her oath of allegiance to the Iredan tribe.'

'I do so permit.' Replied a surprised sheriff loudly.

'Luka, daughter of Ardan, child of the Iredan tribe and senior huntress, agree to abide by the rules and teachings of The Huntress.' The Magistrate continued.

'I do so agree to abide.' Luka replied more firmly this time.

'You may kiss the relic.' The Magistrate concluded.

Then in his mind, Oswald heard a strange voice. *"This is not a correct set of declarations. Please help Initiate of The Light Bringer."* A more familiar voice from his time out cold in Brother Michael's infirmary then said, *"Agreed"*. Oswald noted that Emily had nearly fainted from shock but managed to keep her feet. As Luka approached the statuette, Oswald boomed.

'Luka, daughter of Ardan, child of the Iredan tribe and Senior Huntress make these declarations with an honest heart and of free will. That you must hereafter follow the path of The Huntress and Light wherever it may lead. Understand that you are making these declarations in the presence of your chosen god The Huntress, and in the presence of the witness, the god The Light Bringer. Think carefully of your answer Luka, daughter of Ardan, child of the Iredan tribe and Senior Huntress. It is binding for all of eternity, even beyond death.'

Luka looked at him, puzzled and hesitated. Judging by the look on her face, that was far more than she expected. The strange voice then said in his head *"That was not perfect, long term I will need better, but it will do for now. Thank you Initiate Priest of the Light Bringer, you are a credit to your God."*

Helghyer now flew in and landed at her feet and looked up at her. Looking down at her falcon and with a smile said

'I do so declare.'

Oswald looked down at Helghyer. Knowing what must be done and despite thinking this was utterly bonkers said.

'Helghyer, Companion of Luka, hunter of the wild do you agree to accompany her, advise and assist her wherever her path may lead, for all eternity.' Helghyer stood up tall, stretched her neck and gave a very loud long squawk that clearly meant understood and agreed.

After that, a beam of light came forth from the huntress statuette striking both Luka and Helghyer who appeared to glow slightly for a while. The voice of little Isaac amidst the stunned silence of the crowd and carrying across the entire green pipes up.

'I take it your Goddess said yes.'

'That she did.' Was the awed reply of the Magistrate.

15 - THE FIRST TEACHING

The service was over. Everyone was crowding around Luka and Helghyer congratulating them and stroking the falcon. Saying how incredible it was and wasn't she lucky to have her God respond to her directly like that. She must be an exceptional, wonderful person. Luka was utterly bowled over by the attention but tried to keep respectful of those around her. Helghyer after a short while had had enough, reverted to animal behaviour and started to bite fingers.

Oswald was anxious. He had never really expected it all to work, but it had. As the leading priest, in the future, the service would need to be much better, however the gods attending seemed sufficiently satisfied on this occasion, and that's all that mattered. The result was that he had to start teaching. He didn't even know if Luka could read or write. What was worse, he wasn't even sure if it mattered.

His spirit companion wanted him to work out blessings and consecration, then teach those and healing to Luka. Oswald could see the argument in favour of this but was of the definite opinion that was wrong. He hadn't done the blessing himself and even when he worked it out, consecration was going to be a tough one. As for the healing, at a very minimum, it involved combining two fundamentals as he called them to achieve anything. The more fundamentals you combined, the more difficult it became to sustain the level of concentration required to complete the spell. That would be a challenging task for someone new to spell casting. He had had the images and words placed directly in his mind by his God. Those he taught would not have that benefit. He needed something the crowd could see quickly to sustain the interest and reinforce the new belief. Something like

'I was initiated the day before yesterday, have had a few lessons yesterday and now look at what I can do.'

Something everyone could see that would be useful as well. Certainly, Luka would need to learn healing, blessing and consecration very quickly. Especially with new unknown monsters, but what to teach first, something that others could see.

Of course, Oswald thought. He tried it himself. He said his initial prayer. Feeling the palm of his hand tingle as the focus of the spell was created, he summoned the image of the symbol for light into his mind. This time he said the word but without adding any additional power or distance. A very bright light appeared in the palm of his hand. That would be it. Learning Light produced a visible effect, would give Luka confidence and reinforce the belief of others.

His spirit companion took the opinion that it would not be how he would do it, but a visible effect right now would be an excellent all-around benefit both for Luka and with the public at large. He then realised the Magistrate was speaking to him.

'Sorry Lord Mord, I was contemplating what and how I teach Luka. I have not done this before.' Oswald replied.

This was, of course, wrong, at least as far as his companion spirit was concerned. Back at the temple, he had explained plenty to confused novices who couldn't handle the beating attached to a confession of not understanding to the master of novices. That was not what Oswald considered real teaching. His companion spirit pointedly informed him that he disagreed. His method of teaching was far more useful right now than sticks.

'Apology accepted Initiate Shamus. I hope you don't mind the plagiarism, but it seemed sensible in the circumstances. If you don't mind me asking, why the extra bit at the end?' The Magistrate asked.

'I have no problem with the plagiarism. As I understand it, my religion's ceremonies are completely wrong, and only parts of yours are still correct. I have to work out new services. If I happen to get something right, you and Luka will have to use it. As for the addition at the end, I am sorry about that. Your God spoke to me saying your ritual was wrong and could I butt in. Mine agreed, so I improvised what I thought they wanted. The reply I got was "Not perfect but good enough for now".' Oswald replied.

'That must have come as a shock. I was wondering why you got a bit shaky in parts.' The Magistrate observed.

'Indeed, it did. I have sustained some theological shocks recently.' Oswald replied. A thought then occurred to the Magistrate.

'Our two gods were watching, weren't they? I was deemed inadequate.' He said in a downhearted tone.

'Yes, our two gods were present. A two-up like that has not happened in a very very long time. There was no criticism of you at all by either God. I have already been told your rituals while incorrect are the closest, so don't be concerned. I would ask though that you record what we did and said for next time before the memory fades. I must concentrate on Luka for now.'

'I agree. I will attend to it. Can you start right away?'

'Please understand this may take some time. The way this operates is quite a profound experience. I had the symbols placed directly into my mind. Luka has not had that. It could take her several days to commit a symbol to memory, and that's before teaching her how to use it. My spirit companion believes at least a week each symbol.' Oswald warned.

'Then the sooner we start, the better.' The Magistrate looked towards Luka and called her over.

'Now that you are initiated and tied to The Huntress, I wish you to go with our Light Bringer priest and start your training immediately. The sooner you can begin assisting Oswald, the better.'

Oswald wondered if the Magistrate had listened to anything that was said to him. He decided to repeat himself, hoping that this would also assist the now gathered crowd's expectations of Luka.

'My Lord Mord. I will, of course, start teaching Luka as soon as she is willing, but as I said earlier, please remember that even in the days of legend it took a week or more to learn each symbol and the matching word. Even the simplest of spells require two. Then she must become proficient enough to cast them in combat. It will take at least a month I would imagine.' Oswald said.

'My Lord, we have taken a significant step, but my training must be done properly and with all due diligence as we do with all things in our tribe. People get killed if training is conducted hastily as we all know. That has been our tribe's attitude for hundreds of years and has served us well. I will go with Oswald now so we can discuss matters.' Luka responded with a tone of finality.

She left with Oswald and headed for the Inn where they secured a private room to use. They found Emily on the way and asked her to join them, explaining that she could learn much simply by watching. Max insisted she go and observe despite her assertions that there were essential chores to do.

◆ ◆ ◆

The Sheriff and Ablamon approached the Magistrate. 'What do you think?' the Sheriff asked.

'I think our two initiates are developing the necessary presence and backbone to be the high priests required. I haven't been spoken to like that in years. Gentlemen for the first time in hundreds of years we have hope.' Lord Mord replied.

'It's a huge ask of them my Lord Mord.' Was Ablamon's respectful response.

'I know, but I truly believe they are starting to develop the strength they need.' The Magistrate responded.

◆ ◆ ◆

Oswald and the two ladies went to a small quiet back room at the Inn which contained a table and some chairs. Emily got some heavy white cloth and a charcoal stick. Oswald sat in the middle of the long side of the table with the ladies sat either side.

'First, let me explain how I understand spiritual spellcasting works and what it entails. I will explain what I perceive to be the risks and difficulties. Then I will try and teach you the simplest of spells.' He began.

'Spiritual spells come from the connection you have to your chosen God, in my case, The Light Bringer. The spells themselves are cast by creating a focus and then combining various components which I call fundamentals. Each of these fundamentals does a specific thing once.' He paused a second to see if it sunk in.

'You have seen me cast a light spell at a distance. To do this, I created the focus by remembering the connection with my God. I then use the fundamental for light by calling forth the symbol of light in my mind. I then need to move the focus of the spell from the palm of my hand to somewhere else. I achieve this by adding the fundamental for distance calling forth its symbol and pointing it to my mind's image of where the light is to move. When the spell image in my mind is stable, I say the ancient words for Light and Distance.' He paused to let everything sink in.

'You will both have to be careful then.' Emily postulated. 'If, master priest, you had produced fire rather than light, you would have burnt your hand.'

Oswald thought reflectively and after a few seconds. 'I believe you are correct, Emily. The fundamentals happen in the order they are cast in, so there will be situations where care will be needed.'

'So, these fundamentals, are they the symbols on my statue and that wand?' Luka asked.

'That is part of it. Each fundamental has a symbol and a matching ancient word. There are dozens of them. I was given six and have worked out how to use four of those. We can assume that one of the unknowns on the dark wand is darkness.' Oswald continued.

'The first step of spell casting is to produce the focus. To achieve this, you call on the belief in your God. In my case, I remember the time God first came to me, the image of that and the emotions that went with it. If the spell is going to work, it will produce a tingling feeling in the palm of your dominant hand.' Oswald took the white linen cloth and the charcoal stick. He drew the first symbol on the cloth and wrote its ancient word underneath it.

'So, to produce a light, I think of my god, imagine that image in my mind.' He said, pointing to the drawing 'and say "GOLAU" to produce this.' Oswald opened his hand to show a bright white light. Emily gasped.

'Be careful, though. Each spell weakens you. My first spellcasting in battle caused me to collapse while healing at the end.' Oswald concluded. Without any hesitation, he noticed both ladies concentrate hard while looking at the drawing laid out on the table. They both said "Golou". Nothing happened. They both looked disappointed. Oswald looked at Emily and said

'I am afraid it will not work for you as you are not yet tied to a god. What I haven't said is that you must be both ordained into the priesthood and have given a small amount of blood onto a religious artefact at a holy day. I am sorry, but it will not work until I can figure out how to get you properly initiated.'

"Not true" Oswald's companion spirit interrupted. *"Normally that would be correct, but both our God and another were present at the ceremony. Emily actively and willingly took part in the Light Bringer portion as an assistant priest, privately confessed her sins before two gods, and gave adequate oaths during silent praying. These have been accepted granting Emily the status of novice priest of The Light Bringer. She will only be able to do simple single fundamentals. Such are the restrictions on new novices. There are plenty Emily won't be able to cast yet, those that she can cast won't*

be anywhere near as effective and combining or stacking will not be honoured. That requires a high initiate status." Then the voice was gone. It was clear from the faces of the two ladies that they had heard the spirit too.

'Alright then, let's give this a second try. The pronunciation is "GOLAU" not "GOLOU".' Oswald instructed. 'Luka, you first. Remember, think of the meeting with your God and when you were first bonded. Recall the feelings and emotions.'

After a few seconds, 'My hand is tingling, a peculiar feeling like pins and needles.' Luka responded.

'Look at the picture then.' Suggested Emily.

Luka opened her eyes and stared intently at the charcoal drawing on the linen sheet.

'Remember it's "GOLAU".' Oswald said. Luka with a look of enormous concentration, says 'GOLAU'.

The palm of her hand erupted with a bright light, although Luka sagged a little afterwards.

'Very well done Luka.' Oswald congratulated.

'It is rather tiring, though.' Luka responded.

'It gets easier with time, but every spell drains you.' Oswald said. Turning to Emily, he said 'Do you want to have a try. Remember what the spirit said, as a novice priest, your effects will not be anywhere near as powerful.'

He could see Emily's concentration. Eyes closed and in deep thought. After several seconds, she opened her eyes and staring directly at the linen sheet said 'GOLAU'. A dim light emanated from Emily's palm, perhaps the brightness of one candle.

Oswald's companion spirit then commented *"Very well done all three of you. Now ladies you each must constantly draw the symbol for probably about a week until its very image becomes ingrained in your memory. Then you will be able to call it forth without visual aids."*

The spirit went on. *"Every God of Light has certain common fundamentals. By agreement, Oswald can teach you both these. Each God also has fundamentals specific to that God, in our case, things to do with blocking and banishing evil and undead spirits. Luka, I am afraid Oswald is not allowed to teach you those. There are ones specific to The Huntress. She will have to devise a way for you to discover these yourself. Emily, until you are a High Initiate, you can only learn a few of the common ones. Others won't work. Our God won't honour them until you are of higher rank. That will come, though. We are all sure of that."*

'Thank you.' Oswald replied.

'Do we prove anything to anyone?' Luka asked.

'I think it's too soon.' Was Emily's opinion. 'Let's both get the symbol off pat first.'

There was a polite knock on the door, and Emily's parents entered with some bread, cheese and small ale.

'We have brought you some food as it's well past mealtime.' Said Emily's mother. Then she saw the palms of both Luka and Emily's hands and with shock said 'Both of you straight away, even our Emily?'

'Yes. Be aware though that neither are skilled yet and need my help to cast the spell.' With a stern voice, Oswald continued 'This must be kept secret until they can cast several spells with speed and skill.'

'It appears that your daughter privately gave certain oaths in the presence of both gods. They accepted her oaths, and have bestowed the rank of Novice Priest of The Light Bringer. As such, there are a few minor things she can now do once taught. The range and power of what she can do will improve with her advancement in the priesthood.' Oswald concluded.

'Given our earlier conversation about my daughter being killed, I take it that this must be kept a secret from everyone.' Said Emily's father.

'Yes, it must, even from the magistrate sheriff and the others, I am afraid. She will need to be taught how to fight, though. If her life becomes anything like mine has recently, she will need it.' Oswald replied.

'I can arrange that.' Replied Luka.

'Master Priest. Please pass on to your God that my wife

and I are both humbled and honoured to have our eldest daughter be your first Novice and accepted for training as the first spell casting priestess.' Emily's father said.

'We are proud beyond words.' Emily's mother added with a beaming smile. 'We will leave you to eat.' She continued.

Oswald, Luka and Emily discussed what had been learnt over the evening meal continuing until the lights in the palms of their hands faded out. Emily went back to her duties at the Inn, which was busy that evening with people discussing the initiation service.

Emily noticed her parents were frequently asked why she had been involved that day. They said Oswald needed an attendant to help him prepare and conduct the service. Of their daughters, Emily was the most suitable. She had stayed afterwards to act as servant and waitress during Luka's training. People appeared to accept that.

◆ ◆ ◆

Luka took the linen cloth and charcoal stick to continue to practice drawing the symbol. After returning to her lodgings at the magistrates' house, she entered the large room on the top floor to see Tara and Katina relaxing on their beds. Sitting on her bed, Luka opened the linen cloth. Without paying too much attention, thought of the Huntress and remembered the emotions involved, concentrated on the charcoal drawing on the cloth and said 'GOLAU'. Her hand burst into light, and she sagged back on the bed.

'What the . . . . You can cast this quickly. Wow, that is incredible.' Commented Tara.

'It's not proper spell casting. It's only one component, and I have to have a drawing of the symbol to picture it.' Luka replied.

'No telling anyone. Not even Lords Daxx or Mord. This must remain between us. I wasn't expecting it to work.' She continued while noticing that both Freki and Helghyer were looking at her with a "Surely you're not that stupid" look on their faces.

Then something occurred to Luka. With significant reverence and sorrow, she got up and went over to Helghyer. Crouching down Luka gently placed her hand on the back of the great falcon's head then looked Helghyer in the eyes.

'You are no longer an animal, are you Helghyer?'

Tara and Katina watched in contemplative silence. Helghyer stepped forward and headbutted Luka gently in the face.

'And neither are you Freki, are you?' Luka said, looking at the massive wolf. 'You both now have a human level of intelligence, don't you?' Luka continued.

Helghyer repeated the headbutt.

'I am so sorry to have caused you to be changed and bound such.' Luka received an affectionate nip from Helghyer and got the distinct feeling that her falcon was alright with the situation.

'Are you here to help me the way Oswald's companion spirit helps him.' Repeat head butt followed by a "sort of" set of head and wing movements. Then from the stunned silence.

'I have to go home immediately.' Said Katina in a sad, reflective voice.

'What, why?' asked a surprised Tara.

'The tribe's chief and elders must know what is happening here. They must know the existence of the other humans, the Goblin raids, the finding of my uncle and the others, the finding of the temple, the returning of the Gods of Light, and most of all no safe new home. They must know it all and fast. Luka clearly can't go, that leaves only me. No disrespect Tara, but only a hunter can make a trip like that on their own with any chance of survival.' Said Katina. A sad-faced Tara got up, went over to Katina and gave her a big hug.

'I thought perhaps we could delay it a few weeks until I have finished my initial training, then all go together. Have a good hunt around that temple for more information on the way.' Replied Luka.

'Katina is right, I am afraid. The window of opportunity is now. The Goblins are dead or routed, as are the bandits. There are only the two Plains Devils to worry about, and with Ablamon's help, we could get you passed them. You could then split off and go through the castle pass without being seen. If we wait a few weeks the place could well be crawling with Goblins and Plains Devils.

Glumly Luka nodded. She knew the others were right. They waited for the light spell to wear off and went in search of the Magistrate and Sheriff.

After about fifteen minutes, they had found both of them as well as Ablamon in a private room.

'Lovely though it would be to stay uncle, I have decided I must go home immediately. The tribe must know what is happening here, all of it.' Said Katina.

'The place is not yet safe for the tribe to come and live, which was the whole point of us leaving in the first place.' A sad-faced sheriff said.

'Uncle, the tribe must know that.' Katina said.

'The opportunity is now. Katina can act as one of Ablamon's guards. No prolonged farewells and once clear of the lower villages she can split off and head for home away from searching Goblins and other things.' Tara added.

'They are right Daxx. The tribe must know all that is happening here. The guards and I are due back down the river. We have goods to sell and weapons and tools to buy. This way, the same number leave as entered.' Ablamon asserted. The Sheriff looked at the Magistrate, who with a sad face, nodded.

'The benefit to the village of having both the hunters and the elf is huge, especially given Luka's extra training requirements, but your niece is right all the tribes must know and soon.' The Magistrate added.

♦ ♦ ♦

The old man sat on the floor in complete darkness, his long-matted hair and unkempt beard resting on the huge chains that bound both arms and legs to the enormous wall. The old man had sat there for so many aeons he had lost count, which was saying something for him. Unable to even move his limbs due to the tightness of the heavy chains, he remained stationary. Slightly turning his head was all that was possible. Not that he had anything to look at in the darkness.

He turned his head and looked at the grotesque form of his dying son, then had an idea. He had been in the pitched black for so many years it had been such a long time since he had had a thought.

He could see his son. Only just and in the dimmest of lights, but still his son could just be seen. That could only mean one thing, at least some of his other children had believers. For the first time in so long he had hope, he actually had hope. He must convince his grotesque dying son to remain in existence.

16 - THE FIRST OF THE DEVILS

In the morning, Ablamon and his guards organised themselves without any fuss beyond a few goodbyes. Katina surreptitiously added herself to the team while they were preparing to depart for Izellameth. As they were leaving Arturous approached Katina who was sat on a cart and said

'It has been a privilege to fight beside you these past few days. Have a safe journey.'

'It has been a privilege to fight beside you also.' Katina replied.

'I had a look this morning, no birds.' Arturous added. Katina listened and nodded secretly. She pulled her quiver of arrows out from under the canvas behind her, removed several of her arrows, checked them returning the arrows and quiver on top of the replaced canvas. Ablamon and his guards all noticed. Ablamon's expression being "Really". Each surreptitiously in turn loosening sword ties and quiver caps as they left.

The two carts rolled slowly along the road towards Izellameth. Katina had seen the villagers watching glumly as about half their combat veterans, and one of their scouts returned to their day jobs. Katina was aware the village had a high level of combat experience amongst them despite being a rural backwater. While others had prepared for the initiation service of Luka the day before, Ablamon had gone asking questions. His findings were staggering. It was quite clear that in a short space of time, the Sheriff and former Major Partten would be able to form a very capable militia. Investigations of various village elders had discovered most families had at least one person who had seen combat or was an ex-soldier. They didn't appear to have the level of training her tribe had, but her uncle could rectify that in time as all seemed to have the aptitude and desire to serve.

While sat on her cart, her horse tethered behind, Katina looked around the village they were departing. With horror, she saw her team quietly head up the road inland towards the Partten's farm.

'Oh, dear.' She muttered out loud with a voice full of sorrow.

'What's up?' Asked her companion, then on turning saw the movement and continued 'Oh I see. That's a hard one to watch.' He said in a firm voice 'Ablamon'.

Ablamon turned in the saddle to look at her companion, saw where he was looking and furtively looked also. To those that didn't know him he gave nothing away, but for those that did . . .

'I don't know what is worse, watching your friends go into combat against devil spawn without you, or knowing you're the bait.' Katina quietly said to her companion. He gave an understanding nod and a sad smile.

The wagon continued slowly along the road down the river, the tall grass growing either side of the road. Unlike the previous journeys, the guards were positioned differently on this occasion. While as normal Ablamon and a guard were in front, and each cart had a driver and one guard, the last two guards rode beside the two carts on the inland side. All had bows in hand with arrows nocked apart from the cart drivers.

Katina considered matters as they move slowly on the road down the river, Arturous was correct something was out here. There had been no sign of any wild animal or bird since they had left the village. Looking further afield Katina could see what looked like Helghyer in the distance circling on the high thermals.

'Katina, mind if I ask what is going on. So much has happened, and I have missed things while on various guard duties. I didn't ask nearer the village in case we were overheard.' Her companion asked.

'While we were sleeping before Luka's initiation ceremony, Arturous went scouting. He ran across what we believe to be two Plains Devils watching the village. Virtually impossible to see due to skin colouration. One upriver and one in the wood over there.' She replied, looking at the wood inland from the river.

'Impossible to see, not helpful.' Was the reply.

'Not as bad as all that. Wild animals won't stay near them, so no animals equal Plains Devils.' Katina responded. 'That means they are within about a quarter-mile of us right now judging by the lack of birdsong and wildlife. I have seen a falcon in the distance, so I think I know roughly where Tara's team are. Probably checking out the scout Arturous found yesterday.' Katina concluded.

'Ablamon' her companion called. He looked around at Katina's companion who gave various hand signals.

'Warrior sign. I have not seen it before.' Katina said, surprised.

'We don't use it much, only when our conversations can be overheard.' Was the reply. The two carts closed together, and sword straps were quietly loosened as the convoy continued slowly onward.

◆ ◆ ◆

Arturous glanced at the downcast looking Oswald as they all quietly led their horses out of the village square. Both himself and Oswald had wanted to say goodbye to Katina, but Lord Daxx had sternly said they could not. They had to depart on their next mission quickly, quietly, and unnoticed. Arturous had ignored that and gone up to her anyway. Oswald had decided to follow orders and by the looks of him, regretted every second of it.

They quietly passed what had now been renamed Tower Hill and got to the outer edge of the Partten's farm when Helghyer returned. The falcon looked towards the wood and squawked, then looked towards the open grassland and squawked again.

'That settles it. We have to figure out a plan of attack for these things.' Tara said without even waiting for Luka's translation.

'Helghyer, is there still just the one in the wood you saw yesterday?' Luka asked. A single squawk and a headbutt was the reply.

'Alright, is there only one in the grasslands?' She continued. There were many squawks and a head shake.

'Are there more of them than us?' was the last question. A single squawk and a headbutt followed this.

'Well then, we don't want to have a nearly invisible scout behind us in the woods downriver, so we need to take care of him first.' Tara stated.

'It will have to be just Arturous Helghyer and me, with Freki if he will come. You warrior types are never going to sneak up on him.' Replied Luka who then looked at Freki who growled as a response.

'Freki appears to want to stay with his human. Luka is probably right, while I am quite light on my feet, I am not comparable to Luka or Arturous. If what I have overheard is anything like true, we will be discovered by one wrong step.' Commented Agnes.

'Then Arturous and Luka must try and take out the enemy scout, with Helghyer to keep watch.' Tara ordered to receive a derisory squawk from Helghyer.

'We need to know if you two can take out the enemy scout. If you can't, we will have to withdraw.' Tara continued.

'And if they can, we have a chance against the others as they will be concentrating on the merchant train and Katina.' Suggested Oswald.

'You learn quickly master priest. Yes, that is the idea.' Replied Tara.

'We had better be off then. I will follow you Arturous.' Suggested Luka. The pair promptly ran off towards the back of the wood with Luka following. Helghyer took a more direct route to the high branches of a convenient tall tree.

Arturous led Luka inland about half a mile away from the wood, crouched down and stopped.

'From here, we must start being cautious. We are not near it yet as I can't feel anything. When we get near the wood, don't even break a single twig.' Arturous whispered. Luka nodded.

They crouched low and proceeded slowly through the tall grass using whatever terrain irregularities they could to conceal the approach. After a very cautious half hour, the pair reached the edge of the wood and almost crawling proceeded inside. A further few minutes and Arturous could feel the build-up of that horrible pressure at the back of his mind. The enemy was close.

Crouching down and peering around the tree he was hiding behind, Arturous carefully looked around the area, but couldn't see it. He returned to his hiding position and noticed Luka had stopped following him. She was now well hidden a little way away behind a nearby tree and large bush. Carefully taking a further look, where the creature had been previously was clear, but it was not there. Looking further, he noticed strange marks on the tree trunk next to where the creature had hidden. Of course, Arturous thought, it had climbed the tree for a better view. Something significant was concealed in the foliage in the lower branches. After signalling Luka that way and up, she cautiously crawled to a nearby bush and looked. After a few seconds, she returned to her old position and nodded.

Arturous intended to engage in an archery battle, but he loosened his sword tie just in case and readied his bow. He looked at Luka, who appeared to be doing the same thing. After taking a few seconds to compose himself, Arturous ducked back around the tree and released his arrow. He saw Luka do the same thing. While both arrows went into the correct area, he couldn't tell if either of them had hit anything.

There was a horrific guttural scream shortly followed

by the creature making a flying leap at Arturous. Despite being some forty feet away, it flew through the air straight at him. He fired again at the moving target as did Luka. Both missed the creature who hit the elf hard in the chest, knocking him off his feet. Arturous landed several yards away, dropped his bow, rolled to his feet and drew his sword in one movement.

The creature leapt for a second time with both its curved sword and dagger drawn. Arturous dodged the creature's sword attack while jumping at him, parried the dagger and struck hard at its right forearm. The attack achieved nothing, and for a second time, a shoulder barge to the chest knocked him over. Again, he rolled to his feet and parried an incoming attack from a curved sword.

Arturous saw an arrow from Luka bounce off the creature's back armour. He again struck its forearm, jumping backwards to give more space to move around in. The devil crouched to leap again, but as it did so, an arrow from Luka struck deep into its thigh, causing it to fall short and stumble while landing.

Arturous tried to take advantage of the unarmoured neck, but missed with his sword and hit the armoured shoulder instead. Although not an incapacitating blow, he did wound the monster.

The creature rose to its feet quickly and tried to strike with both sword and dagger simultaneously. Arturous also noticed Luka to his right, taking careful aim, so he jumped back out of the creature's way as it tried to strike. Using a manoeuvre he had seen Tara employ, he took one step back and with the full length of his longer Elvin sword did a large circular motion. He captured both the blades of the curved sword and long dagger sweeping them off to one side and entirely out of the way. Then Luka's arrow struck the creature's side penetrating deeply into a small unarmoured part of his abdomen. Involuntarily it lifted its head with a cry of pain.

With both of its weapons off to one side and its head

looking up, Arturous struck quickly sinking his longsword through the creature's throat and out the back of its neck. It dropped its weapons and fell to the ground. Arturous kicked them away and saw Luka shoulder her bow and draw her sword. Before Arturous had a chance to query, she rushed over knelt beside it and with a mighty swing beheaded it in one go.

'What was that for?' Arturous asked, shocked by the level of violence.

'Katina warned me last night. Sometimes they can heal their wounds even after death, causing them to come alive again. We certainly don't want him doing that. It was a tough fight, are you alright? You took several serious knocks.' Luka replied.

'I am fine. Thank you for asking. I think that was it for this area as I don't have that strange feeling anymore.' Arturous said.

'Good. I think we should try and find the rest of the devils. The others will see Helghyer and join us.'

'Hey look, a pouch full of silver coins. That should help pay for lodgings at least.'

'We can't be using the Lord of All Evil's coinage. We will have to hand them over to the Sheriff and Magistrate. I am sure they will work something out though.'

Arturous attached the coin pouch to his belt, and they both headed cautiously across the grassland separating slightly.

Having quietly crossed the grassland Arturous was perhaps a quarter-mile from the road when the familiar oppressive weight returned to the back of his head. He continued and when cresting a small raised piece of ground himself, spotted a line of nine scaly creatures similar in appearance to the one he had fought earlier. They were crouching behind another small raised piece of ground about two hundred yards ahead of him. These didn't seem to have the chameleon-like powers the other one did, but from the road would be very well hidden.

They were all armed with bow, sword and dagger as well as being armoured. One in the middle seemed much bigger than the others.

He felt a presence behind him and turned quickly, partially drawing his sword. It was Freki, he relaxed. They exchanged a look and the huge wolf quietly padded off back into the tall grass. So, the others were about too Arturous thought. That was good, but he was also worried. Due to all the caution everyone was taking, he didn't know where anyone else was. He had even lost track of Luka, though he believed she must be within one hundred yards or so. The enemies weren't attacking the wagons, so he waited for something to happen, bow in hand and arrow nocked.

After what seemed like an age, the enemy, bows in hand all stood up and reached for arrows. Before any of them could do anything, Arturous released his first arrow. Another followed from his right. Both arrows hit, going straight through the neck of one, with Luka's somehow burying itself deeply in the armpit of another. Good, two down, he thought.

The remaining opponents all turned and knelt quickly firing back at Arturous. They were very wild shots all missing their mark as he ducked back behind a small bank of earth. Another arrow from his right hit a Plains Devil's chest armour achieving very little. They then turned on Luka, so Arturous stood up and released another arrow.

This alternative firing continued for several minutes with neither side appearing to get anywhere beyond the initial casualties. Then Arturous heard the heavy sound of several horses galloping.

◆ ◆ ◆

After Freki had come back and indicated he had found the two scouts, Tara cautiously led Agnes and Oswald all three dismounted across the tall grassland towards the plain's devils. When Tara considered they were about halfway, all quietly remounted their horses and slowly walked forward. When satisfied, the enemies were fully occupied and not paying attention to their flanks, Tara quietly ordered the charge. Agnes and Tara proceeded at full gallop. Tara saw Oswald had had to stop and dismount as he couldn't use either of his weapons mounted. He ran in on foot to the nearest opponent wielding his two-handed war mace.

Agnes gallop slightly to the left of the nearest opponent and with an overhead swing brought her large sword down on its head. The massive blow cleaving its skull in two, leaving it twitching on the ground behind her as she rode past through the remaining enemy and slowed down to turn around.

Tara did the same to the next one along and had intended to ride past as well. However, while galloping along the line, the biggest one shoulder charged her horse in the front right forequarter while simultaneously hitting the horse with both of its massive fists. Being about seven feet tall with muscles like an ox, her horse lost its balance and fell. Tara jumped free, curled herself up around her sword and although not elegantly rolled to her knees, holding her sword level above her head. She blocked two incoming blows from nearby devils in the process.

The enemy leader, despite its intentions and size, couldn't stop the sheer momentum of a large charging horse and got knocked flying. It drew two large scimitars while rolling to its feet.

Tara saw a worried-looking Agnes facing two opponents both bigger than her. She was following the standard orders defend, stay alive, and keep opponents off the backs of her more capable friends. She was concentrating on parrying incoming blows with both her shield and sword. Luckily for her, the devils didn't attack at the same time. Tara could see Oswald running in to help.

'Priest help Agnes. Take the scaly one.' Tara shouted.

Puzzled, he nodded, changed direction and ran in screaming some unintelligible war cry. The scaly one who was on Agnes' left reacted by turning to engage Oswald. Agnes kicked her other opponent, knocking him back and giving her a few seconds to attack. Turning her horse slightly, she gave a heavy overhead blow with her large sword at the departing devil's back. Agnes face turned to horror as the blow bounced off its thick, scaly skin. It quickly proceeded beyond her reach, engaging Oswald. She turned back to her remaining opponent just in time to parry an incoming blow.

The largest of the Plains Devils headed towards Tara's back while she faced two others. Her shield having come off in the fall from her horse, Tara parried the blows from her opponents using her bastard sword two-handed.

Just as the biggest opponent was about to get close enough to strike Tara's back, Freki leapt and bit heavily onto a forearm. The creature staggered backwards and dropped one of its scimitars while shaking the wolf loose. Landing on his feet, Freki crouched and leapt again. This time the enemy leader caught him with both hands. Using supreme effort, the largest of the devils threw the huge wolf several yards away. Freki righted himself mid-flight and landed on all fours.

The enemy leader retrieved his dropped scimitars and started to advance on Tara again. Before he managed even two steps, Helghyer hit it in the face clawing at the eyes. The creature covered his face with one arm and tried to strike the falcon with the remaining scimitar. Helghyer was far too quick for him though and flew off low without having a blow come anywhere near her. She circled for another attack.

The enemy leader recovered from the falcon attack but was again faced by the snarling Freki coiled up to leap. The creature advanced on the wolf only to get kicked in the ribs by two rear hooves of Tara's bucking horse who didn't want to be left out.

The delay of the enemy leader had given Arturous and Luka time to run the hundred or so yards and join the hard-pressed Tara, who was now on her feet. With a sweeping parry, she knocked the scimitar of one opponent aside, leaving him open to an attack from Arturous. He hit the side of the creature but was not able to penetrate its armour. Luka did the same for her opponent leaving an opening for Tara. Her sword, being a lot larger and heavier than Arturous' Elvin long sword, penetrated the creature's armour and bit heavily into its chest. Luka followed up with a slice to the neck.

Tara left Arturous and Luka to finish up and looked around for the leader. The animals were engaging him. She wondered, judging by the bite marks, claw marks and hoof prints if they should be just left to get on with it. Agnes, she noted was doing as she was told and was just keeping her opponent entertained without exposing herself to risk. As for Oswald, he seemed to be slowly getting the upper hand. The creature's thick, scaly skin would make it hard for the swords to wound that devil, but the sheer force exerted by his large two-handed war mace knocked everything aside, including it appeared arms and legs as Oswald's opponent went down to a visibly shattered knee.

Tara now advanced on the leader whom she noted not only appeared winded but also courtesy of various bites and claws now just had one eye and one useable arm. It wasn't much of a fight with the leader. Tara went straight for the attack which the leader parried with ease and skill, but having only one working arm left himself wide open to an attack from Freki. He used the standard wolf tactic of hamstringing from behind. The enemy leader went down with a scream, was disarmed and beheaded.

Tara looked round to see Agnes turn her horse slightly, strike her opponent with her shield and then sliced into its neck while it was off balance. Her opponent went down with a gurgling scream. Looking the other way she saw Oswald bring his two-handed mace down on the head of his opponent, smashing it open. A final guttural scream from behind her said it was all over.

Tara looked about to check, and yes, it was all over. For one of the few times in her life, she let out a sigh of relief. Looking back reflectively, as she had been trained to do, she realised her tactics had been ad hoc and dreadful. If it hadn't been for the animals distracting the leader, they would have lost with several people dead, including her. That was not good enough. Casualties always happen in war, but she realised they should not be caused by poor thinking.

Her body then reminded her that she had not got through it freely. Her forehead was bleeding as were both her arms and legs. Thankfully none of her wounds was that serious so long as they were correctly cleaned and bound. Freki was limping, lifting one of his front paws. Agnes having now dismounted was also limping, and Oswald was holding his side. Initially, she thought Arturous was alright, but on a second glance, he wasn't. Luka appeared fine and was casually beheading the fallen.

'We need to get back and cleaned up.' Tara ordered the group.

'Any more of them Arturous?' Asked Luka.

'Don't think so, I can't feel anything, so that means nothing within half a mile or so.' He replied. Luka nodded, then turning to Tara said

'That was dreadful. It was disorganised and could have got us all killed.' Before Tara could put up an apology or response of any sort.

'But we did not and prevailed.' Oswald replied to Luka in a stern, authoritative, no-nonsense tone that Tara had not heard him use before. 'Our responsibility now is priestly matters and undead. Responsibility for combat and tactics now lies with others who will not be second-guessed by us two.'

'Sorry Tara, Oswald is right.' Luka replied stiffly after a shocked second or two. 'I am not used to my new hat yet.'

'We are all getting used to new ideas, ways of working, responsibilities and even opponents. Not everything we do will work the first time flawlessly.' Tara responded. 'The basic tactics worked. Kill scouts, distract, weaken with archery fire and then flank attack. That way, we can inflict casualties before we engage in the general melee. Master Priest, we need to sort you out a weapon for horseback use. I haven't seen a single handed war mace, so perhaps a club for now.' Tara continued. Then turning to Arturous said

'What are you doing?'

'Oh, we found a pouch full of silver coins on the scout. He's just checking these out.' Luka informed everyone.

'I've found another four pouches of silver and a few gold coins too on the big guy.' Arturous replied.

'Lord of All Evil, I assume.' Tara asked.

'Afraid so yes.'

'Typical, can't use any of it.'

'Don't be so sure. Oswald, can you sense anything on them?' Luka asked. He went over and touched many of the coins.

'I can't feel anything, and I certainly did with that wand I came across on the way here.' He replied.

'Maybe they can be melted down and re-used then.' Suggested Luka.

'That must be up to the Magistrate and village elders.' Suggested Tara.

'Enough chatter. We can discuss such things later. I must deal with wounds and then we must get back to the village. We can't risk being caught out in the open.' Oswald commented sternly.

'Arturous and Luka, please gather up the enemy's weapons, bundle them and distribute amongst the horses. Freki lets have that paw.' Ordered Tara. While checking his paw, she asked, 'Any signs of the carts?'

'They kept going to the next village.' Responded Arturous while gathering up scimitars.

At Tara's insistence, Oswald dealt with Agnes first. She had a nasty gash on her right leg where one of her parries had not been as effective as it should have been. Oswald first cleaned the wound with one of his cloths he now carried with him and then attended to his usual prayer. Given it was only two nights ago when two Goblin arrows had hit her, he put more effort into the healing than usual by calling forth his power component twice. Despite her objections, he healed Tara next, then dealt with his ribs.

After all that he noticed everything was set, the horses loaded to include bows, but no enemy arrows which he queried.

'They are useless. Even the heads are crap. If by some miracle they hit something, they would probably break on impact. The bows are pretty good though. They are well made.' Responded Luka.

They mounted and headed for the road before turning upriver to the village. Helghyer perched on the front of Luka's saddle, the whole group moving at a slow walk to allow for Freki's paw. Both Arturous and Luka scouted initially ahead, later inland and finally behind, but there were no further sightings. As they reached the outskirts of the village, both scouts returned, and the whole group entered Warameth together. The Magistrate, Sheriff, Mr Partten and several elders were waiting for them.

'It looks as if it was a tougher fight than Goblins.' The Sheriff speculated.

'It was my lord, but simply because they are more proficient, and our tactics did not work as envisaged.' Replied Tara.

'We killed them all, ten in total. The scout in the woods and nine waiting to ambush Ablamon and the others. He and his men got through without seeing combat, using Ablamon as bait worked well. We took out the enemy scout first and attacked the ambushers by surprise. Archery is not as effective against them as Goblins and melees are more difficult, but they don't cope with multiple opponents or attacks from unexpected directions. Here are some coins we found, all Lord of All Evil I am afraid.' Informed Tara handing a bag of coins to the Magistrate.

'We have brought back the scimitars and bows. The arrows were useless.' Luka added

'Thank you all. Now try and get some rest, I intend to stand you down for at least four days to recuperate.' Concluded the Sheriff.

PART 4 – A LITTLE KNOWLEDGE

17 - THE RETURN OF FEAR

The exhausted, battered, beaten, and dirty group looked at each other with the stunning realisation that for the first time in ages, they had nothing to do. That all the scouting and fighting was, for the next few days at least, somebody else's problem. It was Emily, who had approached the group without being noticed, that got things moving.

'Master Priest, you are wounded, tired and dirty, please come with me and get cleaned up.' The attitude used by Emily was one of no-nonsense. Oswald considered her orders, realising that she was probably right, and quite frankly he was too stiff and weary to argue or even care. He slowly moved in her direction.

'You too master elf. Come along now.' She ordered.

'Why not, I could do with a proper bath anyway.' Arturous inadvertently said out loud. Emily turned and looked at Agnes' mother.

'Mistress Partten, can I leave the ladies with you? I will have my hands full with these two.'

'Don't worry Emily. I will take care of them.' Was the reply. 'Come along ladies. Let's get you cleaned up and fed. Now follow me.'

'You can't take them straight away. We want to know what happened.' Came the anguished tone of a tall, well-built farmer, who like many others had come over to the battered group.

Mistress Partten gave the man a withering look and was about to let loose with a vicious tirade when she was interrupted by little Isaac.

'Didn't you hear? They fought the Devil's monsters and won, just like a few nights ago with the Goblins. They are our heroes and are brilliant.' Mistress Partten's vicious look changed to one of reflection saying.

'The young lad has said all us civilians need to know at this time. I must care for our lady combatants in private.

Now let us leave.' The crowd, murmuring amongst themselves, gave way to the stern gaze of Mistress Partten and parted. She led the three ladies to the family's farm.

'Major Partten, please take the squad you put together earlier and check our immediate area.' The Sheriff requested.

'Certainly, Lord Sheriff. I have included the three captured bandits to test their worthiness and loyalty.' The Major replied.

'I think that is an excellent idea. Please proceed.'

A group of ten armed men joined Major Partten who went to find horses for their first mounted patrol.

'Lord Sheriff, may I remove the priest and the elf from you, so they may get cleaned up and fed.' Enquired Emily.

'Certainly, Emily, please take care of them.' He replied.

'Master Priest, Master Elf, please follow me now.' Emily ordered. She took them to the back room of the Inn, where she had prepared two warm baths. Emily left them to attend to washing but returned after a short while.

'You are both badly cut and bruised. I have been given various ointments and taught how to use them. Apparently far more people die of diseases received from wounds than the actual wounds themselves, so it is important I do this properly. It will be necessary to clean your wounds and apply the ointments to each of you.' Emily said to them both.

'That is certainly the case with mine injuries if not treated correctly.' Arturous informed her.

After Emily had administered the ointments and bandages, she left. The two men quietly dressed and stiffly walked to their usual table at the back of the taproom out of the way. Many of the evening's patrons appeared itching to speak to them, but the glares from the Inn's owners kept curiosity at bay. Max brought them food and mild ale.

'Do not worry about the payment. This is going on the Magistrate's tab.' Said Max in a friendly tone.

'We thank you and your family for all the help. It has

made some difficult tasks a lot easier.' Oswald replied.

'The thanks are from us. None of us dares think about the consequences of you five not arriving when you did. We are all grateful. I must go now and tend my other customers.' Max nodded politely and left.

After about half an hour, the three ladies joined them. Agnes was walking stiffly with a heavily bandaged leg, Tara and Luka walking with the typical gate of fit athletic women.

'Do you ladies wish some food?' asked Max as they approached.

'No thank you Max, my mother has already fed us. We could do with some ale to accompany our companions though.' Agnes responded.

'They are drinking mild ale.' Max said.

'That will do fine.' Replied Agnes

'Mild ale?' Asked Luka.

'It seemed sensible, given the number of unforeseen events around here.' Oswald replied.

'Probably wise. We do drink before a raid or battle to relax, but not to excess as that affects ability.' Tara responded. With that, the Sheriff entered the taproom and came over to the table.

'Pleasant evening to you all. Major Partten has formed a small team that has gone to look around. The road to Izellameth is clear, and the upriver visitor has been chased away by all the activity, but unfortunately not killed. I can confirm you can have a few days of rest.' He said.

'Thank you, my lord, we all need it.' Tara replied, respectfully. Max returned with the ladies' drinks.

Emily cautiously approached. 'I have washed your clothes, gentlemen. They are hung out for drying.' She said quietly to Oswald and Arturous.

'Thank you, Emily. I am grateful.' Oswald responded. As Emily turned to leave 'Please wait a minute Emily. Luka, can you spare the time to continue your education tomorrow, given we have a few days off?' He asked.

'Certainly, master priest.' Luka replied.

'Emily, can you arrange with your parents to attend us as before. It would be much appreciated.'

'I will ask my father, but after my breakfast chores should be acceptable.' Emily responded.

'Thank you. Is after breakfast acceptable to you, Luka.' Oswald asked.

'That will be fine.' She replied. Emily nodded politely and left.

'Luka, can you please see if Lord Mord can let us use some parchment and ink. We need to start recording what we know.' Oswald enquired.

'I am sure he can let us have some in the circumstances.' Luka replied.

The general conversation continued for some time before they all separated. Oswald went to his room and closed the door. He retrieved his cross and holding it in his right hand.

"Are you there?"

"Yes, I am. What do you need?" Was the reply.

"I think it is time to nail down my last two fundamentals. Can you assist?"

"To a degree. What each symbol and word combination does has been fixed since the father of the gods created the universe. The Light Bringer believes that the best way for you to achieve your maximum potential is for you to work things out for yourself. I think you will need help but will follow the desired method of training as best as is practical. What I can tell you is that one of the unknowns is offensive and the other defensive. If you get the defensive one correct, you will feel it work even if you are not being attacked. The offensive one will only work if you cast it at somebody." The spirit replied.

"So, if I try the defensive one first, I will know the offensive combination by elimination, even if I don't know what it does." Oswald suggested.

"Yes, that is correct." The spirit replied in a pleased tone.

Oswald considered his two unknown symbols. One looked like a stick man running, the other like the long shield the southern plains people use. He decided to try the shield and the first word. He invoked his prayer, feeling his hand tingle he called forth the symbol of the shield and said

'Braw.' Shortly followed by 'Ouch' as the prayer exploded in his hand.

"Wrong word." His spirit guardian added rather unhelpfully.

He tried again. Firstly, he invoked his prayer, felt his hand tingle, called forth the symbol of the shield and said

'Rhwystro'

He felt something emanating from the palm of his hand. He called forth the image for power and said

'Grym'

The energy emanating from his hand had grown decidedly bigger and stronger.

"You really do have an aptitude for this don't you, well done. That blocks incoming spirit magic unless the power of the incoming spell is too strong." His spirit guide informed him.

"Thank you. That means the offensive spell is the stick man and Braw, even if I don't know what it does." Oswald confided in his spirit guide. *"Yes, that is correct."* His spirit guide replied.

He decided to leave it at that for the evening and conducted a gentle prayer session to his god, giving thanks generally. Then Oswald spent some time meditating in bed to collect his thoughts on the implications of what he had learnt. Exhausted, he fell asleep. Then there was a polite knock on the door at what appeared to be shortly after sunrise. He berated himself for getting up late.

'Thank you. I am awake now. I will be down after prayers.' The bleary-eyed initiate priest replied. He rose quickly, then realised how stiff he was, dressed and slowly knelt to say morning prayers. Once completed he went downstairs for breakfast.

'Good morning master priest. You are feeling stiff today.' Enquired Arturous.

'I am, the last few weeks have finally caught up with

me. After breakfast, I will go for a walk.'

'Emily is preparing the back room for your studying today, so I will serve you breakfast. Unfortunately, it is only porridge this time.' Said Max, as he placed two bowls on the table.

'We will both be happy with that, thank you.' Replied Arturous.

They ate breakfast, collected their cloaks, Arturous collected his sword and Oswald his quarterstaff, then they went for a walk together around the village. The first thing they noticed was the rapid extension to the blacksmith's shop. It had only been about a week since Oswald had suggested building something to allow the captured weapons to be melted down into new iron for reuse. The building already had foundations of large stone blocks and a nearly complete oak timber frame. Oswald could see the blacksmith building something he didn't recognise. It was a small square stone structure partially open one side and narrower at the top than the bottom.

'Good morning master priest.' The blacksmith called from his work.

'Good morning, goodman. You appear to be progressing well with the extension and something I do not recognise.' Oswald asked.

'Indeed, we are. There is no shortage of cut stone buried hereabouts, so there is never a problem with foundations. The carpenter already had some cut timber, so we have made rapid progress. As for what I am doing, it is a furnace, or at least I hope it is. I haven't seen or used one since my apprenticeship. The furnace itself should be capable of a test firing in a few days and if all goes well producing new iron when the building is complete.' The blacksmith said.

'That is great news.' Oswald responded.

'Even better news is the metal in the swords appears of good quality but hasn't been processed properly. When I have had some practice, I should be able to improve the quality of the iron above that of the swords we seized. A warning though, I am no weapon smith.'

'I believe the Gods of Light will provide.' Oswald suggested.

'After what I have seen lately, I don't doubt that for a second.' The blacksmith replied.

They continued their walk and noticed both Luka and Tara conducting weapons practice on the green, while the Sheriff and Major Partten put a dozen or so militia through their paces. Luka looked at Oswald, signalled Tara to cease.

'On my way master priest.' She exchanged polite bows with Tara then headed back to the Magistrate's house. Oswald and Arturous returned to the Inn.

'I have my teaching to do now, so I must go and prepare. See you later.' Oswald said.

'I will clean and maintain my weapons, especially my arrows as these are seeing much use. I must also see someone about some leather armour.' Arturous replied as they turned towards the Inn.

Oswald entered the back room and sat at the table, collecting his thoughts while waiting. He would need to conduct an assessment of their ability to cast the light fundamental without help. Then on to learning a new one. They also needed to start recording what was known. There was a lot to cover.

After some minutes, Luka and Emily entered together carrying roles of parchment, a wooden board, charcoal sticks, some ink and quills.

'The board and charcoal sticks were my father's suggestion.' Said Emily

'And a good idea too.' Replied Oswald. Emily closed the door.

'Ladies, please sit down. How have your practices gone? Not that we have had much time.' Oswald asked.

Luka opened the palm of her hand and concentrated hard. After a few seconds, she said 'Golau' quietly. The light burst forth from her hand while she sagged a little.

'I can do it now, but it is tiring.'

'Well done. That will get easier with practice. Emily, how are you getting on.' Oswald asked gently.

'As I am your first novice, I have been practising as hard as possible in private.' Emily replied. Her face with closed eyes emanated extreme concentration. Then opening her eyes and hand said 'Golau'. A dim light appeared in her palm while her shoulders also sagged.

'Well done both of you. I am very pleased. Now we need to decide what you should be taught next. I have worked out the matching word for each of my six symbols. Of the two previously unknowns, one is an offensive spell which I have not been able to test, and another a defensive spell that does appear to work.'

'I know you have fundamentals for curing, power, light, distance and now a defensive one. If the offensive combination is unknown, perhaps we should investigate that. Then record the six on a scroll.' Was Luka's suggestion.

'Alright then, let's see what you think of the new symbol.' Replied Oswald as he took the board and a charcoal stick, then drew the symbol on the board.

'It looks a bit like a stick man running.' Suggested Emily

'How can that be offensive.' Queried Oswald.

'If he is running away, it would be.' Suggested Luka. 'Perhaps some form of fear. You will have to try it on me.'

'I can't do that. I would hurt you.' Oswald said in shocked tones.

'There is little choice. Don't put anything behind it, just minimum spell. It is a controlled situation. If it hurts, you can heal me.' Luka responded.

'Alright then, here goes.' Oswald said his opening prayer, called forth the symbol and while holding Luka's hand said 'Braw'.

He sensed the spell bite, and the battle of the two wills

commence when trying to force through his spell. Just as he thought he would be successful, Luka got the hang of resisting and the spell dissipated.

'That was something. It damn nearly worked.' Was Luka's response.

'It was bizarre. It ended up being a battle of wills.' Commented Oswald.

'What did you feel Luka? I could see you resisting something.' Asked Emily.

'It was fear and very strong too. It took all my concentration not to run straight out the door. In the right circumstances, it could be beneficial.' Luka replied.

'Luka did very well in resisting. Now try it on Emily. Remember, concentrate hard on resisting the emotional change the spell causes.' The spirit guide instructed.

Oswald said his initial prayer and called forth the symbol in his mind while holding Emily's hand. After saying the word 'Braw', he felt the full impact of the spell on her mind. The shock was incredible. He could feel the tears of fear swell in her, shortly followed by the notion that she was the first novice and must do better. Over a couple of seconds, she pulled herself together and the spell dissipated. Oswald opened his eyes to the tear-strewn ashen face, steeled with pure determination. But before Oswald could say anything.

'Amazing. Initiate Shamus is immensely strong. For you both to be able to resist him shows incredible control and ability.' Oswald's spirit guide congratulated them. *'I would mention that it doesn't work very well on the highly trained and very brave like the Iredan tribe. It requires some weakness to get through, and they are just too tough. I suggest you teach them both how to use the fear next. I must go and speak to God directly. I will be away for a while.'* And with that, the spirit guide left.

'We had better get on with it then.' Oswald suggested having seen that the ladies had also heard his spirit guide. 'Take a good look at the symbol each of you. I will then wipe it from the board, and you draw it.'

It took them several hours to draw the symbol correctly without copying from visual aids. When Oswald was finally satisfied that they could repeat it accurately.

'The accompanying word is "Braw". Try that.' He suggested.

Luka and Oswald held hands. She concentrated and then said 'Braw'. Oswald felt as if he had been hit in the head by a stone. There was an irrational desire to run far away. Then remembering both the ladies had withstood this, knew he must also. Steeling himself with the experiences he had survived in recent weeks, forcing the irrational behaviour from his mind, the spell then broke.

'That was intense.' Expressed Luka.

'And it nearly worked too. Now you, Emily.' Oswald ordered. Hesitantly she took his hand and concentrated. 'Braw' she said. Again, Oswald fought away the irrational fear and stood his ground until the spell broke.

'Well done, Emily. We will need to practice on each other. For now, though, let us take a break from learning and start writing out what we already know. Luka, can you write?' Oswald asked.

'Yes, to a point.' She replied.

'Then you start recording the fundamentals you know, and I will start to teach Emily to read and write.' Oswald told them.

And so, it progressed for several days. After breakfast and chores, Oswald taught Emily the beginnings of reading and writing, while Luka drew symbols and matching words. She also added a brief description of what it did. Between them, they created a small scroll of known combinations of fundamentals as a guide. They also practised the fear fundamental, the mental image of the symbol becoming more solid and stronger each day.

Oswald also took a close look at The Huntress statuette and noticed some unknown symbols and words. Each side of the statuette had a simple symbol with a word underneath and a far more complex one next to it inside a square box. He tried to memorise some, but they would not hold. Then he remembered he had been given some of the fundamentals common to all gods of light, but there were others specific to each God. So perhaps these were specific to the huntress, being on her statuette.

When the recording of all existing knowledge was complete, and they had a copy each, Oswald asked.

'Luka, I noticed that your statuette has both simple and complex symbols. I have tried to memorise them, but they won't stick. I wonder if they are fundamentals specific to your God. I would suggest you try and seek guidance, perhaps from Helghyer if your connection works like that.'

'I will ask.' She replied.

"I am sorry I have been so long. I have spoken to our God. He is willing to grant Emily a special dispensation and elevate her to the status of Junior Initiate. This will allow her to stack distance with light, fear and spell block for practice or threat to life." Interrupted Oswald's returning spirit guide.

'That pretty much seals it, tomorrow we learn distance.' Replied Luka.

'Spirit guide, can you please thank god for me.' Requested Emily.

"Certainly Emily but suggest you do so directly. It would be more appreciated." The spirit replied.

'I think that is enough for today. We meet after breakfast as usual if that is acceptable to you, ladies?' Oswald asked to various nods of agreement. 'Emily, please have this.' Oswald said, placing his hand inside his robe and taking out a small handmade cross which he gave to her. 'You deserve that.' He concluded.

'Thank you, master.' Emily said with a beaming smile.

'Let's get some air.' Luka suggested.

'Then, I will return to my chores. They are starting to get backed up.' With that, Emily nodded politely got up and left.

Oswald and Luka packed up the scrolls and ink from the day's work, and once Oswald had put his copy back in his room, they went for a walk around the village. Oswald noticed Tara exercising some of the new militia which included two of the captured bandits. Her students looked sore and tired but were improving. Agnes appeared to be teaching Arturous how to ride a horse. They also spotted the sheriff approaching.

'Senior Hunter, Master Priest, good evening.'

'My Lord Daxx.' Luka responded.

'Good evening, Sheriff.' Oswald also responded.

'How may we assist?' Luka asked.

'I wish you to return to duties tomorrow. Major Partten's team have been conducting three local patrols per day plus training, so they need to be stood down. Also I need something further out.'

'We cannot start tomorrow. Maybe the next day, my lord.' Luka replied.

'I have given you many days off. I now need you to return to your duties.' The Sheriff replied.

'Between us, we believe we have the basics of our first offensive spell.' Oswald replied.

'Let them have their day Lord Sheriff. My squad can pull another couple of patrols. I will ease up on the training and give them a lie in. Having an offensive spellcasting capability is just too useful. We must give Oswald and Luka some time at least.' Said Major Partten who had approached from behind with Tara.

'Why don't we let Helghyer and Freki go out tomorrow and have a look around. Both are getting restless and need a hunt anyway. They will tell us if there is any serious trouble in the area.' Tara added.

'For tomorrow we will try it Tara's way then, but after that, I need your team on a deeper patrol upriver. I will inform you of the mission tomorrow evening at dinner.'

'Yes, my Lord Daxx.' Was Tara's response.

Arturous and Agnes joined them. The five took their leave of the two commanders and heading to the riverbank lay down on the grass beneath the evening sun. They talked of past deeds while throwing stones in the river for many hours until the last of the sun was finally gone, the night had arrived, and it had grown cold.

The morning arrived, pre-breakfast prayers, chores and weapons practice were done so as before Oswald went to the Inn's back room. Luka quickly joined him, but Emily took a few minutes longer, having more chores to complete.

'Can your spirit guide help us with the symbols on my statuette? I couldn't get much sense out of Helghyer. Our communication is not up to that yet. It is limited to some visual and emotional responses.' Asked Luka.

"All I can say is that they are specific to The Huntress. The simple symbols are fundamentals like we use, but specific to your God. The complex ones in boxes are full Divine Miracles. I can't help beyond that, sorry." The spirit guide replied apologetically.

'I must try and teach you both the distance fundamental. That will be the third one this week, for something that is supposed to take a week each. I will also have to teach you how to stack fundamentals, and that won't be easy either. Oh well here goes.' Oswald said.

With a sigh, he took the now well used wooden board that Emily had washed overnight and drew the symbol for distance.

'As I explained before, you create a focus, create the light, then apply distance. You must visualise where you wish to put the spell then point the symbol to it.' Oswald concentrated on saying his prayer, his hand tingled. He thought of the light symbol, said 'Golau', then thought of the distance, visualised the desired location and said 'Pellter'. A candlestick on the mantlepiece burst forth with light.

'Now Luka, you try.' Oswald asked.

Luka concentrated, created her focus, called forth the light into her hand and looking at the board tried to move it, but nothing happened. Emily also tried, but again with no results.

"Do not worry ladies. Stacking fundamentals takes a lot of practice and patience. To achieve it first time has never happened. Keep at it. I am sure you will get it in a few days." The spirit guide assured them.

The ladies though were not so keen on giving up and kept trying. The hours passed well into the afternoon. Oswald then thought he hit on something. His pupils were far too adept to keep failing like that. There must be something he does that they do not. He again did his successfully, and the ladies failed with downcast faces.

'When you are casting, do you hold the original focus and fundamental symbol in your mind?' Oswald asked.

'No, I put the first one to the side, then summon the distance.' Emily replied.

'I do that too.' Luka added.

'Then, the failure is my fault for not explaining things properly. When I cast spells, I hold the focus and the first cast fundamental in my mind as I add each additional fundamental to that image of the spell. If you forget any part of the original image the spell breaks.' He replied. Both the ladies looked confused.

"Don't worry ladies, he confused me too, and I've been at this several thousand years." The spirit guide added.

'Alright then, let's try it this way. I will talk you through the casting from scratch. You follow my instructions as I am saying them.' The others agreed.

'Firstly, create your focus and hold it in your mind.' They did this.

'Now add to that focus your first fundamental symbol.' They did this.

'Now then, keep that new picture in your mind. Add to it the symbol of distance and a vision of where you want the focus to move too.' Oswald recommended.

'This is difficult Oswald. I am having trouble with the image.' Responded Luka.

'Me too.' added Emily.

'Keep trying.' Suggested Oswald.

He could sense the slow expansion of both Luka and Emily's power and felt the second symbols simultaneously fall into place.

'Now say the words.' He commanded.

'Golau, Pellter.' They said in unison.

Two candlesticks burst into light. They both tried several times, each becoming quicker and more powerful.

"I am stunned." Added the spirit guide. *"You must now try it with Fear, but don't do the fear first or it will backfire badly."*

Oswald was the first to try the new spell but followed the advice creating a focus, applying the distance portion before adding the fear. The now-familiar battle of wills took place as Emily resisted him. Then Luka tried it on Oswald first, before it was Emily's turn. While Oswald helped Emily master the new spell, Luka recorded it on the scrolls adding a general note on how to stack fundamentals.

"Your progress is amazing. Very well done." The spirit guide added with a very pleased tone. It then asked

"When you ladies were failing to stack the fundamentals you both said you were putting the focus and cast symbol to one side, then created a new image for the distance fundamental. Did you remember them as two separate images?" Both ladies confirmed that was what they had been doing. *"Oswald, can you do that as well, create a focus, put it to one side for a bit then create a second one."* Oswald confirmed he could do that also. *"I need to discuss this with others. I will get back to you soon."* The spirit guide said in a shocked tone.

It was after this that the Sheriff knocked on the door and entered. Luckily Emily had already stood up to pour some wine for Oswald and Luka.

'Good evening. Lord Mord would like you both to attend dinner. It is almost ready to serve.' The Sheriff asked.

'I can tidy up here if you both wish to leave immediately. The Magistrate should not be kept waiting.'

Emily suggested.

'Are you sure.' Luka asked.

'Certainly Priestess. I am fine with this.' Emily replied.

'Then we are at your immediate disposal, my lord.' Concluded Oswald as they got up from the table.

Oswald and Luka followed the Sheriff to the Magistrate's house at the top of the green.

'Come in. Please sit down.' Lord Mord asked politely. Oswald sat next to Tara, while Luka took position next to Arturous. The two servants placed a sizeable joint of beef on the table together with cooked vegetables and gravy. There was also a small cask of ale and some mugs.

'Thank you, now please leave us.' The Magistrate said to the two servants, who bowed and swiftly left. Once they had departed.

'How are things going?' Lord Mord asked, looking at Oswald, who in turn looked at Luka.

'Which one do you want?' She replied.

'I had better take the Magistrate. It wouldn't be seemly for you, as he is your High Priest.' Oswald replied. She nodded and looked at the Sheriff. Her face changed to one of pure concentration. Oswald immediately began his focusing prayer and looked at the Magistrate. They simultaneously said 'Pellter, Braw.'

Oswald felt the fear bite the Magistrate and start to rise. Being completely taken by surprise, it was a little while before he fought it back. Oswald pushed the fear harder and looked round to see the Sheriff gripping the table with both hands knuckles white.

'Enough' Oswald called. Both broke concentration immediately withdrawing the fear from their opponent's mind.

'What was that?' The sweating shaking Sheriff asked in a stunned voice.

'A spiritual fear at range.' Replied the Magistrate with a stunned look. 'And they both pulled back from us. They didn't push it through.'

'It doesn't work very well on your people. It is the degree of professional training and pure inbred bravery, or so I am told. It does work well enough to prove a point. We perfected this one today. Luka, the candle, please.' Oswald replied.

There was a brief moment of concentration followed by 'Pellter, Golau' from Luka. The candlestick lit up.

'In less than a week, your Luka has learned three fundamentals and how to stack them. We have yet to try to use them in combat, but it should badly affect those weak-willed of our enemy.' Oswald told everyone.

'Then it was well worth the extra day. I wouldn't be so convinced it will only affect the weak-willed either. That was tough, and I am a highly trained warrior.' Added the Sheriff.

'Thank you, Lord Daxx.' Replied Luka.

'However, your team must depart on a more distant search first thing tomorrow morning. I want to know what happened to the Plains Devil upriver and the route the Goblins are taking through the valley. I can't ask Major Partten's team to go on longer searches. They need to remain closer to the village in case it needs protection. Agnes was informed earlier and decided to spend the night with her family. She will meet you on the green half an hour before sunrise.' The Sheriff ordered.

Oswald looked at Tara, who responded 'Certainly Lord Sheriff.'

The rest of the evening was spent in light conversation and interspersed with occasional servings from the two servants. After several hours the meal ended with Oswald and Arturous returning to the Inn and getting some sleep.

18 - THERE WERE HUMAN TRACKS TOO

Oswald got up, washed in the bowl of water left for him, got dressed, said a short prayer, put his leather armour on, picked up his weapons and went to meet Arturous.

When they left the inn, Tara and Luka were already dealing with their horses. Both Freki and Helghyer approached silently through the near dawn towards their humans. Agnes, her father and brother, led several saddled horses. When they were all together, she said.

'Father is lending two horses for the trip, so we can all be mounted for travelling at least.'

'Thank you, Major Partten, that is most kind.' Tara replied.

'It's no problem in the circumstances, but we are short of suitable horses. My team will not be able to patrol until you get back. I suspect you have your orders, but more horses would be useful.' He replied.

'Our orders are to go half a day up the river. Have a look around. Come back.' Responded Tara.

There were squawks and growls with the animals looking inland.

'Are we all ready?' Tara asked while Agnes said her goodbyes to her family, and they all mounted their horses.

There was a louder squawk, and a full bared teeth growl looking inland.

'I think your animals want to go to the plains.' Suggested Agnes.

'They do, but we have our orders.' Replied Luka.

'I've only known you and your animals a little over a week, but doesn't that mean there is something over there they don't like?' Agnes asked.

'It does, but we need to find out what is going on with that upriver Plains Devil. Arturous can sense them. We must go up the river and follow orders.' Tara responded.

Squawk growl squawk growl.

Agnes' father appeared to be thinking.

'Your animals believe there is a danger inland right now. We don't know what it is. You must investigate that first. Then swing around and check what is going on with that Plains Devil thing the elf spotted a few days ago. Then come back.' Major Partten ordered.

'There is nothing within half a day we have already checked that. So, whatever your animals have spotted must be within the low foothills roughly north of here. Any closer and we would have probably spotted them. You are a significant portion of our combat strength, so don't be away more than one night. Follow your orders then straight back.' He confirmed.

'I will have a word with the Sheriff and let him know the change of plans. We will keep watch upriver in case of surprises.' Major Partten informed them.

'We shall do as you suggest.' Tara agreed after a few moments' consideration.

'Well let's get on with it, we won't achieve anything stood here yacking.' Chided Luka.

They rode out of the village heading northwards following the already departed falcon and wolf. The group progressed at a slow canter over the uncultivated grasslands following the rapidly moving Helghyer and Freki ahead of them. They covered a dozen and more miles very quickly. Tara called a halt.

'We had better progress more slowly now. Arturous and Luka, have a look around and see if there are any signs of anything. Not too far now.' Tara instructed. Arturous handed the reins of his horse to Agnes and ran off in an up-river direction. Luka remained mounted and headed off the other way. Freki, who was a few miles ahead, stopped and waited. They each stopped occasionally and looked around.

Luka went about half a mile away before ranging in various directions. She occasionally dismounted and checked things. Arturous went a good deal further. Tara led the rest of the team at a walk. After about an hour, both scouts returned.

'Any luck?' Tara asked

'Yes. Significant Goblin activity, but over a week ago, I would say.' Luka responded.

'Same my way, at least forty, but old. Nothing new.' Arturous added.

'That will be the route that the downriver Goblins took for the village attack then.' Tara guessed out loud.

'Helghyer wants us to get moving.' Luka stated.

'Let's get going then.' Tara ordered, and after Arturous had remounted, they rode off at the usual slow canter and headed towards Freki. He was waiting for them eating a few rabbits. Freki looked at Tara, then looked at another hill in the distance and growled.

'Alright Freki, let's see.' Tara replied.

They crossed the small valley quietly and with caution. When they started to climb the hill, Freki turned around in front of them and glared at the horses.

'Guess we dismount then.' Tara said following Freki to the top of the hill, then crouching looked over the crest. There was a broad path which, because of its position, was well hidden from the grassy plains.

'Freki, are there any Goblins or Planes Devils in the area now?' The large wolf looked at her for a second, then looked down the road and growled.

'They passed here last night then?'

Bark.

'Goblins?'

Bark. Tara got up and returned to the others.

'Alright folks, a group of Goblins passed last night going down the valley. Nothing here now.' Tara informed them.

'Let Arturous, and I have a look. We should at least be able to tell how many groups have passed.' Luka suggested.

'And if it's just one group we kill them?' Arturous

asked.

'Yes, just one group, we kill.' Tara responded.

'Great, let's go then.' Arturous said, looking at Luka.

◆ ◆ ◆

They both dismounted and slowly ran down the hill to the path at the bottom.

'This looks like a fairly well made and marked path. What's it doing here, I wonder.' Luka observed.

'It's how they made paths near the mine used for heavy supply and ore carts. I can't tell how many have passed. The surface is too solid for that.' Arturous said in a disappointed tone.

'We know it isn't lots. If it were, stragglers would have left evidence. We will have to tell the others.' Replied Luka. They went back.

'The path is too well surfaced to check what or how many passed easily. I can say that there is no evidence of off-path disturbance, so we are not looking at a significant number. No more than two scouting groups.' Luka informed everyone.

'We had better check then. Scouts near the path, please. We will go from hill to hill. Luka can you ask Helghyer to find them. Freki, can you help too please.' Asked Tara. Freki padded off at a slow run while the two scouts headed for the path. Luka signalled Arturous to take the far side.

From her position, Luka could see Arturous on her left parallel to her on the other side of the path. Freki was on her right slightly ahead and further up the hill. They continued the advance slowly and silently for several miles until both she and Arturous got within fifty paces of the dozen oblivious Goblins. Arturous then signalled her to stop, which she did. The Goblins appeared to be carrying out maintenance tasks on the road and had set up camp nearby. The camp was disgusting and the pack horses in a dreadful state.

Having already decided what she was going to do, Luka began to concentrate, creating her focus by remembering the meeting with her god. Then visualising in her mind, the position of the largest Goblin and added the arrow symbol for distance, but the image wouldn't hold. Luka tried it several times, but it refused to work. She then got a feeling from Helghyer that the Goblin was too far away. Shaking her head in disappointment, Luka quietly crept closer and got into position behind a large evergreen bush roughly twenty paces to the rear of the commanding Goblin.

Luka again looked at the chosen enemy from her new position, created the spell focus and looking at her target called forth the symbol for distance to her mind. This time it fixed itself in place quickly, so she whispered 'Pellter'. Then immediately added the symbol for fear to her image and said 'Braw'. She hit the Goblin leader's mind with the full force of hers and battered her way in. His resolve crumbled immediately dropping his sword, grabbed his head with both hands, screamed and ran directly up the hill.

Within seconds of the leader going crazy, Luka heard the familiar twang of an Elvin bow to her left. A Goblin collapsed with a scream in front of her as the arrow penetrated the leather back armour. To her right Freki appeared out of nowhere. He leapt, shredding a Goblin that had been stood near to the bush he was hiding behind.

Then Luka heard the familiar sound of galloping horses behind her. Turning witnessed Tara's horse run over the fleeing Goblin leader at full gallop. It screamed while being knocked flat by the horse, breaking several of the Goblin's ribs and limbs on the way through. The next Goblin in front of Tara went down to an Elvin arrow in the head. Her second target was falling to an arrow in the back. Luka looked on in amazement as five Goblins were already down before Tara could engage her first opponent. While readying her bow, Luka then watched with amusement as

Freki knocked Tara's next intended victim flat from behind and ripped its throat out.

Luka then picking her target noticed Agnes had taken out two on her own, as had Oswald who was now using a single-handed club while on horseback. Freki was on his third. Luka concentrated on her target and released two arrows in quick succession. Then she noticed the Goblin falling with four arrows in it.

By the time Tara had charged through the Goblins, slowed down, wheeled her horse to return to the combat, it was all over.

'Damn missed it. Well, that's a first.' Tara said.

'Well done team I am very pleased. An entire Goblin party killed at two to one odds against, and I didn't get one.' Tara continued.

Helghyer landed on a tree branch near Luka and gave her a series of very angry squawks.

'I don't need to speak falcon to know how Helghyer feels about it, though. Make sure the bodies are away from the path, so they don't get found. We need them to continue with this path, so we know where to attack.' Tara concluded.

'Do we follow down the river and see where it goes? That is bound to be useful.' Asked Agnes.

'Useful, yes, but not this trip. We need to follow orders. So, we salvage what we can, continue up the valley for a bit, search for the missing Plains Devil, then head to the river and back to the village.' Tara told them. There were several nods.

'Arturous, can you see if you can find somewhere to put the bodies, while we get useful equipment and coins off them.' Tara asked. Arturous nodded and headed off. He came back a few minutes later.

'There is a hollow. We could dump the Goblins in there.' Suggested Arturous. Tara agreed, so the group rescued the seven horses, stripped the Goblins of armour, weapons and coins, then dragged the Goblin remains into the hollow. They cleared the combat area and had the salvaged equipment stowed in about half an hour. Several pouches of brass coins had been recovered and one pouch of silver from the leader.

'Luka and Arturous, can you please scout ahead up the valley. See where this path goes. I think we follow it for five or six miles, then head for the river. We avoid further Goblins and most definitely Plains Devils. We have important information and resources. Time to try and find out what happened to the upriver Plains Devil and go home.' Tara ordered.

'While I like killing Goblins, you are correct.' Responded Arturous sadly.

'If I may ask what happened to the head Goblin? He just lost it for no reason.' Asked Agnes.

'Luka and I have developed an offensive spell. It induces fear in your opponent. It was used for the first time in combat today. How did you find it?' Oswald asked

'It was horrible to force my way into such a mind. Beyond that, a lot easier than some of the practice runs we did. One thing, I feel somehow stronger, more capable by a little bit. Does that make any sense?' Luka replied

'It is nothing I know about. Something we will have to investigate if we get time.' Oswald responded.

Luka and Arturous ranged out quickly and on return confirmed there were no more hostiles in the area. 'It has been a very long day Tara, and it will be dark soon. We should make camp, but I am not at all keen on being out here overnight.' Luka asked.

'You are correct. It would be foolish to camp here. Some of us can easily go all night without sleep. Agnes, Oswald how do you feel about continuing?' Tara asked.

'I pull night shifts watching sheep all the time.' Replied Agnes.

'I believe I will be able to manage.' Oswald informed them.

'Great, then we continue.' Ordered Tara.

After several miles and when it was dark and all they had was the light of the moon, the two scouts called a halt. 'Plains Devils tracks. One came from the wood to our left, met up with some others waiting over there, then all departed up the valley.' Luka somewhat forcibly asserted.

'I don't doubt you, but can you two check for additional tracks.' Tara asked, then seeing objections about to be raised went on. 'I am thinking of tracking where the one from our left came from, and I want to make sure we don't get any surprises.'

'You think it might be my first one from upriver of the village?' Arturous asked.

'Yes, I do, but we need to be sure.' Was the response.

'Of course Tara. I want to take Arturous with me. This will be very difficult in the dark.' Luka replied in a relaxed tone. Tara looked at Arturous, who merely nodded and off they went.

The two scouts ranged out together following the odd tracks of the Plains Devils. They checked either side of the path for about half a mile, then returned.

'The only tracks we found go up the valley, no side tracks.' Informed Luka.

'I did not sense anything either. There is nothing nearby.' Arturous added.

Tara looked at the group. They all looked tired, it was night, with only moon for light. 'Can the two of you follow where this thing came from in this low level of light? I want to make sure it is the tracks of the one we are looking for.' She asked as politely as possible after twenty hours on horseback and combat too.

'If I am honest, not on my own, but with Arturous we should get most of it.' Replied Luka.

'Then we continue, please lead on. We will follow a little way behind.' The two scouts nodded and got to work. Despite the darkness, hour by hour, they followed the tracks through the dense forest. When one lost them or needed a rest, the other picked up the trail. As time passed, dawn came and went. Still, the two scouts continued. Many hours after sunrise, they left the dense forest and entered the grassy plain upriver of Warameth. After a short while of following tracks through the grassland.

'This is near where the first Plains Devil was. It was hiding behind the mound over there.' Arturous said to the others as they arrived.

'Luka, can you head over to the hiding spot and check the tracks. Arturous, please take us back into the forest and to the riverbank. Then we will look for any sign of other enemy around. If none, we go home.' Tara said gently looking at her flagging team.

Luka went on her way with Helghyer gliding above. Arturous took the group to the road running parallel to the river, stopped them, then went scouting. After half an hour or so, he returned, followed by Luka.

'I have found nothing beyond the old tracks of the Goblin attack.' Arturous told the group.

'I think we have a problem, but I am not sure.' They all looked at Luka. 'I found the hiding spot. There are tracks present of one Plains Devil, with no signs of additional Plains Devils or Goblins. My guess is Tara is right we have tracked the one Arturous spotted, and he has gone home.' Luka told them.

'Then what is the problem?' Oswald asked.

'There were human tracks too, a set of male boot prints both to and from the village. I think they are the same age as the Plains Devil. I don't like the implications of that.' Luka concluded.

'Neither do I. We may have a spy then.' Replied Tara. 'Let's go home and think about it.'

She led her exhausted team down the road and back out of the forest heading towards the village. About half a mile outside Warameth they were met by the Sheriff and Major Partten.

'We had better check them out first.' Tara said out loud before they got within hearing range.

'There's no way my father or the Sheriff can be working for the other side.' Said Agnes.

'I don't think so either, but somebody is, and can we be sure.' Replied Tara.

'I am too tired to play this sort of game right now.' Luka said crossly.

'So am I, but we have no choice.' Responded Tara.

'Then there's a way to be sure. I will do it.' Replied Oswald.

When the Sheriff and Major Partten came within talking distance, Oswald walked his horse forward. 'Please take my hand Sheriff.' Oswald ordered. The Sheriff hesitated. Tara shortly followed by Agnes drew their swords, while Luka and Arturous readied their bows.

'Agnes, what are you doing?' Major Partten said angrily.

'Comply with the Priest's request father and hold his hand or we will kill you both right here.' Agnes told her father in a flat, emotionless voice.

'Make no sudden moves Major. When the warriors of my tribe do this, they mean to kill. They will not ask us twice.' The Sheriff told Major Partten, who with a very shocked face returned his hastily drawn sword into its sheath. He kept his angry eyes firmly on his daughter, who had now pulled level with Tara, shield and sword both at combat readiness. He also looked at the two scouts who by now had placed themselves a few yards either side of the two lady warriors.

'Please, Sheriff and Major Partten take my hand. While we are sure you are both good men, we must be certain. I will not ask again.' Oswald said. While the Sheriff put his right hand on his sword, he did offer the now ungloved left hand to Oswald, who grasped it firmly. Oswald looked at the others and smiled. He then turned to Major Partten and presented his right hand. Major Partten grasped it.

'No aura at all.' Oswald stated.

'Then we must take them to the footprint and check. Please note Major, and Lord Sheriff, fail this one, and we kill you, draw a weapon, and we kill you. We are too tired for games.' Tara stated sternly.

Luka led them to the Plains Devil's hiding spot.

'Now Sheriff, Major, please dismount and place the relevant foot next to the human footprint.' Tara requested with sword drawn. The Major's face changed from anger to shock as he realised what the tracks meant and what they were being tested for. The boot prints they were being tested against were a good deal smaller than either of them.

'We have a spy then don't we.' The Major said.

'Maybe.' Replied Oswald.

'What other explanation can there be?' Replied the Sheriff.

'I don't know. I can't think of one either, but we should find out before you start pulling arms and legs off.' Replied Oswald.

'My lord sheriff, can we talk now while the others retrieve the recovered horses.'

'Please proceed Tara.' The Sheriff said with a somewhat strained tone. Tara reported the previous day and night's activities including the road, the ambush, and tracking of the Plains Devil.

'Which is when you came up against the extra footprint.' Added Major Partten.

'Correct sir.' Tara confirmed and then handed over several pouches of coins found.

The Sheriff considered the report while they proceeded towards the village. 'You have done well. The horses are in a bad way, but we can fix that. Now get some rest all of you.' The Sheriff ordered.

'With this latest haul, we will have enough mounts and leather for armour to equip everyone.' Major Partten said. With that, Tara's team dispersed for a well-earned rest.

19 - LUKA'S TOWER

Luka woke the next morning got up, got dressed and went in search of breakfast. She found both the Sheriff and Magistrate in the main hall.

'Good morning, my lords.'

'Initiate, please join us.' Replied Lord Mord as he signalled the servant to get more food.

'Thank you, my lord.' Replied Luka shaking the Magistrate's hand in greeting.

'We won't have long. I have been told of yesterday's incident along with why.' The Lord Mord said.

'Yes, my lord. We didn't think we had much choice.' She replied.

'You didn't. All three of us understand that, though it was a shock. From now on, keep your progress to yourselves.' The servant returned with Luka's breakfast of porridge.

'Thank you. That will be all. You may leave.' Said the Magistrate. His servant bowed and left.

'You will be pleased to know what we showed you at the last dinner worked well.'

'Very Good.'

'I am wondering when we are to go on the next patrol.'

'The plan was this afternoon. Why?' Replied the Sheriff.

'I would like to get my team up that tower. It could be a useful vantage point and is made of stone. I imagine it could be quite useful if we can find a way in.' Luka asked. The Sheriff thought for a few seconds then replied.

'Alright, have a first look. Be ready for patrol shortly after mid-day. Remember though, what happens with that tower is a matter for the village council. Do your investigations, then present your findings to the council.'

After breakfast, Luka decided to go for a walk and found herself looking at the carpenter and his apprentices working on the extension to the blacksmith's shop.

'Excuse me master carpenter, can I have a word please?' Luka asked.

'Certainly my lady. How can I help you?' He said, looking down from the roof beam he was stood on.

'I need a ladder. Would it be possible to borrow one?' She enquired.

'Begging your pardon, my lady, but probably not. Apart from needing them here, us valley folk as you call us, are a good deal smaller and lighter than your lot are, especially with all that armour and weapons and stuff. I could get one of my apprentices to make you a stronger one. Say tomorrow after breakfast?' He asked.

'That will be fine, thank you.' She replied.

Various people were conducting weapons practice and training on the green. Luka saw three men from Major Partten's squad now had hard leather armour and a long shield. She approached.

'My lord. I have made arrangements to look at the tower tomorrow' Luka said.

'Alright, I will work something out.' Responded the Sheriff.

'What do you want us to do today?' Asked Luka.

'A local patrol is all. Cover the outer farms and neighbourhood to make sure we don't have company. I will leave the precise route up to Tara.' The Sheriff replied.

'Thank you. Good day my lord.' Luka left and went in search of Oswald and Arturous. She found them sat on the riverbank watching the world go by.

'Good morning, gentlemen. I have our tasks for today and approval for my suggestion for tomorrow.' Luka informed them.

'I knew it was too good to last.' Oswald replied.

'We managed an hour. Please go on, priestess.' Arturous responded. Luka frowned at Oswald, not taking the joke.

'The lord sheriff wishes us to do local patrols today.

Tomorrow he has approved my suggestion for an examination of the tower.' Luka replied.

'To see if it can be used as a lookout post or something defensive.' Oswald replied.

'Yes and to see if we can find a way in.' She responded.

Having conducted the patrols without incident, Luka woke the next morning, dressed and went in search of the Sheriff. She found him mounted with a few of the new militia about to head out.

'You may investigate the tower.' The Sheriff said.

'Thank you my lord.' She replied. He nodded and led his militia on the first of the daily patrols.

Luka crossed the green looking for Tara but instead found Oswald and Arturous.

'Good morning gentlemen, you two are about early.'

'We thought we would try to discover what we are up to today before finding breakfast.' Oswald replied.

'The Sheriff has already left on the morning patrol. I would like to go and have a look at that tower on the hill. If it's viable, it will make a useful defensive position. Assuming we can find a door. Will you two agree?' She asked.

'Beats riding a horse all day.' Replied Arturous. Oswald laughed.

'Probably right. Let's find Tara and Agnes.' Suggested Oswald. They found Agnes at her family farm and were offered breakfast. They discussed the tower as they ate.

'It has always been there, like the bridge.' Agnes said.

'Nobody has investigated it?' Asked Luka.

'With no way in there is no point.'

'There will be a way inside. It's just a matter of finding it.' Was Oswald's opinion.

'We had better find Tara.' Suggested Luka once they had all eaten.

'Thank you for your hospitality. We are all grateful.' Oswald said to Agnes' mother.

They found Tara at the stables attached to the

Magistrates' house cleaning and tending her horse.

'Morning Tara. I asked Lord Daxx if he is fine with us investigating the tower. The others are happy with this, are you? I have arranged for a ladder to help us get to the top.' Luka asked. Tara thought for a few seconds.

'If it is serviceable and has a way in, it would be useful.' Tara replied.

'We can make one.' Suggested Arturous. They all looked at him puzzled. 'There are ways if it is needed. I used them frequently in mining.' Tara nodded.

'I will meet you at the tower then. I must collect a ladder and some rope.' Luka stated as she headed off to see the carpenter.

As Luka approached the blacksmith's shop, she could see the long ladder and a coil of large rope lying on the ground next to the building they were constructing.

'Good morning Priestess. William, help the lady with the ladder and rope.' The carpenter instructed. A young teenage boy climbed down from the new roof and looked at Luka for instructions.

'Please grab the rope and the end of the ladder.' She ordered. The young apprentice complied but looked at her like he was about to be bitten by a huge snake. With a twenty feet long ladder between them, they walked through the village and up the hill to the tower. The others were waiting. The young apprentice dropped his end of the ladder, put the coiled rope on the ground bowed at Luka then ran for it, presumably, Luka thought, just in case the snake decided to bite him.

'Looks tall enough.' Observed Arturous. They raised the ladder which nearly reached the top.

'My idea, so me first.' Luka said. While Tara and Oswald held the base of the ladder, Luka climbed it and hauled herself over the wall at the top.

'There is lots of weeds and dead stuff up here. I think there is a solid floor somewhere a good few feet below the top of the wall. We will need tools, though. Can someone see if we can borrow spades, shovels, and stuff. Arturous, can you come up with the rope.' Luka shouted down.

'I will go and get some things from the farm.' Agnes said calmly and left. Arturous slung the coiled rope over his left shoulder and climbed the ladder. Luka helped him over the top of the parapet. They then held the top of the ladder, allowing both Tara and Oswald to climb up one at a time.

'This place is big, isn't it.' Commented Oswald.

'Internal diameter sixty-five feet, with walls ten feet thick and nearly three feet above whatever it is we are standing on.' Arturous commented without thinking. The others just looked at him, surprised.

'I am good at distances and numbers. The external diameter is eighty-five feet. Roughly.' He said in answer to the implied question.

Oswald looked around. 'Goblins won't be getting through those walls in a hurry will they.'

'The best I have seen is a wooden battering ram carried by several dozen Goblins, being used against a wooden gate. That has no chance against these walls.' Tara confirmed to the group.

'Ho up there.' Came a voice from below.

'It's Agnes.' Responded Luka.

'Throw one end of the rope down please.' Came the voice from below. Arturous obliged. Agnes tied various shovels, spades, scythes and pickaxes to the end of the rope.

'Up now, please.' Came Agnes' voice. Oswald and Arturous pulled the rope up while Luka and Tara hauled the equipment over the edge of the parapet wall, dropping it on the ground behind them. The second time raised several large buckets. When these were safely brought up, Agnes climbed the ladder and was helped over the parapet by Tara and Luka.

'Wow, this place is big.' Was Agnes' first comment.

'Yep. And it's going to take some serious cleaning.'

Observed Oswald.

They all got stuck in. Scythes first, then spades and shovels. The tall weeds and wild grasses were cut and thrown in bundles over the walls of the tower. Then they turned to the removal of dead plant material and soil that had built up over the years.

'Hey, this place has a stone floor. It's about a spade blade down.' Observed Oswald.

'And I have a stone pillar in the middle with a hole in the top.' Added Agnes. She also found a few feet further out from the central pillar, a smooth circular groove containing what would at one time have been polished stone.

'I have one of those grooves over here. It's about six feet inside the parapet wall.' Added Tara.

'I've got twelve-inch diameter stone balls over here.' Commented Arturous.

'Tara, this is a defensive tower, isn't it. Like in the castles of legend.'

'I think it is Luka, but they are normally a lot taller and not so wide.' Tara replied.

'Can you throw a stone ball that big? It would seriously wreck someone's day if you could.' Enquired Luka.

'I don't think so. Besides whatever device threw it wouldn't be moveable, it would only hit what was in front of it.' Tara answered.

'I wouldn't be so sure.' Arturous added. They all looked at him.

'In the mines, the Goblins had a few devices that they used to haul rocks up shafts from the lower levels. Some had wheels. They didn't work well but done properly it would certainly swivel on that post and lift those balls. Somebody a lot cleverer than us could probably work out how to throw them.' Arturous continued. They could all see in his face that his mind was working on the problem.

'Let's get this tower cleaned up first. If nothing else this top part would make a great place for archers.' Tara ordered.

They worked tirelessly for hours, filling buckets with soil and dead plant material before dumping the stuff over the side of the tower. It was a hard day, but eventually, the top of the tower was cleared. Towards the end of the day when the sun was low on the horizon, a large stone slab was uncovered.

'Shall we move it?' Asked Luka, eyes burning with curiosity.

'It's very late, and we are all hot and tired.' Observed Agnes.

'Why don't we lift it enough to see if there is anything underneath.' Suggested Arturous.

'Confirm that it is a fortification tower or keep, then we close it and go, at least for tonight.' Tara answered.

'Alright, we do it Arturous' way. Open slightly have a quick look in, close it and go.' Tara continued. They all looked at Arturous.

'The best way is to get two picks, slide the narrow blade under the slab, lift and move slightly so we can get a head in to see what's about.' He answered. Arturous used the blade of a shovel under one corner and lifted it slightly. Two pickaxe blades were placed in the created gap, and the slab moved enough for a quick look. Luka and Arturous peeked in.

'I can see some stairs and a floor below.' Said Luka.

'Yep. Stone floor fifteen feet down. There is a huge column in the middle. The room looks the same width as the top deck.' Arturous added. They replaced the cover stone, bundled the tools and buckets, lowered them to the ground, one at a time climbed down the ladder returned the tools to the Partten farm, and headed to the village.

As they entered the green, an elderly gentleman approached.

'He is a very influential village elder.' Agnes informed the group quietly before he got to them. 'Master Machan, how may we assist you?' She asked.

'The elders wish a meeting. The Sheriff and Magistrate are both on patrol. Are you willing to speak to us?' He asked.

'Certainly. We will tell you what we can, but ultimately we are answerable to the Sheriff and my father.' Agnes replied.

'You will talk to us, though?' He asked. Agnes looked at the others who nodded.

'We will, but please understand we are tired dirty and hungry, so please be succinct.' Agnes informed Master Machan.

'Then follow me.' He replied. They were taken to the end of the green where perhaps several dozen family elders and their wives were sat on the grass waiting. When they arrived, a stocky elderly man stood up.

'Firstly, we are all thankful for your collective efforts in the last few weeks. The horrendous Goblin attack, the patrols and the equipment seized from the enemy. The village is extremely grateful. Without your timely help, we would most likely all be dead.'

'Master Modan, your words are most kind and appreciated.' Agnes replied.

'What my long-winded friend is getting at is how long term is the Goblin threat going to last, and how long are you guys going to be here to face it?' Another elder asked. Agnes looked at Tara, who nodded.

'Master Kenwyn, that is best answered by Tara of Iredan.

'Thank you, Agnes. My tribe have been fighting Goblins for many hundreds of years. The Goblins tend to come in ever-increasing numbers until they are either defeated and frightened off or overrun you.'

'Are you suggesting we abandon our homes.' A worried elder asked.

'No.' Replied Tara firmly.

'It wouldn't work anyway. The Goblins would take over this place, then continue down the river a few months later.' Added Luka.

'They are tribal. Each chief is always looking to expand his land so his tribe can get bigger. Apart from a general loose allegiance to a powerful lord, the tribal chiefs operate individually. That is a serious weakness our tribe have exploited very successfully. The Lord Daxx is best equipped to answer questions like this.' Replied Tara.

'Lady warrior, you are doing just fine. How long are you five staying? You are one down already.' Responded Master Machan.

'Our tribe sent the three of us on a mission. Katina has left to complete that mission. The rest of us are here as long as Lords Daxx and Mord require us.' Tara responded sternly.

'Easy Tara, they do not mean offence. They are just used to getting their way.' Agnes said quietly.

'What Tara means is that the five of us are here for the duration.' Oswald responded.

'And when you are called to your church in Kersladen, which is bound to happen given your capabilities.' Master Machan said above a concerned murmur.

'I can assure you our High Priest will never be wanting to see me again. Besides, as we all saw, my God wants me here. I will not forsake you.' Oswald replied firmly. 'As my friends have said already, these are all questions for the Lords Sheriff and Magistrate.' Oswald continued.

'As you are all here, there is something we would like to discuss with you, and that is The Tower. We investigated it and cleaned the top. It is a fortification. Arturous, you are better with dimensions than I am.' Luka asked. Arturous cleared his throat.

'The tower has an external diameter of eighty-five feet, and an internal diameter of sixty-five feet. Its walls are ten feet thick, and the entire structure is made of solid granite stone in either blocks or slabs each several feet thick. The top has a solid stone slab covering a staircase to a floor beneath. That lower level is fifteen feet floor to ceiling, is a circular room also sixty-five feet in diameter with a large stone column in the middle, probably to support the huge roof we were stood on. There are signs that the roof held a device for throwing large stone rocks.' Arturous answered.

'Can the walls be breached by the enemy?' One of the elders asked.

'Not by anything we've come across them using.' Replied Tara.

'What we wish to do is explore the tower and see if it can be made available for village defence.' Luka interrupted. There were some general discussions between the village elders, after which.

'We will agree to your continued investigations, but subject to the needs of the Sheriff and Major Partten.' Master Machan responded on behalf of the elders.

'Thank you, sirs. May we depart now? We all need to get cleaned up and rest. The Sheriff will have work for us tomorrow.' Luka replied politely. 'Certainly.' Was the response. With that, the five of them left the gathered elders to their continued deliberations.

'Do you wish to meet after we have cleaned up?' Tara asked.

'No, thank you. I am stiff, tired and behind on my religious observances. Luka will have to do her studies as well.' Oswald replied sadly.

'Unfortunately, our priest is correct. I have religious studies too.' Added Luka.

'Oh well, it was a thought. Meet at the inn just after breakfast?' Tara asked for general approval. 'I will try and find the sheriff and determine what we are up to tomorrow.' Tara and Luka bade them goodbye and left.

'I had better go home too, Bowen will need help.' Agnes added and left also.

◆ ◆ ◆

The following morning while Oswald and Arturous

were eating breakfast, Tara came to them.

'Good morning. I am afraid the Lord Sheriff wants us on patrol again. Out, Look, Back. No combat or being seen. The others are getting the horses ready.

'Really, no punch-ups?' Arturous asked.

'Definitely, a sneaky look-see is all. No killing master elf.' Tara replied in an amused tone.

'We will get our things and be out shortly.' Oswald interrupted.

The pair returned to their rooms to collect their equipment. On leaving the inn, they saw the others already on horseback and two saddled spares. Both mounted quickly and followed the group down the river. Once clear of the village, she called a halt.

'Now we are clear of the village, our task this time is to find that new Goblin path, see if we can work out where it goes for a few hours, but no more. Then back to where we left it before, cross through the forest to the river and back home. Everyone alright with that?' Tara asked.

'Are you sure we can't kill any Goblins we find?' Arturous asked, hopefully.

'Not this trip I am afraid. We are to check out the activity and get back without being seen. We are a long way from home. Sorry Arturous.' Tara replied.

I suppose we had better get on with it. There are a lot of miles to cover.' Arturous responded glumly.

They rode at a mile eating canter towards the foothills a reasonable distance east of where they had previously encountered the Goblin path. The team occasionally stopped to allow the two scouts to look for signs of enemy activity and give the horses a rest. It was late afternoon before the group reached their objective. While resting, Freki slunk up to them hidden by the tall grass. He looked at the hills they were approaching and growled, then led them behind a nearby copse of trees. Tara got off her horse and approached her wolf.

'Freki, we have an enemy in those hills a mile or so

beyond these trees, don't we?' Freki gave a friendly face response. 'Is it just a few or lots.' Tara asked. With that, Helghyer landed next to Luka and gave her two pecks.

'I take that as a few Helghyer.' Tara said in a calm voice.

Squawk.

'Luka, Arturous have a look. Don't get seen, and no killing or harming. For tactical reasons they absolutely must not know we have found them.' Tara ordered.

'We will be gone for several hours, maybe longer.' Luka responded.

'Understood. We must remain hidden, which will arise suspicion, but there is nothing we can do about that.' Tara replied.

'They can't count, so as long as the group is seen, they probably won't notice two have gone missing. I used to do that a lot in the mines.' Arturous replied.

'Worth a try Tara.' Oswald suggested.

'It is, isn't it. Alright, we will head down the valley slowly.' Tara concluded.

The two scouts headed off into the trees, Freki and Helghyer going too. They proceeded with some caution. Arturous noticed Luka and Helghyer look into each other's eyes. She then said.

'This way round the back of the hill, the Goblins are on the windward side.' Luka said quietly. Arturous knew better than to question Helghyer's scouting, so he nodded and followed Freki further into the foothills, while Helghyer flew climbing to ever-higher altitudes on the warm thermals.

The three of them approached the enemy scout from behind climbing cautiously and unseen, the Goblin being utterly unaware of the death that lay behind it. Arturous unslung his bow from his shoulder and nocked an arrow. An easy target, the Goblin was not even watching. There was a hiss from his left and looking over saw Luka with a stern face shaking her head. Giving a quiet sigh Arturous realised that she was right of course, they must follow orders. The Goblins must not know they had been discovered. He put the arrow back in its quiver and shouldered his bow, then crept back down the hill out of sight.

As Luka approached 'I know, I just like killing Goblins.' Arturous said quietly. Luka gave an understanding smile and nod of the head. 'Let's check out the new path while we are in the area.' Arturous continued.

'We must find the second Goblin scout first.'

'Same place, next hill along.'

'Alright, the path it is then.' She concluded.

They moved between bush and tree with the usual high levels of caution and silence ever deeper into enemy territory until they came to the new Goblin path. Being free of Goblin interference and with clear signs of animal activity, Luka signalled Arturous to approach. At that point, Freki padded across to some bushes and lay down.

'Freki, have you been able to tell Tara where we are, the way Helghyer tells me?' Luka asked.

Bark.

'Thank you.' Luka responded.

They gave the area a thorough search and found heavy cart tracks. 'What is this, I wonder?' Luka asked, picking something up off the grass. Arturous looked at it.

'Oh, that is our food rations at the mine.' Arturous replied.

'Eww, yuck.'

'No, it's not great. Village food is much nicer.' Arturous replied.

'It also means there is enough need for a supply truck to go down here. That would be a lot of Goblins.' Luka observed.

'Or slaves. It's what they fed us. I don't know what Goblins eat.' Arturous replied.

'Why don't we go down the path a few miles, see if we can find anything then head back to the plains once we are clear of the two Goblin scouts.' Suggested Luka.

'Alright then.' Arturous responded.

They headed off down the path one on each side a little way into the bushes. The evidence of significant enemy activity was abundant. Once clear of the two enemy scouts they crossed back to the plains, hid in a copse of trees and waited for the arrival of the others, which didn't take long.

'We had better get back. Lots of activity heading down the valley.' Luka informed them.

'We found evidence of a heavy cart carrying slave ration bars. Some fell off.' Arturous added.

'Slaves?' Tara asked, surprised.

'Possibly. The bar we found is what they fed us at the mine. I can't say what the Goblins eat. It is a grain, meat, fat mix and is horrible. Max and his wife's cooking is much much better.' Arturous responded. The others grinned.

'We must get back to the village.' Said Oswald.

'Are we being watched?' Tara asked the scouts.

'Absolutely.' Luka responded.

'Then we continue our patrol upriver and circle round as planned.' Tara ordered. They all nodded.

They followed the planned route near the foothills quite openly, continuing up the valley and into the forest. A mile or so in, they cut across to the river, then travelled the old road downstream towards the village. Come sunrise they were on the grassy plains near home.

As per usual, they were met slightly out of the village by the Sheriff. Luka gave a full report of the scouting.

'So, these ration bars, how many could you feed with them?' The Sheriff asked.

'Us slaves were given one per meal. A cart held roughly one thousand bars judging by the ones I saw at the mine. So that's three hundred and thirty days' worth of meals.' Arturous replied.

'So, one cart could support four Goblin squads and leader for a week.' The Sheriff suggested. Arturous nodded.

'If so, they are in the foothills at least a day's ride down the valley.' The Sheriff suggested.

'Yes, they are downriver of Izellameth, but not by much.' Luka added.

'Noteworthy, but not an immediate threat. Now get cleaned up and rest. Tomorrow you can go back up the tower and try and find the door. From what the elders have told me, it could be useful.' The Sheriff ordered.

'If Iredan had one, we wouldn't need to leave.' Luka responded.

The following morning Luka and Tara collected Oswald and Arturous. When they reached the tower, Agnes had already brought most of the tools to its base.

'Good morning all, are we ready for another climb?' She asked them.

As previously the two scouts went first, then lying flat on the wide parapet wall held the top of the ladder while the others climbed up. The equipment was hauled up by rope.

'Alright folks, a suggestion. We limit this trip to two aims, find out if anything hostile is in the tower, and where the door is.' Tara suggested. The others agreed. The group, with the assistance of various tools, moved the stone covering the stairs to one side.

'Why is the floor moving?' Asked Oswald.

Arturous put down his iron bar and looked in. 'Rats. Large ones too, the body is about two feet long by the looks of it.'

'So, this is where they came from. The rats have been terrorising our sheep and cattle for decades.' Agnes informed them as she unslung her bow and nocked an arrow. She aimed and fired. Her first shot was dead centre of a rat's body. It collapsed.

'Agnes, you are quite good. Why didn't you use it on our various Goblin missions?' Tara asked.

'I am not anywhere near as good as you are, but I am alright at killing rats and foxes. There were so many of them I used to get lots of practice.' Agnes replied.

'Let's see if we can find that door.' Added Luka casting a light spell at the bottom step. Oswald also cast one as far round the large column as he could. Between them, they removed most of the shadows from the room. Lots of scurrying of little feet could be heard as the rats ran for cover.

They decided to go in, with Tara going first. Her chainmail clad hard leather boots clanking on the stone stairs as she descended.

'There are lots more of those boulders down here and thousands of arrows. There are also barrels of hard black stuff.' Tara shouted up.

The others started to come down the stairs, all banging weapons on shields to make as much noise as possible. The remaining rats that had not fled the light ran for it down the second set of stairs on the other side of the large stone column in the centre of the circular room.

Before everyone reached the bottom of the stairs, Tara walked round to the other side of the column. Using her long dagger, she slew the few remaining rats that had not escaped from the light and noise.

'Oh my, we have the remains of swords, armour and shields here. The armour is solid plate mail. We can't make that anymore. I wonder if our new armourer is good enough to copy this?' Tara queried out loud.

'Look over here, hundreds of longbows. The strings have gone, but the bows look alright.' Luka informed everyone testing a bow out on her knee. Then on further examination.

'They all have symbols carved into them at the top. Don't recognise them though.'

'Neither do I.' Oswald said after going over and having a quick look. 'We will have to work that out later. Shall we check the stairs down before our light runs out?' he continued casting another light spell on the bottom step of a further staircase down.

They could see a stout stone wall at the side of the steps. Again, Tara being the most armoured descended the stairs first while the others followed banging weapons on shields. Rats scurried away from the light and noise. This level was the same size as the one they had just left. Luka cast a second light spell as far around the central pillar as she could, illuminating most of the rest of the room.

'This place is dreadful.' Tara observed looking at the decaying remains of tables, chairs and stools that lay amongst many nests of giant rats.

'True, but it also has a door.' Arturous said, walking over to the other side of the room. 'The door has mostly rusted away. Some door though, several inches thick of solid iron.' Arturous observed.

'We should leave now and report our findings. We need a proper plan for this place.' Tara suggested.

'Back in a minute.' Arturous said, heading down a further set of stairs on the other side of the room drawing his sword and dagger on route. He came back a few minutes later, blood on both sword and dagger.

'There is at least one more floor under us of the same size as this one, but it is crawling with giant rats. I think there is another floor under that, as there is a large stone slab on the floor.' Arturous informed them.

'We should consider this in a place of safety, not in here.' Tara observed.

They heard rats returning and headed back up the stairs to the roof. Then heaved the heavy stone slab back into place. Packing up the tools, they lowered them on the rope before all climbing down the ladder.

'Shame, we don't know where the door is. We could use the local farm dogs to kill all the rats. It's what we trained them for.' Agnes said once they were all down.

'How many dogs?' Tara asked.

'Every farm has several. I could have two dozen dogs within the hour. If only we knew where the door is.' Agnes replied.

Arturous looked the tower up and down, pointed at a spot on the tower at the ground and said. 'Sure we do, Eighteen feet straight down.'

'How do you know?' Asked Tara.

'Relative distance on the level or vertical is a skill I learnt mining and have used for several hundred years. Trust me. It's down there.'

'That's good enough for me. The real question is, why have it underground.' Oswald observed.

'True, but that's not important right now. We have a door and occupants so need to report this and get permission for Agnes to borrow a few dozen hunting dogs.' Tara ordered. Freki growled.

'It's alright cherished one. I wouldn't have you hunting rat.' Tara replied. The growling stopped.

'Tara, why don't you see those important people about this place while Agnes gets a few dogs to stand guard. The rest of us will start digging.' Arturous suggested.

'Why do we need the dogs now?' She asked.

'Because some of the rats went through the doorway. They must have an underground nest outside the tower.' Arturous replied.

'Alright then, you do your bits, I will try and find someone suitable to talk with.' Tara left with Freki beside her. Agnes also went in search of a few hunting dogs.

'This is more my area of expertise. Mind if I lead.' Queried Arturous and paced out a rectangular area straight out from the tower.

'We start with that. The further we go down, the wider the sides will become to avoid collapse on those digging.' Arturous informed them.

They were making good progress when Agnes came back with some of her farm dogs.

'Bowen has gone to fetch some more from our neighbours and will be here soon.'

Agnes then joined in the digging. Slowly a slope down began to appear. When the tower end got to about head height, Arturous had them widen the trench from the top down, in deep yard steps. Once the lower end of the slope was about ten feet deep, there was evidence of rat tunnels. The dogs were let loose, but none came out.

It took all that day, most of the following day and some extra help to clear enough of the doorway to allow the dogs to get in. When the sun was low in the sky, several dozen farm dogs were let loose into the tower while the digging continued outside. The growling and screaming continued for about an hour. Some rats came out of the door only to be killed by the remaining dogs outside. A fair number of the dogs had been bitten quite severely needing attention. When they checked inside the number of dead rats was staggering, as was the blood and mess.

'These will need burning.' Stated Agnes.

'Do not worry dear sister. I will get help and attend to it.'

'Thank you, Bowen. Also, have a word with someone on the council about getting this place cleaned up. It will be useful.' Then looking at the others said, 'Let's check down the stairs.'

As usual, Tara and Agnes went first being the most armoured. As with previous trips, Oswald cast his light spell at the bottom step which moved and squealed to an arrow from Arturous. On the far side of the circular room, several giant rats had survived the slaughter, and now cornered were hissing with bared teeth. Prompt archery killed them before they attacked.

'A barracks room.' Suggested Tara.

'There is a large stone slab possibly covering more stairs down.' Added Arturous.

Without discussing further, they searched the room. A few more hidden rats were flushed out. Once these were dealt with, they used iron crowbars to lift and move the stone slab enough to look down.

Oswald peered in casting another light spell at the bottom of the stairs and gasped. 'A library. Look at all the scrolls, incredible.' He said in an amazed voice.

'Including its librarian, judging by the dead guy on the chair.' Added Agnes. Luka cast a light spell on the chair the corpse was laying on.

'He's holding a scroll by the looks of it.' Luka observed.

'It's got something written on the outside of the scroll.' Agnes added.

'Raedan Nuda.' What does that mean?' Asked a confused Arturous.

'It's in the old tongue and roughly speaking means "Read Now" '. Oswald replied.

'Shame, it will be too old to read. The stuff we found at the temple of The Huntress crumbled after being touched.' Said Luka.

'This is written on vellum and should be alright if handled with care.' Oswald replied. Reverentially he approached the deceased and saying a prayer gently removed the scroll from the mummified hand, then opened it.

'Oh, dear, I was afraid of that. An important message from history, written entirely in the old tongue.' Oswald observed in an exasperated tone.

'If I dare ask, can you?' said a concerned Tara.

'Back at the temple, with time and the translation dictionaries we have developed, maybe I could have translated it. Without them, it would be challenging. I have experience though. As a new initiate, I was tasked with translating an old scroll. It took me a long time, but I was successful on that occasion.' Oswald replied.

'How safe are these scrolls?' Asked Luka.

'As long as we put that stone cover back on properly, pretty safe I would imagine.' Oswald concluded.

'We had better secure this room and report our findings.' Tara suggested.

'It's a big ask for anyone to translate all of this lot.' Luka said in a concerned tone.

'Perhaps some of the "Read Me Now" scroll would do for the time being.' Arturous proposed.

'I do remember some of the words so I can try.' Oswald promised.

They all left, replaced the large stone slab over the stairs down to the library. Then the group went looking for the Magistrate who was on the green talking with several elders.

'Good evening, all. How did your investigations go?' He asked.

'We have fully investigated the tower. It is a powerful fortification of many floors. The roof once held a device that hurled twelve inch diameter stone balls. Under that is an armoury, then there are two floors concerning soldiers' quarters. There is another floor below that.' Tara reported.

'My brother and some friends are disposing of the dead rats. We are going to have to dig out the entrance thoroughly. The sides have loads of rat tunnels in them. Once those are cleared, and the inside cleaned, it will be a useful place.

'The stone walls are ten feet thick. Fit a new iron door, and the Goblins won't be getting in. You could probably fit the entire population of the village on just one floor and have lots of spare space for food storage and the like.' Oswald observed.

'We must discuss this with the other elders. Kenwyn and Modan can you ask them if a meeting can be arranged.' The Magistrate asked. Modan agreed, and the pair left.

'Alright, what are you lot not telling me?' Lord Mord asked once they were alone.

'The lowest level has a library of scrolls written on vellum, so they should still be readable with care.' Oswald informed him.

'It also had a librarian, long since dead, holding a scroll written in the old tongue with "Read Now" written on the outside. Do you know the old tongue?' Asked Luka.

'Afraid not. So, we have an important message from the past written in a language we can't read. Great!' The Magistrate replied.

'Oswald has done translations from the old tongue before, so he may know some.' Tara suggested.

'I don't know what your plans for us are, but our priest needs some time to decipher the scroll.' Luka added.

'It was bound to happen. I will talk with Lord Daxx and Major Partten. They will need to consider how they want to play this.' The Magistrate concluded.

'I will go and start now.' Oswald said and left for the inn.

20 - SURPRISES IN THE NIGHT

And so it was, the team separated for several days. While Oswald was spending day and night trying to translate the scroll into the modern language, the rest were split between digging out rats' nests by the tower's entrance, cleaning the inside so that it was fit for use, and training new volunteers in combat.

Three days later, at evening mealtime Oswald went to the Magistrate's house and asked if he could join the meeting. All of his team were there, as was the Magistrate, the sheriff and several village elders.

'Get our priest some ale. He looks as if he needs it.' The Magistrate ordered his male servant. 'Have you been able to translate the scroll?' He asked.

'Not in a manner that would be acceptable to my church, but I believe I have the overall meaning of several sections.' Oswald replied.

'Please proceed with what you can master priest.' Lord Daxx requested.

'All right then. I think the dead guy was the author of the scroll. His name was Arthfael, last of the elemental magi, and governor of the fortified provincial capital Fenglas Caester. It roughly translates to Princess' City. The tower was part of the city's fortifications and major defence for the upriver port quarter. It goes on to mention that also in this quarter were some smaller towers, a fortified gatehouse and city walls. The place successfully resisted a siege by the Lord of All Evil for over a year. Then the undead turned up.' Oswald informed them.

'The defenders were outnumbered twenty to one, but they attacked the besieging army anyway with machines of war, magic and a violent storm. They had no priests of light and so were defeated but killed or routed three quarters of the opposing army before they were finally overcome.' Oswald told them.

'Killing three quarters of the enemy and still lost. Ouch.' Observed Master Machan.

'That must have been the battle my father and family elders wanted our priests to help with. We didn't and got conquered anyway.' Arturous added sorrowfully.

'The history lesson is interesting, but how does it help us now?' Asked Master Kenwyn.

'I am getting to that. To stop Fenglas Caester from being used as a base of further operations against humans, the remaining magi used elemental magic to bury the towers in the earth and knock over the walls. That's the first information of use.' Oswald continued.

'So we have the remains of some very serious defensive fortifications if we can find and rebuild them.' The sheriff interrupted.

'Oswald, you said buried and knocked over. Is that an accurate translation?' Arturous asked.

'Yes, I believe so.' Was the response.

'Then I have an idea on that.' Arturous added. The servant distributed further ale all around.

'Master Priest, you said the first piece of information. You have more?' Lord Mord asked.

'Oh yes. I have a rough translation of another section. During the siege, when the defenders realised the undead were coming, they tried to retrieve a portion of the Tree of Life. The aim was to plant the cutting in the city to defend it against spirits of the Evil Lord in the way the "High Temples of Old" used to be protected. Apparently once a cutting was planted, and an ancient ritual conducted, no undead or evil spirit could enter the temple without being killed. They located the tree of life, one week's ride both ways. They got to where it was but couldn't retrieve a cutting for some reason I couldn't make out.' Oswald continued.

'It must be in this valley then.' Lord Mord interrupted. The male servant dropped his tray of drinks.

'I am most sorry, my lord. I will clean it up and fetch

more.' The servant stammered apologetically. He picked up the dropped tray and goblets and departed.

'So we have to locate this tree of life on top of all the other tasks we have going on.'

'True Master Machan. But IF we can find and rebuild the defences, and IF we can find the tree of life, and IF a sapling can be planted, and IF the correct ritual can be carried out, THEN nothing The Lord of All Evil can throw at us living or dead can get in.' Luka clarified to them all.

'That is a lot of "IF's".' Added the Magistrate.

'Which will be why we have had all this divine help lately. We're it. We are the ones to stop and repel the Lord of All Evil.' Tara replied.

'That's a huge ask of a small farming village of three hundred people.' Observed Master Kenwyn.

'But ask they have.' Luka replied solemnly.

There was silence for a long while as they all stared at the table deep in thought.

'Well, I offered service to my god wherever it leads, so stand and serve I must.' Oswald declared. Luka solemnly nodded in agreement.

'This village has been good to me beyond all my possible dreams. I will stay and serve throughout on one condition. That the first opportunity we get, we go free my people.' Arturous asked.

'Agreed.' Said Oswald, Luka, Agnes and Tara in unison. The Magistrate, sheriff and three elders nodded.

'Masters Machan and Kenwyn. We daren't tell the others, not yet. This is too big. Feed it in little chunks over time?' Master Modan asked them respectfully. The other two elders nodded glumly, the shock revelations sinking in.

'So much for a safe new home.' The sheriff concluded wryly.

'Shit, Katina doesn't know.' Commented Luka.

Several hours of talk later and Oswald Shamus had had enough. Time to walk off the ale before I find my bed,

Oswald thought to himself. So he said his pleasantries and left returning to his room at the inn.

After placing his Light Bringer religious symbol that housed his spirit guide on the table next to his bed, he said out loud

'This time, I am leaving you behind my friend. It's only a short walk.'

Picking up his heavy woollen cloak and quarterstaff, he left his small bedroom that was now home. The door to Arturous' room was open, but he was already asleep having got bored of the discussions sometime before Oswald had. Quietly he left the elf and descended the stairs throwing his cloak around him as he went, nodding to Max behind the bar as he left the inn.

On the green, the blacksmith was still hard at work despite it being very late. The extension to house the furnace appeared to be progressing well. It had a solid timber frame including roof supports and half-built walls. He continued through the grass of the village green and the grazing sheep. Bowen Partten was watching the flock, longbow over the shoulder and sword at his belt walking around them, making sure they didn't get in anyone's way.

A few days earlier, Oswald had seen several people working on the riverbank, which he thought created a circular route of about a mile. A long enough walk to clear his mind and refresh the senses. So he strolled along the road towards Izellameth stopping at the spot where those weeks ago he had helped fight off the Goblins. There were still a few signs such as the occasional bloodstained rock or piece of wall.

About fifty yards ahead of him, there was the three-yard wide gap between two field boundary walls. He walked along the narrow lane this created listening to the night birdsong and observing the wildflowers. When he got to the river, the path was no longer grass and mud but a straight line of exposed stone blocks. Each one was several feet wide and as long as the height of a man.

Oswald slowly walked along the part buried stones to the bridge watching a hawk hunt small fish.

He had never seen a bridge made of stone before coming to Warameth. Stone arches supported the roadway of the bridge that was several hundred feet long and ten feet wide. The middle of which would be some twenty feet above the river, high enough for a rowed barge to proceed underneath. As he approached the bridge, a large area of stone blocks, perhaps thirty feet square had been exposed on the side of the bridge. The meaning of his translations of the old scroll now made sense. Clearly, things had been knocked over or buried.

Oswald slowly started to cross the bridge treading lightly on the massive stone blocks of the roadway, listening to the insects and bird sounds of the night. He felt the stress and woolly-headed thinking start to lift as he leant against the nearly three-foot-high stone walls that edged the roadway of the bridge.

For some time he just stayed there watching the world go by. Then something occurred to him. The world wasn't going by, but hurrying home. The water voles and rats scurried for their holes in the banks of the river and amongst the tall grass. Birds that are both prey and hunter flew side by side down the river at their fastest pace. Then the sound of night was silence. There was no bird noise, no insect, no small creatures, just the hammering of the blacksmith.

The silence is wrong, time to go back, Oswald thought. Turning towards the village, he started to run, then stopped suddenly as the village end of the bridge shimmered.

'Shit. Plains Devils.' Oswald said out loud without meaning to. He turned and ran the other way, hearing several running feet behind him. In front of him shimmered as well. Oswald swore, I'm trapped, he thought as the shimmering stopped, the bows of the Plains Devils came off the shoulder and arrows nocked. Oswald looked over the bridge wall. I've got to chance it, he thought. Grabbing the top of the wall, Oswald flung his legs over. Two arrows hit him in the back as he went over the top.

Struggling, he tried to get to the riverbank but was going more down than across. Eventually, he made it, collapsing on the far bank with exhaustion. The two wounds from the now dislodged arrows were bleeding, but not severely. Pulling himself out of the water, several large calloused hands grabbed him and forced a cloth bag over his head.

'Gotcha.' Said one hoarse voice.

'Now let's slit his throat and get outta here before that bloody elf and wolf show up.' Said another hoarse voice. As a wolf howled in the night.

Oswald felt a sharp pain in the back of the head, and all went black.

◆ ◆ ◆

Emily was washing tankards when she heard Arturous shouting upstairs. Then swearing as a door slammed, followed by the elf running down the stairs shouting.

'Where's Oswald.'

'Gone for a walk, perhaps fifteen minutes ago.' Replied her father.

'Shit.' He shouted as he ran at full speed through the taproom, sending tables chairs and customers flying in all directions. Emily put the tankards down and followed Arturous out the door. She missed the first shouts but did catch

'Get anyone you can summon in one minute then follow me immediately.' Arturous shouted as he headed round to the side of the inn to the stone bridge.

Bowen Partten started blowing his cow horn as he ran after Arturous, shortly followed by the giant wolf. Within seconds by Major Partten and Agnes, both mounted galloped across the green to the bridge sending sheep scurrying in all directions. She ran to the corner and saw Arturous pick up a Quarter Staff lying on the ground most of the way across the bridge. He handed it to Agnes. Some words were exchanged, and the whole group disappeared into the darkness across the grasslands with two of the night watch a few yards behind.

Emily hurried to Oswald's room and crying, picked up his cross from the table.

"Hello, can you talk to me please. It's urgent." Emily asked.

"I know Emily. The enemy has captured my charge. He will be dead as soon as his captors stop running. It looks like I've lost."

"Then he's still alive now." The tears were subsiding as realisation dawned.

"You have relaxed. What am I missing?"

"Arturous, Freki, the Partten family and the two former bandits have already left, heading across the grassland over the river. Some minutes before I got here."

"That explains all the running then. I would run if that lot were after me. Now listen to me, Emily, you must keep safe now. You are the only Light Bringer spell caster at this time, so you are going to be temporarily upgraded in rank. Our God has already instructed me that the power fundamental will be honoured in times of emergency and for solitary practice. We have been watching and know you have been privately studying."

"Can I speak with you for guidance?"

"Like this when you are touching Oswald's cross, yes. I am not your spirit guide, as we are not mind linked like I am with Oswald. I can't sense things or listen in to conversations."

"So for now, I have been temporarily upgraded to High Initiate. I am stunned. Thank you, but I hope I don't get to keep it long."

CONTINUES IN BOOK 2 with Katina's trip home

Printed in Great Britain
by Amazon